...to be living in the ... ...ce. She is als...
...nough to write for the ... ... Boon Medical
... line. A primary school teacher in a former
... is now a qualified paramedic. She loves to
... and dance, drink champagne, and spend time
... daughter and her friends.

... vith a poor sense of direction and a
... ...ty to read, **Annie Claydon** spent much of
... hood lost in books. A degree in English
Lite... ... followed by a career in computing didn't
lead ...tly to her perfect job—writing romance
for M... & Boon—but she has no regrets in taking
the ... c route. She lives in London: a city where
... st can be a joy.

THE PARAMEDIC'S UNEXPECTED HERO

ALISON ROBERTS

A RIVAL TO STEAL HER HEART

ANNIE CLAYDON

MILLS & BOON

First Published in Great Britain 2020
by Mills & Boon, an imprint of HarperCollins*Publishers*
1 London Bridge Street, London, SE1 9GF

The Paramedic's Unexpected Hero © 2020 by Alison Roberts

A Rival to Steal Her Heart © 2020 by Annie Claydon

ISBN: 978-0-263-27971-9

MIX
Paper from
responsible sources
FSC® C007454

This book is produced from independently certified FSC™ paper
to ensure responsible forest management.
For more information visit www.harpercollins.co.uk/green.

Printed and bound in Spain
by CPI, Barcelona

THE PARAMEDIC'S UNEXPECTED HERO

ALISON ROBERTS

MILLS & BOON

CHAPTER ONE

Oh, *man*...

It was clearly going to be one of "those" days. Ari Lawson could hear the shouting as soon as he pulled his helmet off, having shut down the engine of his powerful motorbike and secured it on its stand. Checking the house numbers in this outer suburban London street confirmed that one of the people engaged in this heated argument was standing in the doorway of the address he'd been dispatched to but it definitely wasn't the person he'd been asked to check up on. This was a belligerent man in his mid-thirties—about Ari's age—who was waving his fist at the middle-aged woman from the next-door terraced house.

'Mind your own bloody business,' he was yelling.

'It *is* my bloody business,' the woman yelled back, 'if you're punching holes in walls that I'm on the other side of. I've called the police.'

'As if they'll listen to you, you daft old bat. They never have before.'

Ari had lifted his kit from one of the panniers on the back of his bike. He walked towards the house.

'Who the hell are you?' the man demanded. He

looked Ari up and down, his expression disgusted. 'Get lost, whoever you are. You're not wanted here.'

'I'm here to see a Vicky Tomkins. This is where she lives, yes?'

'There you go.' The next-door neighbour folded her arms across an ample chest. 'Vicky's called for help. 'Bout time, if you ask me.'

'Nobody asked you,' the man spat. 'And she didn't call anyone.'

'Yes, I did.'

Everybody turned instantly towards the woman now framed by the doorway behind the angry man. An obviously pregnant woman who was pale enough for alarm bells to start ringing for Ari.

'I called my midwife,' she said. 'She said she couldn't come but she'd find someone who could.' But the younger woman was sounding hesitant now. 'Another midwife…?'

'That's me,' Ari confirmed. 'Your midwife—Yvonne—is busy at the hospital in the middle of a delivery at the moment so she asked if I could come and see you. I'm a midwife, too.'

The moment's silence didn't surprise him. Ari was quite used to people finding a male midwife an unusual concept. Add in the fact that he was well over six feet tall, wore a leather jacket to ride his motorbike and kept his shoulder-length hair up and out of the way in a man bun for work hours and the reaction from others could often be a lot more than bewilderment. It wasn't the first time he'd heard something like the raucous burst of laughter from the man in front of him.

'You have *got* to be kidding me,' he said. 'A midwife? Well, you're not getting anywhere near *my* wife, mate.'

For the umpteenth time, Ari had to wonder why it was such an odd concept that the only appropriate male role in pregnancy or childbirth was that of an obstetrician. At least he was quite familiar with dealing with this kind of prejudice.

'I think that decision is up to Vicky,' he said calmly. 'She's the one who called for help.' He caught her gaze and held it, doing his best to convey reassurance that she could trust him. 'You're experiencing some abdominal pain, yes?'

She nodded. 'And I'm bleeding,' she told him. She had a protective hand on her belly and her voice dropped to a shaky whisper. 'Please... I'm scared...'

The man wasn't about to move but Ari was a head taller and he wasn't about to let this client down. He knew she was less than thirty weeks pregnant and, if she was in pain and bleeding, she could be in real trouble. He could hear a siren not far away, which reminded him that he could well need to call for back-up sooner rather than later.

'There you go.' The neighbour sounded satisfied. 'That'll be the cops on their way and they'll sort you out. I hope they lock you up this time.'

Sirens were commonplace in any huge city and this area of London had more problems than many so Ari thought it unlikely that they would be responding to a minor disturbance like this, but Vicky's husband was incensed, stepping sideways and raising his hands as well as his voice so that he could grab the fence railing between them and shake it. Ari used the opportunity to step closer to the person who had called for help.

'Are you safe here?' he asked quietly. 'Or do I need to get you somewhere else to check what's happening?'

Vicky shook her head wearily. 'He'll settle down,' she said. 'He just gets wound up sometimes, you know?' There was curiosity in her glance this time. 'Are you really a midwife?'

'I really am. But if you're uncomfortable with that, it's okay. I can refer you to hospital for an obstetric check.'

'I don't want to go in there. I'd have to wait for hours and I'm supposed to be working tonight. *Ow…*' Vicky clutched at her belly with her whole arm as she bent forward. 'Oh, that really hurts…'

'Come and lie down somewhere.' The sound of the siren was fading rapidly as Ari put a supporting arm around her shoulders. 'Couch or bed—whatever's easier. We need to find out what's going on.'

A very short time later, he ended his phone call, hoping that he would be hearing another siren from an emergency vehicle in the very near future—from the ambulance he had just summoned.

Paramedic Kelly Reynolds shut down the lights and siren on the rapid response vehicle she was driving as she approached the suburban address she'd been dispatched to. Parking directly behind a large motorbike, she jumped out of the driver's seat to go to the back hatch of the SUV to collect the gear she might need, slipping her arms through the straps of the backpack that contained an extensive first-aid kit. One hand was then free to carry the life pack with its monitoring and defibrillation capabilities and Kelly took a deep breath as she took her first step across the road.

As a rapid response paramedic it was her job to either arrive first to assess and stabilise what could be a serious case, or back up an ambulance crew that needed expert assistance. Sending an officer that worked alone—especially a female officer—into a potentially volatile situation was not ideal but when a call like this came in, it had to be the closest available vehicle that got dispatched and, this time, that had been Kelly.

She wasn't about to stand back and wait for the back-up of the ambulance that she had heard being dispatched at the same time she had received the Code Red, urgent priority callout, on her radio. Not when there was a pregnant woman and a midwife on scene who needed assistance. She just needed to remember her training. To keep a clear escape route behind her at all times and to carry a heavy bit of kit like the defibrillator in front of her so that, in the worst-case scenario, she could throw it at someone to make her escape easier.

There was a woman leaning on an iron railing fence that separated her property from the house they'd been dispatched to.

''Bout time someone got here,' she told Kelly, with satisfaction. 'He's kicking off again.'

Kelly acknowledged the greeting with no more than a nod. She could hear a raised voice coming from inside the house so she walked past the neighbour and rapped on the open door.

'Ambulance,' she called loudly.

The hallway was empty. The man's angry voice was coming from a room to one side.

'It's her own bloody fault. I reckon she got pregnant on purpose. How do I even know the kid's mine?'

It was the cry of pain from a woman that made

Kelly move, her hackles rising as she got closer to what turned out to be a living room. She held the heavy life pack in front of her body as she'd been trained to do—poised to hurl it if she found herself under attack. The angry man wasn't making an assault on anyone, however. He had a can of beer in his hand and he was simply standing in the doorway to a kitchen. The woman who sounded as if she was in severe pain was lying on a couch and there was another man crouched beside her.

An extraordinary-looking man, with olive brown skin and his hair pulled up into a bun that was a lot higher than the one Kelly always used to tidy her own hair for work. A lot messier, too. He was wearing jeans and a leather jacket of all things but he had what looked like a professional medical kit open on the floor beside him with a stethoscope and blood-pressure cuff visible. And he was placing his hands on the woman's pregnant belly. Large, capable-looking hands, she noticed, but even from this distance she could see—or sense—how gentle his touch was. Kelly wasn't the only one watching.

'Get ya hands off her,' the man yelled. 'Nobody touches my wife without my say so.'

He lunged towards the couch but Kelly was faster as she stepped into the room at the same moment to get between him and the pregnant woman. He stopped in his tracks and swore vehemently but then backed off a little. He was a bully, Kelly realised, lowering the defibrillator. He might thrive on making threats but he was actually unlikely to follow through on them. Not that that made the abuse or interference with medical care any more acceptable, of course.

'It's not my fault,' he muttered as he stepped back.

'It's that cow next door. She's the one who's causing all the trouble round here—not me. So we were having a bit of a barney...so what? Who doesn't?'

'What *is* happening here?' Kelly only took her gaze off him for an instant because, while she thought she had the measure of this man, he was still clearly posing a threat. Her swift glance over her shoulder was long enough to see that the woman on the couch was looking distressed and far too pale. It was also long enough for the man who was crouched beside her to look up and meet her gaze.

Dark, dark eyes. A serious expression on a very intelligent-looking face.

'I'm Kelly,' she introduced herself. 'From the ambulance service.' She was still a little confused about who this man was. 'And you are...?'

'He's a midwife,' the man in front of her sneered. 'A *boy* midwife. And you're a *girly* medic. Who let you out to play all by yourself? If you ask me, the world's gone bloody mad...' He crumpled his beer can, hurled it towards the corner of the room and then turned back towards the kitchen. 'I need another drink...'

Kelly ignored him, her gaze fixed on the midwife. She could sense that, beneath that calm expression, he was worried about his patient. Seriously worried.

'I often work with the obstetric and neonatal flying squad,' she told him. 'Do we need to call them?'

The flying squad was a specialised team with a dedicated ambulance that was mainly used for transport of premature or sick babies to a hospital like the Kensington, which had a neonatal intensive-care unit, but it could also cater for any obstetric emergency like a home birth going wrong or a complication like a post-partum haemorrhage or obstructed labour. The team could include an obstetrician and/or a neonatal specialist, midwives and paramedics and had an incubator as part of their equipment in case an out-of-hospital birth or transport was needed for a fragile infant.

'Maybe.' There was a hint of a smile on his face as the midwife spoke to Kelly for the first time but it was ironic rather than amused. 'For now, it's good that you're a "girly" paramedic. Between us, we might be able to properly assess how much blood Vicky's actually losing.'

Any hint of that smile had faded but his glance still communicated the fact that this man was well aware of the threat that Vicky's husband posed and that his attitude to a male midwife being here was exacerbating that threat. He wasn't about to let it stop him doing his job, which deserved serious respect as far as Kelly was concerned. That simple reference to her being "girly" conveyed both an understanding of the kind of prejudice that could come with crossing perceived career boundaries or trying to assert authority and the kind of humour that meant he'd learned long ago how to deal with it. That earned more than respect from Kelly.

She *liked* this man.

As an advanced paramedic whose expertise had been requested, Kelly was theoretically now in charge of this scene but she wasn't about to ask this midwife to step back if it wasn't necessary. He had looked as though he knew exactly what he was doing when he'd been checking both the position of the baby and how tender or rigid Vicky's abdomen was, and now he was about to move her clothing to check on her blood

loss—something they both needed to assess as rapidly as possible.

A split second later, however, he reared back as an
open beer can, spewing froth, whistled through the
air to narrowly miss his head. Vicky cried out in fear
and shrank back against the couch, even as the midwife moved to shield her, and it was in that instant that
Kelly knew this woman had been struck in the past.

Maybe they should have waited until they could
have taken Vicky out of there and into an ambulance
before starting any assessment or treatment but this
was most definitely not the time to start thinking about
how she could have improved her management of this
scene. Abuse of any kind was totally unacceptable and
the midwife—who'd come into this situation alone
with the sole intention of looking after a vulnerable
woman—could have been seriously injured by that can.

With anger driving her muscles, it only took Kelly
three steps to get to the other side of the room, although
it was long enough for a hole to get punched into a wall.
Not that that slowed Kelly down. If anything, she was
even more furious as she faced up to the violent thug
that Vicky was unfortunately married to.

'*Get in there,*' she shouted, jabbing her finger in the
direction of the kitchen. 'If you so much as put a foot
back in this room while we're looking after your wife,
I'll have the police here so fast you won't know what's
hit you. And, believe me, they'll make sure you don't
get to cause any more trouble for anyone for a very,
very long time. Now...*move...*'

Wow...

Ari had his stethoscope in his ears because, having

seen the alarming amount of blood Vicky had already lost, it was a matter of urgency to check on the baby's status, but there was no missing the absolute authority in that voice. This paramedic—Kelly—might be blonde, pretty and as "girly" as they came, but she was not about to get messed with and that was exactly the kind of medical back-up he had hoped would arrive. He moved the rounded bell side of his stethoscope to pick up the baby's heartbeat, which was reassuringly rapid and steady...for now.

'Have you been feeling the baby move today, Vicky?'

'Yes.'

'How long ago did the pain start?'

'I dunno. Maybe an hour. Or maybe a bit longer. The fight started because Brendan didn't like what I was making for lunch and he...he...'

Ari lowered his voice, even though the kitchen door had been slammed behind Brendan. He knew that Kelly was coming back to this side of the room and would be able to hear him.

'Did he hit you, Vicky? Is that how the pain started?'

'N-no...he just...shook me a bit, that's all.'

Again, his gaze met that of the paramedic for a heartbeat. He could see that Kelly, as a frontline member of the emergency services, had seen it all before. He could also see a fierce determination to help a vulnerable mother-to-be. He recognised that determination easily because it was something Ari had lived with himself for almost as long as he could remember. A need to protect and care for those more vulnerable than himself. Especially babies. Including babies that hadn't been born yet and had no idea how tough life could be.

Kelly had her fingers on Vicky's wrist but Ari knew she wouldn't be able to locate a radial pulse because that had been the first thing he'd tried to assess. The tiny frown that appeared between her eyes was confirmation that she'd taken on board the warning that they needed to move fast. An absent radial pulse was an indication that the blood pressure was far too low.

'Vicky?' Kelly's tone was reassuring. 'I'm going to put a mask on you so that we can give you some oxygen. And I'm going to put an IV line into your arm, love. You've lost a bit of blood and we need to give you some fluids to get your blood pressure back up again. Then we're going to get you into hospital. Is that okay with you?'

Vicky nodded wearily, lying back as she closed her eyes, her response no more than a mumbled assent. Kelly must have noticed that Ari was watching her rather intently because she flicked him a sideways glance. One that acknowledged what they both suspected—that Vicky's placenta could be separating from the uterine wall and the amount of blood she was losing could put her into haemorrhagic shock that could be life threatening—both for this young mother and her baby.

There was a question in Kelly's eyes. 'You okay with staying here?' she asked quietly as she opened her backpack and took out an equipment roll. 'Want me to call for police back-up? There's an ambulance on its way but we could try and get Vicky next door in the meantime.'

Ari kept his voice just as low—no more than a murmur that Vicky probably couldn't catch. 'I'd prefer to get her stable before we move her. Her GCS is dropping already. I reckon we can handle this between us...' He tilted his head towards the kitchen door. 'In fact, I think you could handle it all by yourself.'

A brief curl of one side of Kelly's mouth acknowledged the compliment but her nod was an agreement with his preference to stay put and get some fluid resuscitation started. Movement could make the loss of blood more rapid and Vicky's condition could deteriorate rapidly, tipping her into a possibly irreversible state of shock. Kelly had the tourniquet and the foil packet containing an alcohol wipe in her hands, ready to start establishing an intravenous line.

Ari reached for a cannula, peeling back the plastic cover before holding it out for Kelly to take as soon as she cleaned the skin over the vein she'd chosen in Vicky's forearm. In that moment, they became even more of a team than they had when they'd agreed to stay here and try to stabilise their patient's condition.

'Vicky? Sharp scratch, love, but it's only for a second.' She slid the needle in, slid the cannula into place and released the catch on the tourniquet so swiftly and smoothly it looked like a single action.

Impressive.

'There's a bag of zero point nine percent saline in the kit. Top pocket.'

Ari pulled it out. Then he read out the expiry date for her.

'Thanks...' Kelly paused, a finger pressed onto the vein above the small, plastic tube in Vicky's vein as she reached for the Luer plug he'd left beside her knee. 'Sorry... I didn't catch your name.'

'We didn't exactly get the chance for introductions.' Ari was unwinding the giving set to poke the spike into the bag and then run enough fluid through the tubing to remove any air bubbles. 'I'm Ari. Ari Lawson. I'm a midwife attached to Kensington Hospital.' He held the end of the tubing out to Kelly who took it to attach to the Luer plug. With the IV line securely taped, she worked just as swiftly and smoothly to attach ECG electrodes to Vicky's chest and flick the defibrillator into monitoring mode. Almost immediately, an alarm started sounding.

'She's tachycardic,' Kelly noted. 'And look…' She pointed at the screen, where the bizarre shapes of ectopic beats were interrupting a trace that was rapid enough to have tripped the alarm. She silenced the alarm but it seemed like it had triggered a new wave of tension. Chaos, even?

The kitchen door was flung open behind them.

Ari could feel the surge of adrenaline that made every muscle in his body tense as he started to get to his feet. He could sense the same reaction from Kelly as she gathered her inner resources to face whatever new threat might be coming. After what he'd seen earlier, Ari had every confidence that she *could* deal with it but, this time, he was going to be the one in front. Protecting her.

Or maybe he didn't need to. He could hear a commotion coming from the hallway of this small house. Loud shouting that told him that the police *had* apparently responded to the neighbour's call—perhaps because they knew an ambulance officer had been dispatched and might be in need of back-up?

He could also tell that the arriving officers were both male because it felt like the wave of testosterone arrived in this room before they burst in, and although their equipment like telescopic batons, pepper spray and handcuffs were still attached to their belts or stab-proof vests, it felt like they were demanding attention and advertising their ability to enforce authority. Ari found himself turning his glance towards Kelly again. She'd had the authority to command respect without any kind of weapon, hadn't she?

Except...

She looked different now that these male officers had arrived. Okay, her head was probably dipped because she leaning in to try and calm Vicky, who was trying to sit up and pull her oxygen mask off at the same time, but, for a split second, it almost seemed to Ari that Kelly was ducking her head for another reason. Trying not to be seen, even?

'Brendan...' Vicky was still trying to push past Kelly's hands. 'Don't do anything stupid...'

Ari moved to help Kelly keep Vicky still. The last thing they wanted was an increase in the rate at which she was losing blood.

'It's really important that you keep still, sweetheart,' he said. 'We've got this, okay?'

Even if Brendan hadn't been drunk enough to make it difficult to stand up straight, he would have been incapacitated within seconds by the two police officers.

Ari wondered if one of them, in particular, was enjoying the opportunity to use physical force to restrain someone a little too much as he flourished his baton and raised his voice. He was a big man with buzz-cut blond hair that accentuated uncompromising features, including a very square jaw. Kelly was watching as well as the officer twisted Brendan's arm behind him with enough force to make him cry out in pain.

Kelly's expression made Ari suspect that she shared his opinion that too much force was being used here. It certainly looked like her desire to protect an underdog was automatically overriding any desire to remain in the background. She jumped to her feet, although her words were almost tentative.

'H-he hasn't hurt anybody,' she told the police officers. 'He's drunk, that's all. Noisy. He was just…making some verbal threats.'

She was being ignored as the officer issued a rapid, almost bored-sounding caution.

'You do not have to say anything. But it may harm your defence if you do not mention when questioned something which you later rely on in court…'

What Kelly had said wasn't exactly true, Ari thought as he reached for Vicky's wrist to feel for her pulse again. Throwing a full beer can as a weapon was definitely assault. But ambulance staff often got to know local police officers pretty well when they were working in the same area of a city. Was she minimising what had happened here as a form of protection because she knew what this officer might be capable of in the heat of the moment?

Finishing the caution, the big, blond officer pushed Brendan towards his partner and then stepped closer to Kelly. Rather too close in Ari's opinion. Any further and he would have been able to touch her ear with his lips but Ari could still hear what he said.

'You called for us, Cowbell. So why don't you just let us do our thing and look after you, okay?'

Oh, *man*…

How humiliating was this?

Kelly could actually feel the bright flash of colour that was heating her cheeks. She certainly couldn't miss the way Ari's jaw dropped as he heard that patronising tone and the dismissive nickname either. Or the expression in his eyes, even though his gaze only grazed hers for a heartbeat. He didn't understand, did he? He'd seen her stand up to an aggressive, obnoxious drunk with no more than her voice and determination as weapons so why was she letting another bully take charge?

Kelly didn't understand it herself. It was more than two years since her relationship with this man had ended. She should have been over it long ago. She had proved she was strong enough to keep herself completely safe from any other disastrous entanglement. Stupid nicknames should have lost any power long ago as well but, apparently, they could still sting.

Cowbell... Or maybe Kettlebell, because that's all you are, sweetheart. A useless lump...

At least it was chaotic enough for anyone's impressions or embarrassment to be so fleeting that they were unlikely to be remembered. Brendan was being dragged, shouting, from the room at the same moment that paramedics were coming in with a stretcher laden with more equipment. Vicky was crying and another alarm was sounding on the defibrillator. The focus needed on her patient was welcome. Kelly knew that treating a critically ill person was at the top of that list of things she was *not* useless at and she was going to use every one of those skills right now, for the sake of Vicky and her unborn baby.

Vicky's heart rate was climbing. Her blood pressure, oxygen saturation and level of consciousness were dropping. They needed to increase the rate of fluid resuscitation with another IV line. They also needed to get this patient to hospital. Fast.

Only minutes later, Kelly was making sure that all her monitoring equipment for continuous measurements of blood pressure, oxygen saturation and heart rhythm were functioning. One of the back-up paramedics was going to drive her SUV back to the hospital so that she could stay in the ambulance with her patient.

Ari had gathered his own equipment while they'd got Vicky ready for transport. He appeared at the back of the ambulance just before the doors were slammed shut. The flashing lights had already been activated.

'Where are you heading?' he asked.

'Kensington. It's the nearest hospital set up for obstetric and neonatal emergencies.'

'Great. I'm heading that way myself. I'll be able to check up on Vicky later, then.'

Kelly could see him kicking his bike into life and starting to follow them before the ambulance reached the end of the street. She cleared her throat as she received acknowledgment from her radio handset that she'd been patched through to Kensington's emergency department.

'We're coming to you with a thirty-seven-year-old woman—Vicky Tomkins,' she told them. 'Pregnant, almost thirty weeks gestation, sudden onset of acute abdominal pain and bleeding approximately ninety minutes ago. Suspected placental abruption. She's on her second unit of saline but her blood pressure's dropped to ninety over forty and her GCS has dropped from fifteen to twelve in the last ten minutes or so. Estimated blood loss of at least a litre. We'll be with you in about six minutes…'

Another glance through the rear window showed Kelly that her rapid response SUV was right behind the ambulance. Just beyond the SUV was a large bike with a tall man in a dark leather jacket and a black helmet.

Ari Lawson—the astonishingly different midwife who had unexpectedly dropped into her life less than an hour ago—was riding shotgun.

For some inexplicable reason that she wasn't going to allow any brain space to analyse, knowing he was close by was making Kelly feel safer. Protected, even.

And it was a good feeling.

CHAPTER TWO

THE FLASHING BLUE lights and the fluorescent red and yellow stripes on the back of the ambulance were easy enough to keep in sight. Weaving his way through the gaps available to a motorbike in the heavy London traffic was so automatic for Ari he was able to think about other things at the same time and, as he noticed the ambulance turning a corner ahead, he was thinking about what was going to happen to Vicky when she arrived at Kensington's emergency department.

He had plenty of background knowledge to draw on. Ari had trained as a nurse before going into midwifery and he had particularly enjoyed his time in Emergency. His fascination with medicine in general continued to fuel his need for further postgraduate study and so far he'd clocked up qualifications in managing high-risk pregnancies and dealing with complications of childbirth and he was currently enrolled in a part-time course on the out-of-hospital care of premature newborns.

By the time he had the ambulance in his line of sight again, having turned the same corner, Ari had decided that Vicky would have as much time as needed in Emergency to support her circulation with aggressive fluid resuscitation and she might be given a blood transfusion as well. If a placental abruption was confirmed, the specialist obstetrician might want to take some fluid from her uterus to reduce the pressure but it was more likely that they would go ahead and deliver the baby by Caesarean section as quickly as possible and then deal with any complications that might follow.

Yvonne would want an update on her client and Ari should have just enough time to duck into the delivery ward on his way to the outpatient department of Kensington's maternity ward where he was due to start an antenatal clinic at three p.m. It was going to be a busy one, with about six women at various stages of pregnancy who needed clinical assessment, any questions answered, reassurance given if needed and advice for the next stage of the journey they were on.

If there was anything abnormal found, he would need to arrange further care and he'd be fielding phone calls as well—from an obstetrician who'd decided to induce a client, perhaps, or from someone who needed to cancel or change an appointment or home visit. Like Yvonne, he could have a client who went into labour unexpectedly and that would throw his schedule into complete chaos, but the prospect didn't bother Ari. He thrived under that kind of pressure and somehow making it work.

Something was bothering him, however, as he had to wait and watch the ambulance go through the red light of an intersection ahead of him. As the emergency vehicle got further ahead, Ari realised what it was that was niggling at the back of his head. Something about Kelly—the paramedic in that ambulance—had got completely under his skin.

He'd been blown away by her courage in subduing an angry, intoxicated man who outweighed her enough to have been dangerous. He'd already felt a beat of connection with her when Brendan had been so dismissive of any authority or skill either of them might have in their chosen professions. The recognition of the kind of determination to protect the vulnerable that, given the right circumstances, could make you much braver than you might think you were or that others might think you were was another connection that tapped into parts of Ari's life that nobody he worked with knew about.

He'd also been seriously impressed with her calm confidence and obvious skill in her job to stabilise a patient whose condition was clearly deteriorating. But—and this was what was really bothering him—the way she'd visibly shrunk into herself when that macho idiot of a cop had turned up. He knew the type. A big ego, a bit of a bully. Capable of making sure the people around him behaved the way *he* wanted them to and to use whatever means necessary to do so.

But Ari had also learned long ago what even the faintest smell of fear was like. He'd seen, all too often, the effects that were the aftermath of trauma, whether it was physical or emotional, and he also knew, all too well, what it was like to feel vulnerable. And he'd been aware of all of that in Kelly's body language when that cop had pushed himself into her personal space and put her down with such biting efficiency.

What had Kelly ever done to provoke that kind of treatment? And calling her *Cowbell*? What the heck was that about? Not that it mattered, anyway. The man had been unprofessional to the point where an official complaint might be justified but that hadn't entered his head at the time. No…the only thing that Ari had wanted to do in that moment was to protect Kelly. The way he would always want to protect someone who was vulnerable and under threat.

The urge had been so powerful that, if Vicky hadn't started crying at that moment, he would have been on his feet and by Kelly's side. Telling that cop just how she had taken control of a situation that had been a lot more threatening than the one he and his colleague had arrived into. And that Kelly had gained control by using nothing more than her voice and her determination. She hadn't needed to wave weapons around or cause physical pain.

His intervention hadn't been required, of course. He might have caught a glimpse of the other side of the coin that was Kelly but it had only been momentary. She'd gone right back to doing her job without her focus being compromised one little bit. Strength had won out over vulnerability. That glimpse had been enough, however. Especially given the connection he was already aware of.

Ari was intrigued.

He wanted to know more.

And, yeah…he knew he should just let it go because that kind of interest had created problems before. He'd never had the space for a woman in his life who wanted to depend on a long-term relationship and he didn't have the space for another woman in his life for any reason right now.

The ambulance carrying Kelly and Vicky was turning into the bay right outside Kensington's emergency department. Ari couldn't park his bike there so he had to go further down the road to access the staff car park.

He'd have to walk back this way to head towards the maternity wing, though. Well…okay, it was a bit of a detour and he didn't exactly have the luxury of time to be making detours but…

…but the pull to do that was so strong he knew it might well prove to be irresistible.

Different.

That was what was so intriguing about Ari the midwife.

It wasn't simply that a male midwife was unusual. Or that he wore his hair long enough to need to tie it back to keep it out of the way for work. It wasn't even the strangely hot contrast between the idea that he had chosen his profession because he loved babies and that obvious gentleness in caring for his clients and the sheer masculinity of a big man who rode around on a powerful motorbike and wore leather.

There was something else that Kelly couldn't quite nail down and, now that she had the time to think about something other than the patient she'd just accompanied to hospital, her brain didn't want to let it go. She was in a supply room down the corridor from the emergency department at Kensington Hospital, collecting everything she needed to restock the kit that was in the back of her rapid response car. The task was automatic. And easy, because all she had to do was run back through the scene in her head and pick up a replacement for everything she'd used.

An oxygen mask was first on the list and then it was IV supplies. Kelly added a strip of alcohol wipes to the bag, a sixteen-gauge cannula and a couple of Luer plugs and occlusive dressings. She had to stand on tiptoe to reach the shelf with bags of saline and the packages containing the giving sets.

It wasn't just the treatment she had given her patient that Kelly was remembering as she collected the items. She was remembering the assistance she'd had. How easy it had been to work with someone who could anticipate what she needed and when. He was probably quite capable of inserting an IV line himself but he hadn't given the slightest hint of being frustrated at her taking the lead. A lot of men wouldn't like that, especially if that lead was being taken by a woman. Especially men like Darryn…

And there it was…that thing that had been at the back of her mind that felt important enough to identify. The reason that Ari was so different. It was the contrast between those two men that was almost as blinding as the difference between light and dark. Superficially, that contrast was there for everybody to see. Blond and fair-skinned against a Mediterranean kind of colouring. But the difference that Kelly could now see in retrospect was something only she could be aware of and that was the contrast in how those two men made her feel.

It was pathetic, given that she'd escaped her relationship with Darryn so long ago, that he could still make her feel stupid. Belittled. Afraid of what was going to come next, whether it was something being broken or vicious words or the threat of physical harm that seemed just as bad as any actual violence might have been. Worse, in some ways, because there was no evidence left that might have made others realise that something was very wrong. And why would anyone have believed her when he could be so very charming in public? She wouldn't have believed it herself back in the early days when he'd set out to capture her heart. Now it was hard to believe that she could ever have imagined herself to be in love with him.

And in contrast to that was the feeling of…of *safety*…that Ari had given her. She'd only really noticed it when she'd seen him following the ambulance on that huge motorbike but it had been there right from the moment she'd met him, hadn't it? When she'd seen him crouched beside Vicky as she'd entered that living room. There'd been something in his body language that had made her aware of his total focus on the pregnant woman. Something she could sense in the gentle movement of his hands on her belly that had made her think that if *she* was his patient she would feel safe.

She'd seen that look on his face when he'd heard Darryn taunting her with that horrible, old nickname. As unlikely as it seemed, Kelly could believe that he knew exactly how she was feeling in that moment and he'd almost looked as if he was ready to leap to his feet and come to defend her, but maybe she'd imagined that. In any case, it had been Vicky who had needed his attention far more than she had.

Remnants of that feeling of safety were still there, however, and it was doing something weird to Kelly's gut. Making it feel like it did when she was nervous—a fluttering kind of sensation. Stronger than butterflies. More like birds. It wasn't an unpleasant feeling but it was unusual enough for Kelly to prefer that it would go away. Grabbing a handful of ECG electrodes, she headed back to the ambulance bay where her vehicle had been left to one side. She opened the back hatch and then opened her kit to lie flat so that she could slot her replacement supplies into the pouches they belonged in.

The movement and change of scene seemed to have done the trick in dispelling that strange fluttering sensation. Maybe now that she had identified what had been niggling at the back of her mind, she could now dismiss that as well. It wasn't as if she was likely to see Ari again anytime soon and, even if she did, it wouldn't mean anything. So what if he was the polar opposite of her ex-boyfriend? That didn't mean that she was attracted to him, did it? She hadn't been remotely interested in men since she'd broken up with Darryn and that was long enough now to make her think she might remain single for ever.

Zipping her kit closed, Kelly tightened the safety belts that held the defibrillator and an oxygen cylinder in place and then pulled the hatch shut. She was already fishing for the set of keys in her pocket as she turned to see the tall figure walking towards her. The man she hadn't expected to see again anytime soon. If she'd been trying to subconsciously convince herself that those wingbeats in her belly didn't have anything to do with attraction, she realised in that moment that it was a totally lost cause because just the sight of Ari made them spiral into an intensity that was a shaft of something rather too close to physical pain.

The pain of a barrier being smashed, perhaps?

'Hey…just the person I was hoping to see.'

He was smiling at her. She hadn't seen anything more than the hint of a smile on his face before and it was lovely. Warm. Genuine. Enough to make his eyes crinkle at the corners. Brown eyes, she noticed as he came close enough—just as warm as that smile. It was impossible not to smile back.

'All good?' Ari asked. 'How's Vicky? I was hoping to get here sooner but I got held up with some calls.'

'You would have needed to be quick. I was most impressed with how fast they worked. There was a team waiting for us in Resus. An ultrasound confirmed the placental abruption and also revealed that there was quite a lot of blood trapped behind the placenta so what we saw was only part of the volume she'd lost.'

'No wonder she was going into shock. Did she need a transfusion?'

Kelly nodded. 'They had the first unit running as they took her up to Theatre.' She glanced at her watch. 'Her baby should be being delivered right about now. You'll probably be able to see her on one of the maternity wards later this afternoon. I'm just hoping that they'll both be okay.'

'You and me both.' Ari's smile was long gone. 'Especially if she's going back to that violent thug of a husband.'

'The police involvement was part of the ambulance report so Social Services has been notified. If Vicky wants help, it's there for her.'

'I'll put something in my paperwork as well. My colleague, Yvonne, will be doing the postnatal house calls so I'll have a chat to her. I'd hate to have her go back into an abusive relationship.'

'Mmm…' Kelly had to look away from Ari's gaze. It was too intense. As if he really did see more than he should.

'And what about that cop? I'm tempted to put in a complaint about his behaviour.'

Kelly's heart missed a beat. 'What behaviour?'

'Brendan might be a thug but he was handled pretty roughly. And—' there was a note of anger in Ari's voice '—I didn't like the way he spoke to you either.'

Kelly sucked in a quick breath. 'Don't say anything. Please. It would only make things worse.'

'What things?'

'He's my ex,' she admitted. 'It was over a long time ago and we don't cross paths very often but... I wouldn't want to stir things up. You know...'

There was a beat of silence between them. A beat that was so long Kelly had to look back to catch Ari's gaze.

He did know, she thought. More than she would have been prepared to admit to anyone on first acquaintance. But that wasn't stopping him from wanting to know more. What was even stranger was that she wanted to tell him more. To tell him everything, in fact, and maybe she would have said more right then but as she opened her mouth, her pager sounded.

'Uh-oh...' She glanced at the message. 'Code Red. I need to go.'

'Me, too.' Ari stepped out of her way but didn't keep going. 'I finish work about six,' he told her as she opened her car door. 'Want to meet for a drink or a coffee or something? I might be able to update you on Vicky by then.'

Kelly slammed her door shut but immediately pressed the button that rolled her window down. Already, her focus was veering towards her next callout but that new twist of her gut was sharp enough to make her catch her breath.

'Sure,' she heard herself saying. 'Where?'

'There's a pub on the corner. The Kensington Arms. It's the hospital's local, I believe. See you there at six-thirty?'

Kelly was putting her vehicle into reverse. She flicked a switch to start the beacons on her roof. She could actually feel her adrenaline levels rising. Excitement at not knowing what she was being dispatched to this time? Or did it also have something to do with the prospect of meeting Ari again? Outside work hours. Almost like a date…

'I'll be there,' she told him. Her vehicle was pointing the right way now and her foot was poised over the accelerator. She caught his gaze for a heartbeat, however. She couldn't quite find a smile because this suddenly seemed a little overwhelming and she put her foot down as she spoke, as if she needed to escape. 'See you then.'

"Intrigued" didn't quite cover how Ari was feeling about Kelly by late that afternoon.

He should have known there was a reason why he'd felt such a strong urge to protect her when that cop had demonstrated that he had absolutely no respect for her personal space. An ex-boyfriend? What on earth had she ever seen in him? And if he could treat her like that in public, well after the relationship had ended, what had he been like when they had been together, behind closed doors?

Unfortunately, Ari could imagine only too well and he was sure he was right in his suspicions. Kelly was an intelligent, capable, gorgeous-looking woman and there was only one thing that could have undermined her self-esteem enough to make her personality visibly shrink in front of him like that and that was abuse. Pure and simple. He'd not only seen it too many times in his life not to recognise the signs, he knew what it was like to be on the receiving end. He'd only just met Kelly but he could feel anger on her behalf. And sadness. And...the desire to try and help her.

Just as a friend, of course, because no matter how undeniably attractive she was that was all he could offer, but that might be enough to make her believe in how amazing she was. To help heal whatever damage that bastard had done to her and let her move forward with her life with the kind of confidence that would make sure nobody could ever put her down like that again—in public or in private.

The thought had to be shelved as his last appointment for this antenatal clinic came into the room, a small sample container in her hand.

'Sorry that took so long. I couldn't do much either.'

'Doesn't need much for a dipstick test.' Ari unscrewed the jar on his desk and took out the test strip to dip into the urine sample. He compared the colours in the tiny squares to the chart on the jar.

'It's all good, isn't it?'

'Your protein level's up a fraction. We'll need to keep an eye on that. I might get a culture done to make sure you're not brewing up a urinary tract infection.'

'That's dangerous for the baby, isn't it? I'm sure I read something about protein in urine being bad.'

'If it's there along with high blood pressure, it can be a sign of something called pre-eclampsia and that can be dangerous if it's not recognised in time. But your blood pressure's fine, Janice.' He smiled at her. 'Try not to worry so much.'

'I can't help it. We've waited a long time for this baby, you know?'

'I know. But you're well past the halfway mark now and everything's looking great. Come and hop up on the bed and I'll measure your tummy and we can listen to baby's heartbeat. We can have a chat about whether you want to start making a birth plan as well.'

'Oh…yes… I've been thinking about that a lot. I've even chosen the music I want.'

Ari grinned. 'Maybe we could choose the place you want to give birth as a first step. You were considering a home birth, weren't you?'

'I've gone right off that idea.' Janice lay back on the bed and pulled down the waistband of her maternity jeans to expose her bump. 'What if something went wrong? I'd rather be somewhere safe that had all the experts and medical stuff that I might need.'

'Safety is certainly my number one priority,' Ari agreed. 'For both you and your baby.'

He had his handheld Doppler ready, holding the monitor in one hand and the small transducer in the other, pressing it gently to one side of Janice's bump as he searched for the best place to hear the baby's heartbeat. It took a few seconds for the faint thumping sounds to become clearer.

'There we go.' Ari turned the monitor so that Janice could see the readout. 'One forty beats per minute. Perfect.'

Janice was smiling but her lips wobbled a moment later. 'It gets me every time, hearing that,' she admitted.

Ari had to smile back. 'Me, too.'

The miracle of new life never got old. The emotions

that went with it covered every human experience from anguish to ecstasy and, as Ari chatted to Janice about making her birth plan, he hoped that her experience was going to be as joyful as possible. Some women never had the luxury of any control over how their babies came into the world—like poor Vicky today. Ari had half an eye on the clock on his wall. He wanted to get an update on how Vicky and her baby were doing because Kelly would want to know and he would be seeing her very soon.

If that little Doppler had been anywhere near his own heart right now, it would have picked up that little blip of a missed beat as well as the acceleration that followed. Anticipation, that's what it was. He was very much looking forward to seeing her again.

'Let's wrap this up for today, Janice. I've got a print-out here of all the things you can think about and talk to your partner about. Like pain relief options, what kind of food and drink you might want available in labour, preferred positions or use of water. Even who gets to cut the cord. There's lots to think about.'

'There sure is.' Janice's eyes had widened. 'Thanks, Ari. Do I need to make another appointment?'

'Yes.' Ari opened his diary. 'And I'll be in touch about the results of any further testing on your urine sample. If necessary, I'll refer you to your GP for a blood test or any medication you might need.'

Minutes later, Ari stripped off the scrub top he'd been wearing to replace it with a black T-shirt and then his leather jacket. He collected his satchel from the corner of the room but didn't bother picking up his motorbike helmet. He could walk to the Kensington Arms and come back for the helmet later.

The sound of an incoming text message as he turned towards the door was nothing to worry about. They were almost always about an appointment that needed to be changed. People always rang rather than texted if it was something urgent. Except that this message was something different. Nothing to do with his work and everything to do with what currently had such a high priority in his life.

He read the message and then hit a rapid dial key.

'What's happening, Peggy?' He listened for only a matter of seconds, a frown deepening rapidly on his face. 'Okay,' he interrupted. 'It's okay. I'll be there as soon as I can.'

He had to pick up his helmet and he was walking fast through the corridors of the maternity wing. He still had his phone in his hand, ready to call or text Kelly to let her know he couldn't make it. But…he hadn't asked for her number, had he? He had no way of contacting her because he certainly didn't have either the time or the head space to start searching for and ringing around all the ambulance stations on this side of town. Or to go to find someone who might know her contact details because of her involvement in the flying squad. It would have to wait until later.

Ari could only hope that she would understand but if she didn't that would be just the way things had to be. This was why he'd come back here. To be able to provide support for someone who needed him. The only woman in his life that he'd ever been able to trust completely, in fact, and that was why she deserved everything he could give her at the moment. It was also why he didn't have space in his life for anyone else right now, possibly even a new friend.

* * *

'What can I get you, love?'

Kelly smiled at the bartender, who had a strong Aussie accent. 'I'll wait, thanks. I've got a friend coming.' She glanced sideways at the huge railway clock on the wall. She was a few minutes late herself so she had no right to feel disappointed that Ari wasn't here already.

'No worries.' The bartender grinned at her. 'Lucky guy.'

Kelly shook her head. 'It's nothing like that. He's just a friend.'

Not even that, really. Or not yet. But the possibility was there. Of friendship. Of possibly—okay, a very small possibility but it had to be acknowledged—something more than friendship.

And there were parts of Kelly's body that felt like they were waking up after a very long hibernation. Tingly bits that were not at all unpleasant. Quite the opposite.

The bar was quite crowded and noisy and Kelly was happy to sit on the bar stool and just relax in the convivial ambience as she let herself contemplate that tingle that had resurfaced at quite frequent intervals over the last few hours. It wasn't freaking her out any more. In fact, she had identified something she hadn't felt in so long it was almost a new concept in regard to her personal life.

Hope…that's what it was…

The bartender went past, his hands filled with empty glasses. 'Sure you don't want something while you're waiting?'

Blinking out of that daydream, Kelly looked at the clock and was astonished to find another fifteen minutes had gone by. Still, she shook her head, although her smile was harder to find this time. The atmosphere didn't feel so friendly after that either. Had people noticed her sitting here alone? Was some of that laughter on her account? Oh, God…maybe some of Darryn's mates were in here and talking about her. Passing on those nicknames and a warning to stay clear of someone who was too stupid to live.

Had she really thought that being around Ari the midwife made her feel safer? Well…that trust had been totally misplaced, hadn't it? Right now, sliding off the bar stool, Kelly felt just as humiliated as she had when Darryn had reminded her of how worthless he thought she was.

She'd been stood up. Nobody did that to someone they had the slightest respect for, did they?

Not that she should feel this surprised. Or hurt. She knew better than to trust any man. Even one with soft, dark eyes that told her they could understand. That they wanted to know her story. That they thought she was something special.

Kelly's breath came out in an incredulous huff as she let the pub door swing shut behind her. Who was she trying to kid? They were *especially* the kind of men you couldn't trust. The ones who got under your guard and sucked you in so fast they made you feel things that you thought you'd forgotten how to feel. Maybe even feeling those things wasn't worth it, because when reality came along and smacked you in the face, it really sucked.

'Hey…you're going the wrong way, darlin'.' A group of young men were heading into the pub but one of them had turned back. 'Come and have a drink with us, why don't you?'

Kelly shook her head. And walked faster. There was only one place she wanted to be and that was her little basement flat where she lived alone. Where she had only herself to rely on.

Where she felt genuinely safe…

CHAPTER THREE

Code Red... Suspected opioid overdose. Seventeen-year-old female who can't be woken. Pregnant...unknown gestation...

KELLY HIT THE switches for both the lights and siren on her SUV and put her foot down as she moved into a bus lane to get past the queued traffic at the intersection. The address wasn't far away so she was already planning what to take into the scene and how to handle what was an all too common callout.

Looking for the signs and symptoms of an opioid overdose was a well-practised routine. Pinpoint pupils, cold, clammy skin, slow heart rate and, if more serious, cyanosis with blue lips or nails and respiratory distress that was enough to be causing gurgling or even no breathing at all so Kelly needed to be prepared to deal with a cardiac arrest on her own until an ambulance could be dispatched to back her up.

Her radio crackled into life.

'Control to Rover One.'

'Rover One receiving, go ahead.'

'Back-up from ambulance fifteen minutes away. Do you want a police unit dispatched?'

'Ah...' Kelly thought fast. The treatment for an over-dose of this sort was straightforward with a dose of Narcan almost guaranteed to rapidly reverse the effects of the drugs taken. It also put the patient into withdrawal, however, and this could often cause a degree of agitation that put medics in danger of injury, perhaps from a flying fist.

A tiny flash of memory was so lightning fast it didn't interfere at all with Kelly's thought processes but it still managed to generate a knot in her stomach. She'd coped with the threat of violence only yesterday from someone far more threatening than a pregnant seventeen-year-old girl probably was. Mind you, she hadn't been alone and maybe she'd been braver than she might have otherwise been because Ari the midwife had been in the room and she'd known she had back-up. But, in reality, she *had* been alone—because Ari the midwife wasn't as trustworthy as she'd thought, was he?

That pang of disappointment hadn't faded much overnight, had it? Kelly could feel every muscle in her body tensing as she pushed the unwanted emotion away. It helped enormously that the adrenaline from travelling towards the unknown with her lights and siren on was kicking in.

'Negative, thanks, Control,' she said. 'I'll assess the scene and let you know what I need in the way of any back-up.'

Even an ambulance to transport the patient to hospital was not necessarily going to be needed and, in fact, could tie up a lot of time and emergency services resources if the patient didn't want to co-operate. The main danger of reversing an overdose and then releasing the patient from care was potentially fatal rebound opioid toxicity when the effects of the reversal drug were wearing off, although recent research suggested that was extremely unlikely if the patient had normal vital signs and level of consciousness.

The fact that this patient was pregnant might tip the balance for making that decision for Kelly, however. It could influence whether she gave the drug in the first place, in fact, because giving any drug in pregnancy was only indicated if really needed and where the benefit outweighed any risks. She'd also need to find out whether this girl was getting antenatal care and she might need to contact her general practitioner or midwife if she had one.

And there it was…an unwelcome reminder of yesterday's case. Of a meeting that had been not just memorable for it being a male midwife but because he had been a man who had both sparked and then crushed a glimmer of restored faith in the opposite sex. The opportunity for Kelly to use her air horn and blast a car that was refusing to pull aside to let her past was a rather welcome way to clear her head and dismiss what had happened yesterday. It was highly unlikely that a pregnant teenager who was a drug taker would have a midwife, anyway. It was far more likely that Kelly would need to activate back-up from Social Services.

Today was a new start and, as always, Kelly's complete focus was on the job she loved. She shut down her siren as her satnav told her she was almost at her destination and then killed the beacons as she slowed down to find the street number. It looked like it was that rather nice, rambling old house on the edge of a park, which was a little unexpected. Many calls like this came from deserted buildings being used by street kids or homeless people. Or had a resident found someone in the park behind the house? Kelly put her backpack on and picked up both the defibrillator and an oxygen cylinder.

There was no answer to her knock on the door, so Kelly tried the doorknob and found it unlocked. She stepped into a hallway.

'Ambulance,' she called. 'Where are you?'

'In here...'

The voice was that of an older woman—a little frail and quiet—but it was enough to direct Kelly to a room off the right side of a hallway. A bedroom that had a figure curled up with a duvet covering her body and another person sitting on the end of the bed.

'I'm Kelly, from the ambulance service.' Kelly put her gear down near the head of the bed. She was already assessing the girl lying there and she knew this wasn't an emergency. The patient she'd been called to see seemed to be breathing quite normally and her skin was a good colour. The teenager opened her eyes to glare at Kelly as she reached to take her pulse, pulled her hand away and rolled over with a muttered curse.

'I couldn't wake her up before,' the elderly woman told Kelly. 'And...and I couldn't find my patches... I got scared...'

Kelly nodded as she pushed the button on her radio. 'Rover One to Control.'

'Control receiving, go ahead, Rover One.'

'On scene. No back-up required at this stage, thanks.'

'Roger that.'

Kelly clipped her radio back to her belt and turned

to crouch a little so that she was on the same level as the silver-haired woman who looked to be in her eighties. 'What's your name?' she asked.

'Peggy. Peggy Hammond. And that's Stacey in bed. She just turned up on the doorstep yesterday. We haven't seen her in years...'

'Okay...' Kelly didn't understand what was going on here but there was more to it than an unhappy, pregnant teenager who didn't want to get out of bed. Peggy looked beyond frail. She was very pale and her fingers were gripping the corner of the duvet as if she was afraid of falling. 'Your patches, Peggy...what are they?'

'Fentanyl.'

'You're in pain?'

Peggy nodded. 'I've got cancer, lovey,' she said softly. 'But don't you worry about me. It's Stacey who needs help.'

'No, I don't.' The mutter from beneath the duvet was sullen. 'I just need some sleep. I'm tired, that's all. I didn't take your stupid patches. I told you I don't *do* drugs any more.'

Kelly's priorities had just changed. 'I can give you something for the pain, Peggy. Can I contact your GP and arrange a visit as well?'

'No...no, I don't want to bother her. I'll be fine. I've called my boy and he'll be here any minute. I'm lucky he wasn't too busy at work at the moment. He's come back to London specially, you know...just to help look after me.'

'That's wonderful.' Kelly couldn't help returning the sweet smile she was receiving. 'How many children have you got, Peggy?'

'Dozens,' came the surprising response. 'But I didn't

give birth to any of them. Ironic, isn't it? I was a mid-wife and I delivered hundreds of babies but could never have one of my own. So I started fostering instead. I could never turn a baby away.'

'That's an amazing thing to have done with your life.' Kelly could feel a squeeze in her chest that could easily bring tears to her eyes. 'So Stacey is one of the children you fostered?'

'The last baby.' Peggy nodded.

'Stop talking about me,' Stacey snapped. 'Go away.'

Peggy ignored the command. 'I was nearly seventy then,' she told Kelly. 'I couldn't have managed if I hadn't had a lot of help from my oldest boy. He loved the babies, too. Do you know, the first time I ever saw him smiling was when he'd managed to stop a baby crying. *Oh…*' She doubled over as she gasped in agony.

Something like a sob came from under the duvet. 'Shut *up*,' Stacey shouted. 'And go away. Why can't you just go and die somewhere else?'

There was a sudden, shocked silence in the room. And then, as Kelly got to her feet to help, reaching out to hold Peggy's shoulders so that she didn't slip to the floor, the sound of heavy, rapid footsteps could be heard on the wooden floorboards of the hallway. A figure appeared in the doorway. A very tall figure that was even more of a shock to Kelly than the teenaged Stacey's cruel words.

Oh, my God… Of all people… What on earth was *Ari* doing here?

He looked just as shocked to see her. Or perhaps he'd heard what Stacey had shouted but his focus was instantly on Peggy. Kelly had to back away as

he crouched in front of Peggy and put his hands on
her arms.

'How bad is it, Ma? Have you got a new patch on?
Taken a pill to top up?'

'I couldn't find them, love. I thought… I thought
Stacey had taken them. She wouldn't wake up and tell
me…'

'I was *tired*,' Stacey shouted. 'Why wouldn't I be
when Ari kept me up half the night nagging me about
baby stuff?'

Kelly's breath caught as she watched how gently
Ari was scooping Peggy into his arms.

'We hid your medicine in the biscuit tin last night,'
he told her. 'When Stacey was having a bath. Did you
remember that?'

'Oh…*no*…' Peggy's frail arms were wrapped around
Ari's neck as he lifted her. 'I forgot…'

She looked so small and even more frail in his arms.
When she laid her head against his chest with an almost inaudible sigh, Kelly actually had to blink back
tears. She could feel the love between these two people and it was powerful enough for her to be caught in
the glow. She'd never had someone who cared for her
that much in her entire life. Her parents had been loving enough but distant. In the early days, boyfriends
had seemed only interested in sex and more recently
Darryn had been the final—and worst—of a series of
disasters. To be held like that—to be able to let your
breath go and relax, as if you had absolute trust that
you were safe—how lucky was Peggy?

'I told you I didn't take them.' Stacey's head came
out from under the covers. 'I told you I *wouldn't* take

them but you didn't believe me, did you? I hate you. I hate *both* of you. I don't know why I came back here.'

'Yes, you do, Stace.' Ari's tone was calm. 'You were living on the streets and you had nowhere else to go and you knew it was the right thing to do to come and ask for help. I'm just going to get Mum sorted and then I'll come back and talk to you, okay?'

'Suit yourself.' Stacey pulled the duvet over her head again. 'Just don't expect *me* to listen to you preaching.'

Kelly stared at the shape beneath the bedding. She still had no idea of Stacey's medical history or stage of pregnancy and hadn't even recorded a single vital sign but she could be sure that there was no medical emergency to be dealt with in this room. Silently, she picked up her gear and followed Ari, hoping that he would let her help with Peggy's care.

Part of her heart was breaking for what was going on in this household. A woman who was facing the end of a life devoted to babies and children who didn't have the safety of a loving family. A teenaged girl, who had obviously struggled with drugs in the past, had been living on the streets and was nowhere near ready to become a mother. A man who could show such love for others simply by the way he touched them or the patience that coated his words to someone who wasn't ready to listen.

Was Ari Peggy's oldest boy? The one who'd smiled for the first time because he'd managed to comfort a baby? Kelly was sure that he was. She was also sure that her first instincts about this man had been correct. Despite the way she'd been let down yesterday, he was trustworthy. More than that. He was someone very different.

Special…

So his priorities yesterday had been to be with his family instead of meeting someone for a drink at a pub? She had to respect that. It fitted right in with the impression of this man that she'd had from the first moment she'd laid eyes on him and the least she could do was offer any medical skills or access to other resources that might make the challenges Ari was facing a little more bearable.

At the end of the hallway, a kitchen living area spanned the width of this old house. There was a big, scrubbed wooden table that looked like it had hosted countless family dinners, an old dresser cluttered with crockery and a massive corkboard on a wall that had so many photographs pinned to it that some were almost hidden. French doors at one end led out to a garden and inside there was a huge, battered old couch draped with colourful blankets made out of knitted and crocheted squares.

Peggy squares, Kelly thought, a smile tilting her lips as she watched Ari put his foster mother down, oh, so carefully, on the cushions of the couch. Woollen squares that were handmade and as genuine and welcoming as everything else in a room that was very much the heart of a house. Strictly speaking, Peggy was not her patient and she should probably be contacting the ambulance service's control centre to make herself and her vehicle available again for what could be deemed more of an emergency but she didn't want to leave. It wasn't just that she wanted to help in her professional capacity.

This felt personal. And important.

She did radio through to Control, however.

'I'll be on scene for a while longer,' she told them. 'I have a patient here who needs acute pain management.'

'Is transport required?'

Kelly caught Ari's gaze as he shook his head. Then she saw the tears rolling down Peggy's wrinkled cheeks and the flash of something like despair in the elderly woman's eyes.

'Negative,' she said. 'I'll let you know as soon as I'm available.'

Stacey had done everyone a favour, Ari decided as he watched the care Kelly was taking not to bruise Peggy's hand as she slipped a needle through thin, papery skin into one of those prominent veins.

'It's just going to be so much quicker to give you some intravenous morphine,' she was saying. 'A new patch will take quite a while to be effective and even your pills will have trouble getting on top of this pain quickly now that it's got a bit out of control. You've had morphine before, haven't you?'

'Oh, yes, lovey. Too many times now.'

'Mum was diagnosed with ovarian cancer a few months ago,' Ari told Kelly. 'She's just finished a course of chemo intended to shrink the tumour enough to have surgery, including a full hysterectomy.' He held out the peeled-back package containing the Luer plug for Kelly to screw to the end of the cannula. He had the strips of sticky tape to secure the venous access ready as well. 'Do you want a dressing to go on top of that?'

Kelly shook her head. 'I won't leave the IV in. Not if Peggy's going to stay at home.'

'Of course I'm going to stay at home.' There was a fierce determination in Peggy's voice. 'Stacey needs me.'

'Stacey needs more help than you or I can give her right now, Mum. Like I said last night, you've got to look after yourself right now. You were supposed to be admitted today and now your surgery's going to be put back.'

'It's not as if it's going to cure me. We both know that.'

'It's going to buy you time. Maybe more time than you think. You'll be able to do more for Stace by being around for longer. And for all your other kids. Someone else will be landing on the doorstep before too long. They always do.'

Ari wanted her around for as long as possible as well. He wasn't ready to lose the only woman who'd ever been a real mother to him. The only woman he'd ever completely trusted in his life.

Kelly was holding a syringe up in front of her face, having drawn up the morphine and added saline to dilute the drug. She pushed enough to make a fine spray in the air and remove any air bubbles and then took the needle off to screw the syringe to the plug port. She drew back until she could see blood in the chamber, to confirm that the cannula was still patent, and then slowly injected half the dose of morphine in the syringe.

'You'll might feel a bit woozy,' she told Peggy.

'Mmm... Feels like I've had a big drink of gin.'

Ari smiled. 'That was always your favourite, wasn't it? A gin and tonic on a Saturday night.'

'How's the pain now?' Kelly asked. 'What score would you give it if it was ten out of ten before?'

'About five,' Peggy said.

'We'll give it a few minutes and then I'll give you

the rest if you need it.' She looked up at Ari. 'Are you going to be home for a while?'

'As long as I can. I've got a client in the early stages of labour so I'll have to go as soon as she needs me.'

'Ari's a midwife,' Peggy told Kelly. 'Just like I was.'

'I know.' Kelly was smiling. 'I met him yesterday. Bit of a coincidence, isn't it?'

'Did you?' Peggy's face had brightened considerably now that she was in less pain but she was a little drowsy. 'Why didn't he tell me that?' She was smiling as her eyes drifted shut. 'It's about time he met a nice girl like you.'

'It was work, Mum,' Ari said. 'Kelly came to help with a young woman who was having a placental abruption and needed to go to hospital. She was in a bit of trouble.'

But it had had the potential to have been more than simply a professional meeting. What would have happened if he'd turned up for that drink, like they'd arranged?

'I'm sorry,' he told Kelly quietly.

She was wrapping a blood pressure cuff around Peggy's arm. 'What for?'

'That I didn't make it to the pub. When I heard that Stace had turned up, I had to get home.'

'Of course. I understand completely.' Kelly lifted her gaze as she unhooked her stethoscope from around her neck and fitted the ear pieces.

He knew she had blue eyes. He'd noticed them yesterday as part of that classic combination with her blonde hair. He hadn't noticed quite how dark they were, however, or was it sincerity that was adding that depth of colour? She really *did* understand, didn't she?

'I was kicking myself that I didn't ask you for your number,' he added. 'I was doing something about that this morning, so I could contact you and apologise for standing you up like that.'

'It's okay. No big deal.' Kelly opened the valve to deflate the cuff. 'Blood pressure's down a bit but the systolic's still well over a hundred. We can top that morphine up if necessary.' She threw a quick smile in Ari's direction. 'I've already forgiven you anyway.'

'Just as well.' If Kelly hadn't turned away to reach for Peggy's wrist, he might have got caught staring at her face for too long but who wouldn't, with a smile like that on offer? 'I found one of the doctors from the obstetric and neonatal flying squad but he wouldn't give me your contact details. He said personal information was only available for team members. He also said they could do with another midwife on the team if I was interested.'

'Oh? And are you? Interested?'

Kelly looked as if she might welcome his presence on a team she belonged to but Ari shook his head. 'I spent time with a similar unit in Glasgow and loved it but…that's not why I'm back in London.'

Peggy opened her eyes. 'Ari gave up his job,' she told Kelly. 'Just to come back to London so he could help look after me. I told him he had to have his work as well, though. It's lovely to have him around but I can look after myself. Besides…' There was a twinkle in her eyes now. 'I like hearing the work stories. Takes me right back, it does. I'd have loved to have been on one of those flying squads. You should do it, Ari. You've got a special gift that you should be using, instead of spending your days off looking after a sick, old lady.'

'You're my mum,' Ari told her. 'End of story. Maybe I'll think about it after things settle down around here.'

'And when hasn't life been messy in this house?' Peggy patted his hand but it was Kelly she turned to. 'I didn't normally take older children,' she said. 'But little Ari came along when he was about six or seven and I just couldn't resist. And he just stayed and stayed. By the time he was a teenager I couldn't have managed without him. He was the man of the house. And a... what do they call them these days? Those people who have the magic touch with babies?'

'A baby whisperer?' Kelly was biting her lip, as if she was really amused.

'That's the one.' Peggy was smiling now. 'Poor wee Stacey was only a few weeks old and she was still going through withdrawal when she came here. Her mum was an addict. Never heard a baby cry so much.' She turned her gaze back to Ari. 'She was hard work, wasn't she, love?'

'Still is,' Ari murmured. 'I need to go and talk to her. I'm expecting a call back from her case worker at Social Services. We'll be making a plan.'

'She doesn't need a plan. She can stay here until she has the baby.'

'With all your drugs in the house? When she's only been clean for a few months, if that?' Ari shook his head. 'And I heard what she said to you before. That's not the kind of thing you should have to put up with.'

Kelly obviously agreed with him, judging by the look on her face. Yeah... He already knew that she knew how damaging cruel words could be. Ari could feel a beat of that pull towards Kelly that he'd been so aware of yesterday. That vulnerability hiding beneath such a strong exterior that he wanted to know more about.

'She's upset,' Peggy said softly. 'She came here needing help and found that *I* was one who's needing help now. She's cross, that's all. She's only seventeen, remember. And she's got some big decisions to make about that baby or hers.' Trying to sit up, Peggy visibly winced.

'You're still pretty sore, aren't you?' Kelly glanced at her watch. 'I'm going to give you the rest of this morphine. If you're still in too much pain in another ten minutes, it might be worth considering a trip to hospital to really get on top of it.'

Ari nodded. 'They might even let you keep your surgery slot. The sooner you have that done, the less likely you are to even have this level of pain.'

But Peggy shook her head firmly. 'I'm not going anywhere,' she said. 'Not while Stacey needs me.'

'You know what?' Ari sighed. 'You're stubborn, that's what you are.'

'Look who's talking. Tell you what, Ari. You go and sign up for that flying squad so you can do something you'd love and I'll go and have that operation.'

'You mean that?'

Peggy nodded. 'I'll have Stacey here to help look after me when I get out.'

Ari saw the way Kelly's eyes widened at that suggestion but he'd learned long ago that Peggy's instincts were usually correct.

'Okay…how's the pain now?' Kelly asked.

'So much better. I can move.' Peggy sat up to demonstrate. 'I don't need to go to hospital.' She looked up at Ari. 'So, is it a deal?'

'Is what a deal?'

'You join the flying squad and I'll go and have that operation as soon as they give me a new date.'

'It's a deal.' Ari would work out how to care for Peggy if Stacey wasn't around by then.

It was Kelly's hand that Peggy patted this time. 'He would have joined anyway,' she said in a stage whisper. 'That way, he gets a chance to get to know you properly. You're just the sort of girl who'd be perfect for my Ari.'

Kelly made a slightly strangled sound but then cleared her throat. 'Let me take this IV out, Peggy. And then you'll need to press on it firmly for a few minutes to stop any bleeding. I'm going to have to get back to work now.'

There was a pink flush to Kelly's cheeks that hadn't been there a minute ago. And it felt like she was avoiding looking at him but Ari didn't get the feeling that she was too embarrassed by Peggy's comments. If she had been, she wouldn't have paused when he was seeing her to the door a couple of minutes later. And she certainly wouldn't have offered to give him her phone number.

'In case you do sign up for the squad,' she said. 'I can give you a few tips on how it all works.'

'I'll have to sign up now, won't I?' Ari opened his phone to input the number. 'Once Peggy's settled on a bargaining chip, she's not likely to give it up before she gets what she wants.'

Kelly's smile lit up her face when she finished giving him the number. 'She's a bit of a character, your mum.'

Ari's smile felt a little wobbly round the edges. 'She's the best.'

Kelly lowered her voice as she glanced at the bedroom door behind him. 'Good luck,' she murmured. 'I could also steer you in the direction of some organisations that might be able to help if you need support.'

It sounded like Kelly actually wanted him to call her. Was the fact that they could be considered professional rather than personal reasons just a disguise? Ari wasn't blind. He could see that flicker of interest in her eyes. Or maybe he was feeling that connection getting stronger between them. So strong, it was tempting to keep following Kelly towards the front door, just so he could keep her in sight a little longer. But the tiny sound from the bedroom behind him reminded Ari of exactly why he couldn't do that.

'Thanks,' he said. 'I'll keep that in mind. See you around, Kelly.'

He turned back then, and kept moving till he was beside the shapeless lump that was Stacey bundled beneath the duvet.

'Okay, Stace. Are you going to tell me why you're acting up? Is Mum right? Are you angry that she's not well enough to look after you?'

'It's not that she's "not well".' Spiky red hair appeared above huge brown eyes. 'She's *dying*, Ari. And that means I don't have anybody.' She burst into tears as Ari sat on the bed beside her and wrapped his arms around her.

'I know,' he said. 'It's horrible. And it's hard. But she needs our help, Stace. And, hey…you've got me, haven't you? I'm not nobody.'

He'd felt like it once, though, hadn't he? When he'd been a small boy that nobody wanted. When the world had seemed huge and terrifying and he'd been deemed worthless. Until Peggy had wrapped her arms around him, like he was doing for Stacey right now. Until he'd had the love and support that meant he could find his place in the world and follow his passion for helping others in the same way he'd been helped.

It was a foster sister who was half his age that he was focusing on at this moment but he couldn't quite dismiss that thought that was insisting on lingering at the back of his head.

Who loved Kelly enough to provide that kind of support? He had to wonder if she even had anybody at all, if verbal abuse from an ex-partner could make her shrink into herself as if she'd been physically assaulted. At the very least, surely that was something he should find out? Something he needed to find out to give himself some peace of mind. Because nobody should ever be left alone like that, even if it was their choice to keep their secrets and push others away.

Sometimes, just knowing that someone else understood—that you weren't alone—could be enough. And there was no excuse not to find the time to do that.

CHAPTER FOUR

THE SMALL SEMINAR room in Kensington Hospital's maternity wing was full of new faces, which was only to be expected when this was an introductory meeting for volunteers who wanted to be involved with the obstetric and neonatal flying squad service. Kelly recognised a few of them. One was someone she'd worked with at her last ambulance station and another was an emergency department nurse.

And then, of course, there was Ari, who was following through with his promise to his foster mother. Kelly could just imagine the smile on Peggy's face when he'd told her where he was going this evening. She had probably had a very similar smile on her own face when she'd seen him walk through the door because seeing him again just made her feel good. Happy… He was now sitting in the top row of this tiered room, whilst Kelly was down at the front with an obstetric consultant, Phillip Jones, who had just introduced himself.

'Kensington Hospital has the distinction of being one of the first hospitals south of the Scottish border to form and maintain an obstetric flying squad to provide emergency back-up to GPs, ambulances and midwives.'

Kelly's glance shifted back to the only midwife she

knew to be in the audience this evening. It had been nearly a week since the call that, in retrospect, may well have changed her life. If she hadn't met Ari again under those very particular circumstances, she would probably have never spoken to him again. She might have dismissed him, like pretty much every man she'd met in the last couple of years, as being untrustworthy and to be avoided at all costs. Not only had she been deeply touched by the closeness of his relationship with Peggy, she'd done something that would have been unthinkable even a week or two ago. She'd given her phone number to a man she'd only just met. She'd even given him a reason to contact her and Ari had done just that, messaging her only a couple of days later.

What do I need to know about signing up for the flying squad?

Your timing is perfect. There's going to be an introductory session for new team members on Thursday night if you're free.

I'll do my best to be there.

His best obviously hadn't been sabotaged by any domestic crisis this time and it was a little disturbing how Kelly's heart had lifted at the sight of him arriving. Her breath had actually caught in her throat when he'd smiled at her. Even now, having had time to give herself a small lecture about the dangers of trusting anyone too much or too fast, finding him watching her so that their gazes caught for a heartbeat was enough to give her a tiny ripple of sensation deep in her abdomen.

Attraction…that's what it was. Mixed with perhaps more than a dollop of hope…

'Our ambulance service does an amazing job…' Phillip gestured towards Kelly, who tilted her head in acknowledgment of the compliment '...but, like a specialist trauma retrieval team, our purpose is manage serious emergencies on scene and to stabilise both the mother and baby so that they can be safely transported to a hospital such as Kensington that is equipped with adult, neonatal and paediatric intensive care facilities. Because we are a leading tertiary centre in this field, our flying squad is also used as a retrieval service to transport premature or sick babies from other hospitals.'

Kelly had heard all this before. Many times, in fact, so it was no wonder that her attention was slipping a little. Had Peggy been given a new date for her surgery? And what about Stacey? Had she had some antenatal assessment? How far along was she in her pregnancy? Was she still in that big old house with Peggy and Ari? What was going to happen after her baby was born?

So many questions and they barely scratched the surface of what Kelly wanted to know because the answers wouldn't tell her anything more about Ari. Why had he had to go into foster care in the first place? How had he turned out to be as caring and gentle as he obviously was when a lot of children with a similar start in life ended up going in a completely different and destructive direction?

And...did he have anyone else significant in his life? Like a girlfriend?

Kelly could feel her gaze being pulled back in Ari's direction again but she resisted, keeping it firmly on the man who was still speaking.

'The difference between our flying squad and a trauma retrieval team is that our team members and our ambulance are chosen and equipped for a specific purpose. We carry a state-of-the-art incubator and re-suscitation gear and the team will always include an on-call obstetrician and/or paediatrician, depending on availability and what the job is. What we couldn't do without are the ancillary volunteer members of the team who are rostered to be here twenty-four seven to assist us.

'You are all experienced paramedics, midwives, nurses and drivers who are prepared to give up your time and use your skills to help us provide a service that has been demonstrated to save the lives of both mothers and babies. So…thank you all for being here and…welcome. I'm going to hand over to Kelly now, who's one our long-standing paramedic volunteers and has now trained to a level where she might be leading the team if our specialists are unavailable.'

Kelly could feel how every glance was on her now and she could feel her muscles tense. She didn't want to be the centre of attention or get praised to a point where you might have people expecting you to be per-fect. For them to be watching your every move, ready to pounce on any perceived faults and put you back in your place. She especially didn't want Ari to think that she had an overinflated ego. Was he staring at her as well? Kelly actually ducked her head to avoid looking up but she knew the answer to that question because she could feel that tingle in her gut again and it was as strong as some kind of electrical current.

'Kelly's going to give you a brief outline of the types of obstetric emergencies you might expect to go to and the management from a pre-hospital perspective.' Phil-lip was moving to sit down. 'One of our neonatal pae-diatricians will talk about our protocols for caring for premature infants after that, and that'll be enough for your first session. We have regular training evenings that will get you up to speed to assist with things like neonatal resuscitation and the use of incubators.'

'And we regularly finish those training evenings over at the Kensington Arms.' Kelly smiled at the group as she stood up. 'It's not all work and no fun, I promise. And I can tell you from personal experience that you're going to meet some amazing people and learn a great deal about managing specific kinds of medical emergencies. Like our more common obstetric challenges such as major post-partum haemorrhage, a retained placenta, or an obstructed labour.'

Kelly paused and looked around a group of people who were giving her their full attention. They were putting their hands up because they wanted to make a difference to women—and their babies—who might be in serious trouble and that was something she respected.

'You know, I've given an introductory talk like this many times in the four years that I've been involved with the flying squad,' she told them. 'And I usually show you some flow charts of the protocols we follow and throw in a few boring statistics about how often these types of cases happen and what the outcomes might be but tonight I'm going to do something a bit different.

'I'm going to tell you a story about a case I went to only a week or so ago where a midwife was clued up enough to know that something serious was happening. It wasn't a callout to the flying squad but it could well have been. And it's the kind of job where you know that you've made a difference because I can tell you about how it ended for both a premature baby and a young mother—let's call her Susan—and that outcome is why we do what we do. And why I, for one, have found being a part of this team to be life-changing.'

Kelly was about to tell the story of how they'd met, wasn't she?

Ari was that "clued-up" midwife, and the compliment meant quite a lot, coming from someone whose work he respected so much. He could feel his lips were curling up on one side as, yet again, Kelly's gaze sought him out in the far corner of this group.

There was no doubt that Kelly had been pleased to see him turn up tonight. About as pleased as Peggy had been when he'd told her where he was going.

'Oh, I'm so happy. If you see that lovely Kelly again, invite her to dinner. I want to thank her for taking such good care of me last week.'

She wanted to do a lot more than that, of course. Ari had no intention of passing on an invitation that was such a blatant attempt at matchmaking but he did want a chance to talk to Kelly. He listened to her describing Vicky's signs and symptoms and refrained from joining in when she invited the group to guess what their provisional diagnosis had been.

'Premature labour?' someone suggested.

'That could certainly explain some abdominal pain but not the amount of blood loss.'

'Placenta praevia?'

'Good thought.' Kelly nodded. 'But the classic presentation is painless bleeding in the third trimester.'

'Trauma,' a young man near the front offered. 'I work as a nurse in ED and I've seen that kind of presentation. Had Susan had a car accident she thought was only minor at the time? Or a fall?'

'That wins as being the closest differential diagnosis,' Kelly told him. 'And I could add that, due to the situation we found ourselves in, we had to consider the possibility of domestic violence.'

A ripple of increased interest ran through the group. Many of these people were used to working in a controlled, clinical environment where there were security guards and plenty of colleagues if they found themselves in a dodgy situation. They were signing themselves up for frontline work in the community with all the unknowns that could bring, but they were up for it. Excited by the prospect, even. As Ari was. While there was still the worry of not being immediately available if Peggy needed him if he was on a night shift for the squad, this was exactly the kind of thing that fed his passion for the work he did. And Peggy wasn't about to back down on that deal they'd made.

Having been given the clue that what they were dealing with had very similar signs and symptoms to abdominal trauma in pregnancy, it was an easy step to discuss placental abruption and the treatment given before rushing "Susan" to hospital. Kelly finished her story with the successful outcome of the timely Caesarean and two lives that had been saved, and that was why Ari wanted to talk to her. He could give her an epilogue to that case history because he'd been up to visit Vicky earlier today when he'd been on the labour ward for a delivery.

Any chance to talk had to wait until this introductory evening was over and the group, other than those on call at the hospital, drifted down the road to the pub.

And then he had to wait even longer because there were so many people keen to talk to Kelly and ask questions about her experiences with the flying squad.

'Do we really need to know everything about the settings for neonatal ventilation pressures and for the incubators? It sounded incredibly complicated.'

'The more you know, the better you can assist the specialists but you'll never be sent somewhere on your own, don't worry. If there are no doctors available for whatever reason, the job is taken over by the ambulance service—usually with a rapid response vehicle, like the one I work in, followed by transport options of either an ambulance or a helicopter.'

Even the bartender in the Kensington Arms wanted to talk to Kelly, judging by the grin on his face as he came to take her order.

'Hey…it's you again. Hope you're not still waiting for that idiot who stood you up last week.'

It was becoming familiar, that feeling of connection when Kelly's gaze caught and held his own, but this time it was a whole heap stronger. He could see amusement dancing in her eyes but, below that, he could sense what he already knew—that Kelly understood why he hadn't turned up that night and she'd not only forgiven him, she respected him for his choice.

The bartender hadn't noticed anything significant in the blink of time before Kelly smiled back.

'He's far from an idiot and it wasn't his fault. You must be used to us medical types.'

'Some of the stories I hear being told make my hair curl.' The bartender shook his head. 'And meals that get abandoned by people rushing off to an emergency? Don't know how you all do it. Now, what can I get you?'

'A glass of white wine, thanks. Small one. Ari—can I get you something?'

'Just a soda water for me. I'll have to be on my bike in a few minutes.' He took the glass from Kelly a moment later. 'I just wanted to let you know about…you know… Susan?'

'Oh?' Kelly turned back swiftly after picking up her wine. 'I've been wanting to follow up on her.'

'I just caught her packing her bag. She's about to be discharged, having made a good recovery from that emergency Caesarean.'

'And the baby? It was a boy, wasn't it?'

'It was. He's still in NICU but doing well, apparently. And…even better, there's some support in place for dealing with domestic abuse. If…um… Susan wants to take it, that is.'

'Mmm…' Kelly glanced over her shoulder but the other members of tonight's group were busy getting to know each other and weren't close enough to overhear. 'That can be tricky. People—even intelligent people— can get caught in dysfunctional relationships. It can be quite hard to escape.'

That tiny frown line between her eyes was a dead giveaway for Ari. She knew what she was talking about because she'd been there. It was as if she was offering an excuse for having been stupid enough to have been caught herself. He wanted to touch that line and smooth it away. Instead, he just made the connection that came automatically with their eye contact.

'I know how hard it can be,' he said softly. 'But thank goodness some people are brave enough to make that escape, however long it takes. Let's hope Susan is as well.'

The way Kelly's eyes widened was almost invisible but, thanks to that connection, Ari was quite sure that she'd received the message that he understood more than she might have realised. And that he applauded the effort it might have taken for her to make that escape. Not that this was the place or time to talk about it.

'How's Stacey doing?' Kelly asked hurriedly. 'And Peggy?'

'Stace is okay, I think. She finally went to an antenatal appointment. They're not sure of a due date because the best time to estimate gestational age by ultrasound is between weeks eight and eighteen. It gets less accurate after that and this baby may well be small for dates given the lifestyle Stace has been living, but she could be nearly eight months along.'

'She's still with Peggy?'

'Yes. And seems to be behaving herself. Peggy's not about to let her go back on the streets and you already know how stubborn my mum can be. Hence why I'm here tonight so that she rings the hospital tomorrow and hopefully gets a new date for surgery.'

'How's *she* doing?' That frown line had reappeared but this time it was there from a sincere concern for someone else's welfare and Ari's heart melted a little. Kelly the paramedic was a genuinely kind and caring person and the thought that anyone could have treated her badly was unacceptable.

'She's doing well,' Ari said. 'Her pain's under good control. She wanted me to pass on her thanks to you for helping her so much last week.'

'It was a real pleasure.' Kelly smiled. 'I like your mum a lot.'

'She likes you, too.'

That smile was doing something weird to Ari's brain. It seemed to be reminding him that Kelly might need someone to tell her how amazing she was. That she might need a friend. Telling him that he was quite capable of *being* that friend and ignoring any attraction that might be there. It was also undermining that resolve about what he *wasn't* going to tell her.

'She also wants you to come to dinner with us so that she can thank you herself. If that's not unethical or anything, given that she's been your patient?'

There was surprise in Kelly's eyes now but the way she caught her breath suggested that the surprise was not unpleasant.

'That depends…'

'On what?'

'On whether Peggy was simply a patient or whether I can consider her to be a patient that's the mother of one of my colleagues from the flying squad. Or, even better, a friend's mum.'

'That's an affirmative.' Ari nodded solemnly. 'On both counts.'

It was true. He was looking forward to working on the same team she was so passionate about. He could also be a friend, if she wanted him to be—the best friend it was possible for anyone *to* be. It certainly seemed as if she liked that idea, judging by the sparkle in those amazingly blue eyes, but her tone was just as solemn as his had been.

'That's okay, then,' she said. 'I'd love to come to dinner.'

Well…this was a bit awkward.

There she was, having just knocked on Peggy's door

and a text message pinged into her phone at the same moment the door was opening.

'That'll be Ari,' Peggy told her as she opened her message. 'He just rang me to say he's running a wee bit late.'

'Mmm…' Kelly was scanning the message. Ari was certain it was a false alarm but his client was anxious enough to need further reassurance so he was meeting her at the hospital.

'Come in, come in,' Peggy urged. 'And never mind about Ari. This will give us a chance to have a chat.'

The crinkles around Peggy's eyes made her smile so utterly welcoming that any awkwardness simply evaporated. Until Kelly arrived in the kitchen, that was, and found Stacey sitting at the kitchen table, glaring at her. This was the first time that Kelly had seen her properly and the teenager's face looked too thin beneath eyes that were as dark as Ari's. Her bright red hair was in long spikes on one side and shaved on the other and she had a silver ring through the bottom of her nose. Her stare was definitely unfriendly.

'What's *she* doing here?'

'I told you that one of Ari's friends was coming to dinner.' Peggy patted Stacey's shoulder as she walked past. 'Don't eat that whole bag of crisps, okay? You'll spoil your appetite for proper food.'

'She's Ari's *girlfriend*?' Stacey shook her head. 'Nah…he's never brought a girlfriend home in his life, has he?' Her huff of sound was dismissive. 'They've never lasted that long, that's why.'

'I'm just a friend,' Kelly told her. 'Ari and I are going to be working together sometimes.'

'On a *flying* squad.' Peggy made it sound like the

most elite working environment possible. ''Specially for mothers and babies. Real emergencies. He'll sleep at the hospital sometimes to do a night shift. Maybe with Kelly.'

Stacey snorted. 'He'll be sleeping with Kelly?'

'No.' Peggy and Kelly spoke together in a mix of indignant and admonishing tones and then they looked at each other. For a beat, as they made eye contact, Kelly could see that Peggy was hoping there might be something more than friendship in her relationship with Ari. Kelly had the uncomfortable feeling that Peggy might be able to see exactly the same thing in her eyes but, if she did, it just gave the two women an understanding that closed any gap between them. And it made them both smile.

'Can I do anything to help with dinner?' Kelly asked. 'It smells wonderful but I'm not sure you should be on your feet too much.'

'It's just a roast. The oven's doing all the work. And I'm good, thanks, lovey. I've got my pills and patches sorted out so I'm not in any pain at all at the moment.' There was a mischievous twinkle in her eyes. 'Maybe I don't even need that operation.'

Kelly grinned. 'You wouldn't go back on your half of the deal, though, would you?'

Stacey held up her crisp packet to tip the last crumbs into her mouth. 'She's having the operation in a couple of weeks,' she informed Kelly. 'And I'm going to be looking after her when she gets home.'

So there...her tone suggested. You're not needed here...

Or maybe it was more like a warning to stay away from Ari? Kelly remembered Peggy saying that Ari had looked after Stacey when she had first arrived—a miserable baby going through drug withdrawal—and that it had been hard work, even for a baby whisperer. How many hours had he spent soothing that baby? she wondered. And how strong would the bond between them be? Did Stacey know her biological father or had Ari been the only man to help care for her as a young child, even though he would have only been a teenager himself back then? Anyway…she could understand why Stacey might feel possessive.

'It's good that you'll be here,' she told Stacey. 'I'm guessing it's quite hard to stop Peggy doing more than she probably should be doing.'

'Oh, pfff…' Peggy flapped her hand. 'Come and sit down somewhere comfy. Would you like a glass of wine? Or a cup of tea?'

'A cup of tea sounds wonderful. Oh…and I brought this for you…' Kelly handed over the box she was carrying. 'Just something for dessert. A mud cake. It can go in the freezer if you don't need it.'

'Ooh…that's your favourite, isn't it, Stace? Mud cake?'

Stacey shrugged. 'I've kind of gone off chocolate.' She pushed herself to her feet, the baggy, purple corduroy dungarees she was wearing almost hiding her bump. 'I'll be in my room,' she told Peggy.

'Don't mind her.' A few minutes later Kelly carried the tray with the teapot and cups down to the other end of the kitchen where they could sit on the couch. 'She's got a lot to cope with at the moment and she's trying hard. She's actually got a heart of gold hidden under all that angst.'

Kelly smiled. 'You must have been the best foster mother. You see the good in everyone, don't you?'

'I try, lovey. Yes, milk and two sugars for me, thanks.' She accepted the cup with a sigh, took an appreciative sip and then caught Kelly's gaze. 'We've all got things that can hide the best of us, haven't we?'

'That's true.' Kelly knew she'd been hiding for a long time. Being here, in this house, knowing that Ari would also be here very soon, felt like she was stepping out of that hiding place and it could have scary, except that she was with an extraordinary old lady who had the ability to make you feel safe.

Like Ari did...

'Sometimes those things are a bit hard to get past,' Peggy added quietly. 'And the hardest thing of all to rebuild, after it's broken, is trust.'

Kelly swallowed hard. How could Peggy know this much about her? What had Ari said?

'I think I told you that Ari came to me when he was just a little lad?'

Kelly nodded. 'About six or seven?'

'Mmm... His mother had taken him out to a children's playground somewhere. Hyde Park, maybe? Anyway, it was supposed to be a special outing—a treat for his birthday. She must have waited until he was too busy playing to notice and she just walked away. Abandoned him. He didn't speak for weeks. Took a year to see him smile.'

Kelly's heart was breaking for that little boy. For a trust between a mother and child that should be unbreakable to have been shattered in such a brutal way. She remembered something else that Peggy had told her, too. That the first time she'd seen him smile had been when he'd been holding a baby and had managed to stop it crying. When he'd been protecting someone even more vulnerable than himself.

She had to blink hard now. That said so much about the kind of person Ari was, didn't it? It was no wonder she felt safe around him. No wonder Stacey wanted to look out for him. As she blinked away the threat of tears, Kelly found herself focusing on the blanket she was sitting on. Trying to centre herself in the present. Trying not to duck back into that hiding place because she was feeling exposed and potentially too vulnerable.

'I love this,' she told Peggy. 'It's the sort of blanket that even looks like a cuddle.'

'I've made a few of them in my time, I can tell you. Too many. I give them away now, although I've started a new one for Stacey so she can wrap herself up when she's feeding the baby in the night. If she decides to keep it, that is.' Peggy closed her eyes for a heartbeat, as if she was in pain, but she was smiling brightly again as soon she opened her eyes. 'I meant the baby,' she whispered. 'It's not hard to keep a blanket, is it?'

Kelly smiled back, taking the hint that the atmosphere needed lightening. 'I've always wanted to learn to knit,' she admitted. 'I'd love to make something like this.'

'It's the perfect way to learn, making granny squares. Do you know they're actually called Peggy squares, too? After the little girl who started making them in the Depression. And, there's no time like the present, I always say.' Peggy put down her tea cup and reached into a cavernous bag beside her end of the couch. 'I've got some needles and wool right here.

Look, I'll cast on for you and you'll be knitting by the time dinner's ready.'

It always felt like home letting himself in through that red front door but it was even more of a comfort this evening.

Maybe it was because Ari was starving, having missed lunch and then been caught late at the hospital when he was more than ready for his dinner. The enticing smell of a roasting chicken was the first thing he was aware of as he stepped back into his childhood home. The second thing, almost simultaneously noticed, was a peal of laughter. A laugh he'd never heard before but he knew instantly that it was Kelly who was laughing and knowing that she was enjoying herself even if the evening hadn't started off quite as planned gave Ari a ripple of pleasure. Or maybe it was the sound of that laughter that was giving him that sensation. And maybe that ripple wasn't simply pleasure because it came along with a knot in his gut that felt very different from something as shallow as mere enjoyment. But it didn't feel quite like attraction either. It actually felt like a knot. Complicated and hard to unravel.

He passed Stacey's room on his way to the kitchen and paused when he saw her lying on her bed through the open door.

'Not hungry, Stace?'

'Nah…'

'You want to come and keep us company, anyway?'

'What, you and your *girlfriend*? No, thanks.'

Ari took a step further into her room. 'She's not my girlfriend.'

That knot tightened another notch so that it was almost painful and, at the same time, his stomach rumbled. Perhaps it wasn't being caused by anything emotional at all and it was nothing more than hunger, which could be easily fixed.

'She's just a friend.' He added, as further reassurance to a young girl who seemed to be looking for reasons why she wasn't wanted, 'As if I've got time for a girlfriend when I've got you and Mum to look after at the moment.'

There was a beat of silence broken by the sound of a frustrated groan from the direction of the kitchen, followed by a murmur from Peggy and then more laughter.

'She's trying to learn how to knit,' Stacey told Ari. 'And you know what?'

'What?'

'She sucks.'

'Hey…' Ari put on a stern face. 'We all suck when we try something for the first time. What counts is sucking that up so that you can get to be good at it.' He turned away. 'You might not be hungry but, man, I could eat a horse and whatever Mum's cooking smells amazing.'

He could hear the sound of Stacey's boots hitting the floor behind him as he left the room.

'Maybe I am a bit hungry, after all,' she said.

CHAPTER FIVE

'ARE YOU SURE you've got time for this?'

'Absolutely.' Kelly opened the back doors of the ambulance that was parked in a reserved slot at the edge of the bay outside Kensington's emergency department. 'Unless there's a call for the flying squad, in which case I'll be in exactly the right place, won't I? Jump in,' she invited. 'If you're sure you've got the time?'

'I'm back early from house calls.' Ari climbed into the ambulance. 'I've got at least half an hour before my outpatient clinic starts. Unless I get a call myself, of course. Babies have a mind of their own sometimes.'

'Don't they just? Pull those doors shut so we can keep the rain out.' Kelly could feel goosebumps where the tunic of her scrub suit left her arms bare. Was it just the chilly weather or did it have something to do with being shut in a confined space with Ari Lawson? It certainly seemed to accentuate his size and that sheer masculinity.

Kelly cleared her throat, hurriedly searching for something else to focus on. 'So…here we are. This is our squad truck. It's set up a bit differently from a normal ambulance. We've got the two incubators, in case we dealing with twins, and the seating for the two crew members. If we're transporting the mother as well, she sits up front with the driver or, if it's an obstetric emergency we're usually backing up a normal ambulance crew so they've got the stretcher. Our third crew sits up front, too, if we've got someone on an orientation shift. Has someone contacted you or have you put your name down for one yet?'

'Not yet. Peggy's waitlisted in case there's a gap due to a cancelation so she might not get much notice for her surgery. Could be any day. I'll put my name down as soon as we know what's happening.' Ari was looking around at all the monitoring equipment and the built-in storage for a wealth of supplies. 'You look set up to deal with major interventions here.'

'We have two main kinds of scenarios. One is to cut out-of-hospital time for a sick baby as much as possible so we do low-level interventions like a peripheral IV, nasogastric tube, oxygen and then we hit the road. What we like to call a "swoop and scoop" job.'

Ari was listening intently, his gaze fixed on Kelly. It was easier to hold that eye contact when she was talking about something professional like this but it didn't stop that frisson of something that was certainly not at all professional which eye contact with this man always seemed to generate.

'And the other main scenario? Is that a "stay and play", like we had with Vicky?'

The reminder of how they'd met and her first impressions of Ari made Kelly realise how much their friendship had developed since then. There was a familiarity about his company now and after that visit to his home and getting a glimpse into what was important in his life, it seemed like Kelly was further along a path to them becoming so much closer and that was tantalising. Scary but compelling at the same time. Even listening to his voice was delicious because it was as deep and dark as his eyes and it had just a hint of a gravelly edge to it. Everything about Ari was classically masculine. Apart from his job, that was. And the way he wore his hair. Maybe that was all part of the attraction—the things that made him stand out as being so different...

'Pretty much.' Amazing how thoughts—and feelings—could flash by so fast nobody else would ever guess what you might be thinking. Ari hadn't even noticed any hesitation in Kelly's response. 'That's where we stabilise the baby as much as possible before leaving the referring hospital or scene and that might involve intubation, arterial or central venous cannulation or sometimes it might be something like artificial surfactant administration for extreme respiratory failure or a chest drain to deal with a pneumothorax. Depends what expertise we have on board. They're not cut-and-dried boundaries either. Often it ends up being a combination, although it's preferable not to have to stop to initiate anything major, like intubation or CPR.'

'How do you manage CPR on a baby in an incubator?'

'We get it out. Look, there's a great feature on this travel incubator with a slide-out mattress.' Kelly demonstrated how easy it was to get the kind of access they would need to start CPR. 'Quick as...'

'That's very cool.'

Ari moved to help Kelly slide the mattress back into place and, as his hand brushed hers, she felt her breath catch. Skin contact was even more charged than eye contact and had far more effect than the sound of his voice. Was Ari aware of the same sensation—as if one's skin had suddenly become a whole lot more sensitive? If he was, he was hiding it well. His attention was on the features of this state-of-the-art transport incubator.

'So…those tubing ports are to allow for monitoring leads for the ECG, continuous blood pressure and pulse oximetry without heat or humidity loss,' Kelly told him. 'Did I hear that you've got a qualification in neonatal resuscitation? The team were really impressed with the postgraduate study you've clocked up.'

Ari nodded. 'That was an amazing course. I'd done the basics, of course, but there was so much to learn about the physiology, especially with resuscitating premature babies. It's a delicate balance, isn't it? The first priority is to get lungs inflated but you have to be so gentle with how much pressure you use and so careful about oxygen administration.'

'Mmm…' Kelly's gaze was on Ari's hands as he spoke. She'd seen him working so she knew how capable and gentle he was with his touch. She could imagine him working on tiny babies that he could probably cup in the palm of his hand, and this time it wasn't so much of a tingle of attraction that she was aware of. More like a squeeze of something rather more poignant. Like seeing a fireman holding a tiny kitten could spark, or a burly guy stopping to help an old lady across a road. The thought of that little old lady was enough to distract her completely from what was supposed to be a purely professional meeting to show Ari the way the flying squad's ambulance was set up.

'How's Peggy?' she found herself asking. 'I was a bit worried the other night. She didn't eat much of that lovely dinner she'd cooked, did she? Is she worried about the surgery?'

'Only because she won't be around to keep an eye on Stacey. She's worried she might go back to the group she was living with. There's a boy involved, by the sound of things.'

'The father of the baby?'

Ari shrugged. 'Don't know. Don't think so but, if it is, she's not saying. I suspect Peggy's the only person she really trusts but I get that. Hope you weren't offended by her attitude.'

Kelly shook her head and then smiled. 'She doesn't like me much, does she?'

'She doesn't like anyone or any*thing* much right now. Including herself. I'm not too sure of the best way to handle any of this—I've been away from home for too long. I haven't even seen Stace since she was about fourteen.'

'She's lucky to have Peggy in her corner.'

'Anyone who gets Peggy in their corner is lucky,' Ari agreed.

His smile was enough to give Kelly's heart another huge squeeze. 'I've only just met her,' she said quietly, 'but I feel lucky that she's touched my life as well. She's an extraordinary woman, isn't she? Her house… that dinner we had…it felt like, I don't know…a real family.'

Ari's smile widened. 'Complete with the angsty teenager.'

'I was an only child,' Kelly told him, 'and my parents were very absorbed by their academic careers. I never really got that feeling of family and I've always felt like there was something missing from my life.'

'You'll find it,' Ari told her quietly. 'You can create your own one day.'

Kelly shrugged. 'Maybe.' She hadn't found anything like that so far, though. Quite the opposite.

'Biology creates relatives,' Ari added. 'It's love that creates family and it's never too late to find that.'

'So friends can be family?' Kelly caught his gaze again, a tiny part of her brain almost counting down to when that frisson would arrive.

'Absolutely.' The gaze from those dark eyes softened and it felt like a comforting touch.

And…there it was. Only this time it was strong enough to feel painful. This wasn't simply attraction, it was desire. Strong enough for the scary element to be noticeably ramped up, given the disaster that had come from the last time she'd given in to feelings like this. Her time with Darryn had been so destructive that she'd run from any hint of interest from—or in— another man.

But this felt safer.

Perhaps it was because of Stacey's dismissive comment the other night about how girlfriends never lasted long enough to be invited home. Or Peggy's gentle warning about how hard it was for Ari to trust women. Kelly might be attracted but there was no chance at all that she was going to make the first move. She knew what it was like to find it hard to trust. How easy it was to get scared into running back to a safe place— the way she'd been running for years.

And, if Ari did that, she wouldn't be able to spend time with him. Even if they could only ever be just friends, it was something she definitely didn't want to risk losing.

'Let me know when Peggy's surgery is scheduled, won't you? I'll be there as soon as she's up for visitors.' Her smile felt slightly wobbly. 'I want to show her the squares I've knitted. It's taken nearly a whole ball of wool but I'm getting better at it. I might even go and buy some more wool.'

'I remember going to charity shops with Peggy when I was a kid. There's usually a basket of odd balls of wool in a corner somewhere. She'd let me choose all the brightest colours. She made me a blanket when I left home and I've still got it.'

'Bring one of those blankets in, when she's admitted,' Kelly suggested. 'If I was in a hospital bed, it would make me feel better.'

'That's a great idea.' But Ari's face looked sombre. Thoughtful. 'You're a nice person, Kelly. Special…'

Kelly swallowed hard. Look away, she told herself. Don't make this something it isn't. But it was Ari who looked away first. Abruptly.

'Is that the time? I'm going to have to run.'

To the maternity wing's outpatient department? Or to his safe place?

Not that it mattered. Kelly might not be running from the awareness of how attracted she was to Ari but she still needed those boundaries as much as he did. And perhaps that was where the real feeling of safety was coming from—knowing that you could step behind that invisible line and the safety it provided was going to be not only understood but respected.

The woman in the charity shop who took Kelly's money for the balls of wool a day or two later looked almost as old as Peggy. She cast an admiring glance at Kelly's uniform.

'You work on the ambulance, don't you?'

'I do. I've got a few minutes spare at the moment, though, because I'm on my lunch break—I'm not really skiving off to go shopping.'

'I'm sure you're not.'

The balls of wool were being counted as they got put into a paper bag. Kelly had bought a few more than she probably needed but she wanted to replace the one that Peggy had kindly given her, along with that first pair of knitting needles. She wasn't that far from the old house, in fact, so she might have time to pop in for a quick visit.

'Wonderful job you folk do,' the woman continued. 'I needed an ambulance once myself, you know…when I took a funny turn at the supermarket. I— *Oh…*'

They were both startled by the loud thump and rattle of someone hitting the plate-glass window of the charity shop behind the woman who was in charge of the till. For a moment, as she saw the look of terror on the elderly woman's face, Kelly was worried that she might have to deal with another "funny turn", but her attention swiftly shifted to what was happening on the other side of the window. An unkempt and angry young man had shoved a girl so that her back had slammed into the window. He still had his hands on her shoulders and he looked as though he was about to start shaking her. The glass was fortunately thick enough not to shatter under the impact, but it wasn't thick enough to totally mute the swearing and insults being thrown at the girl.

'Why can't you just do what I tell you to do, you stu-

pid, ugly bitch? Too stupid to live, that's your problem. Can't think what I ever saw in you...'

'Oh, my...' The charity shop volunteer had her hand to her chest. 'Young people these days...it must be drugs or something, surely? Should I call the police, do you think?'

Kelly could only see the girl's back but she'd known instantly exactly who it was. Nobody else could have that half-spiky, half-shaved scarlet hair teamed with a pair of purple dungarees.

Kelly shook her head. 'I'll see if I can deal with it. If I can't then I'll call the police on my radio. They might get here quicker that way. You stay in here.'

It was a very good thing she was in her uniform, Kelly decided as she stormed out of the shop. Not only did she have that radio clipped to her belt so she could call for urgent assistance if needed, just the sight of someone in uniform was enough to startle and then intimidate the man who was threatening Stacey. He gave her another shove against the window, hard enough to make the glass rattle again, and then spat on the footpath as he took off, pushing through the knot of people who had stopped to see what was going on.

Stacey looked frozen for a moment as she took in the fact that her attacker had gone, that she was being stared at by a small crowd of people and that Kelly was standing beside her, looking official in her uniform.

'*What*?' she shouted at the onlookers. 'Take a picture, why don't you?'

Kelly could sense how scared the teenager was under her aggressive bravado. 'Come with me.' She put a hand on Stacey's arm. 'My car's just over there. I'll take you home.'

Stacey shook her arm free. 'I don't want to go home.'

'You want to talk to the police instead? The lady in the charity shop might have rung them already.'

That lady was coming towards them, in fact. 'Here,' she said, handing Kelly a paper bag. 'Don't forget this.' She stared at Stacey. 'Are you all right?' she asked. 'Who was that lout and why was he hitting you?'

'He wasn't hitting me,' Stacey muttered. 'And it's none of your beeswax, anyway, so shut up…'

'Well, I never…' The older woman tutted at the rude tone. 'Keep it away from my shop in future. Go and break someone else's window. I know what you look like, young lady, and I can give your description to the police.'

'This way…' This time, Kelly's hand didn't allow her hand to get shaken off. 'In the car. Now—before you get yourself into any more trouble. And put your safety belt on. I'm taking you home.'

She started the vehicle and pulled into the traffic. 'So…who was that? A friend of yours? Boyfriend?' If he was the boy Ari had heard about, he looked like trouble.

Stacey turned to stare out of the side window, clearly having no intention of responding. All Kelly could catch a glimpse of was the back of her head and her hunched shoulders. Taking a slow breath in, Kelly tried to channel some of Peggy's patience. What actually came into her head, though, was an image of a young Ari holding a tiny, miserable baby who was suffering from the effects of the drugs her mother had been taking while she was pregnant. She could imagine those strong arms sheltering the infant. She could even imagine how it would feel to be within that hold and, suddenly, that was more than enough to give her the patience and strength not to allow herself to be irritated enough to step back from this troubled girl. To try and step closer, even, and find a connection that might help.

'Maybe it isn't any of my business,' she said quietly. 'But I've been there, Stacey. That boy might not have been hitting you hard enough to leave a mark but even getting yelled at and being called names is still abuse. You don't deserve that. Don't let him put you down.'

She'd been watching the road as she spoke but, from the corner of her eye, she could see Stacey's head turning. She could feel the disbelieving stare.

'*You've* been there? What's that supposed to mean?'

'I was in an abusive relationship. For a lot longer than I should have been.'

'Is that what you told Ari? To make him like you so much?'

The words slipped past but Kelly knew she'd be thinking about that later. Not about the idea she might try and use her story to garner sympathy, though. What really mattered from those words was what "so much" might mean and why Stacey might have got that impression.

'Actually, you're the first person I've ever told,' Kelly said. 'It's not something a lot of people can understand—unless they've experienced it themselves.' She was silent for a moment. 'I'm sorry you're being treated like that. You deserve better.'

'What would you know? You don't even know me.' Stacey had wrapped her arms around herself. 'I'm nothing like you. My boyfriend's right—I'm rubbish. Just a nobody.' The words were flooding out now. 'Look at me. I'm only seventeen and I'm pregnant and I don't even know who the father is. I don't know who *my* father is and my mum did a runner years ago.' She was sobbing now. 'I've never had a family…'

Kelly pulled the SUV to the side of the road and sent up a silent plea that her radio wasn't about to crackle into life and demand that she take off somewhere else.

She reached for the box of tissues in the central console and handed Stacey a handful.

'That's not true,' she said. 'You've got two of the most amazing people that I've ever met in your life. Peggy's been caring about you since you were born. So has Ari. I've only spent one evening in your house and it felt like a family to me. It's something special and I think you know that.'

Stacey didn't bother with the tissues, ignoring the tears streaming from her eyes and her running nose. 'Peggy's going to die soon and Ari'll disappear back to his flash job in Scotland and they'll take my baby away to give it to someone who can look after it properly and then what?' Her voice rose. 'I'll have nothing. No one…'

Patience could be pushed just a bit too far. Kelly could feel anger building at the way Peggy and Ari's love for this teenager was being dismissed. She could also feel immense sadness that Peggy might be close to the end of her life and having to deal with an attitude that was so completely undeserved.

'I know you're only seventeen,' she said, keeping her tone level. 'And I know life hasn't been easy for you but…here's a newsflash, Stacey. It's not always all about *you*.'

Stacey's hiccup was a shocked sound but she had stopped crying.

'You've got good people in your corner—amazing people—and you've still got your whole life in front of you,' Kelly continued. 'There's no reason you can't turn things around and become whatever you want to be but right now it's Peggy who needs to be cared for. She's given you so much and all you can think about is how you're going to be affected when she's gone. Can't you see how selfish that is? You know what she's doing? The present she's making for you?'

Stacey's gaze was downcast, her chin tucked into her chest, but she shook her head.

'She's knitting peggy squares to make a special blanket. She wants you to be warm if you're up in the night feeding your baby. The way she probably got up in the night countless times to feed *you*.' Kelly was close to tears herself now as she reached for the paper bag that she'd tucked in beside the tissues and pulled out a ball of wool. 'Here.' She shoved it into Stacey's hands. 'Take this and give it to Peggy from me. She might need it to finish that blanket.' She turned away and put her hands on the steering wheel. 'You can walk home from here. It's not far.'

She had to clear her throat as a beep announced an incoming radio message.

'Rover One, are you receiving?'

'Rover One,' she replied. 'Receiving you loud and clear.'

'Code Red call. Stand by for details.'

'Standing by...'

Stacey had already unclipped her safety belt. Kelly dismissed her with a nod as the teenager opened the door and climbed out of her vehicle. She had turned on her beacons by the time the door was slammed shut and was ready to program the address into her satnav before she pulled out onto the road again and took off, flicking her siren into life.

There was a child choking only half a mile away. Kelly didn't look back.

Ari Lawson glanced up at the clock on the wall of the waiting room and then closed his eyes for a moment. How could time be moving this slowly? Peggy had only been in Theatre for a little over an hour but it felt like he'd been waiting for a lot longer.

'You're still here... I thought I might be too late.'

His eyes flew open and something with the force of a fist slammed into his gut. In a good way, that was. Seeing Kelly was the best surprise he could have had. A reprieve from being alone in this vigil with his memories and fears for what the near future might hold. 'Too late for what?'

'To keep you company. I had a feeling you'd be pacing around in here.' Kelly's gaze raked the otherwise empty room. 'Stacey didn't come in?'

'She said she hates hospitals. And she's got stuff she wanted to do. I said I'd ring as soon as Peggy's out of Theatre.'

'How long since she went in?' Kelly perched on the chair beside Ari.

'Over an hour ago.'

'Did they tell you how long it might take?'

'A while. They couldn't be precise. They're doing a full hysterectomy and probably need to remove a section of bowel as well so it could be quite a while. Don't feel you have to stay.'

He wanted her to stay, though, didn't he? So much so it felt more like a need than a want.

'I don't have any other place to be...' Ari might be getting used to that lovely smile of Kelly's but seeing it was never going to get old. 'And look...' Kelly opened her shoulder bag to show him what was inside. 'I've got my knitting. I can get another peggy square done. Maybe two. I'm getting faster now.'

Ari smiled. 'Peggy will be proud of you. She'll be very touched when I tell her that you came to wait, too. She already thinks that you're some kind of angel.'

Kelly ducked her head, clearly embarrassed. Was she remembering that first time she met his foster mother—when she'd said that it was about time Ari met a nice girl like her? Had she also realised that that dinner invitation had been an attempt at matchmaking on Peggy's part?

If so, it didn't seem to be standing in the way of them becoming friends. Okay, there was that undercurrent of attraction that he was pretty sure was mutual, but he also knew that Kelly wasn't going to act on it and neither was he. It was just there. Something they could ignore because, for whatever reason, neither of them wanted anything more in their lives. And that was fine by Ari because it meant that they could be real friends with no expectations of it turning into anything more than that. No pressure. No strings. It was more than fine, really. More like perfect.

Conversation was easy because they had the same interests, thanks to their work. Ari told Kelly that someone from the O&G department had contacted him to see if he was available for an observer shift with the flying squad on the coming Sunday.

'Really? I'm doing a day shift that day. It would be cool if you had your first shift with me but... Peggy will still be in hospital, won't she?'

'Which is exactly why it might be a good time to do it. If it's not busy, I can visit. It's a day shift so I wouldn't be leaving Stace alone at night. And, if it is busy, I'd have lots to tell Peggy about when I visit on Monday.'

'She'd love that. She really loved her work as a midwife, didn't she?'

'She adored babies. It's sad she didn't get to have any of her own but...if she had, I guess there'd be dozens of kids who didn't get to share that love. Kids like Stacey.'

Kelly's fingers slowed as she carefully wound her wool around the needle. 'And like you. Peggy told me a little bit about how you came to be with her. How long it took you to feel safe. She's the one who's the angel. How hard would it be to be that patient and just keep loving someone until they were ready to love you back?'

Ari had to swallow hard. He couldn't remember those early years that well but, yeah...the love was there—on both sides—and it was so powerful it made the fear of loss hit hard. Another glance at the clock. Nearly two hours now. What was happening in that operating theatre? Was it going well? Well enough to mean that Peggy might be in his life for a bit longer?

He needed to think about something else because if he let his brain latch onto the other possible scenarios, it could undermine the strength he was going to need to support Peggy. And Stacey.

'Stacey's doing some housework. Cleaning the oven today, would you believe?'

'Wow.' Kelly's glance was astonished. 'No, I'm not sure I do believe that.'

'She wants to get out in the garden if it ever stops raining, too. Said she's going to go to the charity shop and see if they've got some gardening tools.' He was watching Kelly's fingers as she looped more wool and did complicated things with the knitting needles. 'She told me she saw *you* there the other day.'

'Mmm.' Kelly didn't look up. 'I was following that good advice you gave me. Remember? About it being a good place to go and get some cheap wool? Did… um…did she say anything else?'

'Not really.' But that was when he'd noticed a change in Stacey's attitude, though. 'Why? Did you say something to her?'

'Kind of…' Kelly sounded cautious. 'She was with a boy who looked like he had some issues. I told her that it wasn't just physical stuff that was abuse and that she should know that she deserves better than that. I might have also said that she was being pretty selfish thinking only about herself instead of Peggy.'

'Well, seems like you got through to her more than I've been able to, so thanks for that. I'm beginning to think I can trust her to do a good job of looking after Peggy when she gets home and that'll make life easier for all of us.'

'Let me know if I can help. I'd really like to…'

The knitting was forgotten as Kelly looked up and caught his gaze. They were that dark shade of blue that made Ari think again that it was emotion that had deepened their colour. Sincerity. An ability to care about others on a level that was a rare quality. Peggy had it. Maybe Stacey had been impressed by it. It was something that touched Ari on a very deep level because it tapped into the very foundations of what had changed his own life so profoundly.

He held Kelly's gaze. 'I will. Peggy would love that. I reckon Stacey would be happy to see you again, too.'

'Really?'

'Really.' Ari could feel his lips curving gently. 'And what you told her? It goes both ways, you know.'

'How d'you mean?'

'You said that Stacey deserved something better than being abused.' His smile was fading but he held that eye contact. 'So do you.'

Oh…help…

Ari wanted to put his arms around Kelly but not simply to give her a friendly hug to convey understanding, or encouragement to tell him her story if she was ready. No…at this moment, he couldn't take his eyes off her face. Her eyes. Her lips…

He wanted to hold her all right.

But what he wanted to do even more was to kiss her. To put his lips against hers and see if there was a reason that this magnetic pull was so overwhelmingly powerful. That desire was just hanging there in the air between them in a silence that was increasingly significant. A balancing act that could have gone either way. All it needed was a tiny push and if that had come from Kelly, he would have been kissing her senseless in a heartbeat. Luckily the push came from an unexpected direction and it was exactly what Ari needed to get complete control.

'Mr Lawson?' The nurse in the doorway of the waiting area was smiling. 'Your mum's out of Theatre now. Would you like to come and see her in Recovery?'

CHAPTER SIX

IT WAS STILL raining on the following Sunday.

Peggy was sitting up in her corner bed by the window but she wasn't looking at the dismal weather outside, like Ari was. She had several brightly coloured knitted squares in front of her and she was beaming at Kelly.

'Look at that. You'll have enough to make a blanket in no time. I'll have to teach you how to crochet around the edges and join them together.'

'I'd like that.' Kelly smiled back. 'You look like you're feeling better today.'

'I'm ready to go home. Three days of lying around like this is more than enough.'

'Don't think so.' Ari turned back from the window. 'You've had major surgery. You need to stay in here and rest for as long as they let you.'

'What's Stacey doing today? I do wish she'd come in and visit me.'

'I think she was planning to tidy up a bit today.'

Ari's glance shifted to where Kelly was sitting on the other side of Peggy's bed and she couldn't miss the twinkle of an understanding that was just between them. It seemed that Stacey's new attitude was continuing and Ari thought that Kelly had influenced the positive change.

'I tried to persuade her to come and visit,' he told Peggy. 'But she's got a real phobia about hospitals.'

'I know...' Peggy sighed. 'She needs to get over that before she has that baby. I don't want her having a home birth. I'd never forgive myself if something went wrong. Has she even been back to those antenatal classes?'

'I'm not sure,' Ari admitted. 'She said she went but who knows?'

'I'll make sure she goes when I get back home.'

'You won't be doing anything to stress you out. I'll be making sure of that.'

Peggy shifted her gaze to Kelly. 'So, how's my boy doing? Have you been anywhere exciting yet?'

'No. Nowhere at all today. It's the quietest shift I've ever had with the flying squad. A bit boring, to be honest.'

Except that wasn't really true, was it? Being in Ari's company could never be considered boring, even if there was absolutely nothing to do. Especially not after what Kelly had imagined had happened just a few days ago in that waiting room. When it had felt like he'd been about to kiss her. She had *wanted* him to kiss her—so badly that the disappointment of that interruption had been crushing at the time, although when she'd relived that moment later, more than once, she'd realised that it was a good thing it hadn't happened. She wasn't ready for anything more than a friendship. It was confusing to even imagine it. Scary. It was just as well there'd been no hint of anything like that today.

'There is a possibility that a woman who's pregnant

with triplets and was admitted for bed rest last week might be having a Caesarean later this afternoon,' she told Peggy. 'If we're still here we might be allowed to be in Theatre to observe.'

'I'm not bored at all,' Ari protested. 'I'm reading up on all the protocols for handling preemie babies. We've got special plastic bags to put them in so they don't get cold. What did you do, back in the day, Ma?'

'We certainly didn't have all the bells and whistles you've got these days so we just did what we could and hoped for the best. I do remember things changing after President Kennedy's baby died. Suddenly there was more money and research being done.'

'JFK? I didn't know he lost a baby.'

'Oh…poor Jackie Kennedy had a terrible time of it. She had a miscarriage and then a stillbirth before she had the two babies that survived. And then there was the preemie baby who only lived a couple of days because of respiratory distress. We were all talking about it at work. I think I remember that they put that poor wee baby into one of those chambers for people who have diving accidents.'

'A hyperbaric chamber?'

'That's the one.' Peggy shifted a little and winced but ignored any pain she was having. 'It was to try and force oxygen into his lungs.'

Again, Ari and Kelly shared a glance. They would be talking about that soon, she thought. About how barbaric the treatment seemed now that they knew the damage that too much oxygen could do and about the improvements in managing the risks that came with undeveloped lungs—like giving the mother steroids if there was time before the birth or giving the babies artificial surfactant as protection. But that discussion was going to have to wait. Kelly's pager sounded at the same moment she caught Ari's gaze.

'Ooh…what's happening?' Peggy tried to sit up as Kelly was reading her pager and this time the pain made her gasp.

'Just rest,' Ari told her. 'And tell your nurse that you're hurting. You're allowed as much pain relief as you need, you know.' He turned back to Kelly. 'Do we need to go?'

Her nod was crisp. 'Looks like we're needed. Finally…'

'I'll be back later,' Ari told Peggy. 'If you've rested enough, I'll tell you all about it.'

'It sounds complicated,' Kelly told him as they sped down a staircase and headed for the emergency department and their vehicle. 'Premature labour but the ambulance crew can't get to her yet—there's a flooded stream that's made part of a bridge collapse. Even worse, she's trapped in her vehicle. The fire service is on its way but they're under pressure due to this weather. We might well be on scene before them.'

The call out got even more complicated when they arrived in ED to be told that they had a driver— Bruce—but there were no obstetricians or neonatal paediatricians that were available to go with them. Apparently, the Caesarean for the woman carrying triplets had just become an emergency and all staff were needed in Theatre.

'What do we do?' Ari asked.

'We'll still go,' Kelly said. She opened a cupboard to hand him a heavy-duty raincoat with fluorescent stripes. 'We've got equipment that's not available otherwise and I'm qualified to use it.' She bit her lip. 'I just prefer to be assisting the real experts.'

'You know what?' Ari raised his voice against the sound of the heavy rain as he followed Kelly outside.

'What?'

'I've seen you in action and I know how amazing you are. You can handle anything.'

'I don't know about that.' Kelly automatically dismissed the compliment, although a part of her brain—or perhaps it was actually a part of her heart—registered and liked the fact that Ari thought she was amazing, even if it wasn't true. 'Let's hope we can both handle anything. You're being thrown in at the deep end, that's for sure. Your first callout and you certainly won't be just an observer.'

This was way more exciting than Ari had expected. Not only was it the first time he'd been in an ambulance under lights and sirens but they were heading into a situation that could be life-threatening for both a mother and baby. That they had the weather against them as well added another degree of difficulty and the fact that he was with Kelly, who'd been dispatched as the lead medic for this advanced back-up in an emergency, made it all the more thrilling.

He'd meant what he'd said about her being able to handle anything but he could sense that she was nervous and he was going to give her whatever assistance he could. And maybe it was just a side effect of so much adrenaline in his system but Ari had the feeling that the two of them could make a perfect team. That, together, they could both achieve way more than if either of them was working alone.

Twenty minutes later, when they turned down a side road, having cleared one of London's outer suburbs and arrived on the scene of this emergency, it was Ari's turn to feel a beat of nervousness. He'd never had to deal with anything like this in his life. A police car was blocking the road that led to a narrow bridge. An ambulance was parked just beyond that but its crew was simply standing beside their vehicle. The beacons of both emergency vehicles flashed brightly against the driving rain and were reflected in the tumbling water of the swollen stream.

The far bank had collapsed, presumably due to the pressure of water combined with already saturated ground, and a car had come off the road and was tilted down at the bottom of the bank and seemed to be wedged on the driver's side amongst low-lying branches of a weeping willow. The water was flowing swiftly around the front tyres of the car and Ari could see a police officer on the bridge.

'Stay here, Bruce,' Kelly instructed their driver. 'Keep the engine running and the heat up as high as you can. We'll go and find out what's happening here.' She caught Ari's gaze as she handed him a heavy-duty torch. 'Ready?'

Ari took the torch, having slipped his arms into the straps of the portable kit. 'Ready,' he confirmed.

And he was. Any nervousness evaporated at that instant, replaced by adrenaline and backed up by catching some of that determination he could see in Kelly's eyes.

It was noisier than Ari might have expected. The rain and wind and the rushing water of the stream was a background to the sound of radios crackling, voices shouting, the faint sound of a siren in the distance, which could be more emergency vehicles coming their way and…more disturbingly, a cry that sounded like that of a terrified woman. He was right beside Kelly as they went past the police car blocking the road and got to the ambulance.

'We've been told not to go any further yet.' One of the young paramedics looked frustrated. 'The fire service is on its way but the car needs to be secured. There's a danger it'll get washed out from where it is and could roll. That stream is getting deeper in the middle. Plus, they don't know how stable the rest of the bridge is and they don't want any more weight on it.'

'But you know there's a pregnant woman in the car? In labour?'

'We're going on what's been relayed by the police officer on the bridge. Her name's Zoe and she's thirty-six weeks along. Her contractions had started before she went off the bridge. Her foot's caught under the pedals or something and she can't get out, even though the doors on the other side are open.'

'How far away are the firefighters?'

'Don't know. Feels like we've been waiting for ever.'

Ari turned to catch Kelly's gaze. They'd only been on scene for a matter of minutes but it already felt like far too long a delay to being with their patient. He raised his eyebrows in a silent question that Kelly seemed to understand instantly and she apparently agreed with his summing up of the situation so far— that they weren't necessarily going to comply with or- ders from the police officers on site if they were not in the best interests of their patient. He and Kelly could weigh up the risks and make their own decisions about what could or could not be done for the woman trapped in her car.

'Keep your truck as warm as possible,' Kelly told the paramedics. 'If we can get her out, we might need to deliver a baby in there.'

And if they couldn't get her out, what then? Would they be delivering a baby in a car under threat of either being washed away or submerged in flood waters? This was dangerous but it didn't feel like Ari had a choice. That Kelly was brave enough to be prepared to go with him made him feel proud to be with her. Proud *of her*. He lengthened his stride. There wasn't a minute to lose and the police officer on the bridge must have sensed that neither he nor Kelly were going to be put off getting to the accident victim.

'Be careful,' was all he said. 'That ground's unstable and so is the car. The bridge is still falling apart as well. The firefighters have had to go around the long way to get to this side of the bridge. If you wait another ten minutes, they could be able to secure the vehicle.'

'*Help*...' The cry came from the car beneath them. 'Please...someone, *help*...'

'Can't wait, mate,' Ari told the police officer. 'I think we're needed.' But he turned back to Kelly before stepping onto the rubble between the bridge and the bank. The urge to protect her from danger was too difficult to suppress completely. 'Maybe you should stay up here?'

Kelly simply shook her head, dismissing the suggestion.

Ari was tall enough to reach a tree branch to use as an anchor as he started to pick his way down the slippery mud on the bank. He held his other arm out as a safety barrier for Kelly and it was needed almost immediately as she began a slide that only stopped as she grabbed hold of his arm.

'Hold on tight,' he told her. 'I've got this.'

It got easier as they got further down because the branches were lower. They could see the open, crumpled doors of the passenger side of the car. They could also see the pale face of the terrified driver.

'Oh, thank God...you're here. Please... I can't get out and I'm having... *Ahh*...' She screwed her eyes shut as she cried out in pain.

Ari was almost at the side of the car.

'You want to be in the front or the back?' he asked Kelly.

He expected her to want to get in the front passenger side to be able to get to the woman more easily. She was in charge here after all and he was only supposed to be an observer. But Kelly said she would get into the back seat.

'You've got way more experience than me in assessing how close someone is to giving birth. Put the kit in the back seat as well. There'll be more room for me to open it there.'

'Okay.' Part of Ari still wasn't happy with the idea of Kelly getting into the car at all but he couldn't ask her to stand back and watch and he wasn't about to suggest that she stay somewhere safe because he admired her courage and he wanted to work with her. He *needed* that extra dimension that the two of them could make as a team. But he touched her arm.

'Don't get in until after me, okay? If there's any danger that changing the balance is going to push the car into the current, it's best if it's only one of us in there.'

It was already darker than normal for this time of day due to the weather conditions. Now they were beneath a veil of leafy branches and the interior of the car made it feel like night-time. Ari flicked on his torch.

'Hey…' He eased himself carefully onto the front passenger seat of the car, praying that it wouldn't be enough of a change to give the current the power to do more damage. 'It's Zoe, right? I'm Ari. I'm a midwife.'

The pain from Zoe's contraction was clearly easing and her expression changed from pain to something more like horror. It wasn't because of his gender, however—simply his specialty. 'A midwife? Oh…no… there's no way I'm having a baby in here. I can't… Oh… *God…*'

'We're here to look after you,' Ari told her. 'You and the baby.' The car wasn't showing any sign that it was going to start moving so he gave Kelly a nod. 'That's Kelly getting into the back seat now,' he told Zoe. 'She's an awesome paramedic and she's part of the obstetric flying squad so you're in good hands, okay?'

But Zoe had a hand covering her eyes. 'I just want to get out,' she sobbed. 'I want to go home…'

'Is anything hurting?' Kelly asked. 'Apart from your contractions?'

'My foot. Ankle. Or it was… It's kind of numb now but I can't get it out.'

Ari leaned closer, stretching one arm into the footwell and keeping the torch in his other hand to try and see what he was doing. The driver's door was badly crumpled inwards and the accelerator and brake pedals were bent and pressed onto Zoe's foot. A brief attempt was all it took for Ari to realise that specialised equipment would be needed to free Zoe. And it was needed soon. There was icy water swirling around those pedals as well. The passenger side doors were well above water level at the moment but it was seeping in on the lower side.

Kelly had the kit open on the back seat beside her. She pushed a blood-pressure cuff and a stethoscope between the front seats.

'Can you get a blood pressure?'

'Sure.' Ari already had his hand on Zoe's wrist. 'Heart rate's one hundred and five. And the pulse is strong so she's not hypotensive. I'll get an accurate blood pressure in a minute. There's a Doppler in that kit, too, isn't there? I'd like to check on baby's heart rate.'

'I'll get it.'

'Tell me about your pregnancy, Zoe,' Ari said. 'Is it your first? Have you had any problems?'

But Zoe didn't answer. She reached out and clutched his hand as she screwed up her face again and cried out. 'This hurts *so* much…'

'We'll get you some pain relief,' Kelly said. 'How long since that last contraction, Ari?'

'Between two and three minutes at a guess.' He glanced at his watch. 'I'll keep time for the frequency and duration.'

'Here…' Kelly handed a methoxyflurane inhaler between the seats moments later. 'It's got the activated carbon chamber inserted and the cap off. Put the loop over Zoe's wrist so it doesn't get dropped.'

There was no point in checking for contra-indications or trying to coach Zoe into using the inhaled analgesic until her contraction was over. Ari also needed to examine Zoe to see if delivery was imminent. With a bit of luck, they might be able to get her into the ambulance before that happened. Above them, from the direction of the road on the broken side of the bridge, he could see more flashing lights and hear people shouting. It seemed the fire service was now on scene with their heavy vehicles and ability to not only stabilise a car in a precarious situation but to cut through and bend metal to make extrication possible.

Ari was able to get a blood-pressure reading as Zoe's pain ebbed. 'One-forty on ninety,' he relayed to Kelly. They both knew it was the high end of normal but that was hardly surprising given the circumstances and level of anxiety. 'Can you try and release the lever on the other side of Zoe's seat? If we could tilt her back a bit, it'll make it much easier for me to find out what this baby's up to.'

'I'm not having this baby here,' Zoe said. 'I can't… What if…? *Ahh…*' This time it was a cry of fear rather than pain and Ari thought he heard an echo of the same sound from Kelly as the car suddenly shifted, scraping over boulders on the creek bed beneath them and tilting down more sharply on the driver's side.

'It's okay,' Ari told them. 'Look…the firefighters are putting a hook on the back of the car. It's only moved because they're making sure it's secure and it can't float away. We're safe… I'm not going to let anything bad happen, okay?'

His words were intended as reassurance for their patient but he knew they were still in a very danger-ous situation—even more so, if that hook didn't have a good grip on the chassis of the car. Kelly had to know that as well but, when Ari turned his head to check that she was all right, he could see that she was also hanging onto his words so he held her gaze for a heartbeat longer. So that she would know he meant what he said and that Kelly was included in his protection.

He wasn't going to let anything bad happen to her— not if there was any way he could possibly prevent it. The urge to protect Kelly was so strong, in fact, that Ari could feel it snatch his own breath for a moment. Had he made a mistake in encouraging her to get to Zoe before the vehicle had been stabilised? Taken advantage of that extraordinary courage she displayed because he wanted her by his side in this challenge? No… she'd been just as determined as he'd been, hadn't she? That determination to help others was one of the traits they had in common. One that, right from the start, had created that connection but right now it felt like more than simply being members of the same team. It felt like a bond that was soul-deep. They were in this together and it just felt…right…

As if they'd done this many times before. As if they would keep doing it, perhaps for the rest of their lives. An unbreakable team.

Soul-mates…

How on earth had she ended up in what had to be the most dangerous situation she'd ever faced in her career? There was water covering Kelly's feet now and the car was beginning to rock in the increasing current of the flood waters. The splashes combined with the heavy rain coming through the open door beside her and she could feel it trickling beneath her raincoat to soak her scrub suit and chill her whole body.

What was even more extraordinary, mind you, was that she could feel she was actually quite safe as long as Ari was there. And somewhere in the back of her mind, as she reached for the lever to try and flatten the back of the driver's seat, was the knowledge that even if the worst happened and this car got washed away, she knew that she wouldn't willingly be abandoning Zoe, even if it was to try and save her own life. Because she knew that it wouldn't even occur to Ari to do that?

She could hear him explain to Zoe how to use the inhaler for pain relief when her next contraction started and, although his voice was muted by the sound of water rushing past and fire officers getting closer to the vehicle and shouting instructions as they brought heavy equipment down the bank, just the calmness of that rumble of his voice was enough to reassure Kelly that he was in control. That *they* were in control of managing their patient, at least. The seat mechanism was still working and Kelly had pulled the back down as far as she could.

'Okay, Zoe, breathe in through the inhaler…hold it…keep holding…now breathe out, still through the inhaler. Kelly? Can I have some fresh gloves, please?'

'Sure.' She found the large-sized gloves in the kit. 'Do you want the Doppler now?'

His hand covered hers as he reached for the gloves and the brief glance told her that there might be more urgent things to do than find out the baby's heart rate. A fire officer was leaning in the open side of the car as Ari pulled on the gloves.

'We're going to break the window on the driver's side,' he told them, 'so we can get that door off and get the patient free. I'm going to put this sheet of plastic over you all to keep you safe from the glass, okay?'

'Okay.' Kelly answered for them both. Ari was busy talking to Zoe.

'I need to check what's happening down below as soon as this contraction is over, Zoe.'

Zoe pulled the inhaler from her mouth. 'I can feel something,' she groaned. 'I need to push…'

'Hang on. Try not to push just yet. Pant for me, sweetheart. Or blow, like there's lot of candles on that cake and you want them all to flicker.'

Somehow, Ari was twisting his big body so that he could reach between Zoe's legs at the same time as the plastic sheet was being stuffed into the interior of the car and Kelly was helping to pull it over them.

And then…there they were. The three of them very close together inside a strange plastic tent. There was thumping and crashing outside and the sound of breaking glass and the noise of pneumatic tools starting up but it faded into the background as Kelly leaned over Zoe's head, holding a torch to try and give Ari some light.

'I can feel baby's head,' he told Zoe. 'Let's see if we can get you into a better position and then you can push on your next contraction.'

There was no way Zoe could move her trapped foot but she was able to bend her other leg.

'I don't want to push,' she sobbed. 'I don't want to have my baby here. Get me out…*please*…get me out of here…'

'It's okay, Zoe.' Ari had his mouth close to his patient's ear. 'We're here with you. Your baby wants to come now and it's okay. We've got this. *You've* got this…'

He caught Kelly's gaze for a second. He didn't need

to tell her that there was a limited time to deliver this baby safely now that it was already this far on its way. Even if the fire service got the door off in the next minute or two and could bend metal enough to free Zoe's foot, they weren't going to be moving her anywhere until this baby was born. Kelly squeezed through more of the gap between the seats to get close enough to hold Zoe's hand and try and help encourage her as her next contraction began.

'You can do this, Zoe. We've got you.' The grip on her hand was crushing her fingers but Kelly barely noticed. 'That's it...you're doing great.' With her other hand she was still holding the torch to provide some light for Ari.

'Push, Zoe.' Ari's voice was commanding. 'That's it. Good girl... Keep it going...push...push...*push*...'

'I...*can't*,' Zoe gasped. 'It's too hard...it's... *Ahh*...'

'You're almost there. One more push...'

'As hard as you can,' Kelly urged. In the spotlight from the torch, she could see the baby's head between Zoe's legs, between Ari's hands as he supported the infant and gently tilted its body to help deliver the first shoulder. And then, with another, sharp cry from Zoe, it was over in a rush, with Ari managing to catch the slippery bundle before it could get anywhere near the water that had risen almost to the level of the seats as the door was being prised off this side of the car.

They were still all inside the plastic cocoon as Ari lifted the baby whose first cry cut through the cacophony of noise from outside the tent as access was gained to deal with the pedals trapping Zoe's foot. Kelly had to move now. To find what they needed to cut the umbilical cord and what she had that she could cover the infant with to prevent hypothermia. And then they needed to get him to a safe space as fast as possible but, for a heartbeat, she was caught by the look on Ari's face.

A lot of what she could read in his expression was reflecting the same relief that she was feeling—that the baby *was* crying and not in need of resuscitation in an impossible setting but she could see much more than that in his eyes as well. The whole miracle of birth was amazing enough in any circumstances but to snatch a victory in what could have been a disastrous situation was…well…it was overwhelming enough to bring the prickle of tears to the back of her own eyes. Kelly was never going to forget this moment. Or the way Ari was looking at her right now. As if they had been a team forever and nothing was going to break that bond of trust.

For a heartbeat, Kelly actually believed that she could return that trust. That it might be possible to re-capture that dream she'd once had of finding a person that she could trust—and love—enough to want to spend the rest of her life with them, and it was something that she wanted to believe so much that it hurt. But this was not the time to allow what was an emotion rather than a coherent thought any more than that tiny blink of time.

Already, Kelly was turning away, the conscious part of her brain listing the items like the clamps and sterile scissors and foil survival sheets that she needed to locate in the kit. It was time to cut this baby's umbilical cord and wrap it up to carry to a safe, warm place where they could complete an accurate Apgar score and check that all was well. It would only be moments before Zoe could also be lifted from the car and carried to the warmth of the ambulance for a proper assessment and transport to hospital, probably with the third stage of her labour happening en route.

Maybe later—much later when the chaos of this call out had finally been sorted—she might get drawn back to that moment and find that it would be only too easy to conjure up that sense of longing for a lost dream again. Or maybe it would be better to simply leave it where it was, as part of an extraordinary, once-in-a-lifetime experience that would never happen again.

Like holding this newborn baby in her arms, wrapped up in the foil sheet, as firemen reached in through the open doors to take the kit out of the way and then help her out of the vehicle and up the bank to safety. At the same time, more rescuers were lifting Zoe from the car. As Kelly made sure she had a secure grip on the precious bundle she was holding as someone draped a blanket around them, a quick glance over her shoulder showed her that Zoe was now in Ari's arms. He was standing knee deep in the swirling, icy water of the stream and his head was bent so that his mouth was close to Zoe's ear, as if he was saying something he wanted only her to hear. It must have been something reassuring, Kelly thought, judging by the way Zoe wrapped her arms around his neck and tucked her head beneath his shoulder and against his chest—as if she'd found the safest place in the world.

Or maybe that was how anybody would feel once they were in the circle of those arms? Kelly shook the notion away almost as quickly as it surfaced. Errant thoughts, imagining what it might be like to be a lot closer to Ari Lawson than was appropriate for a colleague—even one who was a good friend—were becoming a bit of a habit. A bad habit that had the potential to undermine her focus on her work. It only took a shift of her glance to the tiny face visible in the crook of her elbow to regain that focus and the pressure of supporting hands on each side of her was, quite literally, another step in the right direction.

'Let's go, baby,' she whispered. 'We've got this…'

CHAPTER SEVEN

'IT'S NOT BROKEN.' The orthopaedic registrar was staring intently at the computer screen where the X-ray of Zoe's ankle was illuminated. 'Looks like just some bad bruising.'

Ari caught Kelly's glance. 'Exactly what you thought,' he murmured.

There was a glow of satisfaction in her eyes. 'Had to get an X-ray to be sure, though. How's that paperwork going?'

'Almost done.'

Ari was adding the clinical description of his part in Zoe's rescue and the birth of her baby to their report, including the third stage with the delivery of the placenta that had happened as they'd travelled back to hospital with Zoe in the second ambulance, which had had both a stretcher and baby carrier available. Her baby had been well enough to travel with the new mother, having not needed the incubator in the flying squad's ambulance.

They were in one corner of the larger resus room that had been ready for Zoe on arrival at the Kensington and, until a few minutes ago, it had been a crowded space. Members of the obstetric team on call had joined the emergency department staff, paged to check that there were no complications from Zoe's dramatic labour under such challenging conditions, but apart from a minor tear, it appeared that all was well. The paediatrician who had also been paged had been quite happy with the condition of the baby, who was now cradled in Zoe's arms, sound asleep after all the excitement.

Bruce, the volunteer driver for the flying squad, had come to tell Kelly and Ari that the squad's ambulance was cleaned up and ready for a new crew and that he was heading home with their shift done and dusted. A police officer had also come in not long ago to tell Zoe that they had managed to contact both her husband and her parents and they were all on their way to see her.

'I'm pretty much done with the paperwork, too.' Kelly pushed back a strand of her hair that had come loose. 'Did you know that there are reporters waiting outside and a television news crew? They've already got pictures of the scene and some of the story from the police but they'd like to talk to us before they come in to get an interview with Zoe and some close-ups of the baby.' She grinned at Ari. 'We might be a little bit famous.'

'It's the kind of story everybody loves, I guess.' Ari signed the bottom of the patient report form. 'Some real drama and danger and not just a happy ending but a cute baby as well.'

The kind of story that Ari knew would be a career highlight and one that he would remember for the rest of his life. And, professionally speaking, it had been an experience that only he and Kelly would ever share. Nobody else could ever truly understand the flash of fear that had come with the scrape and rock of the car shifting on the rocks, with them both knowing that if it got washed away it was quite possible that neither of them would survive. And nobody else could relate to that astonishing wash of relief on hearing Zoe's baby cry for the first time because it could only have been that intense due to the unusual combination of factors—not just the danger and the tension but the fact that he and Kelly had been working so closely together under that plastic tent.

That bond of being a team that Ari had been aware of as they'd started that job had strengthened tenfold now and, even though his clothing was still damp enough to be chilling his body and he had mud splatters from head to foot, including in his hair, he wasn't in any hurry to leave this room. Or perhaps it was Kelly's company he didn't want to leave because he didn't want to break this new bond. Or to turn his back on the kind of glow that Kelly had right now—the kind that advertised the confidence and satisfaction of an exceptionally challenging job well done.

The kind of glow that Ari would want her to have as often as possible because it meant that she was happy with who she was. Proud of herself—as she should be. He would prefer to make sure that it would be remembered so well that Kelly could tap into it if—or probably when—she had moments when she doubted her own self-worth. Like maybe the next time her path crossed that of the bastard of an ex-boyfriend and he tried to put her down again.

When they'd said goodbye to Zoe, brushed off her heartfelt thanks and admired the baby again, they slipped out of the resus room. They had a choice of whether to head for the locker room, where they'd left their personal items like street clothing this morning, or to go to the waiting area where they knew the reporters had gathered.

'You were amazing out there.' Ari paused to nod towards the doors that led to the waiting room. 'You deserve to be more than a little bit famous.'

'You were the real hero. I think I'd rather have a hot shower and some dinner.'

'Oh...you and me both. I'd better text Stacey and see if she wants me to bring takeaway home.' He pulled out his phone and started tapping even as he kept talking. 'I'd like to pop in on Peggy but I can't go anywhere like this and by the time I've been home and cleaned up, it'll be too late to come back.'

'You could shower here.' But Kelly was staring at Ari's head as they moved, by tacit consent, towards the locker room. 'How did you get so much mud in your *hair*? I think you'll need some heavy-duty shampoo rather than just soap.'

Ari's phone buzzed. 'I don't need to take food home,' he told Kelly. 'Apparently Stacey has a friend visiting and they're making cheese toasties. Hey...why don't we both shower here and go across to the pub? Being almost famous calls for a celebration, doesn't it?'

'I'd rather use my own shower,' Kelly said. 'I'm only down the road a bit. Ten minutes' walk at the most.' Ahead of Ari as they reached the locker room, she turned to glance over her shoulder. 'You could come too, if you like. I'm sure I've got a beer lurking in the back of the fridge behind some wine and there's the best Chinese takeaway almost next door. That way you'd still be close enough to go and see Peggy before you head home.'

There was no reason to take Kelly up on her offer, given that there was a shower available in the locker room and he could find something to eat across the road.

But there was every reason to take up her offer, because it meant that he could put off breaking that new bond with Kelly for a bit longer. Plus, he had to admit he was curious to see where Kelly lived and get more of a glimpse into her private life. That curiosity along with the undeniable reluctance to leave her company won any internal debate with ease.

'Can we take my bike? I've got a spare helmet in a pannier and that way I can be somewhere else in a hurry if I need to.'

'Sure.'

Kelly's smile assured him that it was no big deal but was the slight hesitation he'd been aware of before her answer and the way her glance slid away from his trying to tell him something else? That maybe he'd made the wrong choice here? That he was taking a new turn on a pathway that might be impossible to undo? He brushed the warning off as irrelevant until he was standing very close to Kelly a short time later, his fingers brushing the soft skin beneath her chin when he was helping her fasten the strap of the helmet.

Oh, *man*… Had he ever felt a tingle of awareness quite like that when he'd touched a woman's skin? He didn't dare catch Kelly's gaze because he didn't want her to see any hint of what he was feeling. Instead, he drew in a slow breath and slammed internal doors on that tingle and any significance it might have. He couldn't—*wouldn't*—go there. For both their sakes. A bit of self-discipline was all that was needed here and exerting that kind of self-control had never been a problem for Ari.

'Have you been on a bike before?'

Kelly shook her head.

'You don't need to do anything except hang on. Best if you put your arms around my waist.'

Best for safety, anyway. It might not be quite such a good thought when it came to that self-control, Ari decided when he felt Kelly's arms tighten around his waist and her body pressing against his back but, somewhat to his surprise, it actually helped. By the time he had parked his bike by the steps that led down to Kelly's basement flat, being so close that they were physically touching each other was feeling familiar. No different from any friend he might have offered a motorbike ride to.

Something had changed.

Something big…

Kelly wasn't quite sure what it was but she knew it had happened because of how dangerous that mission to help Zoe and her baby had been. Because circumstances had pushed her and Ari to work alone together in a life-and-death situation. An oddly intimate situation at the most crucial point, in fact, because they'd been cut off from even the rest of the rescue effort by that thick plastic sheeting.

Whatever alchemy had occurred, it had certainly brought them closer together. So close that Kelly knew they were treading the very fine line that could lie between friendship and something a whole lot more significant. It was the same kind of tension that she'd been aware of the other day, when they'd been waiting for Peggy to come out of surgery and she'd been so sure that Ari had been about to kiss her. And, because this wasn't the first time, it didn't make her feel nearly so wary. When Ari's fingers brushed the skin of her neck as he was doing up her helmet, Kelly could feel the buzz of tension as something pleasurable rather than a warning.

Something even more pleasurable than standing in her hot shower now, rinsing away both soap suds and some of the chill of that flooded stream. Ari had insisted that she have the first shower and Kelly had agreed because she didn't need to wash her hair immediately so she could be quicker. Ari was choosing something from the takeout menu for the nearby Chinese restaurant and placing the order while she was in the bathroom and Kelly was going to go and pick up the food while he was having his turn in the shower.

By the time she got back, the gas fire should have done its job to make her small sitting room that doubled as a dining room cosy enough to make them both forget the less pleasant aspects of that damp and muddy mission and, if he was as hungry as she was, the food would be even more welcome.

Kelly couldn't wait. She turned off the shower, hurriedly towelled herself dry and then dressed in her favourite "at home" clothes of her most comfortable yoga pants, an oversized sweatshirt and some old sheepskin boots. She pulled her hair out of its bun and brushed it but didn't bother tying it up again. She wanted to make sure that Ari didn't interpret this invitation to come home with her as anything other than casual. Convenient. The kind of thing that any friends could do and no reason at all to run. Or hide. Those boundaries were still visible and they wouldn't be crossed. Not unless that was a mutual choice.

'Shower's all yours,' she told Ari as she grabbed her shoulder bag on her way through living room to the front door. 'And help yourself to a beer from the fridge. I'll be back with dinner in no time.'

Being the end of the weekend, however, the takeout section of the popular local restaurant was being well patronised and it took longer than Kelly had expected. It was raining again as she came out into the dark of the early evening and gusts of wind were picking up long tresses of her hair to make them tangle around her face. Fortunately, it didn't take long to get home and down the steps to let herself back into the flat, with her bag full of cardboard boxes of steaming rice and fragrant food.

'Wow...that smells amazing.'

Ari's voice came from behind Kelly as she pushed the door shut and she turned to see him coming out of the bathroom, rubbing at his head with a towel. The only clothing he had on was a pair of faded jeans and, while they were zipped up, the top button hadn't yet been fastened. Maybe that was what undid something deep inside Kelly and unleashed a shaft of desire that made her breath catch in astonishment. Or maybe it was Ari dropping the towel around his shoulders to reveal that his hair—that Kelly had only seen sleeked back into a tidy man bun—was loose and falling in soft, damp waves to frame his face and neck.

That little gas fire had certainly done its job in warming this room up. Kelly was suddenly feeling overheated. Because she'd come back in from being out in a cold, rainy evening? No. It didn't take more than a split second to realise that this heat had very little to do with any external source. No wonder people who were good looking were described as being "hot". Kelly was melting right now because she'd never seen anyone who was as beautiful as Ari Lawson was at this moment.

This small room was making him seem taller. Broader. Or perhaps it was because Kelly could see *so* much of that smooth, olive skin covering muscles that her fingers itched to touch the shape of. He looked so different with his hair loose as well. Softer? Or was that impression due to how dark his eyes seemed in the shadows of that tousled hair?

Whatever the reason, Kelly was still having trouble catching her breath. She was still aware of that spear of sensation that was a white heat deep in her belly and there were tendrils of that heat reaching her toes and fingertips to make them also feel as if they were melting. Losing their function anyway, because the handle of the bag Kelly was holding slipped from her fingers to land on the floorboards.

'Oh, *no*...' Kelly dropped to a crouch. 'I'm so clumsy...'

'Oops...' Ari swooped at the same time to rescue the bag.

The waxed boxes were sealed tightly enough not to have spilled their contents but they were falling out of the top of the bag and both Ari and Kelly reached for them at the same time so that what actually happened was that Ari caught hold of Kelly's hand instead of a box.

Time appeared to stop in that instant. Kelly lifted her gaze but then froze as it met Ari's. She felt her pulse suddenly speed up and then trip as it missed a beat but it was the only part of her body that was moving. Even her lungs had given up on the idea of drawing in a fresh breath.

Oh...*my*... Kelly completely forgot about the food she'd been about to rescue. She couldn't even smell it now because she was close enough to Ari to be able to smell the shampoo and soap he'd been using. *Her* shampoo and soap, which made the scent familiar enough to feel safe but, mixed with the background musk of potent masculinity, it was different enough to be arousing her senses in a way that was making everything completely new—brilliantly clear and so sharp and bright it was as if she was using those senses properly for the first time in her life. And, because time had stopped, she was aware of every one of them.

That touch of his hand on her own, almost burning her skin with the intensity of the sensation. Kelly could feel the puff of his breath on her face at the same time because they were that close and she could hear it as a sigh. She could feel the warmth of that breath as well—or was it the heat that seemed to be radiating from his skin? Her gaze finally drifted down to his lips, having torn itself away from the depths of those wickedly dark eyes that she just knew could see every single thing she was thinking and feeling.

Taste... That was the only sense that Kelly wasn't using but, somehow, she knew how delicious it would be to put her tongue against that gorgeous, olive skin. Or to lose herself in a kiss that would totally capture her mouth. Unconsciously, the tip of her tongue came out to dampen her bottom lip as she imagined that kiss and it was then that she heard the change in that breath that Ari was releasing. An almost sound that—if it had involved his vocal cords—could have been a groan of desire. Of lust even…

How could so many impressions and the flash of so many thoughts happen with such speed? There was a warning sounding somewhere in the back of Kelly's mind—something to do with what she'd been told about Ari and how women never stayed long in his life. But at that same instant Kelly had the feeling that those women wouldn't have regretted being there when they looked back, no matter how short the time had been, because they would have shared something very special. As unique as Ari was. She would settle for whatever he wanted to offer her at this moment, even if that was no more than a kiss. Because everything had changed. Or maybe it was only one thing that had changed but that one thing had the power to change the rest of her life.

It wasn't simply the familiar scent of her own toiletries on Ari's skin and hair that were providing a sense of safety, was it? That had been there well before she'd even invited Ari into her home. It had been there at that moment when she'd become aware of that new bond between herself and Ari when they'd heard Zoe's baby cry for the first time and they'd become a real team. A partnership that could accomplish more than either of them could on their own. People who could totally trust each other.

And Kelly had been aware that there was something even bigger than anything professional in knowing that she *could* trust Ari. For a split second she'd known that it might just be possible to go back in time—or at least reset something in her heart or her head that would allow her to trust in someone enough to believe that they would never set out to hurt her. That the dream of finding someone who would be a partner for life might not have vanished for ever.

Her breath had already caught in her throat and now there was a squeeze in her chest that meant she wouldn't be trying to use her lungs anytime too soon. A squeeze that was tight enough to be painful, as Kelly understood that she had already given that trust to Ari without realising that she had. How could she not have known when she'd recognised the danger they'd been in in that car and yet she'd felt safe because she'd had Ari by her side?

She could feel that internal squeeze morphing into something else. Something that was just between herself and Ari and, yes, it had a lot to do with wanting him and the need to touch and be touched, but it there was more to it than simply sex. There was something huge happening here that had the potential to be as full of hope—and joy—as the safe arrival of Zoe's baby had been.

It could only have been enough time for a few heartbeats since they'd both dropped to reach for that bag at the same time but it felt like for ever. Enough time for so much to fall into place for Kelly anyway. And enough time for a silent conversation to have happened. For questions to be asked and answered. For desire to be acknowledged and permission given to explore it, at least a little.

And, still, Kelly hadn't taken a new breath but it didn't seem to matter. She had to close her eyes against the intensity of what she could see in Ari's eyes as he closed the gap between their faces in the same kind of slow motion that the last seconds had been played out in. She wanted to let her eyes drift shut anyway, because all she wanted to do right now was to feel. And taste...

This wasn't supposed to be happening.

Okay, he'd had that warning that he was a little too aware of Kelly as more than a colleague or a friend but he'd been so confident that he could keep his distance enough to make sure nothing got out of control.

But here he was—a heartbeat away from kissing Kelly Reynolds. *Again*... Knowing that it was exactly what she wanted as much as he did. And maybe she needed it to happen far more than he needed it *not* to happen? Right from that first time he'd met Kelly— when he'd seen her confidence and courage shrink before his eyes when she had been faced by that idiot of an ex-boyfriend—he'd sensed that she needed someone to make it obvious how incredibly special she was and give her the confidence to believe in herself, no matter what situation she might find herself in in the future. How much easier would it be to communicate that with a kiss than by trying to find the words that would be convincing enough?

He'd known all along that he didn't have the space in his life for someone like Kelly—that it wouldn't be fair on anyone involved to indulge in his usual kind of short-term fling and that he could never consider anything long term—but he'd also known that the pull might prove to be irresistible. And he wasn't the only one who could feel that pull from Kelly, was he? A brief encounter with Stacey had been enough for his foster sister to make a real attempt to change aspects of her life and Peggy...well, Peggy had been captured by that very first meeting with Kelly. Or perhaps she had sensed a connection that was already there between Ari and Kelly that neither of them had recognised.

'You're just the sort of girl who'd be perfect for my Ari...'

The boundaries had been there, though, despite any attraction and that near miss in the waiting room the other day. They both had their reasons for keeping the boundaries intact. Ari had never wanted to find a "serious" relationship with anyone and Kelly had clearly had her trust in so many things damaged. In men, relationships and, worst of all, in herself. But something had changed today.

It had changed at that moment when the car had lurched and scraped on those rocks and he'd conquered his own fear in order to try and reassure both Zoe and Kelly. When he'd promised he was not going to let anything bad happen to them. When he'd held Kelly's gaze to make sure she knew that he meant what he said. Even now, Ari could still feel how strong that urge to protect her had been and it wasn't just that he wanted to keep her safe from physical harm. He knew perfectly well that emotional harm could have even more far-reaching effects and he also knew that there was a new connection that had been cemented between himself and Kelly today. A connection that was, possibly, as deep as any connection between two people could be.

Trust.

A form of love all on its own and perhaps the first real trust Kelly could believe in for a very long time. A first, huge step towards healing? Ari could sense that if he pushed back from Kelly now, as her eyes were drifting shut, he would be breaking this promise of a kiss that was hanging in the air between them, and that would mean he would somehow be breaking that trust as well.

He couldn't do that.

Besides… Ari could feel the relief as he relaxed his muscles enough to allow him to lean forward and touch Kelly's lips with his own. It was only going to be a kiss after all.

Just a kiss.

What harm could that do?

CHAPTER EIGHT

'OH, NO… I thought Stacey or Ari would be able to answer the door. I didn't want you to have to get up.'

'I'm fine, lovey. Getting better every day. Come in…' Peggy turned to lead the way towards the kitchen at the back of her house. 'Ari's just popped out to collect Stace. She had an outing with her antenatal group today—it's a special one for teenage mothers and I think they went to visit a play centre.'

Peggy was using a walking stick and moving slowly and carefully but, when she turned to smile at Kelly at the kitchen door, there was no sign of her being in too much pain. If anything, she looked much happier than when Kelly had last seen her in hospital a week or so ago.

'I've been telling Ari that I'm quite ready for visitors now. Especially *you*…' Her smile was making the crinkles around her eyes deeper. 'Did you bring your squares?'

'I did. I think I've made enough of them to start joining some up. It's a bit addictive, isn't it? Knitting? People are laughing at me at work because I take it out when things are quiet.'

'I've always found it very soothing, I have to say.' Peggy nodded.

She was making her way to the old couch at the far end of the huge kitchen which was draped with one of the colourful, handmade blankets that Kelly was currently aspiring to create. Kelly offered her a supportive arm as she settled and then put her feet up and, as she did so, she remembered the first time she had ever been in this room and had a clear memory of how tenderly Ari had settled his foster mum onto these cushions and how his touch could reveal how much he loved someone. The memory gave her one of those chest-tightening moments that felt like one's heart was being held in a hand that could squeeze so hard it brought tears to your eyes.

Because she now knew just how tender Ari was capable of being. What the touch of his hands was actually like and how incredibly special it could make you feel. It *could* make you feel genuinely loved, although Kelly was trying to remind herself that it was simply sex and didn't necessarily mean anything more than the fact they were so attracted to each other. The first time had been a revelation, mind you. And the second time, only days ago, had been even more astonishing, so there was something snapping at the heels of that tenderness that made a lot more than her heart feel a squeeze.

Kelly might be getting used to these sensations of pure desire that could be conjured up with no more than a thought about Ari Lawson and create a delicious knot deep in her belly but it didn't make them any less powerful. If anything, they were getting stronger. Strong enough to make her close her eyes as she took a breath and rode the wave of that knot tightening to the point of pain and then ebbing to leave a delicious tingle. It happened even if he wasn't anywhere nearby or she couldn't even hear his voice on a phone call or something.

When he *was* breathing the same air, it took only the briefest eye contact for the need to be alone with him to become almost overpowering but, on the plus side, they were already learning that it could build a tension that could take sex to the next level. To a level that Kelly hadn't ever guessed even existed, in fact.

'Pop the kettle on, there's a love.' Peggy settled back on her cushions with a sigh. 'I'm a bit parched and it's past time for afternoon tea.'

'Do you need anything else? Painkillers maybe?'

'No, thanks, lovey. I'm good. Just pass me that bag of wool over there and I'll see what I can find to edge your squares. A dark colour is usually best. Have you ever done any crochet?'

'No.' Kelly's heart sank. 'I've seen people doing it and it looks harder than knitting.'

'It's easier,' Peggy said. 'You don't have to do an edging—you can just sew the squares together but I think it looks better. Like this…' She traced the dark outline on the squares of the blanket hanging beside her over the back of the couch. 'I think it brings everything together and makes it perfect.'

About to agree, Kelly was distracted by the sound of people arriving as the front door slammed shut. The ripple of laughter made her catch Peggy's gaze in surprise because she'd never heard Stacey laughing before. And then her own lips were curving into a smile as she heard the answering rumble of Ari's laughter and she couldn't look away from the door because she couldn't wait to see him again. To feel that squeeze in her belly and the warmth of a pleasure—so deep it was indescribable—that she knew would touch every cell in her body the instant that Ari's gaze met her own.

And…there it was. Still smiling, Kelly moved to get on with the task of making a pot of tea. Peggy's attention was on Stacey now as the teenager went straight towards her, clearly eager to tell her about the class visit, so the opportunity to agree with her about how those dark edges drew the squares of a blanket together had passed. But Kelly couldn't have agreed more. She caught Ari's gaze again, briefly, on her way to putting the kettle on. Having him back home with Peggy and Stacey and having herself included in this family group had brought things together as well. And it did feel perfect. For now, at least.

And, okay…she knew that it probably wasn't going to go anywhere. Ari was only planning to be in London for as long as Peggy needed him and he didn't do long-term relationships anyway but…but when he made love to her, it *felt* like there was a lot more to it than simply sex. That maybe Ari was falling in love with her even if he didn't realise it himself or believe that it was something that could last.

The voices behind her were just a background murmur.

'You should have seen Stace at the play centre, Ma. She's a natural. I've got a photo of her with a bunch of the kids. I'm going to print it out and put it on the corkboard.'

'They told us there are certificates you can get to be a childcare worker. I reckon I could do that one day.'

'Of course you could, lovey. We'll find out about it, shall we?'

With the kettle full, Kelly flicked the switch to boil the water and opened a cupboard to find cups and saucers. She felt her breath escaping in a long sigh. No matter how perfect things felt right now, she wasn't sure she herself believed that what she and Ari had found together was going to last. What was that saying? Oh, yeah... If something seemed too good to be true, it probably was...

This was shaping up to be a really good day, Ari decided as he cleared up the cups and plates from their afternoon tea.

Peggy was looking the best she had since she'd been discharged from hospital. Better than she'd looked since he'd come back to London, that was for sure. Maybe the surgery she had gone through was going to buy enough time for her to not only see Stacey's baby arrive but to know that the young mother was going to be okay and have a future to look forward to, even if Peggy wasn't here to support and encourage her.

Even better than the positive things happening at home was the fact that Kelly was visiting this afternoon. Ari had loved this house for almost as long as he could remember. When he'd finally learned that he was safe here, there was nothing he'd loved more than coming through that red front door, knowing that he belonged here. That it was *home*. And Kelly somehow just fitted right in as if she belonged here, too. It had, in fact, seemed like that even the first time she'd stepped through that red door and she'd been so gentle and caring in the way she'd treated Peggy.

His mum…

She'd been here since then, of course, for that dinner that Peggy had insisted he invite her to. Right now, she was sitting on a footstool beside the couch and the glow of her blonde hair was almost touching the silver of Peggy's curls as they bent over something they were doing with those knitted squares that Kelly was so proud of. Her hair was loose again today and Ari's fingers itched to lace themselves through those waves. The way he had that first time he'd kissed her.

For a second, his breath caught in his chest as his body reminded him of what it was like to kiss Kelly. Had he really believed that it was ever going to be "just a kiss"? How could any man have resisted the overpowering urge to go further when it was like nothing he'd ever experienced before and the invitation had been there so clearly it had felt like he was responding to a need more than simply a desire.

Maybe it had been a need on both sides. To remind Kelly to believe in herself and that she deserved everything she wanted in her future, and for him perhaps it had been a release that he hadn't realised he'd needed so badly. He'd come to London because his beloved foster mother was dying and the prospect of a life ending was a background sadness to everything else that was happening. Making love with Kelly had reminded him that life was for living as well. That there was magic to be found in not being alone sometimes.

Maybe the feeling that Kelly belonged here, in this house, wasn't because she'd been here before or because she got on so well with Peggy. Maybe it was because she actually belonged with *him*…

The longing that came with that idea was disturbing enough to make Ari abandon the washing up and head out of the kitchen to give himself a bit of space. He had a good reason to go, anyway, because he'd told Peggy he was going to print off the nice photo of Stacey with the toddlers at the play centre. He went into an office where he could download the photos from his phone to the printer but the task wasn't complex enough to distract him completely. He could actually feel an internal battle kicking off.

He *wanted* to believe that he could find someone like Kelly and imagine a perfect future where he had his own house and a family to come home to every day. But he knew that reality could be very, very different and he'd learned long ago that it was safer to assume that good things never lasted because then you wouldn't get crushed when they ended. The lessons learned in how to protect himself—and others—were so deeply engrained they felt like they were part of his DNA so it was quite possible that he would never be able to make himself vulnerable by trusting someone else with something as important as his own future. His own heart.

But the longing was there, wasn't it?

And the strength of it was a warning all by itself.

Holding the printed photo in his hand was a tangible reminder of the reasons he was here in the first place. For Peggy and, because she was so anxious about Stacey, it was of the greatest importance to do whatever he could to sort things for his foster sister as well. They had to be his priority, which made it easy to push aside any wants or needs that were purely personal. And that was a relief because it meant that he didn't have to think about it any more, which only stirred up stuff that was better left back in a past that was so distant it was irrelevant.

'Hey Stace…' He paused by her bedroom door because he could see her feet, which meant she was lounging on her bed. 'Want to see the photo again? It's a belter.'

'Maybe later.'

Something in her tone made Ari pause and peer around the edge of her door. In her favourite purple dungarees, she still didn't look hugely pregnant, especially when she was curled up like that, leaning back on her pillows as she stared at her phone, texting rapidly.

'Everything okay?'

'Yeah…' The tone was aggressive. 'Why wouldn't it be?'

Ari backed off so as not to antagonise Stacey any further but he knew he was frowning as he entered the kitchen again. Something was going on there and his instinct told him he might not like what it was.

Peggy was delighted to see the photo. So was Kelly.

'She looks so happy,' Kelly said.

'I think it would be brilliant if she could work with children.' Peggy nodded. 'I'd forgotten how good she used to be with the littlies, like Ari was. She might even want to become a teacher one day. I'll have to see if she could catch up on her GSCEs at night school or something—while I'm around to help look after the baby.'

Both Ari and Kelly made encouraging murmurs but she caught his gaze for a heartbeat. Peggy's surgeon had been very pleased with how her surgery had gone and her oncologist had said they could hope for a better quality of life but nobody wanted to say how long

Peggy might still have and, unless a small miracle got pulled out of the bag, it was possible it wasn't going to be more than a few months.

'I'll put it on the corkboard.'

Kelly followed him, carrying a teacup that had he'd forgotten to collect earlier. 'I should probably head home. I think I've got the hang of crochet enough to be going on with.'

'No, no…' Peggy shook her head. 'Stay for dinner. We'd love to have you. If you don't mind leftovers, that is.'

'I don't want to make any more work for anybody,' Kelly said firmly. 'And I've got some work to catch up on.' She paused to look at the corkboard as she went past. 'Oh, my God… Is that *you*, Ari?'

'Yeah… I know. But dreadlocks seemed cool at the time. To be fair, I was only seventeen.'

Kelly's grin faded as she looked up. 'And is that baby you're holding Stacey?'

'I guess it must be.'

'It was indeed,' Peggy said. 'It was when she started pulling on those awful dreadlocks that he decided it was time to cut them off—and thank goodness for that.'

Kelly was smiling again, holding his gaze, and Ari could see so much in those gorgeous blue eyes. An appreciation for his love of babies and respect for him going against convention and devoting his career to the most vulnerable people out there, perhaps? No…it was something deeper than that. Something about how she felt when he was holding *her*? Whatever it was, it was touching something very deep in his own chest and…and it almost hurt. It also made it very hard to break that eye contact. He might still be sinking into that astonishing blueness if Peggy hadn't cleared her throat from the other side of the room.

'So...' There was amusement in her voice. 'That's how it is now for you two...'

It was actually more than amusement that Ari could hear coating her words. More than satisfaction that something she'd been angling for had finally happened. It was...it was joy, wasn't it? A deep, genuine happiness, as if she'd been gifted something that she'd set her heart on a long time ago and that was about the best thing Ari could have wished for Peggy to have in her life right now. And to be able to keep for as long as possible.

He couldn't tell her that the new closeness between himself and Kelly was only a temporary thing and it would never be a part of his long-term future. Peggy didn't need to know that. It would be far better if she could spend whatever time she had left on earth believing that he had someone as amazing as Kelly Reynolds to share his life with. That he had the prospect of his own family and happiness in his future.

Kelly had been startled into pretending that she was really focused on looking at some of the other photos on the corkboard but there were spots of colour on her cheeks that revealed her understanding of everything Peggy had expressed in just a few words. And when her gaze slipped back to his, as he pinned the new photo in place, he could see that she understood what he had been thinking as well.

At that moment, it appeared that a silent pact was being made. They weren't going to say or do anything that might undermine Peggy's happiness. As far as they were both concerned, they could keep up the appearance of being in a committed relationship for as long as necessary to spare Peggy any disappointment. It was a welcome agreement because it gave them permission to let them carry on with their new, intimate connection.

It also gave Ari the confidence that everything was going to be okay. That Kelly understood that there were no promises of forever. That it was Peggy who'd brought them together and, when she was gone, that bond would also most likely evaporate. There was relief for Ari as well. He didn't have to rake over his past or emotions. He wasn't falling in love with Kelly and she wasn't going to get dependent on him or ask for anything more than he was able to give.

What they had going on at the moment was just… well, it was just what it was. Something that they both needed at this point in their lives. Kelly because she was on the way to believing in herself and maybe for him this was just a part of what he'd always been drawn to do—to make the vulnerable feel protected. Safe. To give them the gift of having hope for the future.

And if it came with the bonus of mind-blowingly amazing sex?

It was Ari's turn to clear his throat. Peggy certainly didn't need to know anything about that but it was a worry that she had seen so much already by simply witnessing a look between them. Was she seeing rather too much or was it too easy to see because there was more there than Ari was aware of?

Whatever Peggy was thinking now, however, was hidden beneath a carefully casual demeanour as she packed Kelly's squares, some new balls of wool and a crochet hook into a bag.

'Did you drive here today, lovey?'

'No, I caught the bus. So much easier than fighting late-afternoon London traffic.'

Peggy smiled. 'There'll be queues at the bus stops now, though, with people heading home from work. Ari—why don't you take Kelly home on that bike of yours?'

Ari almost shook his head. The suggestion was about as subtle as when Peggy had suggested he invite Kelly home for dinner that time. It was kind of funny now that he'd been so determined not to pass on that invitation because he hadn't wanted to complicate his life any more. Fate had had other ideas, hadn't she?

'It might take a while, even when I can get through most traffic on a bike,' Ari warned. 'It might be past your dinner and bedtime when I get back.'

Peggy was still smiling. 'That's perfect. I want a chance to talk to Stacey about a few things and we can do that over dinner—woman to woman. Then we can have a look on the internet and make a plan about how she could get the qualifications she would need for a job working with children. I don't want her to lose that dream.'

Ari found himself nodding slowly. It would be a very positive thing for Stacey to see something more in her future than being a teenage mother and, given the way she was inclined to push him away at times, like she had only minutes ago, a one-to-one talk with Peggy might achieve more. Peggy certainly seemed pleased with his agreement. Was it his imagination or did he also see her give him the ghost of a wink?

'I won't expect you back anytime soon, love,' she said serenely. 'London traffic is just terrible these days, isn't it?'

* * *

This was about Peggy's seal of approval that Kelly's friendship with Ari had become something more significant. There was a twinkle in her eyes when she kissed Kelly goodbye that made her realise she was only just getting to know a woman who had an endless capacity for living life to the fullest and trying to make it better for others at the same time. How lucky had she been to meet Peggy? And how easy was it to love her this much?

They got through the late afternoon traffic with ease as Ari slipped past the queued cars, trucks and buses at congested intersections. Pressed against his body, Kelly could feel every ripple of his muscles as he tilted even slightly in one direction and then the other and how her own body picked up those ripples and intensified them. She could have just handed Ari her helmet to put in the pannier of his bike and then gone into her basement flat alone but she caught his gaze as she stood beside him to pull the helmet from her head.

Her body was still buzzing from the contact they'd had even through their clothing and there was no way she was going into her flat alone if there was another option. Not just because Peggy had practically asked for time to be alone with Stacey but because the pull between them had just ignited something too powerful to even think about fighting.

They were down the steps even before Ari had pulled his helmet off properly and it was being dropped on the floor as Kelly turned—so quickly that she was already pressed against the solid warmth of his body. The flames of desire that were being fanned kicked up to a white heat as Ari cupped Kelly's face in his hands and covered her lips with his own.

She heard the front door slam shut and realised that Ari must have shoved it with his foot and then Kelly forgot about anything other than the touch of Ari's lips and his tongue and that those clever hands were slipping down her neck to her shoulders and beneath her clothing to find that deliciously sensitive, soft skin at the top of her breasts. Nothing else was going to enter her consciousness for quite some time and that was just perfect. The sound Kelly made as Ari scooped her into his arms to carry her to her bed was one of absolute pleasure. Ecstasy, even...

Ripples of that bliss were still trickling through Kelly's body much later, as she stayed within the circle of Ari's arms, her face against the side of his chest where she could hear his heartbeat and feel his breathing finally settling to a normal range.

'Thank goodness for that bad London traffic,' she murmured.

The rumble of sound from Ari was amused. And full of fondness. 'She's a character, isn't she?'

'She's wonderful. I love her to bits.' The beat of sadness was enough to bring tears to Kelly's eyes. 'I hope... I hope I get a lot more time to get to know her better.'

Ari's arm tightened around her before relaxing slowly. 'It's impossible to say. Like a lot of stuff in life, we need to make the most of it while we have it.'

'Mmm...' Kelly had to swallow hard. He wasn't just talking about losing Peggy, was he? Was he warning her that times like this were also something they

needed to make the most of because they weren't going
to last very long?

The silence hung there as if they were both thinking the same thing. It was Ari who broke it.

'You're amazing, Kel,' he said softly. 'Don't let anyone ever make you believe that isn't true. Ever. Okay?
Don't ever think you're not special enough to deserve
the best because you are. You're the most amazing person I've ever met.'

The knot forming in her belly wasn't renewed desire. It was more like tension. Fear, even, that Ari was
about to tell her their time together was already over?
But she could feel herself smiling at the same time.

'I think you've got the gift of making any woman
feel special,' she murmured. It was so true. His touch
could be gentle enough to feel reverent but then it could
change into something that was so passionate you could
believe it was what he was feeling and tasting that was
inspiring it. And then, when you threw away any in-
hibitions to respond in ways you'd never imagined, he
was with you all the way—encouraging that response.
Revelling in it...

'You need to believe it, though. In here...' Ari laid
his hand on Kelly's breast. Over her heart. 'And you
need to keep believing it, even when I'm not here to
remind you.'

Oh...the trailing ends of that internal knot had just
been given a sharp tug so that it tightened enough to
cause real pain. She might be safe within the circle
of Ari's arms right now but her time with him wasn't
going to last as long as Kelly would want it to.

Which was, she realised with absolute certainty,
for ever.

It wasn't just Peggy who was so easy to love. She'd recognised the trust that Ari had won from her as a form of love but somehow she'd delegated it to the kind of love you could have with a good friend. She'd seen it as a signpost pointing to a future where it might be possible to find the all-consuming "falling in love" kind of love that was so far above the level of even your best friends. The kind of love that made you so sure that you'd found your soul-mate. The person that you didn't want to live without. The lover that you wanted to wake up next to, every day, for the rest of your life.

It had been a signpost all right. But how could she not have seen that it was pointing straight towards Ari Lawson?

That *he* was that person?

That knot wasn't about to unravel but Kelly could feel the tightness loosen a little as Ari's hand shaped her breast and then he bent his head to let his lips take the place of his fingers and the tip of his tongue to taste her nipple. She caught her breath in a gasp—arching her back, even, at the searing intensity of that pleasure.

'That traffic…' Ari's voice was so low it was no more than a whispered growl. 'It's particularly bad today…'

CHAPTER NINE

THE TRAFFIC WAS so much lighter by the time Ari finally headed home it was a pleasure to get up enough speed to lean into the corners and feel the pressure of wind against his body. After the last couple of hours in Kelly's bed, he was still a little drunk on the delights of physical pleasure that had raised the bar of what he'd believed possible. Even a gust of wind could rekindle the buzz. He knew it wasn't going to last that long—his sexual relationships never did—but, right now, Ari couldn't imagine not having Kelly in his life. He could never have had enough of her—in bed or out of it.

Daylight was beginning to fade so it was easy to spot the flashing lights of a police car coming up behind him as he got closer to home. A second police car wasn't far behind, its lights flashing and the siren also wailing. When an ambulance rushed past him only a minute later, Ari knew that something major must be happening in his neighbourhood. A serious car crash perhaps? A stabbing or shooting?

It wasn't just in his neighbourhood either. The emergency vehicles were congregating in his own street. Right in front of his own house…? It was only then that any remnants of the delights of being with Kelly evaporated completely and fear kicked in to take their place. Ari was off his bike in a flash, running down the street as he yanked his helmet off.

'Sorry, sir, but you can't go in.' A policeman was blocking the path to the front door of the house. 'There's been an incident.'

'I live here.' Ari's words were clipped. 'My mother's in there. You can't stop me.'

He pushed past the officer, only to find another guarding the front door. Behind him, in the hallway, he could see an ambulance stretcher. Waiting for Peggy? Or was Stacey having her baby and something had gone wrong? But why were the police here as well as an ambulance?

'What the hell is going on here?'

The question was fired at the second officer but Ari didn't wait for an answer because he was too desperate to see for himself. Maybe this officer had heard him tell the one at the gate that he lived here. Or perhaps it was just the expression on his face that made the policeman step aside to let him in. Ari burst into the kitchen to find Stacey sitting at the table, flanked by two police officers. She was white-faced and sitting as still as a stone and it didn't look as if she was about to willingly communicate with anyone.

What was far more alarming, however, was the crumpled figure on the floor in front of the couch where he'd left Peggy resting comfortably some time ago. Two paramedics were crouched beside a body so still that, for a horrible moment, Ari thought that his mum was dead. He dropped to his knees close to her head but couldn't speak for a moment. He had to focus on taking a breath.

'Ari...' Peggy's voice was weaker than he'd ever heard it to be, even straight after her major surgery. 'Is that you? Oh...thank goodness you're here...'

Peggy's skin was even paler than Stacey's, except for where it was stained by a livid bruise appearing all around an eye that was already almost closed by swelling. Her lip was badly cut as well.

'Blood pressure's still too low,' one of the paramedics said. 'Let's get an IV in and get moving. How's that ECG looking?'

'Sinus rhythm,' his colleague responded. 'But tachycardic.' He looked up at Ari. 'And you are...?'

'He's my boy,' Peggy whispered. Her breath caught in a gasp that could have been either pain or fear. 'I need him...'

Ari had to swallow a huge lump in his throat. 'What's going on?' He had his hand on Peggy's forehead, smoothing back her hair. 'Did she fall? She's just come out of hospital after major abdominal surgery.'

'She didn't fall.' The senior paramedic shook his head. 'Some lowlife assaulted her. He was after drugs that he knew she had in the house, presumably because of the surgery.' His glance slid sideways and his tone hardened. 'Seems like he was a "friend" of the young lady living here.'

Peggy's unswollen eye was fluttering shut. 'Not her fault...' she whispered. 'Ari...you'll take care of Stacey, won't you?'

'Yeah...' But Ari had to push down a rising anger as he remembered the feverish text conversation he'd seen Stacey having before he'd left to take Kelly home. Had she been setting up the visit that had turned vicious? Had she deliberately put Peggy in danger by allowing a drug addict into the house? The abusive boyfriend that Kelly had told him about maybe? 'I'm going to take care of you first, though.'

But he needed to move back to give the paramedics room to work and he could feel the glare coming from the direction of the kitchen table. Anger bubbled and began to colour his words.

'What the hell were you thinking, Stace? Did you even think what the repercussions might be if you let your drug-addict mates know what was in the house? The medications that Peggy needs?'

Stacey said nothing. Her arms were wrapped tightly around her body above the bump of her pregnancy. She looked terrified beneath her resentment, Ari realised. And so, so young… He had to swallow hard.

'Are you okay?' he asked. 'Did he hit you as well?'

His anger might not have penetrated Stacey's stony silence but the concern in his voice did now. Not that Stacey seemed to appreciate his concern.

'As if you care,' she spat. 'You said you'd come back to look after Peggy. You promised you'd help look after *me*, too, but you're not that interested any more, are you?' Her lips curled as she glared at Ari. 'This wouldn't have happened if you'd been here but you weren't, were you? You were too busy, off shagging your girlfriend.'

Oh… *God*…the truth in those words was inescapable. This *was* his fault as much as Stacey's. What had he been thinking to let Kelly take over so much of the free time he had away from work when he should have been spending it caring for the closest thing to family he would ever have? The guilt that slammed into Ari on top of his fear for Peggy was too much. Ari could feel the pressure suddenly build to a point where he had to lash out.

'Who told that scumbag there were drugs in the house, Stace? What were you doing—trying to make a bit of pocket money?' He lowered his voice so that Peggy couldn't possibly hear if she was still conscious. 'If Peggy dies because of this, I'll never forgive you...'

He could see Stacey shrinking. Holding herself even more tightly, her lips now pressed together so hard they had all but vanished.

'What do you know about the person who might have carried out this attack?' the police officer asked Ari.

He shook his head. 'I only know that she's got a so-called boyfriend who's been abusive to her in public. And she had a friend over here for dinner not long ago.'

The night he'd first made love to Kelly, in fact. If he'd gone home that night, would he have met that "friend"? Could he have made it clear he wasn't welcome?

'Was it the same person, Stacey?' the policeman asked.

Stacey shrugged one shoulder but then nodded.

'Did you give him drugs then, too?'

Stacey ignored him.

'I can give you the name of a friend who saw him with her a while back,' Ari told the police officer. 'She'll be able to give you a description.'

'That could be helpful, although we've got a fair idea of who it is. Stacey's been doing her best to give us the information we need and we're confident he's someone who's already on our radar. You might want to know that he broke into the house because he was refused entry. And it was Stacey who called us to report the incident.'

And he'd just laid the blame on Stacey. Because he didn't want to face up to his own share? He'd known all along that he didn't have the room for any more complications in his life but he'd let Kelly in and devoted more and more of the precious time to being with her. But there was no point in trying to apportion blame right now. There was something far more important to worry about. Ari's head swerved back to where the paramedics were still working to stabilise Peggy for transport to hospital. A police officer was being used to hold up a bag of IV fluid. He could see a slightly erratic green line on the screen that was recording Peggy's heart rate and rhythm and equipment was being hastily collected and packed as if it was urgent to get her to hospital as quickly as possible.

Stacey's chair tipped backwards and toppled to the floor as she pushed herself to her feet.

'Don't go anywhere,' the police officer told her. 'We've still got a few more questions.'

'I need to go to the toilet.' Stacey's voice was wooden. 'If that's all right with you?'

'Of course.'

She didn't look in Ari's direction as she left the kitchen but he barely noticed. The stretcher had been brought into the room and the paramedics were being as gentle as they could as they lifted Peggy from the floor and arranged blankets and pillows around the wires of the ECG monitor and the tubing for the IV fluid. Ari could see the trace that told him Peggy was still alive but, looking at that pale, still face and the limp hand on top of the blankets, Ari felt the hollow space in his gut growing into an abyss. He was going to lose the person who'd been the most important to him for so much of his life—maybe a lot sooner than he'd expected.

'I'm coming with you,' he told the paramedics. 'I don't want her to be alone for a minute.'

'No worries. But let's get going, yeah?'

It took a minute to manoeuvre the stretcher through the kitchen door and into the hall, where they were blocked by two police officers.

'She's gone,' one of them was saying.

'What? How did that happen?'

'I couldn't go into the bathroom with her, could I? How was I to know that she was going to climb out the window…?'

They stepped aside to let the stretcher pass. Ari slowed as he followed it. 'Stacey's gone?'

'Done a runner.' The officer nodded. 'But don't worry, she can't have gone far, especially in her condition. We'll find her. Dunno why she's taken off when it's not her that's in trouble.'

Ari simply mirrored the nod. Stacey had stormed off because of what he'd said but right now he couldn't worry about the fact that he'd upset her so much—he had to focus on Peggy because, as awful as the thought was, it was quite possible these were the last minutes he would ever have with her. He lengthened his stride to catch up with the stretcher.

'I'm going to the hospital with my mother,' he threw back over his shoulder. 'You can find me there if you need to.'

He held her hand all the way to Kensington Hospital's emergency department. He was still holding it, more than an hour later, when she'd been admitted to a ward.

She was conscious again and he'd been told that her being admitted was more of a precaution than anything else but he'd never seen Peggy looking like this. So old and shaky. As if life was finally just too hard. It was so typical of his mum that it wasn't herself that she was worried about, however.

'Please, Ari…go and find her. She's probably frightened. It wasn't her fault, you know. Not really…'

'I'd rather stay here. With you.'

Peggy shook her head but the movement made her wince. Her black eye was still swelling and changing colour and it looked horrific. She could see him staring.

'This looks far worse than it is. And after what they've given me, nothing hurts if I don't move. I'm going to sleep, Ari. There's no point in sitting by my bed, love. I'd much rather you went to find Stacey.' A tear escaped the eye that had been closed by the swelling and the whispered words might not have been intended to be heard. 'I don't want to die before I know she's all right… And that poor wee baby—what if it gets born on the streets…?'

So Ari went home. Because he'd decided he could collect Stacey and bring her back. The least she could do was to come into the hospital, no matter how much she disliked the place, to give Peggy the reassurance that would allow her to rest and try to heal from injuries that had to have set her back considerably in her recovery from the surgery.

But Stacey hadn't been found and taken home. The police officer that had been left to secure the house just shook his head at Ari's questions.

'There's too many places street kids can hide out in and that boyfriend of hers probably knows them all. If she doesn't want to be found, it's going to be very difficult.'

Ari paced the kitchen minutes later, the reminders of what had happened all too obvious, from some discarded packaging of IV supplies to blood spots on the polished floorboards and the odd angle of the chair Stacey had knocked over that had been picked up but not straightened.

"Difficult" didn't mean you couldn't try, but he didn't know where to start and...and Ari had never felt so alone in his life. Or maybe that wasn't quite true. He'd felt rather like this as an abandoned six-year-old, hadn't he? When what he'd needed most of all had been someone to love him. Someone who would put their arms around him and tell him everything was going to be okay. There was only one person he could think of who might be able to make him feel less alone.

He pulled his phone from his pocket without giving himself time to think it through and the warmth that flooded his body the instant he heard Kelly's voice told him that he'd been right. She *was* the person he needed most right now. He had to fight back tears as he told her what had happened and his need to try and do something to fix everything but the frustration of not knowing where to start.

'I know a few places street kids hang out in,' she told him. 'I've gone there on ambulance jobs. There's an under-bridge homeless community not far from Kensington Hospital that I've been to. And an old house not far from you. I went there for a drug overdose once.'

'What street is it in?'

'I can't remember the name. I'd know it if I saw it, though, and roughly where the street is. Come and get me, Ari. I'll help you look…'

It felt good to be on the back of this bike because it gave her an excuse to wrap her arms around Ari and hold him tightly. It couldn't have felt more different than the last time she'd been on the back of his bike only hours ago, however, when she'd been aware of every tiny movement of his muscles. Even through the protective layer of that leather jacket over his clothing now she could feel how tense he was—a solid mass of focused human who was probably barely aware of the touch of her arms.

Kelly would have been beyond appalled to learn about a cowardly attack involving physical violence on any frail, old woman but this was Peggy and that made it utterly unthinkable. While she was inclined to agree with Ari's first reaction and blame Stacey for what had happened, she could understand how torn he was and how important it was for Peggy to know that the teenager was all right. Stacey had listened to Kelly once when she'd told her how lucky she was to have Peggy and Ari in her life and it had apparently made a difference so maybe she could help again. She desperately wanted to help. For Peggy, of course, and for Stacey herself but mostly for Ari. The haunted look on his face when he'd arrived to collect her on his bike had been heart-breaking.

As far as they could tell, Stacey wasn't amongst the group of homeless young people who had claimed the area under the bridge that Kelly knew about.

'Have you seen her?' Ari asked someone who had

dreadlocks reminiscent of the hairstyle he'd had when he was seventeen. 'She's got really bright red hair, short on one side. And she's pregnant.'

'Nah, man…she's not here. No one's seen her.'

People were turning their backs on them.

'If you do see her, tell her Ari's looking for her. Tell her to come home.'

They got an even more hostile reception at the abandoned house that was inhabited by squatters—many of whom were no older than Stacey.

'You're not in trouble,' Kelly told whoever had been swearing at her on the other side of the closed door. 'We need to find someone, that's all. Stacey. Red hair. She's pregnant and the baby could come anytime.'

'We've already had the cops here and I reckon that's your fault.' The door opened a crack. 'Get lost or you'll be sorry…'

For some time after that, they rode around the streets, slowing to check shadowy doorways or lanes and stopping when they saw a figure walking alone or hunched on a park bench. It grew later. And colder. Kelly could feel the tension mounting as the realisation sank in that they were looking for a needle in a haystack, trying to find a single teenaged girl in a city of millions of people. There were lines on Ari's face she'd never seen before and he was so focused on his search he didn't even meet her eyes or seem to hear things she said.

It was a tacit acknowledgment that their efforts were futile when Ari finally took Kelly back to her flat. He took his helmet off to talk to her when she'd climbed off the back but he stayed sitting astride the bike as if he wanted to be ready to take off at a moment's notice.

Kelly wanted so badly to try and reassure him. Even if the only thing she could do was to hold him and keep him company.

'Come in. I'll make some coffee.'

'Nah… I'm going to keep looking for a while. Then I'll go back and see how Mum is.'

'I'll come with you.'

'I've already arranged time off work.' Ari still wasn't meeting her gaze. 'You've got an early shift tomorrow and there's no point staying up all night anyway. Like the police said, if she doesn't want to be found, it's going to be difficult.'

'She'll come back,' Kelly told him. 'I'm sure of it.'

'Why would she? She's as upset as any of us and she blames me. She said it wouldn't have happened if I'd been at home and she's right. I would have flattened that bastard before he got anywhere near Mum.'

'I know.' The words were hard to get out. She did know just how protective Ari would have been. She also knew that the reason Ari hadn't been at home was because he'd been with *her*. In her bed. Making love to her that second time… He was blaming himself now. Was he blaming her as well?

'I knew how she felt and I ignored it,' Ari said softly. Finally, he did meet her gaze and the pain she could see in his eyes was unbearable. 'This is more my fault than hers. 'Do you remember—that first time you came to dinner?'

Kelly nodded. Of course she remembered. 'It was when Peggy gave me my first knitting lesson.'

And when Stacey had totally dismissed the idea of her being Ari's girlfriend but she'd known that Peggy was hoping something was going to happen between them—almost as much as Kelly was?

'I almost didn't invite you,' Ari admitted. 'I knew I shouldn't get any closer to you because…well, because I can't do long term and you deserve better than a relationship that isn't going anywhere but, more than that, I knew I owed it to Mum and Stacey not to get involved with someone who was going to distract me from what I'd come back to London for in the first place—to look after Mum. I didn't know Stacey was in trouble but, as soon as I did, I had to look out for her as well.'

'Of course you did. They're your family.' Kelly was still holding her helmet in her arms. Hugging it when she would far rather be hugging Ari.

'I knew how attracted I was,' he continued. 'But I actually believed that we could be friends. I knew that was how it had to be because Stacey reminded me that night. She was really sulky and let me know that it was because she thought you were my girlfriend. And I reassured her. I said, "As if I've got time for a girlfriend when I've got you and Mum to look after at the moment."'

Kelly was biting her bottom lip now. So hard that it hurt. She'd played her own part in all of this. She'd wanted more than friendship. She'd wanted Ari to kiss her that first time so badly that when it hadn't happened, the disappointment had been crushing. She'd wanted it all.

She still did, but she could feel it disappearing. Being gently but irrevocably being taken away from her.

'We can't be "just friends", can we?' I can't be anywhere near you, Kel, without wanting more. Without it messing with my head so much it's too hard to think of anything else. Well…work's okay…' He met her gaze for a heartbeat and there was even a hint of a smile on his face. 'Better than okay, really, because when I'm working with you, it feels like I can do more than I ever could on my own.'

Kelly was nodding. 'I know. I feel the same way.'

Ari's breath came out in an audible sigh. 'Yeah…we make an amazing team but, out of work, it's a different story. For me anyway. If we'd been able to keep our hands off each other, I would have got home in time to make sure this never happened. It *shouldn't* have happened.' The anger in his tone was chilling. 'None of it.'

Kelly's throat was so tight it was hard to take a breath. Or to release any more words but they came out anyway. Because she had to know.

'Including me?' Her voice cracked. 'Us?'

He held her gaze properly this time and there was no way on earth Kelly could have broken it.

'I've never asked for relationships in my life,' Ari said quietly. 'Never expected them. Not after my mother just dumped me and walked out. I never wanted them, I guess, because I knew how they ended. But Peggy just happened and so did Stacey and it feels like I had no choice but to love them—as if the love had always been there for me to find, or something. I have to be there for them and, to do that, I can't be with you. I'm sorry… You're the last person I'd ever want to hurt.'

Or maybe not the last person because there were others who were more important? But Kelly could see the turmoil in those dark eyes—the agony of the loss of his mum that he might be facing, anger for a foster sister he'd held when she was just a newborn baby, that was confused by a compassion he couldn't banish and…and just pain. Even if he loved her as much as she knew she loved him, he had to push her away, didn't he? Because there were others that he felt responsible for. People he cared about who had been in his life a lot longer than she had. She had to respect that.

And, because Kelly loved him that much, she could do the one thing that help him at the moment. She could let him go and make at least this part of the mess easier to fix.

'It's okay, Ari,' she said softly. 'It's going to be okay.'

'How?'

'You'll find Stacey. You can do what you came back for and look after your mum and you don't need to let anything else interfere with that. Maybe, one day, we can be just friends…' Kelly handed Ari her helmet. She needed to get away. To duck down the steps to her flat and out of sight before she started crying. 'If that's something we both want.'

This was unbearable. There were echoes from the past that were trying to gain head space. Darryn's voice…

You're a useless lump… Waste of time… Dunno what I ever saw in you in the first place…

She had already turned away when Ari said something so she couldn't be quite sure what she'd heard but if it was agreement about wanting some kind of relationship in the future, it sounded too tentative to be of any comfort.

'Maybe…one day…'

CHAPTER TEN

BEING NOTHING MORE than friends didn't mean you weren't allowed to care.

Kelly's priority the next day, at the first opportunity she had with a break in her shift, was to visit Peggy in a ward of Kensington Hospital where she'd been admitted for observation and further assessment of her traumatic injuries. It was no surprise to find Ari sitting by her bed, holding his mum's hand, even though she appeared to be asleep, but it was almost overwhelming to find how hard this was going to be—to let Ari go like this. To step back and turn away from a love that she could feel burning in every cell of her body.

He looked as if he'd slept even less than she had last night. Paler than normal skin made his eyes look almost black and the knot of hair high on the back of his head was messy enough to have fronds escaping on all sides. Kelly could see—or perhaps feel—the tension in his body, even though he smiled at her as she came into the private room Peggy had been given. What she wanted, more than anything, was to walk straight into his arms and just hold him as tightly as she could for a few seconds, to let him know how much her heart was aching for him and that she could be by his side for every moment of this ordeal if it would help.

It wouldn't help, though, would it? Their being together was the reason Ari was blaming himself for the terrible thing that had happened to Peggy. He had let down the most important person in his life in the worst way possible and she knew Ari well enough to understand that he had to take control somehow now and put things right. That he had to care for the people he loved. And she loved him enough to let that happen, even if it meant that she might lose him for ever.

He didn't meet her gaze for more than a heartbeat as he offered her that smile of welcome. His attention shifted almost instantly and it was obvious it was slipping straight back to where it had been, probably for many hours—to Peggy's face.

'How is she?' Kelly kept her voice low. Rest was going to be vital for Peggy's physical healing. Having Ari by her side would be equally vital for her emotional healing but how hard was it going to be to get over such an appalling attack? In her own home and when she had been with someone she deserved to be able to trust?

'There's no sign of a significant head injury and she doesn't seem to have suffered any internal injuries from the fall but they're going to keep a careful eye on her for a day or two.' Ari rubbed his forehead with his free hand and his voice was raw. 'She was only just starting to heal from the surgery.'

'I know...' Kelly swallowed the lump in her throat.

'They caught him. The police came in this morning.' Ari sounded as if it didn't really matter now. 'He was out on the streets, trying to sell the tramadol he'd nicked. He's been arrested. He probably won't be out of prison and able to hurt anyone else for a very long time.'

Maybe it didn't actually matter so much to Ari now because the damage had already been done to someone who was precious to him. Damage he should have been able to prevent. If anybody could take any blame for this atrocity, it had to be Stacey, but Ari felt responsible for her as well, didn't he? He probably had, to some degree, ever since he'd held her when she'd been a tiny, vulnerable baby having a rough start in life. And Kelly couldn't begrudge the place the troubled teenager had in his life. It was one of the things she loved about him, after all—that extraordinary ability to love and protect. The quality of being someone you could trust with your life.

And your heart…if he let you get that close.

'Have they found Stacey, too?'

Ari shook his head. 'No sign of her.'

As if she'd heard the whispered name, Peggy's eyelids fluttered.

'Stacey?'

'No sign yet, Ma.' Ari leaned closer to rest the backs of his fingers gently on Peggy's cheek. 'Try not to worry, yeah? They'll find her. I'll go back out to look again later, too, when I know you're going to get some proper sleep. I'll pop home first. Who knows? Maybe she's there and tucked up in her own bed again.'

'Oh…' Peggy still hadn't opened her eyes. 'Go now, Ari. Please…go and check…'

'Soon. I'm not going anywhere just yet. I've got all the time I need away from work. I'm not leaving you.'

'I'm on the road all day,' Kelly added. 'I'll be looking out for Stacey, too. I've already put the word out for any other ambulance officers to help. It's a good thing that she's so easy to recognise with that hair of hers.'

'Oh...' Peggy opened her eyes properly as her head turned towards Kelly. 'You're here too, lovey. I'm so pleased about that...'

'I had to come and see how you were.' Kelly stepped closer to the bed. 'I'm so, so sorry this has happened to you, Peggy.' The threat of tears muffled her words and Kelly could feel a stab of the horrible guilt that she knew Ari was struggling with right now—that she had been in his arms, in blissful ignorance, happier than she'd ever been in her life, while this unthinkable attack had happened to the sweetest old woman she had ever met.

'It's not the worst thing in the world.' Peggy's voice had a wobble in it. 'I'm more worried about our Stacey and that baby of hers. And you,' she added, turning back to Ari. 'You've got to stop blaming yourself, love. This isn't your fault.' Her head sank back into the pillow and her eyes were closing. 'Thank goodness you've got Kelly. She'll look after you...'

Except that Ari didn't want to be looked after. He was the one who looked after others and nothing was going to be allowed to interfere with that any more.

Kelly could almost feel the wall between them and she suddenly realised why his relationships had never lasted. He was the person who could be needed, and relied on, and he would always be there for the people who'd captured his heart, like Peggy and Stacey. But he would never willingly become the needy one, relying on someone else, where you could have your own trust—and your heart—shattered.

Her heart ached for the small boy he'd once been, when that ability to trust had been ripped away when his mother had abandoned him. And it ached even more for the beautiful man he was now, but she couldn't push any closer in emotional terms at the moment because she knew it would only make him run harder and faster and then she might lose sight of him for ever.

Even if…and possibly entirely due to the fact that he felt the connection between them as much as Kelly did. Perhaps he actually loved her already but couldn't admit it. Because it made him too vulnerable? It wasn't possible to force someone to trust you. Maybe Peggy was the only person on earth that Ari would ever trust to that degree. He was facing the loss of something incredibly precious but Kelly couldn't offer him any comfort because being too close would only make it harder for him.

She bent to place a very gentle kiss on Peggy's cheek. 'I'll be back to see you later,' she said. 'Rest and get better, okay?'

Ari looked up as she straightened and, for a brief moment that seemed to stretch for ever, the silent communication encompassed everything that had been running through Kelly's mind. The guilt and the fear of loss, the trauma of the past that made it impossible to trust, the need to care for others and…there seemed to be a heartfelt apology there as well.

It felt like a goodbye and it left a haunting note that stayed with Kelly as her afternoon wore on with call after call to people needing help from the ambulance service. To make it even harder it seemed that fate was making sure that every job had something about it that made her think of the new, significant people in her life. A cyclist had been clipped by a car not far from the charity shop where she'd bought those balls of wool—and seen Stacey being abused by her boyfriend. The elderly lady who was struggling for breath because her heart failure had taken a turn for the worse had silver hair just like Peggy's and there was something about the way that young father was holding his baby in his arms on her last call for the day that reminded her so much of that photo of Ari holding Stacey as a baby.

Except it wasn't quite her last call for the day. The febrile seizure that had terrified the baby's father had not been repeated but Kelly had called for back-up to take them to hospital for further assessment, monitoring and much-needed reassurance. Her radio crackled as she headed back to her station.

'Rover One, please respond to call for back-up from police. You're the closest unit to the bridge on Campbell Road, south of Kensington Hospital. Person threatening to jump.'

Kelly hit the switch to start her beacons flashing. She blipped her siren as well, to warn traffic as she made a U-turn and then sped towards the bridge. Following the theme of her afternoon, this job was also going to remind her of Ari because the area beneath that bridge was one of the places they had gone to last night to search for Stacey. A bridge that had high steel curves on either side. If someone had climbed up to the top of the curve, they could fall onto the roadway instead of the river, which would be un-survivable. Kelly could feel the tension increasing rapidly as she neared the bridge to see the flashing lights of police cars blocking traffic from using the bridge.

Worse, she recognised the silhouette of one of the

police officers standing by his car, his feet planted wide and his arms folded as he formed part of the barricade. Darryn. The last person she wanted to see anywhere but particularly today when she was already feeling the loss so poignantly of what might have been with Ari. Clearly Darryn didn't feel the same antipathy.

'Hey, Cowbell. Can't stay away from me, huh?'

Kelly ignored him, walking past to find whoever was in charge of this scene. She was looking up and her heart sank as she saw that someone had, indeed, climbed up the latticework of steel. They weren't near the top but they were still high enough for a fall to be potentially fatal, whether it was into the river or onto the roadway.

'Don't go too close, darling.' Darryn's voice was teasing enough to be uncomfortably familiar but the undertone was anything but affectionate. 'She might take one look at you and decide to jump. Two for the price of one, there, too.'

'What?' Kelly's head swerved. 'What's that supposed to mean?'

Darryn tapped the side of his head. 'Thought you were smarter than that, Cowbell. The driver that called this in saw her start climbing. She's got a bun in the oven.'

Kelly was shading her eyes with her hand, trying to see into the fading daylight against the over-bright lights of emergency vehicles around her. Maybe there wasn't enough light to see hair colour or the bump of a pregnant belly but Kelly's heart took another dive as she reached for her phone. She just knew that this was Stacey.

She hit a speed dial button on her phone, spoke

only for seconds and then headed behind the police vehicles towards where the curved side of the bridge started its rise on the other side of some railings. There were two sides to the curve connected by steel pipes that looked enough like a ladder to suggest it would be easy to climb.

'Don't go any closer.' A police officer wearing a "Scene Commander" high-vis vest came swiftly in Kelly's direction. 'We've tried talking to her and she said she'll jump if anyone tries to climb up. We've got a police negotiator on the way. She's just a kid.'

'I'm pretty sure I know her,' Kelly told him. 'And I've got a family member on his way.'

More than on his way, in fact. Ari must have run like the wind from the hospital to have got to this bridge so fast. He was out of breath but it didn't stop him cupping his hands to try and make his voice carry further.

'Stace? Don't move… I'm coming up to get you.'

'*No…*' The sound was faint but unmistakable. 'Stay away…'

Ari shook his head. 'No way…' He could have been talking to himself as he eyed the railing and the structure of the curves. 'This is my fault. I can fix this…'

'You're not going up there,' the police commander told him. 'I'm not going to risk escalating this situation. We just need to wait until—' He stopped talking abruptly as another call came from above.

'What?' He shouted. 'Say that again?'

'Kelly…' Again, the words were faint but audible. 'I want to talk to Kelly.'

Kelly could feel everybody staring at her, including Darryn, but she was only looking back at one person. Ari. Holding his gaze. She knew exactly how desperate he was to get closer to Stacey to make sure she could be kept safe. She knew how hard it would be—impossible, perhaps—for him to trust someone else with something this important. She took a step closer and kept holding that dark gaze. Trying with all her might to convince him that she would never do anything to hurt him. Ever…

'Trust me, Ari,' she said softly. 'Please…'

'Yeah, right…' The taunting tone could only have come from one person. 'Wouldn't do that if I was you, mate…'

Kelly head snapped around to face Darryn. 'Shut up,' she told him. 'You're not only being completely unprofessional, you're showing everyone what an abusive bully you are. And you know what?' She didn't wait for any response. 'You don't intimidate me in the slightest.'

And he didn't, she realised. What had Ari said about working with her? That it felt as if he could do more than he ever could on his own? She felt the same way. She had more courage and confidence when she had Ari just standing close to her, let alone working with her. Even if the brief time they'd had together was all she'd ever have, Kelly would be grateful for the rest of her life for what he'd given her. It was this man who'd encouraged her to believe in herself—to believe in love—again.

Darryn—the abusive bully she'd been unfortunate to have had a relationship with—was never going to intimidate her again. Thanks to Ari, she was no longer afraid of this man on any level. She didn't even bother looking at him as she pushed past.

'Now…get out of my way.'

* * *

He'd seen her stand up to an aggressive man the first time they'd met and he'd been blown away by Kelly's courage. He'd also seen her shrink in the face of abuse from this man but here she was, standing up to him with just as much authority as she had dealt with Vicky's husband that day. Darryn was backing away, like the coward he probably was, and even amongst his fear for Stacey and the determination to be the one to protect her somehow and then get her to safety, he felt a burst of pride for Kelly and the satisfaction of realising that she was in the space he had wished for her to be in all along. A space where she could believe in herself and realise that she deserved so much better than anything a creep like Darryn could have offered her.

No wonder it was Kelly that Stacey wanted to talk to rather than him and, as hard as it was, Ari knew that he had to do what Kelly had asked him to do. He had to trust her. And it seemed like he wasn't the only one who was prepared to do that. The police officer in charge had a slightly stunned look on his face as he stood back to allow Kelly climb the railing and gain access to the edge of the bridge structure.

Her face was set in tight lines that Ari had seen before. In that car with Zoe when it had shifted on the rocks in that flood and, for a moment, they had faced the reality of how much danger they were in. When he'd held Kelly's gaze and tried to reassure her that he was going to do anything he could to protect her.

But he couldn't protect her now. Even though it was tearing him apart, there was nothing Ari could do but to stand here and watch.

And trust…

* * *

This was scarier than anything Kelly had ever had to do in her work. Scarier than being in a car in a flooded stream even, but she'd been able to find the courage to cope with that and she could find that same kind of courage now because…because Ari was nearby and that changed everything. Like he felt himself, they were better together than alone and that meant that Kelly could be a version of herself that was only possible because she believed it was. Because Ari believed she was amazing?

She had begged Ari to trust her and now she had to trust herself. She'd got through to Stacey once before by being honest and not holding back. Was that why Stacey wanted to talk to her now? Because she knew that she could trust Kelly to tell her the truth, even if it was difficult to hear?

'Don't come any closer. I could still jump…'

Oh, *God*… The fear in Stacey's voice was heart-breaking. Kelly had to fight back the threat of tears and it took a supreme effort to keep her voice calm.

'No, you won't,' she said quietly. 'You wouldn't do that. Not when it's going to hurt the people who care about you so much.'

'They don't care any more. Why would they? It's my fault that Peggy got hurt. Ari said so.'

'He was upset. People say things they don't necessarily mean when they upset. But they don't stop caring because something bad happens.' Kelly climbed another rung. 'I went to see Peggy today and you know what the only thing is that she's worrying about?'

Stacey was silent for a long moment but Kelly

waited until she felt compelled to ask. To buy into the conversation.

'What?'

'You. You…and your baby. Ari's worried, too. He's down there on that bridge and he's holding his breath, waiting to see that you're okay. He wants to take you to see Peggy. You're a family, you guys. You need to be together right now.' She climbed another rung and then two. 'I'm not just saying this stuff, Stacey. You know I'm telling you what's true.' She was almost close enough to touch Stacey, who was clinging to the framework of the steel curve, her eyes screwed shut and her face tear-streaked and pale.

'I can't…' Fresh tears were rolling down Stacey's cheeks. 'I can't go down.'

'You can.' Kelly swallowed her fear. 'I'm here. I'll help you.'

'No… I can't. My back hurts too much and…and I've wet my pants.'

'Oh…' Kelly closed the distance between them as much as she could. The gap between the two sides that made the curve was wide enough for her climb right up beside Stacey. To put her arm around the frightened teenager. 'You know what this probably means, don't you?'

Stacey's body was still rigid but she was leaning against Kelly as if she desperately needed the human contact. 'What?'

'Your baby might have decided it's time to arrive.' Kelly reached for her radio with her free hand, careful not to rock the weight Stacey was trusting her to support. 'There's a fire truck down there on the bridge with a long ladder and I think it's just become even more important that we get you safely back on the ground as fast as possible. Are you ready?'

'No…they're going to be mad at me…'

'Who? Ari? Peggy? Are you kidding? They love you. You can trust that, you know. Always…'

He had known, deep down, that he could trust Kelly. Always.

It hadn't made it any easier to stand back and watch, however. It was, in fact, the first time that Ari could remember allowing himself to be so vulnerable. To have so much hanging on the outcome of trusting someone else.

He had been too far away to hear anything that was being said between Kelly and Stacey but he had felt the tension rising steadily as Kelly had climbed closer. And then she had her arm around Stacey and he heard her voice coming over the radio of the police officer in charge but, instead of relieving that tension, her words made Ari catch his breath in horror.

'We need the ladder and basket to get down.' Kelly sounded calm. 'And an ambulance called, please, if there isn't one on the way already. Stacey here is in labour. I don't think we're going to have time to get her up to ED at the Kensington.'

An ambulance arrived only minutes later, as the fire officers were getting both Kelly and Stacey safely into the basket on the top of the ladder. Ari watched it being lowered, the extendable ladder folding into itself until the basket landed gently on the ground. Ari was right beside it as the side was opened, ready to add his support to Kelly to get Stacey into the privacy of the ambulance. He could see how scared Stacey was and it was heart-breaking.

'It's okay,' he told her, holding out his arms. 'It's all going to be okay, I promise…'

Stacey took a step towards him but then stopped, crying out as she doubled over in pain. Ari caught her as she leaned so far forward it looked as if she might fall, scooping her up into his arms as if she weighed no more than a child. He carried her to the warmed cabin of the ambulance, with Kelly following close behind, and, seconds later, it was just the three of them in that secure space, with no room for the ambulance crew if it wasn't needed.

'Something's happening,' Stacey sobbed, as Ari put her down on the stretcher. She pulled her legs up as Kelly was peeling the purple dungarees clear. 'It feels weird. Like I have to…have to push…'

Ari had sterile gloves on already. 'Your baby's coming, Stace. I can see the head already. It's crowning.' He knew exactly what to do now to try and protect both Stacey and her baby. He didn't have to trust anybody else but he couldn't have wished for anyone other than Kelly to be by his side in these tense moments of trying to ensure that Stacey's baby arrived safely in the world.

'You're doing so well, Stacey,' Kelly told her. 'Good girl…'

'It hurts,' Stacey groaned. 'It's burning.'

'Don't push,' Ari told her. There was a risk of her tearing if she pushed right now. 'Take short, shallow breaths like this.' He showed her what he meant. 'Pretend you're blowing out a candle on a cake. And…' he took hold of Stacey's hand to direct it '…you can feel baby's head just here. See? That his hair that you're touching.'

'Oh… *Ohh*…' Stacey was touching her baby's head but she was staring at Ari. 'It's real,' she choked out. 'A real baby…' Her words got swallowed by another cry of pain.

'You can push with this contraction,' Ari told her. 'Push as hard as you can…'

He checked to make sure the umbilical cord wasn't around the baby's neck as the head was born and then it took only minutes to coach Stacey through another contraction and catch the body of her baby as it appeared.

'It's a boy…' Ari had never been this close to tears at a birth before. He'd witnessed the miracle of it happening countless times and some of those births had been remarkable enough that he would never forget them— like delivering Zoe's baby in the car, for example, but this was something different again. This was the baby of someone he had cradled in his arms when she had been no more than a newborn herself. This was family and the love for this baby was already there.

Kelly had a soft towel ready to wrap the baby in and then they helped Stacey to take her son in her arms. And, as she cradled him, Ari met Kelly's gaze over the top of the baby and he recognised, in that moment, what had been there all along—he just hadn't let himself see it. He loved her. He had no more choice about loving Kelly Reynolds, in fact, than he'd had in his relationships with Peggy and Stacey.

It felt like his love for Kelly had always been there. How could he not have realised that Kelly had not only captured his heart virtually the moment he'd met her, but that she was the part of it that he'd been missing for ever. He'd felt that bond of trust and been amazed that he could achieve more in his work with her by his side than he could alone but this was more than that. Much, much more. This was about his whole life. His future.

And it seemed that perhaps Kelly understood the tsunami of emotion that was rushing through Ari in those intense seconds as Stacey gazed at her baby with total wonder and he was holding Kelly's gaze with a very similar kind of wonder as he began to see how much his universe had just changed. It certainly looked as if she was feeling exactly the same thing.

This moment—that Ari knew he would remember for ever—would have to be broken very soon. Stacey and her baby needed to be transferred to Kensington Hospital's emergency department to be checked and, as soon as they were cleared for discharge, there was an elderly woman in a ward upstairs who was going to be overjoyed to have her family gather in her room and to meet the newest member. The moment could be held for just a heartbeat longer, though, couldn't it? Enough time for one of those swift, silent conversations that he and Kelly could have from just sharing a long glance.

From letting their souls touch for a heartbeat.

I love you, his gaze told her. *I trust you. I trust us...*

And he could read her reply as easily as if she'd spoken aloud.

So do I. Always and forever...

EPILOGUE

Three years later...

'I WISH PEGGY was here.'

'Oh, but she is...' Kelly smiled up at Ari as she stood on tiptoe to kiss him softly. 'She's everywhere in this house. Don't you feel it?'

She saw his gaze shift to the battered old couch that was still at the end of the kitchen, still draped in those colourful blankets made from knitted squares. Currently it was bathed in sunlight streaming through the open French doors that led out to the garden.

'That's where you were looking after her,' Ari murmured. 'That day that you got called here.'

Kelly let her head tilt so that it was tucked into a favourite spot, just below his collar bone, as she stayed snug in the circle of his arms. 'You carried her to that couch,' she said softly. 'Do you know, I think that was the moment I started to fall in love with you? I wanted to be held like you were holding Peggy. To have someone who could make me feel that safe...that loved...'

Ari pressed a kiss to the top of her head. 'And do you?' he asked. 'Still?'

'More every day. Especially today...' Kelly's heart

was filling again, so much that it brought tears to her eyes.

'I reckon I fell in love with you the moment I wanted to hold you like that.' She could feel the way Ari had to swallow hard. 'There you were, a kick-ass paramedic with a dodgy situation under total control and then, suddenly, I could see the person inside. The Kelly that *needed* someone to hold her like that. To tell her that she was the most amazing person in the world.'

Kelly really had to blink tears away now as she turned to look out towards the garden, where a small girl with brown eyes and blonde hair was trying to tie ribbons around the tail of a very patient, large dog. 'What do you think Maggie's going to say when we tell her she's going to get a little brother or sister?'

'I think she'll say she wants a brother. She adores Jack, doesn't she?'

'Who wouldn't? Stacey's doing such a wonderful job in bringing him up. Peggy would be so proud of her.'

'And of her graduating as a nursery teacher. She was so determined to see her succeed. I reckon that was what made her live so much longer than any of us expected. At least she got to celebrate Stacey getting all the GCSEs she needed from night school.'

Kelly was smiling again. 'She was just as determined that we would get together, too. If you hadn't passed on her dinner invitation it might never have happened.'

Ari's arms tightened around her. 'I can't imagine life if it hadn't happened. And Peggy was still well enough to dance at our wedding. Still there to meet Maggie the night she was born. To know that we had named her Margaret- after her.'

Kelly turned her face back to nestle against Ari and they held each other very tightly for a moment. It was such a poignant memory because that had been the night that Peggy had slipped away from them, not long after holding her precious new grandchild in her arms. She had died in her sleep, surrounded by her closest family. Surrounded by the kind of love that the walls of this house still embraced. So much love but there was still an infinite capacity for more.

Kelly didn't need to tell Ari how lucky she was feeling. Or how much she loved him and how excited she was to know that a new member of their family was on the way. All she had to do was look up and catch his gaze. It only took a moment for one of those lightning-fast silent conversations that could say everything that captured the past, present and future of those three little words.

I love you...

* * * * *

A RIVAL
TO STEAL
HER HEART

ANNIE CLAYDON

MILLS & BOON

CHAPTER ONE

THE YOUNG MAN had a mop of red-brown hair, blue eyes and an easy, engaging smile. Anna Caulder thought she'd seen everything, but the tattoos on the backs of his hands plumbed the depths of bad taste.

'This may hurt a little, Callum. Tell me if it gets too much, and we'll stop.'

'That's all right, *Miss* Caulder.' Callum gave her a cheery smile. Someone must have told him that, as a surgeon, Anna should be addressed as 'Miss' and he was clearly eager to please. 'This place is pretty cool.'

Unfortunately that wasn't going to make removing the tattoos any less painful. Anna's expertise might, but only if Callum could be persuaded to stop looking around at the gleaming worktops and state-of-the-art medical equipment, and keep still.

'I'm going to need you to take a couple of deep breaths, and relax, Callum.'

'Okay. Are you going to do both hands?'

'Just one will be enough for this session, Cal. You'll need some time to heal afterwards,' Dr Jamie Campbell-Clarke interrupted. He did that a lot.

'Are you supposed to be here?' By Anna's calculations, today was a Monday, which was one of the three days a week that Jamie Campbell-Clarke spent working in the A&E department of a nearby hospital. Thursdays and Fridays were usually the days when she could expect to see him here, at the London Central Clinic, accompanying one of the teenagers he'd referred from the youth charity he ran in Hastings.

'I'm only at the hospital for two days this week. So I thought I'd come along and watch you work.' He sounded positively gleeful at the prospect.

'And make sure I didn't bottle out,' Callum reminded him.

'Yeah. There was that to it, as well.'

Jamie's charity aimed to help teenagers like Callum overcome all kinds of disadvantages and make the most of their lives. He was fiercely protective of his young charges, and checked on everything. Which was fine, because he was an excellent doctor, but a trace of professional rivalry sometimes crept into his exchanges with Anna.

'It would get it over with quicker. To do both hands.' Callum's face took on an imploring look.

'Miss Caulder will do as much as she can…' Anna turned and shot Jamie a glare and he fell silent, hopefully remembering that this was *her* consulting room and plastic surgery was *her* speciality.

'I know you want to get rid of these tattoos, Callum…' Anna glanced at the spidery words and the suggestive poses of the stick figures, and looked away quickly '…but it needs to be done properly, which is going to take a little more time than it did to get them.'

Callum nodded, staring at the backs of his hands. 'Yeah, I know. Jamie explained it all… At least they're black ink, so that's easier to get rid of, isn't it?'

'Yes, that's right. But I'm sure that Dr Campbell-Clarke explained that new tattoos are a little more difficult, and I gather you've only had these for a few months—'

'Twelve weeks,' Jamie interjected, and Anna ignored him. Heaven forfend he allowed her to get away with anything as vague as a *few months*.

Callum gave her a sudden smile. 'I understand. Thanks, Miss Caulder.'

He might not be thanking her at the end of the session, when his hand was hurting, but Callum didn't make a sound as she carefully traced the outline of the tattoos on the back of his right hand with the laser. When she'd finished, he gave her another smile, which smacked a little of false bravado.

'That's going to give us the best results we can achieve for today.' Anna decided that Callum needed a little reassurance that the short procedure was actually going to show some benefit. 'I think when the inflammation goes down, you'll see a big difference. Would you like the nurse to put a dressing on your other hand as well, just to cover the tattoos there?'

'Yeah. Thanks. It beats having to keep wearing gloves.'

'All right then. We'll give you some replacement dressings and a leaflet on how to care for your hand. That's really important, to avoid any infection.'

Callum nodded. 'Thanks, Miss Caulder. Jamie's already told me about that.'

'I'm sure he has. I'll leave it to him to check on your hand and re-dress it as necessary.' Out of the corner of her eye, she saw Jamie lay his hand on his chest, as if surprised that she'd finally found something that she could trust him to do.

Anna ignored the gesture. It was just a game that she and Dr Campbell-Clarke played. Each trying to outdo the other. Watching each other like hawks to make sure that the patients that he brought to her consulting room had the best possible treatment. It was harmless enough, and it took her mind off his eyes…

Moss green. On a woman, they'd be stunningly beautiful, and Jamie's dark hair and the strong line of his jaw made them seem like dazzling jewels, surrounded by steel and muscle. Under the clear lights of the consulting room they seemed almost luminescent.

But she had a policy of not thinking about his eyes. They were enough to make any woman's hand shake. Knowing that he was watching her every move and that he'd be quick to correct any mistakes gave her hand the professional, rock-steady quality that any surgeon needed.

He was wearing green today, a dark green flannel shirt with the sleeves rolled up. That was his style when carrying out the business of his charity, casual clothes and first names. It was a little different from the Dr Campbell-Clarke persona that Anna saw when she visited the large, central London hospital where he worked three days a week, but he had the same self-assurance. The same way of daring anyone to question him, which was perhaps why Anna never hesitated to do just that.

The nurse had dressed Callum's hands, and he was ready to stand now, a little shaky still from the procedure. Jamie ushered him outside, to where a neat-looking, middle-aged woman was sitting in the waiting room. Callum sat down beside her, and she gave him a brisk nod, but her hand moved to his back in a gesture of comfort.

'Mary, this is Miss Caulder.' Jamie introduced the two women quickly. 'Callum did really well, and Miss Caulder's very pleased with the results of the procedure.'

Anna could have said that herself. She resisted the urge to push him to one side, and smiled at the other woman. 'I've just done the one hand, and I think that when the inflammation goes down you'll see an appreciable difference. Callum asked us to dress his left hand as well, to cover it up.'

Mary nodded. 'Thank you, Miss Caulder.'

'I'll see him again in six weeks. I'm hoping we won't need too many sessions, and we should be able to remove the tattoos completely.'

'It's very good of you.' Mary frowned. 'I'm sorry—'

Jamie cut her short. 'It's okay. What's done is done and we look forward, eh, Callum?'

Callum nodded, his fingers moving to back of his right hand. Mary grabbed his hand, snatching it away before he could worry at the dressings.

'Maybe you'd like to sit for a while before you go.' The armchairs in the comfortable waiting room were laid out so that patients could sit in groups with their families, and Anna gestured towards the side table. 'Help yourself to coffee or tea.'

'Thank you. I think we'd like a drink before we get back on the train…' Mary glanced at Callum and he nodded.

'Great. Well I'll see you in six weeks then, Callum.' Anna smiled at him, and Mary nudged him.

'Yes. Thanks, Miss Caulder.'

Jamie went to fetch Mary and Callum's drinks, and Anna turned away, walking back to the consulting room. All the teenagers that Jamie brought here had some kind of story, and Jamie's obvious concern for Callum showed that his probably wasn't a good one.

She heard a knock on the open door and turned.

'Nice job,' Jamie said from the doorway.

'Did you expect anything else?'

He shrugged and Anna took a gulp of air into her lungs. The to and fro between them didn't seem to be working as well as it usually did. Maybe because of the green shirt, which made the colour of his eyes so much more prominent.

'Ask. I know you want to.'

If he was going to add mind-reading to his talents, then Anna needed to establish a few more boundaries. But she *was* curious. She gestured towards the door, and Jamie walked into the room, closing it behind him.

'All right then. Callum seems a nice lad, and Mary doesn't look like the type to take any nonsense. What on earth is he doing with those tattoos?'

Jamie quirked his lips downwards. 'He *is* a very nice lad. Mary's his aunt, and she took him in two years ago. Before that, he was neglected and abused by his mother.'

'Poor kid. So he's acting up?'

'Yeah. His older brother turned up three months ago, and Callum disappeared with him. Mary was frantic, and tried everything she could think of to find him, that's how she made contact with us. He came back a week later, his brother had moved on and dumped him.'

'And that's where he got the tattoos?'

Jamie nodded. 'Callum craves acceptance, and like a lot of kids with his kind of background he has a few issues with impulse control. He just wants to please, and he doesn't think about the consequences. Our youth counsellor is working with him pretty intensively, and it's pretty clear that we don't know the full scope of what's happened to him yet.'

'You're getting to the bottom of it, though.'

'Yeah. We will. In the meantime, I just wanted to let you know that we're doing all we can to make sure that he won't be back with another set of tattoos that he regrets. And to…um…apologise. For any embarrassment.'

'I've seen worse. I didn't run out of the room screaming then either.'

'No. Of course. But your non-judgemental approach is just the kind of thing that Callum needs.'

Was that a *thank you*? Anna decided not to push it and ask. 'I'm just glad that they're a single colour and relatively superficial, so they shouldn't be too difficult to remove completely. Something like that won't help Callum when it comes to getting a job or a place in college. Or a girlfriend…'

'Yeah. He didn't grasp the full implications of some of them. Mary asked me to explain it to him…' His brow furrowed. Clearly he'd not found the conversation particularly easy.

'Well… Good luck with him…' The words slipped out before she'd had a chance to think. Jamie quirked his lips down.

'We don't leave things to luck.'

'No, I know. Hard work, determination and expertise.' Along with a lot of caring. Jamie's charity had a policy of tough love, and it worked. 'I'm actually not too proud to take a bit of luck when it comes my way.'

'I'll bear that in mind. Thanks for what you did today. I'll let you get on now.' He turned suddenly, closing the door behind him as he left.

Anna flopped down into her chair. Maybe Jamie was right, and luck didn't come into it. But there were some things that determination and hard work alone couldn't put right.

Maybe it was those eyes that were making her think this way. They tempted her to revisit a past that was done with, and couldn't be changed. If things had been different, then she might have allowed herself to get a little closer to Jamie. But they weren't different, and he probably wasn't interested in her anyway.

Think that. Keep thinking it.

She had no business lingering over Jamie Campbell-Clarke's eyes, or his dedication, or the spark that fuelled their professional rivalry. Anna wasn't in the market for a relationship with him, or anyone else.

She'd fallen into that trap once before. As soon as things had started to get serious with Daniel, she'd told him that she couldn't have children, fully expecting him to leave. When he hadn't, she'd thought she had found that special someone who could accept her as she was. But after a year of marriage he'd changed his mind and left. Once was more than enough when it came to having her heart broken.

Anna puffed out a breath. Jamie was right in one thing. She had patients waiting and she had to get on.

Jamie's characteristically brusque two-line email had imparted the information that he'd visited Callum at home the previous evening, that he was in good spirits and that his Aunt Mary had reinforced the message that his gratitude for the help he was being given should take the form of not worrying at the dressings on his hand. He'd be back in six weeks and was looking forward to losing the unfortunate tattoos. Anna emailed a similarly brusque acknowledgement of the update, telling him to contact her if there was anything else she could do. She imagined there wouldn't be.

And this morning there were new challenges, the first of which didn't take a medical form. The private London Central Clinic was used to receiving patients whose fame required a degree of discretion and anonymity, but *this* patient had stretched policy almost to breaking point. She'd even caught her boss humming snatches of 'Everywhere'.

And the singer responsible for that rock classic was here. Even Anna felt a small flutter over meeting the man who had reached a million hearts, including her own, with the song.

'How's he doing?' She murmured the words to the ward receptionist, who leaned across her desk to whisper a reply.

'Just great. A little taller than I thought he'd be.'

Right. That wasn't the information Anna was after. 'He's settling in?'

'Oh, yes. They took him a cup of green tea and a biscuit.'

Asking what kind of biscuit would only stoke the fires. 'He has someone with him?'

'No, he came on his own. Just a driver and he didn't stay long. Parked on a meter, I expect.'

So fame didn't always guarantee companionship. It

seemed a shame, though. 'Everywhere' had been the song that had spoken to Anna when her life had hit a rough patch, and she imagined she wasn't alone in that. It was all about hope, about kindling a flame in the darkness, to lead the way into the light.

'Okay, I'll go and see him now. Which room…?'

Jonny Campbell was sitting alone in his room. Dark glasses covered his eyes, and his head was nodding slightly to whatever was playing through his high-end headphones. His bag lay on the bed, unopened. One of the ward orderlies would unpack it for him if necessary, but Anna reckoned that Dr Lewis had told them to wait a short while, to see if he'd do it himself. Their patient was nominally here for assessment of burn scars on his arm and the side of his face, but Jon's listless indifference during his assessment interview had raised the possibility of mental health problems as well. Dr Lewis had taken overall charge of his case, and Anna had been told to start treating the burns, but to be aware that there may be other issues.

'Hello. I'm Anna Caulder.'

Her words made him jump. Maybe his eyes had been closed under the glasses. Anna saw his hand shake as he removed his headphones.

'Hi. Jon Campbell.'

'I'm sorry if I startled you. You prefer Jon, or Jonny Campbell?'

His lips curved in a slow smile. 'Jonny Campbell's my professional name. Just Jon will do. You prefer Anna or Miss Caulder?'

'Anna will do.' He seemed so different from his stage persona. And yet somehow so familiar. Anna shook off the feeling. Her job was to find out what the real Jon Campbell needed, not the rock star Jonny Campbell.

'I think Dr Lewis prefers *Dr Lewis*. Or maybe sir…'

Anna laughed. The dry humour that Jonny Campbell put to such good use on stage was there still.

'Yes. I think he does. He's a great doctor, though.'

'I've no doubt of that. But he doesn't have your beautiful blue eyes.' Jon tilted his head towards her, and Anna blushed, fighting back the urge to tell him that she'd been to one of his concerts and loved his songs.

'Well I'm here to take care of your burns.' And to ignore compliments.

Jon flexed his arm. 'Yeah, that would be great. I didn't have much time to get them looked at when they happened, I was touring. I took a handful of painkillers and was back on stage the following evening. Being on stage in front of tens of thousands of people tends to make you forget about everything else.'

'And you never had a doctor look at them?'

'I was in hospital for a week in America. They said that my arm had become infected and gave me a course of antibiotics.'

'You went to hospital for the burns? I didn't see anything about that in your notes.'

'No, I…' Jon shrugged. 'I needed a break.'

If he'd been in hospital for a week, it sounded as if there was a bit more to it than that. 'Would it be okay if we contacted the hospital and asked them to send us through their notes?'

'Sure. Knock yourself out.'

'Thanks. I'll have our administrator follow that up with you.' Anna pulled up a seat, sitting down opposite Jon. 'Can you tell me what happened when you burned yourself?'

'One of the amps wasn't working. I kicked it, and it burst into flames.' Jon shook his head slowly. 'Serves me right. I guess there's a song there somewhere.'

'I'd like to hear it.' Anna bit her tongue. She'd resolved not to mention the songs.

'I'll sing it for you, Anna.'

Right. Another trace of Jonny Campbell's charm. But it was faded and worn, like a mask Jon assumed when he didn't want to face a reality that found him alone in a hospital room.

'Will someone be coming? To visit you…?' Maybe she was overstepping her boundaries a little, but the doctors here were given the time to get to know their patients as people, and were encouraged to do so.

'Didn't you know that I'm here incognito?'

'I did. That doesn't extend to family and friends, though, does it?'

'When you tour, all you have is the band. We've been having our differences lately. That's privileged information, by the way…'

'It's all privileged information here.'

'That's what everyone says.' Jon twisted his mouth. 'Then you see it in the papers the next morning.'

'It's not the way *we* do things.' Anna searched for eye contact and found none. She wished he'd take the glasses off, but guessed he wouldn't for a while at least. 'It's important that you understand that everything you say to us is completely confidential.'

Jon shrugged, as if it didn't really matter one way or the other.

'Blue-eyed Anna… It'd make a great song. Does

that turn you on?' He was retreating again behind the rock star persona, expecting her to go weak at the knees. There was nothing like meeting your heroes to inject a dose of reality.

'Not particularly. Doing my job turns me on, and right now my interest in you is that you have scars that can be improved.'

Jon laughed suddenly, holding up his hands in a gesture of surrender. 'Okay, fair enough. My twin brother is just the same. Being a doctor turns *him* on.'

'You didn't ask for his help? With the burns?' The back of her neck was prickling, and Anna ignored it. Two and two didn't always make four, and the feeling that she knew Jon Campbell was just an illusion, born from his fame.

'Nah. We don't talk. Jamie and I had a falling out.' Jon shrugged. 'He doesn't know I'm here, and he probably doesn't care. The rest of the family isn't much impressed with me either...'

'It's up to you but...sometimes families can surprise you.'

Jon shook his head, taking his glasses off, and suddenly there was no question about it. Anna's words dried in her throat. The jade-green eyes and ravaged face of Jonny Campbell really *were* familiar. His brother was Dr Jamie Campbell-Clarke.

CHAPTER TWO

MAYBE JON CAMPBELL had taken her wordless shock for granted, as the kind of thing that any woman would do when faced with a rock idol. Whatever. Anna couldn't think about that right now. She couldn't think about Jamie Campbell-Clarke either. What she *could* think about was her duties as a surgeon.

She asked Jon if she could examine his burns, and he nodded his assent, rolling up his sleeve. The skin was discoloured, beginning to tighten and contort, showing that the injuries had been given very little care.

It was odd. Whatever it was that made her heart beat a little faster when Jamie was in the room was entirely absent. Now that she'd made the connection, she could see that the brothers were very alike. Brown hair was brown hair and Jon's was longer than Jamie's, but they both had the same strong jaw, the same shaped face. And the eyes left no doubt, even if Jon's seemed just an unusual colour, while Jamie's were compelling.

She retreated to her seat, clasping her hands together. She had to remember that Jon was her patient, and act according to his wishes and in his best interests, even though her first thought was that Jamie would be horrified to find that his own brother was in the clinic and he didn't know it.

'I think that the scars can definitely be revised and improved, particularly the ones on your brow and neck. The one on your arm is a little bigger, but there's a lot we can do there as well.'

Jon nodded. 'Good. Thank you.'

Anna took a breath, wondering how best to ask. 'You said that Jonny Campbell is your professional name. Is your real name Campbell-Clarke, by any chance?'

'Yes, it is.' Jon shot her a questioning look. 'Not many people know me as Jon Campbell-Clarke any more…'

'So Dr Jamie Campbell-Clarke is your brother?'

A flash of defensiveness. 'Yeah. Looks a bit like me. We're not identical twins.'

'You both have the same colour eyes.'

'That'll be him then. You know him?'

'I do, and I should tell you that he sometimes visits this clinic.'

Jon nodded, pursing his lips. 'I didn't know that. Is that going to be a problem?'

'No. It's entirely up to you whether you want him to know you're here or not.' She should make that clear before she started to make the case for telling Jamie. 'I just thought that you should know.'

'Yeah. Thanks.' Jon heaved a sigh. 'When I said that we had a falling out… It was a pretty big one. And it was my fault, he has good reason to be angry with me.'

'Do you think he might also have good reason to forgive you?'

'Not particularly. Look…we were close once and now we're not. None of us gets to change the past.'

'Jamie might take issue with you there. He tries to change things for the kids he works with.'

'That's different.' She saw a flash of anger in Jon's face. 'Look. Sorry, but I can't…'

'It's okay. Just know that I'm here to help, and that I'll do whatever you want me to do.'

'Right. Well, you can tell him if you want. Or don't tell him, it's up to you. But I know what he'll say, and I don't want to hear it. Are we agreed?'

'Agreed. Is there anything else I can do for you?'

Jon heaved a sigh. 'I don't suppose there are any books in this place, are there? Not magazines, something I can get my teeth into.'

'Yes, we have a small collection. I'll send our activities co-ordinator in with a selection and if none of them appeal she'd be happy to go out and get you something that does.'

'Activities co-ordinator.' Jon gave a mock frown. 'She's not going to ask me to make raffia baskets, is she?'

Anna chuckled. 'Raffia baskets don't turn you on?'

'Not even a little bit. I'd like some fresh air…'

'We have a small garden area on the roof. It's secluded and the air's about as fresh as it gets anywhere in central London.'

'Sounds good to me. Jamie's not going to find me up there, is he?'

'No. He's not expected here for the rest of the week, and after that…we'll handle things.'

'Still thinking you might engineer a reconciliation?' Jon raised one eyebrow. 'I can save you a bit of time there, because you won't. Just handle it so that neither of us gets any nasty surprises.'

'All right. Consider it done.'

Lunchtime. Anna pulled on her coat, grabbed an energy bar from her desk drawer, and hurried out of the building. She'd already thought of about a thousand reasons why she shouldn't do this…

Families were out of her sphere of expertise, she knew that. She was the only child of two only children, and the large, extended family she'd married into had sometimes baffled her but mostly delighted her. She'd lost them when she and Daniel had divorced…

The clinic was her family now. Anna always did her best for the families of the patients who passed through, and now Jamie Campbell-Clarke came under that umbrella. It meant crossing the line that she'd drawn between professional and personal with him, but she couldn't step aside and do nothing.

He was sitting alone in the office he shared with two other doctors, the door wide open, and when he saw her he smiled. 'You wanted to see me?'

Why did that always sound like a challenge? Anna swallowed whatever smart retort was about to reach the tip of her tongue. Not the time for it.

'Yes, I did.' Anna sat down on the other side of his desk, keeping her coat on and clutching her handbag in her lap. 'Can we have a private conversation?'

Something kindled in his eyes and Anna ignored it. Jamie closed the door, sitting back down again. 'Sure…'

'We have a new patient at the clinic. He has some recent burn scars for revision, and…he has a demanding job, which has caused a great deal of emotional strain recently.

Jamie nodded. 'And who is this mystery patient? One of your celebrities?'

'Yes.'

He gave her a searching look. 'So you're not going to give me a name.'

Not until she'd reassured Jamie that Jon's condition was stable and he wasn't in any danger. 'He booked himself in earlier this morning. He's being well looked after, and there's no need for any concern.'

'That's always nice to know.' Jamie shot her a puzzled look, leaning back in his seat. He'd obviously decided that she'd get to the point sooner or later, and that he'd wait.

'It's your brother. Jon.'

Jamie's face hardened suddenly. Whatever it was between the two brothers, it was serious. She'd never seen Jamie look so thunderously angry.

'He asked you to come and see me?'

'No. I… He said he had a twin brother, but that there was some bad blood between you. When I realised it was you he was talking about, I told him I knew you and said that I thought you should know he was at the clinic. He seems…alone.'

Anna lapsed into silence. Maybe she'd got this all wrong. Maybe she should have listened to Jon when he'd told her that there was only one answer that Jamie would give to any plea for reconciliation. But Jamie never turned anyone away. It was a matter of pride that his charity would at least try to help any kid that knocked on its door.

'Okay. Thank you.'

That was it? 'I'm sorry if this... I didn't mean to overstep any boundaries.'

Suddenly the boundaries that she and Jamie had drawn had changed and Anna felt crushed within them. She should probably go now, and hope that Jamie would forget this had ever happened.

'That's okay. Jon knows you're here?'

'He said that I could tell you he was at the clinic, but I wasn't to tell him your reaction. He thinks you'll refuse to see him.' Right now that seemed to have been a forward-looking strategy on Jon's part.

'Right. It's good of you to let me know. Is that all?'

That was a clear invitation for her to leave. Anna wanted to ask what Jamie was going to do, even hint that he might tell her how he was feeling about this. But the hard mask of his face left her in no doubt that he'd just tell her to mind her own business.

'Yes. I'd better be going. I have to be back at the clinic in forty-five minutes.'

It was surprisingly hard to get up and leave. She'd come here intending to deliver a message, but now she badly wanted Jamie to let her in and allow her to help him. But he already seemed to have forgotten that she was in the room. As Anna closed the door behind her, he was staring at his hands, which were clenched into fists in front of him on the desk.

Jon. It had to happen sooner or later, and in truth Jamie was surprised that he hadn't bumped into his twin brother before now. But Jon's career only took him on flying visits to London, and hardly ever to Hastings. And in the three years since they'd argued, their family had tactfully contrived to keep them apart.

And the first person who'd brought him news of Jon, beyond what he tried to stop himself from reading in the paper, was Anna. Jamie's first thought had been to lock her in his office until she promised never to set eyes on Jon again. To protect her...

He reminded himself that Anna could look after herself. She'd proved that to him time and time again, meeting him headlong and refusing to back down when she knew she was right about something. She wasn't going to fall for the good looks and the rock star charm.

Jamie shook his head, trying not to think about it. Women *did* fall for Jon. Jamie's own fiancée had fallen for him, and Jon had done what probably came perfectly naturally to him as a rock star, and what any brother would have found unthinkable. Jon could have had any woman he wanted, but he'd taken the one that Jamie had wanted.

Three years. He could still feel the anger and the shock. The clawing pain that two people who he'd loved could have betrayed him like that.

Did that outweigh the thirty-odd years that had gone before? Growing up together, doing everything together? Looking out for each other? His parents and sister had made it very clear that they wouldn't force a reconciliation and that if Jamie didn't want to take the first step they didn't blame him. They probably didn't know that Jon was in the clinic either.

It was probably better to let sleeping dogs lie. But the childhood refrain, whenever Jon had been hurt or upset, wouldn't stop echoing through his thoughts.

What did you do now, little brother?

* * *

It was relatively normal to go for weeks without seeing Jamie Campbell-Clarke. But as luck would have it—and Anna wasn't sure whether the luck was good or bad—he was waiting for her the following morning when she walked into the A&E department of the hospital.

She'd been worrying all night about whether she'd done the right thing. But Jamie hadn't come to the clinic to see his brother so she should do as she'd been asked and let it go. That was easier said than done.

'Hi. Thanks for coming.' He looked very tired.

She'd seen Jamie tired before—his schedule was impressively busy—but today his face reminded her of Jon's haggard features. It didn't look as though he'd had much sleep either.

'My pleasure.' They had work to do, and she should concentrate on that.

'I didn't know you had an interest in syndactyly.' He too seemed anxious to keep this professional.

'I studied under Sir Max Barnes in Manchester for a while.'

'Ah. That explains it.'

It really didn't need any explanation. The clinic made the services of its doctors available to nearby hospitals on a regular basis, as part of an ongoing partnership programme. Jamie would have consulted the list and found Anna's name on it. That was all there was to it. Jon had had nothing to do with his call to the clinic to ask if she might give a second opinion on one of his patients. All the same, there was a formal unease about Jamie's manner that wasn't like him.

The best thing to do was to ignore it. She followed him to a cubicle where a nurse was sitting with a baby.

'This little fella was brought in early this morning. He was abandoned and the police are looking for the mother.' Jamie's face was impassive, but his eyes reflected the same compassion that showed in the nurse's face. In an environment where every case had a story behind it, some were still easier to deal with than others.

'I've examined him, and he's generally surprisingly healthy. But I wanted a second opinion on his hands. You've seen the X-rays I sent over?'

Anna nodded. 'Yes, and it looks to be a case of simple syndactyly. The second, third and fourth fingers on both hands are fused by soft tissue, but the bones are separate. Let me take a look at him.'

The nurse lifted the baby boy from the cradle, and Anna examined his hands carefully. His fingernails were also fused, but it looked as if separating the fingers would be a relatively straightforward matter.

'This is going to take more than one operation, isn't it?' Jamie was watching her intently, but there was none of their usual joking rivalry in his manner.

'Yes, it's not possible to operate on more than one side of the finger at a time, or there's a risk of damaging the blood supply. When the time comes to operate he's going to need probably four procedures.'

'We'll be sending him up to the ward soon—is there anything I need to ask them to look out for?'

'I don't see any signs of a more complex syndrome but they should be aware of the possibility. I'll add my recommendations to his notes.'

'Great. Thanks. Can I leave you to it for a moment?

I'll be right back...' As usual, Jamie had more than one patient to attend to.

'Yes, that's fine. I'll watch him.'

Both Jamie and the nurse hurried out of the cubicle. The little boy began to fret in his cradle, and Anna couldn't resist picking him up to soothe him.

She wouldn't...couldn't have her own child. The nieces and nephews she'd gained when she'd married had never really belonged to her and, along with their parents, had just melted away again after the divorce. And this little one was only hers for a few short moments, before Jamie or the nurse returned. But he didn't know that, all he knew was the reassurance of being held by someone.

'Hey there, sweetheart. Everything's going to be all right.' She cooed the words at him, and he seemed to respond to her voice.

Everything was very far from being all right. An abandoned baby who faced painful medical procedures. It seemed such a cruel twist of fate when Anna would have done anything to have her own child. She felt tears well in her eyes, and blinked them away quickly.

She rocked the baby boy in her arms, singing to him quietly, and his eyes began to close. He was so peacefully unaware of everything that was going on around him.

She could put him back into his cradle, now, but somehow it seemed wrong to do so, as if holding him might add just a drop more love to a life that already needed all the love it could get. When Jamie returned, she was still holding the little boy, the notes untouched. He glanced at them and then looked at her.

'Everything okay?'

'Oh. Yes…'

Jamie finally managed a smile. 'They smell so good, don't they? My sister always had a battle on her hands, getting me to hand her newborns back…'

He shot her a speculative look and when Anna failed to answer he seemed to decide that he needed to delve a little further. 'This little man tugs at the heartstrings.'

Anna's heartstrings were close to snapping. And she'd forgotten to really take in that new baby smell. It was too late now, and it was just one more loss to contend with.

'What's his name?' She asked the question before she'd really thought about it, and Jamie shook his head slowly. Of course. They didn't know.

'He'll be staying here for a little while, while his foster care is arranged. I dare say the nurses upstairs will be giving him a name.'

He took the baby from her arms, and Anna tried not to notice the way his face softened. Jamie's green eyes seemed to be cutting into her heart more painfully than usual. He put the baby back into the cradle, stopping to gently stroke his cheek with one finger.

'I really appreciate your time, thank you.'

'No problem. I'll just write my recommendations up and then I'll be on my way.' Anna decided that everything would go a bit faster if she did them outside, where she couldn't be distracted by either Jamie or the baby. She picked up the notes and headed for the door of the cubicle.

'Anna…' Jamie's voice behind her sounded suddenly strained.

'Yes?'

'How is he?'

There was no need to ask who he was talking about. Jamie wasn't as unconcerned about his brother as he seemed.

'He's fine, Jamie. I saw him this morning and he's settling in well.'

Jamie nodded. 'Thanks.'

Nothing else. No indication that Jamie would come to see his brother, and no message. But she'd done all she could and it was time to take a step back now, and let Jamie work things out. And she did have to get back to the clinic.

Anna turned, getting the distinct impression that Jamie was watching her as she walked away.

Five o'clock. She should be going home, but Jon hadn't had a visitor all day. Anna decided to pop in and see how he was, but when she looked in his room he wasn't there. She found him up on the roof of the building, huddled in a heavy leather jacket and a scarf. As she walked towards him, he slid the headphones he was wearing down around his neck.

'Aren't you cold?' An autumn chill was beginning to set in and the evenings were drawing in.

'Nah, I'm good. I like it up here.' Jon tapped his finger on the book in his lap. 'I have plenty of company.'

Music and books. They were wonderful company but didn't replace a family. Anna wondered where Jamie was, and what he was doing.

'You contacted him, didn't you?' Jon was looking at her keenly.

'Yes, I did. I went over to the hospital yesterday and saw him.' Anna bit her lip. Maybe she shouldn't have let Jon know that Jamie was so close, or that it had been more than twenty-four hours since Jamie had heard that his brother was here. But Jon just nodded.

'I'm not gonna ask you what he said.' Jon shifted fitfully in his seat. 'You think we're alike?'

The question came right out of the blue, and it was a difficult one. The two brothers looked alike, but… Jamie was Jamie. He was unique.

'You resemble each other. You seem different to me.'

Jon laughed suddenly. 'Good answer. We used to hate it when we were kids and people reckoned we were just two versions of the same. We had this aunt who always bought identical Christmas presents for us, even when I was on the road, touring, and Jamie was at medical school.'

There was regret in Jon's face. He obviously missed his brother, and Anna wondered again what had torn them apart. Neither of them seemed to want to talk about it, and in that they were identical.

'I guess that's one of the hazards of being a twin.'

'Yeah. Jamie was always the one who said less but had more going on in his head.'

Anna smiled. 'I can't imagine that the person who wrote "Everywhere" doesn't have something going on in his head.'

'You like that song?'

'Yes, I love it. It got me through a bit of a rocky patch in my life. It's so…optimistic about the future.'

'It's a great song.' Jon's lip quivered. 'Jamie wrote it, you know. I imagine he probably hasn't told you that.'

'No, he didn't.'

'Like I said. Jamie has a lot more going on in his head than I do. I generally used to write the music and he wrote the words, but "Everywhere" was all his own work.'

They must have been close once. If writing songs together wasn't proof enough, then she had only to look at the regret in Jon's face. Maybe she should change the subject, even if the words to 'Everywhere' were now running insistently through her head. The hope for the future and the determination not to give up made so much more sense now that she knew they were Jamie's words.

'What are you listening to?'

Jon took the headphones from around his neck, detaching the earpieces from their mounting and handing one to her. She pressed it against her ear, leaning forward so that Jon could listen through the other one, and he traced his thumb across the screen of the phone he'd taken out of his pocket.

'Bach! Really…?'

Jon laughed. 'Both Jamie and I had music lessons when we were kids and we played all the classics. Bach was always my favourite. Don't you think this has a lot in common with all song structures?'

'Now you mention it, I suppose…' Anna put the earpiece against her ear again, and Jon began to trace the precise tempo with his finger in the air, like a conductor. When the complex strands of the melody wove together to draw the music to a close, he made a concluding flourish and Anna laughed.

'I see it now…' Anna looked over her shoulder as Jon's gaze suddenly left her face. Jamie was standing by the door that led from the stairs to the roof garden, watching them.

Something about the look on Jamie's face made her

quickly give the earpiece back to Jon and lean away from him. She was just talking to a patient, wasn't she? Maybe Jamie thought that she was taking sides, because he shot her an injured look.

'Jon, I...' She turned back to Jon, whose face was moulded into a look of stony shock. 'I didn't know he was coming.'

Jon didn't reply. His attention was all on Jamie, who was walking towards them, and the closer his brother got, the more agitated Jon looked. This whole situation was turning into a nightmare. Something was about to explode...

'I heard you were here.' Jamie's voice was quiet, his face impassive.

'Yeah. I'm here.'

Jamie sat down, without even looking at Anna. The two brothers regarded each other steadily. It would be good to leave right now, but Anna wasn't going anywhere until she knew that they weren't going to start arguing as soon as she turned her back.

'Let's take a look at your arm, little brother.'

Jamie's quiet words seemed familiar to Jon, and he gave a stiff smile as he pulled up the sleeve of his jacket to expose the bottom half of the burn scar. Jamie turned the edges of his mouth down.

'Looks as if it hurt. Probably still does.'

'Yeah. The doc says she can sort it for me.'

Jamie nodded, turning to Anna with the hint of a smile. 'You don't mind if I step on your toes?'

He'd never asked before, but then they'd never been in this situation before. She stood, flashing a smile at Jon. 'I'll leave you to it, if that's okay.'

Jon nodded, and Jamie turned his attention again to

his brother. When Anna reached the door that led to the staircase, she turned and saw him examining the scar on Jon's arm carefully. Then he gestured towards his brother's face, and Jon turned his head so that Jamie could see the scars on his brow and neck.

She shouldn't stay. But her heart was beating like a drum in her chest. One spark and the fragile reconciliation could all go up in smoke. Jamie and Jon were talking, and Jamie gestured to the book on Jon's lap. Jon picked it up and began to read aloud, and Jamie leaned back in his chair.

That was an odd thing to do. But it seemed to be part of an old bond that she knew nothing about, and the taut lines of Jamie's body began to relax a little. As they did so, Jon began to smile. Anna shook her head. Whatever worked for them. She turned, opening the door. One last look told her that neither of the brothers was even aware that she was leaving.

CHAPTER THREE

HARD? THIS HAD been much more than hard. More than any of the adjectives that Jamie could apply to any given situation. But he'd known he had to come, and when he'd shrugged on his jacket and left the hospital it hadn't even occurred to him to call ahead. He just wanted to see Jon, and make sure that he was all right.

The receptionist in the ward knew him, but she gave him a second look when he asked for Jon, as if she'd only just noticed the resemblance and put the two names together. It had been a long time since anyone had asked whether he and Jon were related, and Jamie guessed it was because their lives were so very different.

He'd reached the top of the stairs and stopped short, shock gluing him to the spot. Anna was leaning towards Jon and they were both listening to the same piece of music. He always noticed everything about Anna, and now he saw that her blonde hair, usually tied back when she was working, was loose and falling forward across her shoulders. Just inches from Jon's hand.

The intimacy was obvious, and he wanted to grab Anna and pull her away. But Anna wasn't his to protect, and she had every right to spend time with Jon if she wanted to. Then Jon saw him, and the two started almost guiltily.

Rage flowed through him like a tide of molten lava. He couldn't do this. He couldn't see Anna with Jon. But he somehow managed to get himself under control and walked towards them.

An hour later, he'd brought Jon back down to his room, and bade him goodnight. His head was spinning, and he didn't want to see Anna. But his legs didn't obey the command of his head, and he walked towards her office, knowing he'd find her there.

'You're still here?' He stood at the open door, trying to feign surprise.

'Yes. I've been trying to make up my mind about whether I did the right thing or not. And wondering if there was going to be an explosion…' She gave him a nervous smile.

'No explosions. You did the right thing.'

She nodded. 'Come in. I'll get you some coffee.'

Jamie walked into the office, sitting down in the chair on the other side of her desk. 'No coffee. I don't think I'll be sleeping much tonight as it is.'

'I'm glad you've patched things up. Whatever this argument was about…' She waved her hand, as if that didn't matter.

She didn't know. Jamie told himself that it made the intimacy he'd seen between Anna and his brother a little less shattering, but he still couldn't put it out of his mind. He reminded himself that he'd seen Anna many times with patients, and that her manner was always caring and kind. He should look at it in that context.

'We haven't so much patched it up as… We're not talking about it.'

Anna shrugged. 'Whatever works…'

Who knew whether it was going to work or not? Right now it was about the only option as Jamie still couldn't talk about what had happened without betraying his anger, and right now Jon needed his care.

'Do the rest of the family know Jon's here?' There were a lot of questions he hadn't asked Jon, and Jamie realised that he'd been saving them for Anna.

'Not as far as I'm aware. Jon said that if you weren't coming then he didn't want the rest of the family to have to take sides.'

'That was decent of him. Unnecessary, though. I'll call my sister tonight. My parents are in Australia for three months, but I'll email them and let them know.'

'Sounds like a plan.' Anna's obvious approval began to cut through the haze of uncertainty that Jamie felt. 'You'll be back?'

'Tomorrow morning. The charity can do without me for a couple of weeks, and I'll be staying up in London full time.'

Anna nodded. Another little shard of warmth, something concrete to hold onto.

'If you'd like, you can use my office to work in while you're here. I'll mention it to my boss but I doubt he'll have any problem with the idea. You work with us on an informal basis anyway.'

'You're keeping me here for as long as you can?' Jamie flashed her a smile.

'That's the general idea.' She smiled back. Honesty was one of Anna's more endearing traits.

'Thanks. That would be really helpful and… I

should spend as much time as I can with Jon, but it would be nice to have a bolthole as well.'

'I thought that might be the case.' Anna leaned back in her chair, regarding him thoughtfully. 'So what's with the reading?'

She didn't know *that* either. It was no secret, but Jamie's habit was to compensate for his dyslexia as much as possible when he was working. 'I have mild dyslexia. When we were kids, Jon used to read to me. It was usually comics then, he used to do different voices and act things out.'

'Ah. So that explains the planner on your office wall, then.' She smiled at him. 'And your diary. I thought you were just terrifyingly organised.'

Both his diary and his calendar were colour coded, allowing Jamie to see what was most important at a glance. It was one of the many small techniques he employed that most people didn't even notice, even if they knew about his dyslexia.

'Yeah, I find that colour coding makes things a bit easier. Although I wouldn't want to dissuade you from your belief in my organisational skills.'

'Okay. I'll remain suitably terrified.' She shot him a smile. 'Jon says that you both made music together when you were young as well.'

Jamie knew exactly what Anna was doing. She was gently probing, getting him to talk in much the same way as she got all her patients and their families to. Soon he'd find himself tempted to tell her about his darkest fears, the way they did.

He'd meet that problem when he came to it. Jamie wondered if Anna knew that he'd been concentrating on the things they'd shared before the bust-up as a way of reconnecting with his brother, and decided that she'd probably already worked that out.

'Yeah. He was always the showman, though. The one who liked to get up and sing.'

'He told me that you wrote "Everywhere". It's one of my favourite songs.'

Her smile made his heart beat a little faster. Maybe Anna had let his words into her life, as she'd sung along to them on the radio… The thought made his hand tremble.

'I…um…was at a bit of a turning point in my life when I wrote it. I'd applied to medical school and they'd accepted me, despite the dyslexia. It was a dream I never thought I'd be able to accomplish, but I was also a bit concerned about how I might cope.'

Anna nodded her head. 'That's what I like about the song. It seems to me to be all about hope and accomplishing your dreams. Maybe not in the way you thought you would, but doing it anyway. Suddenly your charity makes a lot more sense.'

Jamie dragged his thoughts from wondering where she'd first heard 'Everywhere' and what she'd been doing, and focussed his mind on his charity. That usually gave him a bit of clarity.

'The charity only exists because of the royalties from the song.'

'And you and Jon did that together.' She gave a little nod of approval.

Much as he liked the feeling of having made a connection with Anna, Jamie couldn't think about it any more. In retrospect, 'Everywhere' had been the beginning of the end for him and Jon. It had blasted his brother into the stratosphere of fame and set their paths on an ever-diverging trajectory.

'Yeah, look… I'd like to see Jon's notes.'

Anna pursed her lips. Maybe she was about to give him the lecture about stepping on her toes and leaving her to get on with treating her own patients. Jamie flashed her an apologetic look.

'You're asking as a doctor? Or as his brother?'

That was the nub of it. Jamie had always imagined himself a doctor first, beyond anything. 'His brother.'

'Fair enough. I'll have to check with Jon first, of course.'

'Of course.'

'Right, then.' Anna got to her feet, and Jamie took the hint. He should be going now. But when he started to rise from his seat she waved him back down again. 'Stay there. I won't be a minute.'

She was actually a little more than a minute. Jamie stared at the wall, trying to rearrange his thoughts, but everything seemed jumbled, like words on a page that wouldn't respond to any of his normal reading techniques. He was out of his depth, and the old panic about whether he'd be able to make sense of anything had returned. And he was hanging on to Anna for dear life.

He wondered if the families of her other patients felt like this. That she could be trusted to steer them through the myriad of decisions that faced them, all of which seemed frighteningly incomprehensible. He guessed they probably did…

'All right.' Anna bustled back into the room, making him jump. 'I've spoken to Jon and he was very pleased you were taking an interest. My only reservation is that you remember who you are…'

'You're his surgeon, Anna. I'm a concerned family member, who happens to understand the issues involved a little better.'

'Perfect. In that case, we could go for coffee and something to eat if you like. I skipped lunch…'

He hadn't eaten either. Jamie wondered if her reasons were the same as his, and let it go. And suddenly he found himself at a loose end. He wouldn't be driving back down to Hastings tonight—after all, his place was here with Jon, and he'd stay in his London bedsit for as long as it took.

'That sounds great.'

He followed her out of the building, and she crossed the road, obviously making for somewhere. Jamie didn't much care where.

'Italian okay for you? They do food upstairs in the evenings, and it's pretty quiet around this time.' She led him through winding back streets to a bustling coffee bar.

'Yeah. Anything…'

Anna nodded. Upstairs the restaurant area was quiet, just a few evening diners, and she led him to one of the booths that lined the far wall, which afforded them some privacy. Jamie managed to remember to help her out of her coat and lay it down on the bench that ran around the table.

A waiter approached them, wearing a smile and handing Jamie two menus. He passed one to Anna and fixed his gaze onto his own.

The closely typed words seemed to be moving in front of him, locked in a complicated dance, and not heeding his silent exhortations to just sit back down in their usual places and behave. Tonight they were breaking free of the framework he usually applied and continuing with their hedonistic movement.

'Mmm…' Anna was studying her menu. 'Lasagne looks nice… Or tagliatelle. They do a really nice carbonara here, but I think I'm a bit hungrier than that…'

Was she reading the menu to him? Jamie decided that he didn't care if she was. So what if he could usually manage without betraying his difficulties. This evening, he was too stressed out to use his usual coping strategies.

'I think I'll have the carbonara.'

She nodded. 'Yes, I think I will too. We can always have a second course. Are we having wine?'

'Don't let me stop you. I'll stick to water.'

'Okay.' She closed the menu decisively and beckoned to the waiter.

Jamie was obviously struggling. Whatever the argument between him and his brother had been about, it must have been bad. Something life-changing that had parted brothers who had once been close. Since it was clear that neither of them were going to talk about it, Anna had to quell her curiosity and just hope that they could work it out between themselves. The way that Jamie had responded to the knowledge that Jon was in hospital made it quite clear that he *wanted* to work it out.

And he'd written 'Everywhere'. The song that gave people hope. In the dark days after her marriage had ended so abruptly, she'd sung it at the top of her voice, along with all the other survival songs in her break-up playlist.

And now she had to get Jamie through tonight. She

could see him eyeing the folder that was sticking out of the top of her handbag, and when the waiter brought her a glass of white wine, she took a mouthful and gave Jamie his brother's medical records.

He opened the folder, running his finger under the printed words. She'd seen him do that before and had thought little of it. But he seemed to be struggling rather more than usual, probably because of the stress he was under.

'This doesn't make any sense.' He wiped his hand across his face. 'Or is it just me…?'

'No, it's not you. When Jon first came to the clinic he made an outpatient appointment with Dr Lewis— he just said that he was away from home and needed general medical advice. He asked primarily about the burns, but he also complained of a whole raft of other unconnected symptoms and Dr Lewis suspected that there were other underlying issues. He told Jon that he wanted to give him a more thorough assessment, which Jon agreed to, so he was booked into the clinic, and referred to me for scar revision.'

'Right. You're saying he has something else wrong with him?'

'We found out that he'd been in hospital in America about six weeks ago. There's a summary of the notes that they sent through on the next page.' Anna reminded herself of Dr Lewis's advice to her this morning. Tread carefully. Answer questions and let both Jamie and Jon take things at their own pace.

Jamie turned the page, running his finger along the printed lines. It stopped at the list of medications that Jon been prescribed. 'These are strong anti-depressants. What aren't you telling me? And why on earth didn't you tell me before?'

That was an unequivocal expression of intent. Jamie wanted to know everything. Anna took another sip from her glass, resisting the impulse to gulp the lot down.

'Second question first, I didn't tell you before now because I didn't have permission to do so. It's up to Jon whether you see his medical records or not. So you can thank him for letting me show you this when you see him tomorrow.'

'Okay. That put me in my place.' The signs of strain were showing on Jamie's face, and Anna longed to reach out and touch him.

'I have to do everything properly, Jamie. You must understand that.'

He nodded, taking a sip of water. Jamie knew all this, but he was asking the same things that any concerned family member would. 'Okay. And my first question?'

'I don't have a final answer to that, yet. We've talked to Jon about his previous stay in hospital, and all he says is that he just lost it for a while. Apparently he'd locked himself in his hotel room and wouldn't come out, and everyone just left him there for two days, until the hotel staff raised the alarm. We know that he's exhausted and very probably depressed, but we have to rule out any physical causes for his symptoms.'

Jamie nodded his head, flipping the pages and reading through the rest of the file. 'So you're still in the diagnosis stage at the moment. What does Jon say about that?'

Anna shrugged. 'We've explained everything to

him, and he just tells us to go ahead and do whatever we want. He doesn't seem to care. He says he wants to stay and get the burns sorted out, but my opinion is that the clinic is a safe place for him at the moment. A refuge.'

Jamie heaved a sigh. The pain in his eyes was almost tearing Anna's heart out. 'He didn't want me to know, did he? Everything was falling to pieces, and he didn't want me to know...'

Anna had come to the same conclusion, and glossed over it for Jamie's sake. 'Maybe he thought you wouldn't come. But he was wrong about that, wasn't he?'

'I took my time.' He shot her an anguished look.

'You came. That's all that matters. Don't beat yourself up about it, there are plenty of more constructive things you can do with your time right now.'

He pinched the bridge of his nose with two fingers, shaking his head as if he were trying to clear it. 'That's your standard advice, is it?'

There was a trace of the confrontation that seasoned any discussion they had about a patient. But this time it was bitter, with no hint of a smile.

'I may have said it a few times before. That doesn't mean it isn't true, Jamie. I don't underestimate my patients' families. Did you think for one minute I'd say anything different to you because you're a doctor?'

For one moment she was lost in his gaze. Those searching eyes that seemed to need so much from her at the moment. Then he smiled.

'You really *are* trying to put me in my place, aren't you?'

'There's nothing wrong with knowing your boundaries, in any particular situation. Being a great doctor isn't going to help you now. Jon needs you as a brother. I know that's difficult for you, on lots of different levels.'

He nodded. 'All that matters at the moment is that he needs me. So I should remember to eat and sleep, and just be there for him. Because concentrating on his medical care is just my way of distancing myself from the emotional issues.'

'Yeah. You're getting it now.' Jamie always had been aware of what his patients and their families went through emotionally, and now he got to put that knowledge into practice.

He smiled, that same smile that he always wore when she'd prevailed in one of their debates. Jamie could never be accused of being a sore loser.

'Thanks, Anna. I really appreciate what you've done here.'

She could feel herself beginning to blush, the way she always did when Jamie spared some praise for her. She took a gulp of wine, hoping the gesture might cover her pleasure, or at least explain the redness of her cheeks.

'No problem. All part of the service.' That was an obfuscation too. Anna had longed for brothers and sisters when she had been growing up, and then she'd found a family and lost them again. Losing each other must have been ten times harder for Jamie and Jon. She'd go to any lengths to make sure that the fragile reconciliation between them took root and flourished.

CHAPTER FOUR

'I DON'T LIKE sleeping here.'

Nine-year-old Darren greeted Anna and Jamie with a frown. Jamie had been at the clinic all day yesterday, and had arrived at the crack of dawn this morning, and Anna had given in to the inevitable and asked him to come with her to see Darren. He'd been working with the boy and his family for the last two years, ever since Darren had been scalded by hot water. The long process of medical care and counselling had been successful, but the skin graft on the boy's leg had failed and Jamie had arranged for it to be replaced here.

'No?' Jamie sat down beside the boy's bed. 'Why not?'

'This place stinks. And my leg hurts. I want to go home.'

'All right. The thing is, I don't think your leg's going to hurt any less at home.'

Darren rolled his eyes. 'I don't like it here.'

'Your mum will be here soon. Will that make you feel a bit better?'

'No. They're only going to go home again, and I'll be on my own.'

Jamie considered the matter carefully. Anna liked

the way he always took the youngsters in his care at their word, listening carefully to their concerns and never dismissing them.

'You've got a point. So if I tell you that I'll do something about that, will you let Anna take a look at your skin graft?'

'You *have* to do something.' Darren was obviously upset, and he wasn't going to let this go.

'I'll sort things out. You have my word on that.'

Jamie's word was clearly enough for Darren. That kind of trust took a lot of work to build, and Anna watched as Jamie took his phone out of his pocket, handing it over to the boy. He brightened instantly.

'You've got the new game!'

'Yeah, I thought you'd like it. You can show me how to play it.'

Darren was losing no time. As Anna carefully removed the outer dressings on his leg and examined the skin graft, he was already tapping on Jamie's phone, wrinkling his nose when something went wrong.

'Darren, stay still for me…' The boy nodded in response to Anna, his concentration on the phone. Her observations told her that the graft she'd transplanted the day before was in good condition.

'That looks really good, Darren…' Jamie had to nudge him before he responded. When he did, he gave Anna one of the bright smiles that he'd given her yesterday.

'Thank you, Anna.'

'You're very welcome. Now I want you to do something for me.'

She leaned towards him, and Darren momentarily

lost interest in the phone. It slid from his fingers, and Jamie caught it before it fell onto the floor.

'I've got some things to do now.' Nothing was as important as Darren at the moment, but she would find something to occupy her time. 'Jamie's going to ask you what we can do to make you feel a bit happier here. I want you to tell him, because I really want you to be happy.'

Darren nodded, and Anna glanced at Jamie. She'd relied on him before to talk to their young patients, and find out what was bothering them, but this time there was no trace of the customary adversarial looks that flashed between them. Just warmth. A warmth that made her heart beat a little faster and tingles run down her spine.

'And Anna will sort everything out for you.' Jamie flashed her a delicious smile.

'Will you make me a list?' Anna tore a piece of paper from the notepad that she carried with her, and laid it on the bed. 'Maybe different colours...?'

'That sounds like a plan. We'll colour code it, shall we? Red for the things you really don't like, eh?' Jamie took a red pen from his pocket. 'We'll do those first.'

Anna wasn't sure what to expect when she made her way back to Darren's room. But the boy seemed cheerful and Jamie rose, patting his pocket and giving him a conspiratorial smile. Leaving him to play with his phone, he ushered Anna outside.

'All right. Let's have it.' She held out her hand, and Jamie gave her the folded paper.

'It's... This is what he said.'

The paper was divided into three. At the top, written in red, were the things that were really bothering Darren. Anna scanned Jamie's neat, clear handwriting.

'Custard. Okay that's easy enough. No more custard.' Anna read the next entry and frowned. 'Really? There's a ghost in his room…?'

'That's what he said.'

And that was what Jamie had written down. Of course he had, he always took what his young charges said seriously.

'Well…' Anna decided to play along. 'What *kind* of ghost exactly?'

'He says it's a sparkly white woman. She appeared by the television at midnight. He checked the time.'

'And the TV wasn't on? Maybe it had been on standby.'

Jamie shook his head. 'Nope. I asked him that, and he said it wasn't *on* the TV, it was in front of it.'

'Midnight. Well, perhaps it was one of the nurses. Darren was recovering from surgery, and he may well have been disoriented or drowsy…' Anna shrugged.

'I mentioned that too and he told me he knows the difference between a nurse and a ghost.' Jamie grinned. 'I imagine that ghosts don't bring you custard and expect you to eat it.'

'No, I imagine they don't.' Anna put her mind to the problem. 'Well, we have another room that's empty at the moment. If it makes Darren feel better then he can move to that one. And we can arrange for an extra bed if his mum would like to stay with him overnight.'

Jamie nodded. 'That would be great. His mum's on her own and has younger children, but she has a sister who helps out. I can arrange for one of our outreach workers to go and stay with them if her sister can't manage.'

'Okay. We'll do that, then. Anything else, apart from the custard? Does his leg hurt him?'

Jamie smiled, pointing to the green list at the bottom of the page. 'It hurts a bit but he says it's okay. I took the liberty of checking…'

Of course he had. But it felt less like a liberty and more like a helping hand. 'That's great, thanks.'

Anna scanned the rest of the list. Nothing there, apart from the usual dislikes that everyone had of hospitals. 'Perhaps you'd like to take Darren up to the roof garden this afternoon if he'd like a breath of fresh air. I think we have some binoculars somewhere, I'll see if I can find them. He might like to do some sightseeing with them.'

'I think he'd like that.' Jamie shot her an uncertain look. It wasn't like him to hesitate before he asked for something for one of his patients. 'Are you…? Is someone going to be in Darren's old room tonight?'

'I doubt it, there are no new patients coming in today. We're not going to fill it with garlic and brick up the door, though.'

'Garlic's for vampires.' Jamie grinned suddenly. 'They're entirely different. If I've learned anything thing from Darren's games, it's that you need to be armed with the right weapon when you face any given opponent.'

'Well, whatever the right weapon is, we're not going to be using it. Darren's a little boy in a strange place who thought he saw something.'

'He told me exactly what he saw. More than once.'

Anna puffed out a breath. She knew what Jamie was doing, and it was the right thing. He was listening to the most vulnerable person first, and believing what they said.

'Jamie, you can go and look around the new room with him, and check it out. We need to do everything we can to put Darren's mind at rest and help him to heal, but there's no ghost. It's all very well to believe what he says, but there has to be some filter of whether it's actually credible or not.'

Jamie gave her a reproachful look. If he could just wear contacts or dark glasses it might help. His moss-green eyes spoke to her on a level she couldn't resist.

'I filtered. I still can't work out what he saw. You don't believe in ghosts, then?'

Anna shrugged. 'I like to think I have an open mind. That doesn't mean I won't look for an explanation for something I don't understand. And you've got too much time on your hands. If you want something useful to do, you can help us move him.'

Darren's mother arrived, and Jamie took her down to the coffee lounge to explain everything to her. Once she'd approved the plan, the new room was made ready for Darren. His things were gathered together, and then Jamie lifted him out of his bed, carrying him across the central nurses' area, his mother walking alongside.

Anna swallowed hard. The thing Darren most needed right now was love and care, and Jamie was giving him just that. He'd make a great dad. And she suspected that making babies with him would be an ultimate pleasure. One that she'd never enjoy. She turned her back, hurrying away.

'Everything okay?' Anna had spent the evening in her office, doing a few jobs that could have waited. The ward was quiet now, and in darkness.

'Yes, Darren settled down to sleep and his mum's

with him.' The nurse gestured towards the closed door of Darren's new room. Anna nodded, turning her gaze towards the half-open door of the room he'd occupied last night.

'Is he there?'

The nurse grinned and nodded. Anna walked towards the door, slipping inside the darkened room.

'So you decided to try your hand at ghost-hunting, did you? Or do you just have nothing better to do on a Friday night?'

Jamie's smile was traced by light, filtering in from outside. Intimate in the shadows. Like the smile of a lover in the half-light.

'I could ask you the same questions.' He murmured.

Anna wasn't going to answer either of them. Particularly the one about having better things to do on a Friday night because she didn't. She spent more evenings here than she liked to admit, and the clinic often felt more like home than her flat did.

'You're not going to stay here all night, are you?' She wouldn't put it past him. Jamie's unswerving belief that Darren *had* seen something, and his determination to find out what, was mesmeric. Attractive in a way that moved her beyond any physical thrill.

'It's gone half eleven. I'm just curious, I'll give it another hour and then I'll go.'

'And you're absolutely sure that it wasn't one of the nurses that Darren saw?' Anna had privately made up her mind that that was the most likely explanation.

'He told me twelve o'clock. The nurses make their rounds on the half hour and I checked the notes for last night. The nurse on duty wrote down when she'd checked on him.'

'This is crazy, Jamie.'

'Yeah, okay. I'll see you tomorrow, then.'

He was calling her bluff. Jamie had slid a long bench across from under the window, and placed it as close as he could to the side of the bed, so that he'd get the same view of the room that Darren would have done last night. Anna sat down beside him, and they lapsed into companionable silence together for a few moments. The temptation to sink into the darkness with him was almost unbearable.

'I heard there was an impromptu concert on the roof this afternoon. Jonny Campbell unplugged.'

She heard Jamie chuckle quietly. 'Yeah, I fetched a guitar from home for him, and asked if he'd like to play. It was a sell-out, we had a crowd of more than a dozen when the nurses' shift changed.'

'Not quite what Jon's used to, then?'

'It was a lot better than he's been used to recently. Jon's been talking about getting back to his roots, and he was enjoying it as much as Darren was. I think it meant something to him. Darren's a brave kid, and making him smile helped Jon, too.'

'It sounds like great therapy. For both of them.' There were some things that the hospital couldn't give to its patients, and this was one of them.

'Darren's mum was pretty thrilled as well. Jon sang "Everywhere" for her, and I took some pictures.'

'You didn't join in?'

'Nah. We're not quite there yet.'

Making music together had been such a bond for Jamie and Jon. Maybe it was too much to expect of their fragile new relationship. 'Next time maybe.'

'Maybe.'

She wanted so badly to touch him, to comfort him.
Jamie had put all his own feelings aside and had turned
his attention to helping Jon and Darren. He was making a great job of it for both of them, but at some point
he was going to have to confront his own emotions.
Anna moved her hand, laying it on Jamie's arm in
what she hoped would be construed as a friendly gesture of concern.

She felt muscle flex beneath her fingertips. She
should move away, but she couldn't. Then she felt Jamie's hand on hers as he leaned towards her. She could
hardly breathe.

'It's nearly midnight. Are you frightened yet?' He
whispered the words in her ear.

Terrified. Afraid of what might happen if she sat
any longer with him in the darkness. The supernatu-
ral world had nothing that rivalled this for sheer, un-
thinking dread.

Then she saw it. A pale figure that seemed to shim-
mer slightly on the other side of the room. Anna let out
a gasp, feeling Jamie's arm move protectively around
her shoulders. Suddenly she was clinging to him, feeling the beat of his heart quicken against her cheek.
Then he let out a low chuckle.

'So *that's* it.'

Jamie didn't have an extensive knowledge of ghost-
hunting, and had always assumed that it was a ruse,
intended to entice a girl closer. If that was the case,
then this had unexpectedly worked like a charm. He'd
assumed that his night-time vigil would be spent alone,
but suddenly Anna had slid towards him and was in
his arms.

It was obvious now, what Darren had seen. But his first glimpse of the illusion had taken Jamie by surprise, and he'd automatically reached for Anna, seeking to protect her from the unknown.

'It's…um…a trick of the light.'

'Yes, I can see that.' Anna didn't move away, though.

It was proving extremely difficult to move away from her. The scent of her hair, and the feeling of having her close was driving him crazy. He almost wished that something fearsome and dreadful *had* appeared before them, so he could hold her a little closer.

He drank in the feeling, knowing that it wasn't going to last for long. Then she shifted in his arms and he let her go.

'Had me fooled for a moment, though.' He murmured the words and she nodded.

'Yes. Me too.'

And after that moment the shocked reaction had turned into an embrace. Jamie had wanted to hold her, and it had been very apparent that Anna had wanted it too. The thought was far more disturbing than anything that the night could throw at them.

Jamie got to his feet, walking over to the door, and looking out. He saw it all now. 'It's the night nurse. She's standing at the end of the counter at the nurses' station in front of the work lamp so that she can read the notes before she goes on her rounds.'

'And the light's reflected in the mirror…' Anna gestured towards the full-length mirror that was fixed to the bathroom door.

'And then reflecting again on the screen of the TV…' Jamie moved towards the large screen on the wall at the end of the bed. 'The refraction is giving it an almost 3D quality.'

'But why hasn't anyone seen this before? This room's generally occupied.'

Jamie shrugged. 'Maybe they've moved the work lamp. Or maybe because they left Darren's door open last night to keep an eye on him, and usually the doors are closed.'

The figure disappeared suddenly, and the door was pushed open. The ghost was standing in the doorway, an enquiring look on her face. Anna got to her feet.

'Katya, come and sit over here. We've found our ghost.'

The night nurse looked puzzled, but did as Anna bade her. Jamie decided to stay where he was. The idea of any other woman clinging to him, so soon after he'd felt Anna close, was unthinkable.

He watched Anna walk over to the lamp, and motioned her to the side a little, so that she was standing in exactly the same place that Katya had been. Then he heard a gasp behind him.

'What…! So he *did* see something.'

'Yeah.' Jamie's eyes moved to the blurred figure reflected in the TV screen. This time it seemed a far more alluring ghost. 'Did you move the lamp recently?'

'Yes, we got a new one, and the lead wasn't as long, it won't stretch far enough so we can sit at the desk and read the notes. We were going to ask for an extension cable, but in the meantime I've been standing at the end of the counter…' Katya's hand flew to her mouth. 'Poor little Darren, no wonder he was so upset.'

'Well, at least we've got to the bottom of it now.'

Jamie beckoned to Anna, and the form in the TV screen disappeared as she walked back to the doorway.

'I'm so sorry. I thought he was just having nightmares, so I comforted him and sat with him until he went back to sleep.' Katya's mouth turned down. 'I'll move the lamp straight away.'

'You couldn't possibly have foreseen this, none of us did. And don't move the lamp just yet…' Anna flashed a look at Jamie, as if she already knew what he was about to say.

'Yes, I'd like to show this to Darren in the morning. If that's okay.'

'Of course. I might even come and do a turn as the friendly ghost.' Anna's smile seemed luminous in the interplay of light and shade in the doorway, and Jamie wondered if Darren would see it too. A beautiful, friendly ghost. Who seemed intent on picking the pieces of his heart up and stitching them back together. It was complex surgery, and Jamie doubted that even Anna was equal to it. He was too broken, and there would always be a little chink missing that let in the doubts and the mistrust.

But he could still walk Anna back down to her office. Still enjoy her scent, which, now that he'd noticed it, was more intoxicating than he'd ever imagined. And when she turned, flinging her arms around his neck and then retreating away from him almost as quickly, he felt his heart beating in his chest.

'What was that for?'

'Because you believed Darren.' Anna gave a shrug. 'I mean, we all believed that was what he *thought* he saw, and we took it seriously. But you believed him, and you found the answer.'

The warmth of her praise was working its way through him. If it reached his heart he wouldn't be able to stop himself from kissing her. 'I didn't discount the idea that it might have been his imagination.'

'But you waited up, all the same.'

'Oh, and you're not really here?'

She wiggled her fingers and whoo-whooed at him, in a laughing impression of a ghost. 'Maybe. Maybe not…'

'So how are you getting home?' Now that Jamie had betrayed the protective streak he felt for Anna, he may as well go the whole hog and not just fret about whether she got home safely.

'I'll call a cab. Would you like a lift?'

'I'm only twenty minutes' walk. I could do with the fresh air.'

She made the call, and when the cab arrived, he walked her down to the main reception area and out into the street. Opening the back door of the car for her, he suppressed the impulse to warn the driver that he was carrying precious cargo and stepped back onto the pavement, watching as the cab drew away.

A walk would do him good. The last few days had been all about trying to find something to say to Jon that would encourage him and make him feel better, and ignoring the elephant in the room. But Anna had turned everything that he'd thought he knew on its head, and made anything seem possible.

CHAPTER FIVE

THE SOUND OF raised voices came from Jon's room. Anna supposed it was inevitable as Jamie and Jon couldn't keep ignoring whatever it was that they'd argued about. But when she approached the door, she found that she'd been wrong. They seemed to be managing to ignore it *and* argue at the same time.

'Hello…' Anna pushed the door open a little further. 'Am I interrupting anything?'

They both looked up from the crossword they'd been discussing, and she thought she saw a flash of relief in Jamie's eyes. 'Hi. What are you doing here on a Saturday morning?'

'I was going to help you show Darren his ghost, remember?'

Jamie nodded. 'The ward sister says that I can pull down the shades and try it out after lunch. She's interested as well.'

'So am I,' Jon chimed in. 'Poor little chap, he must have been frightened. Waking up like that and seeing things. I'm glad you managed to explain it for him.'

There was a note of sadness in Jon's voice. Anna wondered what the silent hours of the night had held for him. Demons, maybe, fuelled by exhaustion and depression. She smiled, sitting down opposite Jon.

'How are *you* today?'

Jon shook off his reverie. 'Okay. Thirteen down's giving us a bit of a problem.'

Anna picked up the paper, examining the cross-word. 'Humerus.'

'Of course!' Jon took the paper, filling in the word. 'You should have got that one, Jamie. What's the point of medical school if you don't know the name for a clown's arm?'

'Upper arm, technically.' Jamie frowned. His mood seemed to have darkened suddenly. Anna put the folder containing her notes down on the table, and decided she should get down to business.

'I wanted to talk to you about your arm, Jon.' She glanced at Jamie and he gave her a questioning look, then got the message.

'Okay, I'll leave you both to it, then.' He got to his feet.

'Stay.' For a moment there was an imploring look in Jon's eyes, but it was quickly masked. 'You never know, you might learn something.'

Jamie ignored the jibe, and sat down again. 'If that's okay.'

'Yes, of course.' Anna settled the matter as firmly as she could. 'So how is the burn feeling now, Jon?'

'Okay. It doesn't itch so much.'

'Yes, I'm happy with the way that the cream has helped moisturise the skin and take down some of the inflammation.'

'You'll be doing the procedure soon?' Jon's restless

anxiety was never far from the surface and he shifted in his seat.

'That's what I'd like to talk to you about. You've already had a couple of sessions with our counsellor, and Dr Lewis has prescribed medication for depression. In view of that, and the fact that you're also very run down, we both think it would be best to postpone any surgery on your arm until we've tackled those important issues.'

Jon frowned. 'My arm's a mess. *Anyone* would be depressed.'

Anna had anticipated some resistance from Jon, and decided that the most straightforward answers were the best. 'It's normal to have feelings in reaction to an injury. But that's not necessarily the same as depression.'

Jon shook his head. 'I want this done. I want rid of it.'

'Anything we do to modify the scars on your arm and face will make them more painful in the short term—'

'I don't *care* about pain. If it hurts, it hurts. It's not as if everything else is rosy at the moment.'

That was exactly what Anna and Dr Lewis had discussed yesterday. Jon was in a world of mental pain and confusion, and they needed to address that first. The pain from a medical procedure might serve to take his mind off his other problems, but it would do nothing to solve them.

'We feel that these other issues are more pressing and should be addressed first. We'll still keep up with the cream and massage, and that will improve the skin around your burns and make it more likely that surgery will be successful.'

Jon shook his head, cursing under his breath. Then got to his feet and started to pace. 'This is… Why can't you just do as I say?'

Anna shot Jamie a warning look, hoping he wouldn't intervene, and he ignored her.

'Hey! You think you're the most important person in the room? You're not, Anna is. Because she's your surgeon and you need to listen to what she's telling you and follow her advice.' Jamie's voice was quiet but very firm. And it worked. Jon calmed down suddenly.

'Sorry. I don't much like sitting around, doing nothing.' Jon's moods could turn on a sixpence, and now he seemed the picture of contrition.

'You have nothing to apologise for. I know it must be hard, and frustrating, but both Dr Lewis and I feel that this is the best way forward. If you agree, he'll take over sole responsibility for your care for the foreseeable future, and you can come back to me when you've worked together to resolve the most important issues.'

Jon shrugged. 'Okay, whatever you say. Although I'll miss my beautiful Anna's visits.'

Anna saw Jamie stiffen, and felt herself blush. It was just a compliment and it meant nothing to her. It would have meant a great deal more on Jamie's lips…

'It's not a beauty contest, mate.' Jamie's tension showed beneath his smile. 'Anna's here to do her job.'

He was right, but he hadn't needed to say it. Jon's words were harmless.

'I'll always take a compliment.' She tried to diffuse the tension that had built suddenly in the room.

Jon chuckled, and Jamie looked at her as if she'd just slapped his face. Whatever was going on between them was one of the things that needed to be resolved.

A knock sounded at the door and Anna jumped to her feet to open it.

A woman of about her own age was juggling a baby and a large bag. Her resemblance to Jamie and Jon was obvious.

'Look who it is! Is that Joshua…?' Jon was animated again, and even Jamie looked a little less grumpy.

'Yes, I thought you might like to get to know your new nephew.' The woman turned to Anna. 'I'm Caroline, Jamie and Jon's sister.'

'I'm Anna Caulder. I was Jon's surgeon until about five minutes ago.'

'Jamie's told me all about you. Thanks for looking after my big brothers.' Caroline grinned, clearly reckoning that *both* of her brothers had needed some looking after. 'And this is Joshua.'

'Hey, Joshua.' Jon's voice was cracked with emotion and he was staring at Caroline and the baby. Caroline planted a kiss on her son's brow and pointed towards Jon, waving at him. Joshua imitated his mother, and Jon waved back.

'Don't let me interrupt…' Caroline smiled at Anna, and Anna shook her head. This was exactly what Jon needed.

'We're finished. I'll leave you to your visit.' Anna shot Jamie a pointed look and he got to his feet. Despite his obvious annoyance, he too understood that Caroline and Jon needed some time together, and that baby Joshua was a very special visitor too.

Jamie ushered his sister to a seat then followed Anna out of the room. She closed the door and Jamie paused, looking at her thoughtfully.

'Is there something *you* need to talk about?' Strictly

speaking, and now that she was no longer Jon's surgeon, that was Dr Lewis's question to ask. But Jamie was a friend.

'Yeah, actually, there is.' She saw a trace of annoyance in his eyes.

'Right, then.' She turned on her heel, beckoning to him over her shoulder. 'My office.'

Anna walked into her office, perching herself on the windowsill and folding her arms. 'All right. What gives?'

She was going to push it. Right now probably wasn't the time.

'Nothing…'

'Don't *nothing* me, Jamie. You've been swallowing something for days, and it's got something to do with me and the way I've been treating your brother. So let's have it.'

'You've done everything right. I think that the decision to have Dr Lewis take over is an excellent one.' Jamie decided that the best course was the least antagonistic one.

'And…?'

Okay. If she wanted to know so much… Maybe it was something that he should have mentioned to her before. Sitting down would be good, it might make him feel less angry, but somehow being confined in a seat was unthinkable.

'I think… Jon's very charming. Charismatic…'

'And…?'

Jamie puffed out a breath. 'Don't be fooled by it. He just loves the attention and he's broken a few hearts.'

His heart. Jon had broken his heart as well. Jamie swallowed down the thought.

A slight flush spread across her cheeks and as it did so, Jamie's stomach did a somersault. Not Anna. He couldn't bear to think that she might have fallen prey to Jon's charm.

'You think that I haven't been professional?'

'No, but now that you're no longer his surgeon, that's not an issue, is it?' Jamie shook his head. 'This is just... friendly advice.'

Anna's eyebrows shot up. 'Friendly advice? You think I need *friendly advice* to keep my hands off the patients?'

She was angry now, and deliberately misunderstanding him. Jamie felt his own anger begin to bubble furiously.

'No, of course not, we both know how to act professionally. But I've seen how you look at him, the way you were listening to music together up on the roof the other evening...' Jamie couldn't even think about it.

'How *dare* you?' She marched across the room, stopping just inches in front of him, her face suddenly cold with rage.

'Anna, I'm not suggesting you've done anything wrong. I just don't want to see you getting hurt.'

'No, Jamie. You're telling me that I've been inappropriate with a patient. I found him sitting up there on the roof on his own, and I took a moment to talk to him. You understand *talking*, don't you? If you saw a reaction from me when you arrived, maybe it was because you were looking daggers at me.'

Her indignant fury left no room for doubt. He'd allowed his own feelings for Anna to get in the way of his judgement, and he'd jumped to the conclusion that had been presented to him by his own relationship with his brother. Jamie suddenly felt very ashamed of himself.

'Do I get to apologise?' Maybe she didn't want to hear it. Not after what he'd said.

'Damn right you get to apologise. I'm not entirely sure how much good it'll do, though.' Anna's face had softened a little as she threw down the challenge.

Jamie took a breath. He had to make this good. 'Then I apologise. Unreservedly. I was wrong to suggest that your motives were anything other than kindness. And you're right, my reaction was nothing to do with you, and everything to do with me. I've been trying not to lash out at Jon, and I lashed out at you instead. I'm sorry.'

He could feel the tension in the room lifting. He wanted to hug her, but he didn't dare. In the silence between them, he felt himself begin to shake with emotion.

'That's a very nice apology. And it's accepted.' Anna moved her hand, brushing her fingers against his trembling hand, and he felt desire flood through him. No. She was just being a kind friend. He wasn't going to mistake that for something else, not so soon after he'd made such a similar, horrendous mistake.

'Thank you. I don't really deserve that. I...um... think I need to get some fresh air.'

She frowned. 'Where are you going?'

He'd thought flowers. Maybe something bright and happy. Friendly rather than romantic.

'I'm not sure you want me around right now. I wouldn't blame you...'

'And you're getting out while the going's good?'

'Yeah. Something like that.'

She smiled, and Jamie felt relief flood through him. They'd said the words, but her real acceptance of his apology was in her smile.

'I want you in that chair. Right now.' She pointed to the seat on the other side of her desk, where Jamie had set up his laptop to work.

Jamie swallowed hard. That was rather more costly than the price of a few flowers, but then Anna had never shied away from difficult. It was the least he could do. He sat down, expecting her to retreat to the other side of her desk, but she pulled up a chair and sat beside him.

'Jon's not the only one who needs a bit of help, is he?'

'I'm dealing with it.'

'I can see that.' Her lips quirked into a half-smile. 'How do you reckon that's going? On a scale of one to ten…?'

Messing up with Anna had made him realise two things. He couldn't just forget about what Jon had done, and he cared for Anna. Right now the level of pain and confusion he was feeling was off any scale he could think of.

'I haven't made much of a start. Nought out of ten would be pushing it.'

'You're here. You're helping your brother. That's huge, Jamie, and I think that entitles you to at least a five.'

'That's generous of you.'

Anna took a breath, regarding him for a moment. Jamie didn't really want to know what she was thinking, but he didn't get to duck away from anything right now.

'What did you argue about? You and Jon?'

'It was… I guess *in the past* isn't going to wash, is it?' So many of the kids he dealt with talked about things that were in their pasts that still held sway over them now.

'No. I think you know the reasons why not. Whatever this is, it's tearing you up and you need to talk about it. If not to me, then someone else, but I really want to help.'

Jamie took a deep breath. 'When it happened, most of my family insisted on taking sides. Caroline was so furious with Jon that she wouldn't even speak to him. I hated it, and I reckoned that if I never spoke about it then they'd come round eventually. I didn't want our argument to rip the family apart, but it did.'

'Caroline's here now.'

'Yes, but it took me a while to convince her to come. I don't want you to think less of Jon, the way my family did. You're his surgeon, he needs you.'

'We practise medicine without fear or favour, Jamie. You know that. Anyway, I *was* Jon's surgeon. I'm not any more.'

'I just didn't want you to feel a conflict.'

'I don't. I know exactly where I stand. You're the person who matters to me, and if you ask me to make no judgement then I'll do my best to respect that. I might have an opinion, but I won't allow it to change the way I act.'

The sudden warmth in his chest almost made him choke. *He* mattered to Anna. Maybe she'd been giving

Jon a little extra attention for his sake, and the thought made his accusations seem even viler.

'It'll stay between you and me?'

She nodded. 'Yes, of course. Between friends and in the strictest confidence.'

Jamie leaned back in his seat. Suddenly this felt like the safe place where he could admit to his feelings, without making the situation worse.

'Thanks. I'd like that.'

CHAPTER SIX

WHATEVER IT WAS, it was bad. But she'd told Jamie that she wouldn't judge and so she should just listen, and take whatever he said at whatever value he chose to give it.

'It was Christmas, nearly three years ago. Jon had landed back in the country the previous week, and he was staying at a hotel five minutes from my parents' place. I went up there the day before Christmas Eve with my fiancée, and Caroline was going to drive over with her husband and children on Christmas Day. The idea was that we'd be close, without giving my mother all the extra work of having house guests for a week.'

Fiancée? Anna resisted the urge to take just that one word from everything else that Jamie had said, and nodded him on.

'It was good to see him again. We'd grown apart since I'd gone to medical school and he'd gone on the road…' Jamie shrugged. 'Gill hadn't met him before, but of course she knew him by reputation. She was really thrilled to meet him.'

'Gill, your…erm…' Anna waved her hand, not wanting to say the word.

'Fiancée, yes. She and Jon got on really well, and I

was tired, I'd been working pretty hard in the run-up to Christmas. I went to bed and left them talking. I woke up the next morning and she wasn't there.'

'Wasn't…where?' Anna felt her throat dry suddenly.

'Wasn't next to me in bed. She'd been in Jon's room all night.'

'Talking?' Anna decided not to jump to the obvious and most devastating conclusion.

'No. My twin brother slept with my fiancée, after only knowing her for a matter of about six hours. On the night before Christmas Eve. While I was sleeping a couple of rooms along the corridor.'

'He… She…' Anna clapped her hand over her mouth before she said something stupid, feeling her eyes fill with tears. 'Oh, Jamie…'

'Yeah.' He was clearly fighting for control over his emotions. 'Don't say it. Whatever it is, it's not going to help.'

'No. I don't imagine it will.'

'I looked for her, and then knocked on Jon's door to see if he knew where she'd got to. I was worried about her…' Jamie shook his head. 'She was there, with him. Both dressed in those towelling robes that the hotel provides for guests.'

'And…they'd definitely…' This line of questioning wasn't working very well. She couldn't imagine any sane woman choosing Jon over Jamie, and she couldn't put it into words.

'Like a fool, I just took it for granted that it was all innocent and for some reason Gill had decided to use Jon's shower instead of ours. She followed me back to my room and told me. She was sorry, but Jon had swept her off her feet. She'd found something special and she had to follow her heart.'

'I can't...' She *had* to pull herself together. 'I mean, I believe what you're saying to me. I just can't believe it happened.'

'Neither could I. I didn't trust myself to say anything, I just walked away. I must have walked for miles, and then I decided that I had to talk to them both and went back to the hotel. They'd both packed their things. Jon had the decency to look pretty shamefaced about it all, and I was pretty angry.'

'I think you had a right to be.'

'It didn't help much, though. I tried to keep my cool, but I couldn't. I ended up shouting, asking Gill why she couldn't have just stopped and thought about it before she decided that sleeping with my brother was a good idea, and she burst into tears and turned to *him*. I decided there was nothing more that I could say, and I wasn't going to trade insults, so I turned and walked out. I went to my room and stayed there until after they'd left.'

'Where is she now?' Anna wondered whether Gill was still with Jon but had stayed away from the clinic because of Jamie.

'I don't know. She and Jon broke up after a couple of months, and I heard she was back in England, but she never contacted me. I didn't want to contact her, to be honest. The thing that hurt the most...' Suddenly Jamie's composure cracked and he shook his head.

Anna reached forward, taking his hands in hers. He'd already shown a lot of restraint in telling his story, and maybe that was the real problem. Now that he'd finally accessed his emotions, he needed to own them.

'What was the worst thing, Jamie?'

He looked up at her, his eyes brimming with tears. Anna held onto his hands tightly.

'Stick with me. The worst thing, what was it?'

He pulled one of his hands away from hers, brushing it across his face. But the other hand was still hanging tightly onto hers.

'The worst thing, was the fact that it didn't last. If it had really been something special, and they'd found true love, then maybe I could have come to terms with it. But they'd broken my heart and thrown me away for…a couple of months.'

'And now you're trying to forgive him.'

'He's my brother. I have to forgive him before the rest of the family will. I *want* to forgive him…'

'Do you know why he did it?'

'We never spoke about it.' Jamie shrugged. 'He did it because he could, I guess.'

'I'm so sorry this happened, Jamie.' There was nothing else that she could say, no way to make sense of it all. Maybe just being here was enough.

It seemed enough, for this moment at least. They sat in silence, holding hands. It felt as if there was a measure of healing there, but there had to be more than this if Jamie was ever going to truly leave this behind.

'Could I suggest something?'

He smiled. 'Go ahead. I'm out of ideas in finding a way forward.'

'You haven't talked much about this, have you?'

There was a flash of understanding in Jamie's eyes. 'There are counsellors attached to my charity. I never really got around to talking to any of them…'

'They might not be the best people to talk to, you

know them and have a relationship with them outside the counselling sessions. Jon's benefitted from the sessions he's had here, at the clinic.'

'You think I should take part in his sessions?' Jamie shook his head. 'I'm pretty sure that neither of us are quite ready for that.'

'I don't imagine you are. But maybe if you talk to someone here, who's working within the same framework as his counsellor, that might turn into a reconciliation network for you both. When you and Jon are ready.'

Jamie thought for a moment. 'It…makes sense. It might work. Nothing ventured, I suppose…'

'And you both have a lot to gain. Even if you can't truly forgive him, at least you might know a bit more about what happened and how you feel about it. And you'll have tried.' Anna smiled at him. 'Made the best of what you have.'

'Now you're throwing my own words at me.' Jamie's charity was all about teenagers making the best of themselves. 'Don't you have any scruples at all?'

Anna chuckled. 'No. Not many.'

None at all when it came to Jamie. Right now, she'd do anything to help him feel better about this.

'It's a good idea and I'll think about it. Very seriously.' He gave her hand a squeeze and Anna squeezed back. 'Where are you, in all of this?'

That was a question that bore thinking about.

'Practically speaking… Our tissue viability nurse can deal with Jon's burns, and now that we've delayed surgery I'll be taking a step back. I'd like to speak to Dr Lewis and make it formal that I'm no longer Jon's surgeon.'

Jamie knew what that meant. She still had a duty of care to Jon because he was a patient at the clinic, but she was more free to dictate the nature of her relationship with *him*.

'And...' He was still uncertain. Jamie needed her to say this.

'It means I have no part in Jon's counselling or yours. I'm just your friend.'

His moss-green eyes became suddenly luminescent. Slowly Jamie raised her hand and even though his lips barely touched her fingers the effect was electric.

'There's no *just* about having you as a friend.'

Jamie was sitting in the cafeteria with a young girl of around ten. *Young lady* described her better. Her dark hair was done in a neat plait and she wore a pink sweatshirt with matching pink baseball boots and jeans. A pretty blue backpack hung over the back of her seat, and both she and Jamie were sipping their drinks from cups and saucers. A book with a sparkly pink cover lay on the table between them.

It looked like the kind of conversation that shouldn't be interrupted, and Anna decided to collect her coffee and drink it in her office. But Jamie saw her and raised his hand, beckoning her over.

'Anna, this is Jessica. Will you join us?'

Jamie's invitation was obviously sincere, and Jessica turned and smiled too. Anna pulled up a chair and sat down.

'Hi, Jessica. I'm Anna.'

'Anna's my friend,' Jamie explained to Jessica, who nodded, taking the information at face value even if it prompted a small quiver in Anna's heart. 'Jess is Caroline's eldest.'

'We're having tea.' The tone of Jess's voice indicated that this was an established ritual between Jamie and his niece. 'It's nice to have an adult conversation sometimes.'

Jamie chuckled. 'Yeah, it is, isn't it? Jess has younger brothers and between them things can get a little loud.'

'Do you have brothers?' Jess turned to Anna.

'No, I'm an only child.' Since this was an adult conversation, a little honesty was in order. 'I had loads of adult conversation when I was your age. I often wished I had brothers or sisters.'

Jess considered the thought. 'I like my brothers. Most of the time.'

'How many do you have?' Anna had seen Caroline with the baby and an older boy, and Caroline had joked that she was bringing the children to see their Uncle Jon in instalments so they could each get to know him on their own terms.

'Three.'

'The twins are five. And then there's Joshua, he's going to be a year old next month.' Jamie elaborated.

'That sounds like a lot of noise.'

Jess nodded. 'Yes, it is sometimes. They're not allowed in my room. Mum says that's just for me.'

Anna imagined that Jess's room would be neat and tidy, probably with a bit of pink and a lot of sparkle. Her special place. And she had her Uncle Jamie to take her for tea and some adult conversation. It was nice of him to think of doing that.

Jess had finished her drink and was sliding her book

carefully into her backpack. Jamie grinned. 'You're going back upstairs to see your mum and Uncle Jon?'

'Yes. Don't forget what I told you, Uncle Jamie.'

Jamie spread his hand across his heart, in the expression of innocence that always made Anna smile. 'No, of course not. You remember the way…?'

Jess rolled her eyes. 'You don't need to come with me, Uncle Jamie. I can go on my own.'

'Yes, of course you can. I'll just walk you to the door, then, I'm going to get some more tea.' He flashed the hint of a wink at Anna.

She watched as Jamie lingered by the entrance to the cafeteria, obviously watching Jess along the corridor and towards the stairs that led straight up to Jon's ward. He turned, pulling his phone from his pocket and speaking a few words into it, before going to the counter and ordering a cup of coffee. Presumably Caroline now knew to expect her daughter's arrival at any moment.

'That's very sweet of you…' Anna smiled at him as he sat back down.

'You think so?' That innocent look again. 'I'm always up for a bit of adult conversation too. Jess has decided she wants to take me in hand.'

He pushed his half-drunk cup of herbal tea to one side and took a sip of the coffee. Clearly he and Jess had their own set of rules for tea drinking, which stipulated they should both have the same herbal blend, but Jamie preferred coffee.

'She knows about you and Jon?'

Jamie shrugged. 'She was old enough when the argument happened to know that something really bad was going on. Not old enough to understand it properly. That's not easy for her.'

Anna's own childhood had been full of carefully explained things, all of them age appropriate. She'd never had brothers and sisters, or uncles and aunts, whose actions were a mystery to her.

'But you've explained things to her.'

'She knows that her twin brothers argue, and then make up and turn into the best of friends again. I told her that when you're grown up things sometimes get a bit more complicated, but that I'll always love her and so will her Uncle Jon.' Jamie quirked his lips down. 'Caroline will make sure that Jon keeps to his end of that bargain.'

'Not you?'

Jamie laughed suddenly. 'You and Jess would get on like a house on fire. She's made me a list of five things I have to do.'

'She has? Good girl! I hope you've taken note.'

'I did. I take note of everything you say as well.' The humour in his eyes couldn't conceal their warmth. 'I told her that taking him shopping to get him a present wasn't really our style, so we agreed on going to the pub for a quiet drink together. Although we'll have to choose our spot if we don't want to be besieged by Jon's fans.'

Jamie's easy relationship with his niece was nice, he was the protective adult who kept his niece from harm, but they could still talk as equals. Anna had been fascinated by the complex interactions of a large family when she'd been married, and she missed them. Now the only place she could find them was here, at the clinic, and she felt pretty much the same as Jess obviously did. If she could make peace, she would.

'Your…um…name came up. In my counselling session.' Jamie was staring into his coffee now.

'Yes? That's okay, you don't have to explain. It's between you and your counsellor.' Anna could feel her ears starting to burn all the same.

'There's nothing that says I can't mention it either.' Jamie shot her a thoughtful smile.

'No. There isn't.' Anna was holding her breath. This was stupid, Jamie's counselling sessions were none of her business. She still wanted to know what he'd said about her. Or maybe she didn't…

'I was talking about the weekend. You know I'm taking Jon down to my place in Hastings on Saturday, and Caroline's bringing the children over?'

'Yes, Caroline mentioned it the other day. Seems like a good idea. Jon's been much better these last few days and it'll do him good…' The words dried in Anna's throat. This wasn't about Jon. It was about Jamie.

'I was saying that you'd supported us both in keeping the lid on things. I wasn't sure how we'd do on our own. Caroline's great but she's too close to it all and she gets upset when there's any hint of an argument between Jon and me.'

'He's been baiting you, hasn't he?' Anna had noticed the jibes that Jon aimed at his brother from time to time. Jamie was one of the most easygoing people she knew, and he ignored them, but Anna could see him making an effort to hold his anger back.

'Jon's always been the more impatient of the two of us. He's making a good show of things, and claiming he's better and stronger now, but he's still fragile. My role is to keep the peace and help him as much as I can.'

It was an approach. One that clearly took more heed of Jon's needs than Jamie's. 'You might be right. What do you want of me, Jamie?'

'It's a big ask...' He quirked his lips down. 'Not much notice either, you're probably busy...'

'All right, so you've supplied me with an excuse to say no. You'd better give me a chance to use it.'

Jamie chuckled. 'I was wondering if you fancied joining us. Not as an arbiter between me and Jon, just for a day out and some lunch together. Although I might glance in your direction from time to time, just to remind myself that I *do* need to keep a lid on things.'

Jamie needed this. Badly. He wouldn't have asked if he hadn't.

'This is your family day, Jamie. Won't Caroline feel I'm intruding?'

'I mentioned it to her and she thought it was a great idea, if you'd like to come. She was expecting that her husband Harry would be there, but he has a meeting with a client who's only in the country for a couple of days so it had to be Saturday. Harry runs his own architectural practice and this client wants to talk about a new project, so Caroline told him he must go and that she'd be all right on her own. I think she's rather hoping she won't end up being the only adult in the room.'

'And what are you hoping?' Jamie had tried so hard to keep his feelings under control and Anna had seen the toll it had taken on him.

'I'm *planning* on being the perfect host. Caroline knows that, but she thinks your presence might remind both Jon and me that we still need to make an effort.

She reckons that you have us both twisted around your little finger at the moment.' He shot her his most compelling innocent look, and Anna's heart jumped in her chest. 'I haven't a clue what she means, and I told her that she was imagining things.'

Twisted around her little finger. It was a breath-taking thought, not so much where Jon was concerned but Jamie… And he wanted her to be a part of his family day. Anna felt herself flush.

'I've embarrassed you. It's a bad idea, I shouldn't have asked…' Jamie's face registered concern, and he was back-pedalling furiously now.

It would take just one nod to take everything off the table. They could finish their coffee, and Anna could go on to put the finishing touches to her non-existent plans for Saturday. That might be the best way forward, but Jamie needed her. If she needed reminding that he was just a friend, then she could imagine the look he gave her when he said it. As if friends were the most important thing in the world.

'You *should* have asked. Because I'd like to come.'

'Really?' He seemed genuinely surprised.

'We could have an adult conversation, if you like. About the weather, or something inconsequential.'

Jamie laughed. 'That would be fantastic.'

CHAPTER SEVEN

SATURDAY MORNING WAS gloomy and overcast, but when Jon walked out of the clinic, with his brother by his side, he greeted the drizzle of rain and the open air with a broad smile.

Anna had hung back, wondering if Jon would take the front seat, but he held the door open for her and then climbed into the back of the car. Jamie didn't even seem to notice his brother's show of gallantry, and Anna settled into her seat. As they drove out of London the skies seemed to clear a little, and by the time they reached Sussex, the sun was out.

The old farmhouse stood back from the road a little. A silver SUV was parked in the drive outside, indicating that Caroline was already here with the children, and when they approached the door it flew open.

'Uncle Jamie…' The twins ran towards Jamie, and he bent to pick them both up, one under each arm, and whirl them around.

'What have you two terrors been doing?'

'Making gingerbread men. Mum said it was all right for us to cook.'

Jamie chuckled. 'Oh, she did, did she? I'll be having a word with your mother if she's left a mess. Did you make one for Uncle Jon?'

'Yes!'

Jon had been watching, still a little reserved around the children. He broke into a sudden smile, and Jamie put the twins back down onto their feet. 'Why don't you show him, then?'

Ben, the more reserved of the two, hung back, but Thomas took Jon's hand, pulling him into the house. Jamie smirked, pleased with the welcome, and Anna followed him inside. Coats were taken off and piled onto the hallstand, and Jon was propelled through the hallway and into the kitchen.

There *was* a mess, along with the smell of cooking, but Jamie didn't heed it. Caroline was doing her best to get icing out of her baby son's hair, while Jess had a stack of fine china plates in front of her, none of which matched, and was clearly deciding which plate went best with which gingerbread man.

'That one's yours, Uncle Jon.' Thomas waved his finger towards a figure with a large yellow splodge of icing around its chest. 'We made a guitar.'

'That's great.' Jon was all smiles now.

'Did you make one for Anna?' Jamie asked Ben, and he nodded.

'Of course we did. You're the one with the yellow icing all over your head, Anna.' Caroline grinned at her. 'A bit like Joshua. The twins reckoned it was a good idea to ice him as well.'

'Go and sit down, I'll make the coffee while Jess finishes putting out the plates.' Jamie smiled at his niece, who grinned back at him.

'No, I need to clear up a bit...' Caroline protested, but Jamie was shooing everyone out of the kitchen.

'I'll do that. It's easier when no one's making icing-sugar footprints all over the place.'

'Oh! The carpets... Thomas and Ben, take your shoes off,' Caroline wailed, and Anna bent down, helping the twins with their shoelaces.

Order was restored, and Jon lowered himself into an armchair, seeming tired after the journey. The children were left to play by the fireplace, and Anna had a moment to look around.

Jamie's sitting room was...different. The room had obviously been stripped back at some point, but no effort had been made to cover the cracks in the brickwork over the fireplace, they'd just been filled. The old polished floorboards were pitted and stained from years of wear, and the deep brick fireplace had obviously seen many years of use. But above it the long wooden mantel was pristine and gleaming, with glass lamps at either end. The sofas and chairs were all spotless, and the book cabinets and furniture gleamed. It was a suffusion of old and new, comfortable but with a lot of character.

'Nice, isn't it?' Caroline had seen her looking around.

'It's lovely. If I'd known that *not* decorating could be so effective, I wouldn't have gone to all the bother at my place. Although I imagine that quite a bit of thought went into this.'

'Yes, it did. When Jamie bought this place, it was pretty run down. He decided that anything you touched would be new and clean. Anything you didn't touch would be left as it was. I was a bit sceptical, but my husband Harry's an architect and he got it. I do now too, I think it works.'

As long as you had the eye to pick out furniture that didn't match but which went together well. Chairs and sofas that were all different but were upholstered in complementary colours, dark reds and russet tones. It seemed artless, but there was a cohesiveness of thought behind it all.

Jessica appeared, carefully holding two plates, each with a gingerbread man on it. She gave one to Jon and one to Anna, and Anna thanked her for choosing the prettiest plate for her. Jess confided that it was her favourite too, then disappeared back into the kitchen for the next two. Jamie brought the coffee, and the twins were persuaded to sit down in a couple of wooden children's chairs that stood by the fireplace.

'So…why have I got green hair?' Jamie was regarding his plate with a smile.

'The green icing was meant to be for your eyes.' Caroline shrugged. 'Call it artistic licence.'

'Yes. Of course.' Jamie bit the leg off his gingerbread man. 'They taste great, Jessica.'

Jessica gave him a little smile, obviously pleased that her part in it all hadn't gone unnoticed by her uncle.

'You've done a lot here since I saw it last.' Jon was looking around the sitting room. 'It looks great.'

'You want to see the rest?' Jamie asked diffidently.

'Yes, thanks. That would be great.'

There was a restrained courtesy about Jamie and Jon's conversations, but they were talking and it obviously meant a lot to Jon to be asked here. A shared glance between her and Jamie was enough for Anna to tag along with them, curious to see what he'd done in the rest of the house.

Jamie's eclectic style was everywhere. In the dining room, a large polished table was surrounded by cabinets filled with books and a collection of plates, glasses and silverware, some matching and some not. Jamie walked straight past a corridor that led to the other side of the one-storey house, and Anna guessed that the bedrooms lay in that direction. Jon ignored it as well, which was probably just as well.

Only the kitchen and bathroom showed no trace of the building's ancient shell, with gleaming floor-to-ceiling tiles and mirrors in the bathroom, and wooden cabinets in the kitchen. When Jamie led the way out of the kitchen door, Anna found herself on a long veranda.

'This must be lovely in the summer.' The view was spectacular, farmland and open countryside stretching off into the distance.

Jamie nodded. 'I like it in winter, too. I've a couple of space heaters, and it's quite cosy out here. Last year I sat and watched it snow.'

The thought of him sitting alone seemed a little sad. But the house was full of noise and activity now, some of which was heading their way. The twins burst out onto the veranda, and Thomas ran up to Jamie, pulling at his hand.

'Why don't you show Uncle Jon our cars…'

Jamie grinned, squatting down in front of the two boys. 'What cars?'

'The ones we're building, silly… Uncle Jon would like to see them.' Thomas turned to Jon for confirmation.

Jon was clearly torn, unable to say no to his nephew

but clearly wanting to show how much he appreciated Jamie's hospitality as well. 'I'd like to see them later, Thomas. Uncle Jamie's showing me around right now.'

The twins chorused their disappointment and Jamie smiled.

'Okay, why don't you two show Uncle Jon your model cars now, then? He might have some ideas about what colours to paint them.' Jamie glanced up at Jon. 'The garden will still be here later.'

'Okay. Thanks.' Jon grinned, holding his hands out to the twins and they started to pull him back into the house.

It was a nice gesture. The two boys were still a little shy with Jon, and Jamie seemed determined to include his brother as much as he could. He knew how much that meant to Jon.

He watched Jon go, and then turned to Anna. 'Looks as if we have ten minutes for one of those adult conversations you promised me. Would you like to see what I've done in the garden?'

'Yes. That sounds great.' Anna glanced down at her high-heeled boots. 'I've got a pair of trainers in my bag. Caroline said that I might need them if we all decided to go for a walk.'

Jamie nodded. 'Yeah, good idea. I'll wait for you here…'

The garden was much the same as the house. Seemingly artless, but everywhere there were things that made you want to stop and look. An old, worn stone birdbath nestled amongst the foliage. Blackberry bushes, forming a wide mass of ripening fruit that could be picked and eaten straight away, and the soft yellows of a brick-built outhouse contrasted with the new, dark slate roof. It was shaped by nature, but Jamie's guiding hand had given it a touch of magic.

'How long have you been here?' They strolled together along a winding pathway that led away from the house.

'Six years.' Jamie looked around at the garden. 'It's not really finished yet.'

'It looks like one of those things that will never quite be finished.' There were no straight lines about this place, it seemed as if it might constantly evolve.

'No, I'm not sure it will.'

'I expected something different. A bit more under control.' Anna smiled up at him and he gave her a *Who? Me?* smile.

'You think I'm a control freak?'

'You have goals, don't you?'

Jamie chuckled. 'That's a different thing. I have goals, I just don't make myself any promises about how I'm going to find my way to them.'

That made sense. The way that everything fitted together neatly, without necessarily matching. 'Caroline said the place was pretty run down when you bought it. It must have taken a lot of work.'

'It's the closest thing I have to a hobby. I work hard, and then when I come down here I relax and go with the flow of the place.' Jamie turned, his hands in his pockets, looking back at the house.

'I had an inkling of its potential when I bought it, but after I'd had the rubbish and old furniture from the last owner carted away, it started to take shape. The plaster was damaged and rotten, but once that was stripped out and the carpets were lifted there was this amazing space. It seemed somehow wrong to cover it all up.'

'Is that what they call *arrested decay*?'

Jamie shrugged. 'Not entirely. I removed the worst of the decay, rather than arresting it. I wouldn't like to say what you'd call this.'

So he wasn't even going to give it a name. Anna could see how that was Jamie's version of therapy, a break from the exacting work that he did. Or maybe in its own way it was another version of his work. Knowing where he wanted to be, and letting the journey define itself.

'Isn't it a bit lonely here sometimes?' Anna bit her tongue. It *was* a large house for just one person, but then Jamie had probably never intended to be alone here.

'Being on my own wasn't in the plan.'

'Sorry. I didn't mean to…you know.'

'That's okay. It happened. Things aren't what I expected but I'm lucky in lots of ways. Whenever I feel the urge to fill the house with kids, I just give Caroline a call. She's generally got a few I can borrow.'

So he'd wanted children. Of course he had. He was so good with his nephews and niece and they obviously thought the world of their Uncle Jamie. It was a sobering reminder that getting too close to him would only lead to heartbreak.

'You never wanted to settle down?'

'I'm settled. I have a flat and a career.' Anna deliberately avoided the obvious intent of his question.

'Yeah.' He started to walk slowly away from the house again.

Perhaps she'd been a bit short with him. There was no reason why she shouldn't give him the basic facts.

'I was married six years ago, but it didn't take. We split up after a year.'

'I'm sorry to hear that.'

'It's okay. We never really should have been together. We wanted different things.' Anna and Daniel had actually wanted exactly the same things. They'd both wanted children, and even though he'd promised that he would be happy with their family of two, he'd changed his mind.

'It changes your view of things, though, doesn't it? You think you're going in one direction and suddenly you find you're not.' Jamie was looking at her thoughtfully.

'Yes, it does. But that's in the past now. I love my job, and most of my energy goes into that.'

He didn't answer. Maybe he didn't believe her, the married-to-my-job thing hadn't sounded totally convincing. But Anna had said all she was going to say, and thankfully he left it alone.

'Would you like to see the beehives?' They were wandering further and further from the house.

'You have beehives? How much land do you have here?'

Jamie pointed to a line of trees in the distance. 'It goes down to there. We planted an orchard, and this year I'll have some apples. There are bees and a wildflower meadow, and…you see down in that dip?'

Anna followed the direction of his pointing finger. 'Marshlands?'

'It's more a small dip that collects water at the moment. But I'm hoping it'll grow and encourage some wildlife.'

'How do you do all this?' Even Jamie's voracious appetite for work wasn't equal to what had been done here.

'I have help. A couple of the lads from the youth club that the charity runs couldn't get jobs when they left school. They decided to do something for themselves and started a gardening business. I advised them on some of the practicalities and got them onto a course, and then became their first customer.'

'They've done well.' Anna might have guessed that Jamie's nurturing of the land would also extend to nurturing the talents of his young charges.

Jamie chuckled. 'They made up in enthusiasm for what they lacked in experience at first, and we had our share of disasters. But they got things together, and they've got a nice little business going now. They spend a day a week here, and pretend not to mind when I interfere, so it works pretty well.'

'I'd like to see the orchard.'

'No appetite for bees?' He grinned at her.

'They get a bit bad-tempered in the autumn, don't they? I'm not sure I want to be stung.'

Jamie chuckled, turning onto a path that led to the left. '*My* bees are very good mannered. But since you prefer apples, the orchard's this way.'

He led her towards a collection of young trees, planted far enough apart to allow for more growth. Jamie pointed out the different varieties, some for cooking and some for eating.

'That one looks about ready.' He pointed up at a red apple in the branches above Anna's head. 'Want to try it?'

'I'd love to, thanks…' Anna reached up, and even when she stood on her toes her fingertips didn't quite make contact. 'Can you reach it?'

'They taste better when you've picked them yourself, straight from the tree.' Jamie hesitated and then held out his hand. 'You want a boost?'

The apple was hanging right above her head, just begging to be picked. 'Um…yes, okay.'

She felt his hands around her waist and he lifted her against him. Anna curled her arms protectively over her chest, feeling her own body stiffen. The thick layers of clothing between them didn't seem to be doing anything to mitigate the effect of being so close to Jamie.

'Um… It would help if you hung on…' Anna could hear the strain in his voice. She was dead weight in his arms, and Jamie was clearly struggling a bit to support her.

'Sorry…' Winding her legs around his waist was easier than she'd thought. More natural. And when she clung to his shoulder with one hand, it seemed almost the proper thing to do.

'That's better.' He balanced himself and Anna suddenly felt safe and strong. She reached for the apple, turning it in her hand.

'Oh. This one has a hole in it.'

'Pick it anyway, it can be used for cooking. What about that one…?'

The apple that hung a little higher was ruby red and perfect. When she bent it upwards, the stalk separated from the branch easily, a sure sign that it was ready to harvest.

'Got it.'

He let her down carefully. When her feet hit the ground again it was almost a disappointment to have to step away from him. Anna inspected the apple carefully for any holes or damage.

'Now close your eyes.' Jamie's lips curved. It was

the kind of smile that no woman in her right mind would want to miss a moment of, but Anna closed her eyes, sinking her teeth into the apple.

It tasted fresh and sweet. So much more like a real apple than the ones she bought in the supermarket.

'This is gorgeous. You want a taste…?' She opened her eyes.

He nodded, his eyes darkening suddenly. Moss green, and glistening with a desire that provoked an immediate response in Anna's chest. Suddenly she forgot all about the apple.

When she stepped towards him, his hand touched the waist of her jacket. So softly that she didn't even feel it. She wanted very badly to feel everything about his embrace, and everything that told her she shouldn't was shattered beneath the weight of expectation of his touch.

She had to move. Either forward or back. Forward was the only way that seemed clear at the moment. Anna reached up, allowing her fingertips to brush his cheek.

It was a sweet, slow give and take. Staring into each other's eyes, watching for the response to each new action. The increasing pressure of his hand on her waist. Anna laid her hand on his shoulder and they were almost in an embrace. One that she wanted so very much. She stood on her toes, kissing his cheek lightly, and felt him pull her a little closer.

This was delicious, but it could end at any moment. He could decide that he'd misinterpreted all the signs, or that he needed something more definite and draw back.

'I want to kiss you.'

Jamie smiled. 'I'd love to kiss you back.'

That was that, then. Still he didn't move, waiting for her to take things at whatever pace she wanted. Head-spinningly fast seemed like a wonderful option. Anna stood on her toes, kissing his lips.

She tasted apple-sweet and dew-fresh. When he drew her a little closer, Jamie felt her arms tighten around his neck, pulling him down. In a moment of sheer exhilaration he realised that she wanted this just as much as he did.

He couldn't conceal his hunger. When he kissed her again, she responded and Jamie felt his whole body harden. She was so soft and yet so strong.

'Did I forget to tell you how beautiful—?'

She stopped his words with another kiss.

'Yes, you forgot. You mentioned that my hair was coming loose from my ponytail the other day.'

'Ignore me. I'm a complete and utter jerk.' One who noticed everything about Anna. One who'd been dreaming of this moment for far too long, and telling himself it mustn't happen.

'You're forgiven. After all, this isn't really in your plan, is it?'

A sudden dose of honesty that jerked him back to his senses. 'No, it's not.'

'That's okay. We both have a little baggage.'

So there *was* more to it than she'd said. Jamie had suspected that was the case—no one got married and divorced within a year without a few scars to show for it.

'Both of us?'

'There's no story to tell, if that's what you mean.'

'Everyone's got a story. But if you don't want to talk about it, that's fine.'

'Okay. I don't want to talk about it.' She looked up at him, and Jamie suddenly forgot everything other than the pale blue of her eyes. 'But since we both seem to have settled on the same eventual outcome, then I guess a diversion doesn't matter.'

'*You* are never a diversion.' *That* mattered. That Anna knew how important she was to him, and that this had meant something.

She smiled up at him. 'Thank you. In that case, you can kiss me again.'

He didn't need to be told a second time. If this was the only thing that he could share with Anna, then he wanted it to matter. Jamie kissed her, feeling her move against him, her arms tightening again around his neck.

He'd found another side of Anna. She was passionate and giving and yet she knew how to end things. She made him feel that this hadn't been one big mistake, a lapse of self-control that should be forgotten as soon as possible. No apologies and no regrets. Just an understanding that they should stop before it led somewhere that neither of them was ready to go.

Jamie's head was fine with that. His heart would follow if he repeated the words enough times, but right now it didn't know how to beat without taking up her rhythm. Without thrilling at her smile as they collected cooking apples that had fallen from the low cordons at one end of the orchard, filling their pockets with them.

'Apple and blackberry?' They'd started on their way back to the house, and Anna stopped by the bushes. Jamie nodded, cupping his hands to receive the blackberries as she picked them.

'We'll give them to Caroline. She can use them for a pie tomorrow.'

Anna nodded, popping a blackberry into her mouth. 'Mmm… They're sweet. Try one.'

She laughed as he shrugged, his hands too full to comply. Anna made a show of searching amongst the branches, curved and heavy with fruit, until she found a large blackberry.

'This one looks nice.' She popped it into his mouth, and Jamie smiled.

'Yeah. That's the best one.'

'Hold on a minute…' She raised her juice-stained fingers to his mouth, and he felt her wipe away a smudge. 'That's better.'

He could do this for the rest of the morning, and the better part of the afternoon as well. Then he could sit by the fire with Anna, maybe roasting a few chestnuts as the evening closed in around them. But he had guests and it was about time he made a start on lunch, even if it was just a matter of putting the lasagne he'd made into the oven and taking the salad out of the fridge.

'We'd better go back. You have important work to do today.' Anna was smiling up at him.

'Yeah. Though to be honest, I'd rather be here…'

'I know. But this is an opportunity that you can't miss.'

His family, together again. It was something that Jamie wanted, even though it was hard. Out here he could forget about the anger that was never too far from the surface every time he saw Jon. Anna seemed to know, and she turned without another word, leading the way back to the house.

CHAPTER EIGHT

THE DAY WAS going well. They'd had lunch, and then Jessica and the twins had gone out into the garden. Jamie had lit the fire in the sitting room, leaving Jon to doze in front of it, and when Caroline had chased him out of the kitchen, he'd meandered out into the garden to see what the children were up to.

'He's great with the kids.' Caroline had reached the end of a long succession of plates and pans, and picked up a teacloth to help Anna with the drying up. 'It's a shame…'

'That he doesn't have any of his own?' Anna tried to clear the lump that was forming in her throat.

'Yes. I can't blame him for being cautious, not after what happened with Gill. He'd be happier if he could leave that behind, though.'

'Maybe he can. He and Jon seem to be patching things up.'

'You think so?' Caroline didn't look convinced.

'I don't really know. They seem…'

'Polite. They're mostly polite with each other. Apart from when Jon's baiting Jamie, and Jamie's trying not to notice.'

Anna sighed. 'Yes. But it's a start.'

Joshua was starting to fret a little in his baby bouncer, and Caroline picked him up. Anna made a face at him, and he chuckled.

'Will you hold him while I put everything away?' Joshua was reaching for Anna, and Caroline put him into her arms. She sat down at the kitchen table, and the little boy started to grab at her hair.

'He has green eyes!' The resemblance to Jamie took her breath away.

Caroline laughed. 'Yes, it's not fair, is it? I got stuck with muddy brown in the genetic lottery, and now my son has gorgeous green eyes. I thought they might get darker as he gets older, but my mum said that Jamie and Jon's were exactly the same, so I'm keeping my fingers crossed.'

Anna hugged the little boy and he gurgled happily, clutching at her sweater. This was as close as she'd ever get to knowing what it would be like to hold Jamie's child, and even though it hurt she couldn't let him go. She felt a tear roll down her cheek, and brushed it away before Caroline could see it.

'He's so precious…' She heard her voice falter as she said the words.

'You're reckoning on having some of your own?' Caroline lifted a pile of plates into one of the cupboards and then grinned over her shoulder.

If only. If she could give Jamie a green-eyed, happy little boy like this, Anna would have let things between them go much further. She'd have hung in there and shown him that the heartbreak they'd both suffered was in the past and could be turned around. But that was all wishful thinking.

'I don't know. I'm pretty busy with my career.' Anna shrugged trying to shift the pain in her chest.

'The two aren't necessarily mutually exclusive. I've put things on hold a bit workwise, but I still work two days a week. It keeps me relatively sane.'

'What do you do?' Changing the subject from babies to Caroline's job would be good right now.

'I'm a midwife. Harry and I decided that Joshua would be our last. I wouldn't mind more, but there's the small matter of raising them to contend with. We have our hands full as it is—people say that twins are more than twice the work, and it's true...'

Caroline was talking still, but the words seemed to fade into background noise. Anna had come to terms with her inability to have children, and after Daniel had left her she'd pulled herself together and got her life back on track. She should forget all about things that she couldn't do and concentrate on the ones she could. But the child in her lap was making that very difficult.

Caroline walked over to the window, looking outside. 'The kids are amusing themselves out there so let's have some coffee, eh?'

'Oh. Yes, that would be nice.' Perhaps she could give Joshua back to his mother and the terrible, instinctive tug would begin to subside.

'Where's Jamie, I wonder? He might want...'

Caroline fell silent as voices from the sitting room floated through into the kitchen. They were getting louder.

'You just walked away, Jamie!'

'Oh. Right. And that made it all okay, did it? Sleeping with my fiancée was obviously the only response possible to my career choices.'

'Oh, no! Just when I thought things were going so well…' Caroline wailed, her hand flying to her mouth.

This didn't sound good. The two women ignored Joshua's innocent babble, straining to hear.

'I needed you. We had a dream, and you turned your back on it.'

'You had a dream, Jon. It was all about you. It always is.'

A thud sounded from the sitting room as if something had been thrown. Caroline jumped, tears beginning to roll down her cheeks. She must have been dreading this.

Anna stood, putting Joshua into his mother's arms. 'I'm going to stop this.'

'How?'

'I've no idea…' All she knew was that she had to. For Jamie's sake. She marched into the sitting room and saw the two of them on their feet, each trying to stare the other down. The book that had been sitting on the coffee table, next to Jon's chair, was lying upended in the grate.

'Stop it!'

Jamie flinched at the sound of her voice, taking a step back, but Jon flailed his arms towards his brother.

'That's right. Play the injured party, why don't you…'

'I said stop it.' Anna pushed between them, feeling Jamie's hand on her shoulder, gently trying to move her out of the way. She shook it off, facing Jon. 'Sit *down*, Jon.'

'Why me?' Jon growled at her and she felt Jamie trying to move her away again.

'Both of you. Back off and sit down.'

For a moment there was silence. Then Jon turned and sat down. Jamie backed away too, sitting down in a chair on the other side of the fireplace. Anna took a deep breath.

'You should both be ashamed of yourselves. If you want to shout then you can do it out of earshot of Caroline and the children. Don't you think they've suffered enough?'

Jamie's face, set in an expression of anger and stress, softened a little. 'I'm sorry. I'll go and see if they're okay—'

'You aren't going anywhere, Jamie. I'm not finished with either of you yet. What's all this about?'

'He—' Anna silenced Jon with a wave of her hand.

'No, Jon. You both need to stop blaming each other and start taking responsibility for your own actions.'

Jon stared at her, clearly not comprehending her meaning. But Jamie knew, she could see it in his face. If he could just lead the way, maybe Jon would follow. Maybe they could turn this into progress.

Rage. Jon had been baiting him, and he'd lost control of his temper. And then shock when Anna had pushed herself in between him and Jon. Now Jamie felt ashamed of himself for destroying the fragile peace that had been carefully brokered between him and his brother.

But Anna wasn't going to take shame. She wouldn't take apologies or excuses, or promises to keep his cool in the future. She wanted more than that, and there was no denying her. It occurred to Jamie that she was very beautiful when angry, but he dismissed the thought. Anna didn't want to hear that either. She was standing, her arms folded, waiting for someone to say something, and he knew exactly what he had to do.

'When we were kids…you remember, Jon, how you used to help me with my written work?'

'I remember.' Jon glared at him sullenly.

'I never thought I'd be able to cope with medical school. But you gave me the confidence, you told me that I could do anything.'

'I meant…' Jon puffed out a breath. 'I meant *we* could do anything. We could write songs and perform them. We were going to take the world by storm…'

'All right.' Jon's voice had started to rise, and Anna shot him a warning look. 'Were you good?'

'They were very good.' Tension still hung heavily in the air, and Caroline's voice made Jamie jump. She was standing in the doorway, holding Joshua in her arms.

'You were just a kid.' Jon pursed his lips, but his tone was quieter now, more measured.

'We *were* good together, Jon.' This felt like an admission. Jamie realised that he'd never really voiced it before. He'd been so determined that he wanted to be a doctor that he hadn't allowed himself to even think it.

'So why did you break up the partnership? You could have been famous. It sounds like a nice life to me.' Anna allowed herself a smile.

Jamie shrugged. 'I just felt… I suppose that music was something I did. A doctor is what I am.'

'And you explained that to Jon? After everything he'd done to help you?'

Jamie felt himself redden. 'No, I don't think I did. I'm sorry.'

Anna turned her gaze onto Jon. Jamie felt a prickle

of sympathy for his brother because he'd just been subjected to that look and he hadn't been able to resist it.

'Music is what *I* am. I wanted it to be what you were too, but…' Jon shrugged. 'I guess that's life. We don't always get to choose.'

'It sounds as if you resented the way that what each of you wanted led you in different directions.' Anna spoke gently.

Jon let out a grim laugh. 'He wasn't so much fun. I got the band together and we sang "Everywhere"… It was *his* song, but half the time he was too wrapped up in his books to even notice.'

'I noticed. I was really proud of you. I thought it all went to your head a bit, though.'

'A bit? Trust me, when you're nineteen years old, and you're standing in front of thousands of people all shouting your name, it goes to your head. It loses its charm a bit after a while, though. Everyone seems to want a piece of you.'

Jon had never spoken of this before. Or maybe Jamie had just never listened. 'I should have been there for you more over the years.'

'You had your own gig. Your studies and then that charity of yours… I hear it does a lot of good things.'

There was one more thing that Jamie had to do. He got slowly to his feet, flashing a glance at Anna, and she nodded him on.

'You helped me overcome my dyslexia, and gave me the confidence to chase my dreams, Jon. The charity's just a way of passing that down.' Jamie held his hand out to his brother. It was no longer a struggle, he really meant it this time.

The handshake turned into a hug. He heard Caroline's squeal of delight, and she rushed over and kissed both of them. When Jamie turned, looking for Anna, she'd flopped back onto the sofa, as if the effort of this had been too much for her. But she was smiling.

'I've brought you both something.' Caroline delivered baby Joshua into Jon's arms and hurried out into the hallway. When she reappeared, she was holding the battered box that contained memories that had seemed lost for ever a moment ago.

'You brought the games!' Jon smiled suddenly.

'It's been a long time since we all played.' Caroline started to unload the board games onto the table. 'I thought we might give it a go. If you'd like to.'

'It sounds like a great idea. I'll make some tea, and fetch the kids in from the garden, shall I?' Jamie volunteered.

There was one thing more that he needed to do before any of that. His gaze found Anna's and she rose, following him into the kitchen.

'Hey. Thank you.' Taking her hand seemed acceptable, and when he did she smiled up at him.

'Are you good with this? Really?'

She'd seen through the pretence and had known that his initial reconciliation with Jon was what Jamie knew he must do, rather than something he felt in his heart. This, more recent, one went a lot deeper.

'I'm good. I mean it this time.' Jamie heaved a sigh. 'All that you said, about taking responsibility for our own actions, telling each other how we felt... I knew that. It's what I tell the families I work with...'

'It's easy to say. Harder to put into practice when you have all the emotion to deal with as well.'

'Are you letting me off lightly? That's not like you.'

She rolled her eyes. 'No. You still don't get any free passes from me. There's a lot of work to do still.'

There was. He and Jon hadn't even got to the point of discussing what had happened at Christmas three years ago. But this was a start. Jamie was beginning to see that it wasn't just an isolated incident but that the resentment had been brewing for years.

Suddenly she stretched out her arms in an invitation that he took straight away. Her hug was comforting and yet sexy all at the same time, and everything he needed right now.

'You can be a bit scary when you want to be.'

He heard her laugh against his chest. 'I can be *very* scary. Don't you forget it.'

'No, ma'am.'

'And I could *really* do with a cup of tea.' Anna looked up at him, mischief in her eyes. 'So you can leave the talking for another time and get on and make me one.'

Caroline's idea of board games was a hit with everyone. The older twins, Jamie and Jon, each paired up with one of the younger ones and faced each other across the board with mock scowls. Jessica added a more ladylike note to the proceedings and sat next to Anna, discussing their next moves in a whisper behind her hand. Baby Joshua sat on his mother's knee, keeping his strategies to himself but holding up his arms, babbling with glee along with everyone else, when someone made a killer move.

A family. One that was weathering a storm but who were all focussed on the same thing. Love had held them together, and maybe it would bring them safely home. For now, Anna was a part of that, but it wouldn't last. She shouldn't get too comfortable here, and she definitely shouldn't think about the green eyes of baby Joshua or his uncle Jamie.

When Caroline packed Jon and all the children into her SUV and drove away, the house seemed suddenly quiet. The plan had been that Jamie would take her to the station so that she could go back to London tonight, but he walked straight past their coats, hanging in the hallway, and stood by the hearth in the sitting room, staring at the glowing coals.

'It feels as if it's been a long day.' Anna was searching for something to say to break the silence.

'Yes, it does.'

'So what are you up to tomorrow?'

He looked up at her, smiling suddenly. 'I have the Hastings Hustlers first thing tomorrow. We're a multi-disciplinary team, but at the moment we're concentrating on basketball.'

'What else do you do?'

'Anything that takes our fancy. We make a mean baseball team, and we play football as well. And tennis. A couple of the girls do gymnastics and we have a chess player too.'

'And they're all Hastings Hustlers?'

'I got the sweatshirts. It seemed a shame to waste them.' Jamie paused for a moment, letting the silence hang between them. 'Would you like to come along? You could meet some of the kids and see something of what we do.'

'I'd love to. Another time perhaps. I'm not sure I

can get back down to Hastings for first thing tomorrow morning.'

'You could stay over. You have jeans and trainers and that's all you need to join in. My guest room has plaster on the walls, a proper carpet and all the furniture matches.'

That was a disappointment. Going to sleep in one of the characterful rooms that reflected Jamie's taste would have been nice. But Anna suspected the real piece of information he'd been intending to convey was *guest room*.

'And you get a team sweatshirt. But only if you play.' He shot her a look that was beyond tempting.

'What colour sweatshirt?' Decorum dictated that she should pretend that the idea wasn't one that demanded an immediate *yes*.

'Red. Only I don't think we have any of those at the moment. Orange, yellow, green, blue, black or violet.'

'No indigo?'

He grinned. Jamie knew that her assent to the plan was only a matter of time. 'Have you tried getting an indigo sweatshirt printed? Black was the closest they could do.'

'Hmm. Violet might be nice. As long as it's not really purple.'

'You can decide for yourself. And I'll stand you lunch afterwards. You can throw some things into the washing machine tonight and they'll be clean for the morning.'

'You know how to tempt a girl, don't you?' This was suddenly so easy. Jamie had staked out the boundaries, and she knew exactly where she stood. A kiss didn't mean that they couldn't just be friends, however explosive it had felt at the time.

'You want temptation? Wait till you see the sweatshirts.'

He led her through the kitchen and into a large office, which caught the best of the early evening sun. It was decorated in the same eclectic style as the sitting room, although a large colour-coded wall planner gave a more businesslike feel. A chrome-legged, fifties-style desk with a shiny red top provided a splash of colour and the sleek computer equipment and shelving contrasted with bare brick walls and a wooden door, knotted and scarred with age. Storage boxes were stacked up against the wall, and Jamie heaved a couple of them to one side, opening them.

'There you go. Pick whichever one you like.'

Anna sorted through the plastic-wrapped sweatshirts. The violet was nice, and she pulled a pile out, sorting through the sizes, which ran from five-to-seven years to extra-large. 'This one will fit.'

'You can't take it out of the bag until you promise to play.' A smile hovered around his lips. Anna tore the plastic, unfolding the sweatshirt and holding it up against herself.

CHAPTER NINE

ANNA WOKE IN a comfortable bed, early morning sunshine filtering through the windows. Unlike her flat in London, the house wasn't overlooked, and she'd left the curtains open, welcoming the glimmer of a harvest moon slanting across the cream-painted walls. Waking at dawn brought the sound of birdsong and not traffic.

The quiet created a sense of peace that the ever-present sounds of the city couldn't reproduce. She'd discovered last night that Jamie didn't own a TV, and they'd sat by the fireside, roasting chestnuts and talking. London was his inspiration, full of the clamour of every different kind of professional and cultural stimulus, but his heart was here.

Her clothes and the new sweatshirt were folded neatly on a chair. Anna gave her T-shirt a shake, deciding that the creases from the washer/dryer would have to fall out with wear, and made for the en suite bathroom.

She found him in the kitchen, wearing a dark green Hastings Hustlers sweatshirt, the white lettering on the back beginning to crack from having been washed and worn.

'Morning. Did you sleep well?'

'Yes, thanks.' Curled up in the bed, wearing borrowed sweatpants and a T-shirt that somehow bore his scent even though they were fresh out of the washing machine. Maybe that had been just in her dreams. There was only one thing that would have been better, and that was on the other side of the boundaries they'd set.

'I've got eggs, bacon, toast... Um, coffee, bananas, peanut butter...'

'Sounds great. Everything but the peanut butter. I'll take the banana for later.'

He gave her a smiling nod. 'I was rather hoping you wouldn't go for a sliver of toast with a dash of low-calorie marmalade. Not that I *have* any low-calorie marmalade.'

'You have regular marmalade, though?'

'I have honey. The bread's from a local bakery and the eggs and bacon are from the farm shop.' He smiled. 'They could probably tell you the name of the hen that laid the egg, but that's a little too personal for my taste. I have absolutely no idea who grew the banana.'

'Sounds delicious.'

An hour later, after a leisurely breakfast that tasted of the countryside instead of the supermarket, they were on the road. Jamie drove into the centre of Hastings, parking the car on the edge of a small park, where a line of basketball courts was currently filled with kids in Hastings Hustlers sweatshirts.

Two older boys were already practising, hotly contesting possession of the ball. There were girls and boys of all ages, and Anna wondered how that was all going to work when it came to picking teams. Jamie

seemed satisfied with the turnout, though, and when
he got out of the car and they walked over to the basketball courts, everyone crowded around.

'This is Anna, everyone.' A chorus of *hellos* followed and Anna gave a smile and a small wave. 'Shall
we pick teams?'

Everyone knew what to do. The two older boys were
the team captains and everyone else lined up in order
of size. Jamie settled an argument between two girls
about who was taller than the other, and then went
down the line, dividing everyone up into two teams. He
produced a printed chart from his pocket, and started
to note down who was playing where.

Callum appeared from the crush, taking off one of
his fingerless gloves and displaying the back of his
hand. A few black lines still remained and the skin
looked a little red, but the letters and shapes of the tattoos could no longer be made out. Anna smiled at him.

'That's looking great, Callum. You've obviously
been taking good care of it.'

'Yeah. Can we do some more now?'

Anna laughed. 'When the inflammation's gone right
down. We'll book an appointment soon.'

'Great.' Callum turned to Jamie. 'Shall I go with
Freddie?'

'Yep, that would be great.' Jamie turned his attention back to the chart, while Callum sauntered over
to a young boy in a wheelchair, who was sitting on
one side. The two exchanged a high-five and Callum
pushed the wheelchair onto the court.

'Callum with *two* "l"s.' A girl of around seventeen
with orange hair and a matching sweatshirt was looking over Jamie's shoulder.

'Ah. Yes.' Jamie squinted at the chart and then passed it over to the girl. 'Do me a favour, Jen…'

The girl nodded, and took over, writing everyone's names in the positions that Jamie assigned to them. Jamie clearly didn't mind asking for help here, and Anna guessed that it was all part of the culture amongst the group. Everyone helped everyone else.

'You said I could play…' She tugged at Jamie's sleeve, and he turned, smiling.

'I didn't forget. We're going to have a throw-around first, though. You might like to sit that out, to get an idea of the rules.'

Something told her that the rules probably weren't in any book. Anna nodded, walking over to one of the benches by the side of the court as the teams took up their positions. A middling-sized boy in glasses blew the whistle that hung around his neck, and play started.

It didn't make a lot of sense to Anna. The team captains were engaged in their own private tussle for the ball, but when it was passed to a younger child, they stood back. There was a group of mothers standing on the other side of the court, and Anna wondered whether she might go and introduce herself and ask for an explanation.

'Hi. I'm Jen.' The girl with the orange hair had made a beeline for where she was sitting, and sat down next to her. On the other side they were joined by a girl with heavy black make-up around her eyes, dyed black hair and a black sweatshirt.

'Hi, I'm Anna.'

'Yes, we know. That's Spark.' Jen gestured towards her companion. The two girls were sitting close on either side of her, and Anna had the feeling that she'd been ambushed. Maybe they were the two head girls in the group, and had decided to let her know about it.

'You came with Jamie?' Spark fixed her with a not-too-welcoming look.

'Yes, I work with him.'

'In London?' This time Jen asked the question.

'Yes, that's right.'

The two girls exchanged looks. Clearly this *was* an ambush of some kind.

'You're going out with him?' Jen asked.

Spark gave a knowing nod. 'Out here on a Sunday morning? They're going out.'

'No, we're just friends.'

Jen flashed her a disbelieving look. 'Okay, if that's the way you want it. Just friends.'

How did you explain the difference between pretending you were just friends and *being* just friends? Jen and Spark had clearly decided the question between themselves, and Anna had to admit that Spark had a point. Being here this early on a Sunday morning did raise a few questions about the nature of her relationship with Jamie.

She wondered what Jamie would have wanted her to say, and the answer came straight away. Be honest. Anna took a breath.

'You know, the kind of just friends where you're really going out together but you don't want anyone to know.'

Jen's lips curved in an expression of triumph. 'Yeah, we know.'

'Well, Jamie and I aren't that kind of just friends. We're really just friends.'

'Oh.' Jen gave her a searching look and Anna returned her gaze. Clearly that convinced her and she nodded. 'Well, we just thought…'

'And you decided to look me over?' Anna smiled. That was okay. It was actually quite nice that the girls cared enough to do it, however challenging they seemed.

'We didn't much like the other one, did we?' Spark wrinkled her nose.

Jen shook her head. 'Nah. She turned out to be a nasty piece of work.'

'He never gave her a sweatshirt.'

'Just as well. She didn't play… And after what she did, I'd have ripped it off her back.' Jen's lip curled.

'You and whose army?' Spark gave her friend a dismissive look. 'You were going to get on a plane and find her, were you?'

'Wait…' Anna shouldn't interfere, but she wanted to know. 'You know what happened?'

'Yeah, 'course we do.' Spark rolled her eyes. 'She went off with his brother. Jamie looked proper sorry for himself for a while.'

'He told you about it?'

'No, we saw pictures of them on the internet. Jamie didn't say anything.' Jen wrinkled her nose. 'We made him fairy cakes.'

'Oh. Well, it was nice of you to go to the trouble…'

'We *bought* the cakes,' Spark corrected her friend. 'Then we iced them. I put black icing and a skull and crossbones on mine. He didn't want to talk about it, but I reckon he got the message.'

'Yes, I expect he did.' Anna wasn't so sure, but the girls meant well. 'I'm sure it cheered him up.'

The ref's whistle sounded, and she looked up at the

players. Jamie had turned towards the bench, and he frowned suddenly. 'Hey. Spark, Jen, aren't you playing?' Clearly he recognised an ambush when he saw one.

'Nah, we're explaining to the rules to your *friend.*' Jen's words didn't seem to reassure him at all and he shot Anna a questioning look.

'We won't be a minute. I think I'm getting the hang of this,' Anna called across to him, and he nodded, turning back to the other players.

'So what *are* the rules, then?'

Jen grinned. Clearly Anna had proved herself with the girls. 'You can only try and get the ball if the person who's already got it is the same size as you. You can pass it to someone who's bigger or smaller, but you can't take it from anyone smaller than you.'

Anna frowned. 'Doesn't that mean that those two bigger boys just hog the ball to themselves, though?'

Spark shook her head. 'You *have* to pass the ball, and you get extra points depending on who you pass it to. Don't worry about that, the ref works it out. Just don't throw the ball to Jamie or the team captains and you'll be fine. Everyone else is smaller than you.'

'Ah. I see. I think...' Anna watched as the teams started playing again. It was all making a bit more sense now.

'You'll get the hang of it.' Jen stood up. 'You wanna play?'

'Yes, thank you. I'd like to very much.' If Anna could survive Jen and Spark's interrogation tactics, she reckoned that the Hastings Hustlers basketball rules would be a breeze.

* * *

Jamie had shot her another querying glance when she walked onto the court with Jen and Spark, and she'd ignored it. Anna was beginning to enjoy herself. It was just a matter of passing the ball to as many different players as possible, so that the little kids could catch it and play too. Easy.

A howl went up as a little boy ran across to Jamie, clutching the ball to his chest, and threw it up towards him. Jamie hadn't touched the ball yet, preferring to run up and down and encourage the others, but the ref's whistle sounded in a signal that everyone should back off and give him a turn.

'No-o-o-o!' Jen's shout echoed across the court, and when Anna looked round she saw both Jen and Spark flapping their arms in her direction. 'Get him!'

Fair enough. Anna ran towards Jamie, and he deftly avoided her. She ducked under his arm, turning to block his path, and saw him smile. He was quick, and his reach was longer than hers, but she was quicker...

She managed to tip the ball from his grasp, but after a few bounces he got it back. She heard Jen and Spark howling with disappointment and redoubled her efforts. Finally she managed to get the ball and break free of him, bouncing the ball as she ran madly for the hoop.

Just as she slowed, ready to take her shot, he caught her, lifting her up off the ground and over his shoulder. Anna kept a tight hold on the ball as he walked back towards the other end of the court. The ref's whistle peeped frenetically, and Jamie ignored it.

'Cheat!'

She managed to get the word out through clenched

teeth. Jamie was holding her tightly, and she resisted the temptation to kick him. Any minute now she was going to drop the ball and slide down into his arms, and that wouldn't do. Particularly after she'd just been at such pains to make it crystal clear what kind of *just friends* they were.

He reached the other end of the court and put her down, his green eyes full of mischief. The ref jogged up to him, and he backed off, grinning, as the boy waved his arms.

'Penalty!' The ref clearly took his responsibilities very seriously. 'And you're benched, Jamie. Ten minutes.'

Jamie took his punishment without question. Anna only just heard his murmured words as he walked past her.

'It was worth it.'

'Watch this.' Anna pulled a face at him, walking back to the other end of the court. She stopped well short of the place where he'd picked her up, in a spot behind the three-point line. Gauging the distance carefully, she reckoned she could make it. Jamie was sitting on one of the park benches now, shaking his head and motioning her closer to the hoop.

Everyone was watching to see what she'd do. Whether she could make the shot. Anna looked round and saw Spark, who gave her a thumbs-up sign. That was it. She *had* to make the shot now.

There was silence as the ball arced through the air. And then a howl of applause from both teams as it bounced against the backboard and through the hoop. Jen and Spark both careened towards her, hugging her and slapping her on the back.

'You trashed him...' Jen gestured towards Jamie, who was on his feet, applauding with all the others, seemingly unaware of his complete humiliation. The ref peeped his whistle, motioning everyone back to their places.

She was on the team now.

'So what were Spark and Jen saying to you?' Jamie had a feeling that the two girls had been doing a little more than just explaining the rules to Anna. The two of them could be difficult at times, but Anna had seemed to take it all in her stride.

'Oh, just girl talk.' She climbed into his car, smiling at him.

Heaven help him. Anna was ferocious enough on her own, and Jamie wasn't quite sure how to view a potential alliance between her and the girls.

'That was a hell of a shot.'

Anna grinned at him. 'Wasn't it exactly what you wanted me to do?'

Maybe not quite. The Hastings Hustlers were a tight-knit group, and while they welcomed other teens in their number they could be wary of adults, who they saw as authority figures. He'd reckoned a little outrageous cheating might break the ice and get them on Anna's side, and it had. But she'd outdone him.

'It didn't occur to me you were a basketball aficionado.'

'I played a lot of netball at school and it's not so different.' Anna grinned at him. 'And the ref did a pretty good job of putting you in your place.'

Jamie chuckled. 'Yeah, Andrew's a good kid. He's our chess player and he doesn't much like running around with a ball, but he's a great referee. Very impartial and he knows all the rules by heart.'

He leaned forward, twisting the key in the ignition. 'What do you fancy for lunch? There's a great fish and chip restaurant down by the promenade.'

'Sounds good. I'm hungry.'

The fish and chip restaurant had a fifties vibe, with shining chrome, tiled walls and red leather seats. They found a table by the window, and a waitress with a check apron came to take their order, putting a carousel with red sauce, brown sauce, salt, vinegar and cutlery down onto the table.

Anna was staring out at the iron-grey sky, which merged into an iron-grey sea. It was starting to rain, and people were hurrying past, anxious to get out of the biting wind.

'So you got on pretty well with Jen and Spark.' What Jamie *really* wanted to know was what the girls had been saying to Anna, but that had already been asked and answered.

'You just can't let it alone, can you?' She grinned at him.

'I'm just…' Jamie shrugged. He was actually just being protective, but Anna wouldn't like that. 'Just curious. They have their own agenda sometimes.'

'Oh, they definitely had an agenda. They'd decided that I was your girlfriend and that they'd give me a once-over to make sure I was good enough for you.'

Jamie winced. 'Ouch. Sorry…'

'That's okay. I thought it was rather sweet of them.' She paused, drawing circles with her finger on the tablecloth. 'Did you realise that they knew about what happened when you broke up with your fiancée?'

'What! No.' Jamie felt the hairs on the back of his neck suddenly spring to attention. 'I never mentioned it. I didn't want anyone to know.'

'Well, they're teenagers. They know how to use the internet. What Jon does and who he's with tends to get photographed and reported.' Anna's expression softened suddenly. 'And they said that you'd seemed upset about something.'

'And I thought I was doing so well.'

She shot him a look that made his heart melt. If he'd known Anna then, he'd never have been able to keep silent.

'No one can hide a broken heart. Particularly not from a bunch of kids. They see what's going on a lot better than adults do.'

'Yeah, I guess so. Especially *these* kids. A lot of them have good reason to be watchful, they've been let down by the people around them.'

He didn't dare ask what Spark and Jen had thought about it all. What Anna had thought. When she brushed her fingers against the back of his hand, he knew exactly what she thought. Anna was there for him in a way that he couldn't have expected.

'They said they bought you fairy cakes. They wanted to make you feel better.'

'Fairy cakes?' Jamie thought back. 'Oh, yes, I remember now. They had enough for the whole team, and they gave me a bag to take home with me. They had black icing...'

A lump rose suddenly in his throat. He'd felt so

alone then. If he'd just opened his eyes and seen, he'd have known that he hadn't been.

'There's nothing that says *Cheer up, we've got your back* quite like black icing and a skull and crossbones.' Anna grinned. 'I hope you got that message.'

'I suppose I did, in general terms. I remember thinking it was very nice of them, and that things couldn't be that bad after all.' A thought occurred to Jamie. 'They told you all this?'

'I generally find that when people ambush me for information it's because they're worried about something. If I tell them what they want to know, in plain and simple terms, then they respond to that and tell me what's bothering them. Jen and Spark think a lot of you, and they don't want to see you hurt again.'

Jamie was overwhelmed. No thought, just the feeling that there was so much he'd missed. So much he'd got wrong.

'I've been a fool, haven't I?'

Anna shook her head. 'I don't think so.'

The waitress arrived with their plates, and he took cutlery from the carousel, and then some tartare sauce to go with his fish. He watched as Anna shook the bottle of tomato sauce, dribbling some onto her plate, then dipping one of her chips into it. Everything she did was enchanting, and it seemed that she was all he had to hold onto.

'Great chips.' She gave him a smile that seemed achingly intimate. As if she knew all his secrets and she didn't judge him for them. She just wanted to eat chips with him on a wet, windy day and watch the sea.

'I think… I could have done a few things differently.'

'You're in good company. You, me and everyone

else on the planet.' She put another chip into her mouth, but she was watching him steadily.

'I could do a few things differently in the future, then.'

Anna smiled. 'That's a bit more to the point. The future's something we can change.'

'I've been thinking that the business with Jon and Gill was just one thing, and that it came out of the blue. It happened and I could keep it to myself, and control it.'

'And you've learned differently.'

'Well, clearly there were a few issues that had been brewing before that. And I wasn't in control, I couldn't just keep going without anyone noticing.' Jamie thought for a moment. 'Maybe I should mention that to my counsellor.'

'What, that you're not completely in control of everything?' Anna gave him a knowing look.

'I sat down with her last week, and outlined the way I expected it all to go.' He allowed himself a rueful smile. 'What the issues were, and how I was going to resolve them.'

'I'll bet she just loved that. Where's the job satisfaction in counselling someone who's already got everything worked out?' Anna was teasing now.

'Yeah, okay. Just don't stop giving me a hard time, will you?'

'Of course not. That's what friends are for, isn't it?'

Jamie nodded. Being friends with Anna was so much more than he'd dared hope. And suddenly he had an appetite for the food in front of him. He picked up his knife and fork and began to eat.

CHAPTER TEN

WHEN ANNA'S PHONE had beeped yesterday, she'd thought that Jamie had just sent a message wishing her a good Monday morning after a weekend that had been so full of different emotions. He *had* done so, but the purpose of contacting her had been something else entirely. Something she'd been dreading.

She knew that Jamie had taken an interest in the abandoned baby that had been brought to the hospital two weeks ago. So much so that the nurses on the paediatric ward had named the little boy *James*. Anna had visited him once more, but had then stayed away, knowing that this day was going to come.

It wasn't until she'd arrived at work on Tuesday morning that she realised she'd dressed for the occasion. A dark skirt and jacket with high heels wasn't her usual style as she preferred the more informal look of a bright top with trousers. But today the distance of formality was her only armour.

'Hi. You okay?' Jamie seemed much the same as always. Tall and broad, deliciously handsome, and seeming to notice everything about her. *That* wasn't what she wanted to think about either.

'Yes, fine.' Anna pressed her lips into a determined

line. 'I've got a pretty full schedule today, so...' Don't stop and talk. Just get it over with and leave.

'We'll make it quick, then. They're in one of the family rooms.' Jamie got the message, starting to walk purposefully towards the paediatric unit.

'Have they found the mother?' They stood alone in the lift together, and Anna couldn't help but ask.

'Yeah. She's very young and the social workers say that she wants to go ahead and have the baby adopted. Apparently everyone's in agreement that it'll be the best way forward for both mum and baby.'

Anna swallowed hard. 'So the couple we're seeing today...?'

'They're foster parents for the time being, but they've been on the adoption list for a while, waiting to be matched with a child. If everything goes to plan, and I'm sure it will, they'll adopt James.'

Anna thought she saw a hint of pride in his face. A baby named after him. That was what any man wanted, wasn't it? 'Do they like the name the nurses gave him?'

Jamie shrugged, and the lift doors opened. 'What's not to like about it?'

His version of hurrying was to give the smiling impression that he had all the time in the world but still get straight to the point. Anna was introduced to Marianne and Neil, and she sat down, trying not to notice the glow in both their faces as they looked at the baby in Marianne's arms.

'I understand you'd like to know what the operations for syndactyly are going to entail.'

'Yes.' Marianne tore her gaze from the baby, and nodded her head. 'Whatever it takes, we'll be there for him. We'd just like to know how we can best care for him.'

Anna nodded. 'Well, the good news is that there's no reason why his fingers shouldn't be separated successfully. It'll take some time, and I'd advise you to discuss all the options with your surgeon. There are a number of centres of excellence that specialise in syndactyly.'

Neil nodded, reaching across to stroke little James's hand with his finger. 'We've seen the list you sent, thank you. He's perfect as he is, but we know that surgery can give him a lot more than he has at the moment, and we want to make sure we do things right.'

That was a great start. Anna reached into her bag, pulling out the information folder that she'd put together and handing it to Neil.

'I've got some fact sheets and a few web addresses for you. I'll just run through some of the main points, and then I know you have some questions for me...'

'Nice people.' Jamie had walked Marianne and Neil out to the entrance of the paediatric unit, holding the door open as they manoeuvred the new pram through it. Anna had hung back.

'Yes.'

'He's going to a good home. He'll be fine.'

Anna wanted to retort that he had no way of knowing that. But Marianne and Neil had been through the demanding process of being accepted as potential adoptive parents, and everything had been done to make sure that baby James would have all the care he deserved. Jamie had just picked up on her mood and was trying to reassure her. Maybe himself, too.

'Yes, you're right. He'll be fine.'

'So...you need to be getting back?'

She'd said that, hadn't she? And now she was standing, staring dumbly at the door, as if Marianne and Neil were going to bring baby James back for one last hug. The one that Anna hadn't dared give him.

'Yes, I do.' Anna smiled briskly up at him. 'Will I see you on Thursday?'

'I'll be there.'

'Good. I'll remember to clear a space on my desk for you.' Anna shouldered her bag, and walked away.

As she hurried through the main reception area of the hospital, she saw Marianne and Neil again, with an older couple who were bending over the pram. Probably baby James's new grandparents, who hadn't been able to wait to get a glimpse of him. Thankfully they didn't see her, and Anna made for the doors as fast as she could go without careening into someone.

Marianne and Neil were embarking on a journey that Anna would have loved to take. She'd begged Daniel to take it with her, but he'd refused, saying he wanted his own biological children. Anna hadn't tried to persuade him any further. Daniel had already changed his mind about not wanting children, and had left her. They would never have been the kind of couple that could look after an adopted child, the way that Marianne and Neil were.

She should just forget all about it. Baby James would be well cared for. If it seemed that he'd left a gaping hole in her life, it was only because that hole had always existed and was never going to be filled. Not with anyone, least of all Jamie.

Anna had become attached to baby James. That wasn't in the least surprising, the little boy's happy temperament belying his difficult start in life, and he'd been

a favourite amongst everyone at the hospital. Jamie
had got a little too attached himself, but he knew that
everything was being done to make sure that both the
baby and his biological mother were being properly
cared for.

All the same, her reaction had puzzled him. He
could have understood if she'd given him a hug and
brushed away a tear, the way that the paediatric nurses
had done. But Anna had been clearly struggling to hold
her feelings back, and that piqued his curiosity. Anna
was generally in the habit of telling him exactly what
was on her mind.

Maybe she'd got to thinking about the kiss, and had
decided it had been inappropriate. But she greeted him
with a smile when he arrived at the clinic on Thursday,
and the brush of her fingers on his arm told him that
she was thinking nothing of the sort. Which was just
fine, because Jamie didn't regret it either.

'We're playing baseball on Sunday morning.'

They'd been sitting in silence, both concentrating
on the papers in front of them on Anna's desk. Actually, Anna had given every appearance of concentrating on her paperwork, while Jamie had been wrestling
with how to phrase his invitation.

'Yes?' She looked up at him. 'I heard that the fore-
cast was for rain over the weekend.'

He'd heard that too. And if getting thoroughly cold
and wet with Anna seemed like a taste of heaven to
him, he didn't blame her for finding it an unenticing
prospect.

'I should probably book an inside court.'

'Yes, probably.' Her gaze shifted to the papers in
front of her again.

This wasn't going quite the way he'd planned. Anna had sensed his ulterior motive and was already backing away from it. He should have been a great deal clearer about what he was asking of her.

'Jon's going to be staying with Caroline this weekend. I'm going to leave them to it, and was wondering if you're free...' Anna didn't look up at him, but Jamie lapsed into silence as he saw the tops of her ears redden.

'Jamie. Don't embarrass me...'

He hadn't meant to. And the only way that this could embarrass her was if she was about to say no. He liked spending time with Anna, and he knew that she liked spending time with him, but they both needed the reassurance of having a reason to be together. Just wanting to be together wasn't enough.

Without looking at him, Anna picked up her pen again and started to write. The tops of her ears were still burning red, and the silence in the room was pressing down on him like a ten-ton weight.

Long minutes passed. Her phone was going to ring any moment now, calling her away, or it would be time for him to go and visit Jon's room to have lunch with him. The subject of seeing Anna again would have been dropped, and with every moment that passed it would become increasingly unlikely that it would ever be broached again.

'Look, Anna. Neither of us has any plans for a relationship right now. So could we take that off the table, please?' Jamie blurted the words out.

She looked up at him. Then she smiled. It was a little watery, but it was a smile all the same.

'Yes. You're right, we should do that.'

'So keeping that firmly in mind... I'd like to be your friend and spend some time with you.'

She thought for a moment. 'I'd like that too. I'm free at the weekend.'

The weight lifted from his shoulders and Jamie suddenly felt as light as a feather. 'That's great. I am too, so maybe we could do something together.'

Now that a relationship had been taken off the table, it had allowed everything else to be added. Jamie had mentioned that the trees in the orchard were laden with fruit, ready to be harvested, and Anna had suggested they do it together. They'd driven down late on Friday evening, only giving themselves time for a nightcap before he went to his bedroom and she went to hers.

Jamie had slept peacefully for the first time in weeks, just knowing that she was in the house, even if he couldn't hold her. In the morning, he'd cooked breakfast, and they'd walked down to the orchard together, Anna carrying the boxes for the apples and Jamie taking the sturdy ladder that would be needed to reach the highest branches.

'I think that's about it...' They'd gathered up the windfalls, and sorted the apples into two boxes, ones that were perfect and those that were damaged.

'There are still some on that tree, over there.'

Jamie shook his head. 'They're not ready to pick yet.'

'Just as well probably. What are you going to do with all these?' Anna gestured towards the four large boxes of apples.

'Um... Caroline will take some of them. And I can

pack the undamaged ones and put them in the outhouse, they'll keep for a while.'

Anna nodded. 'What about picking some blackberries and making pies with the windfalls? You could freeze them.'

'Good idea.' There hadn't been so many apples last year, and Jamie had given them all to Caroline, because making pies would have reminded him that he'd had no one to eat them with. Now it felt like a *real* harvest.

He carted the boxes back to the house while Anna picked blackberries. Two boxes were set aside for Caroline, and Jamie put the box of windfalls on the kitchen table.

'Do we have enough?' Anna surveyed the apples and blackberries, and Jamie laughed.

'Enough for what? How many people were you thinking of feeding?'

'I meant enough butter and flour for pastry.'

Jamie opened the refrigerator, pulling out half a packet of butter. 'No, I guess not.'

'We'd better get some, then.'

Going to the supermarket felt like an excursion to heaven. Weaving through Saturday shoppers with a trolley, standing patiently as Anna changed her mind for the third time about how much flour they'd need, and then loading everything into the car. Stopping for coffee and a sandwich on the way home, because they had too much to do this afternoon to contemplate cooking lunch. He'd done this a thousand times, and it had slipped past him like all the other irrelevancies in life. Today it felt special.

'How are you at pastry-making?' Her face was shining as they re-entered the kitchen. Anna was enjoying herself too, and that made it all perfect.

'I can give it a try. Caroline does it all the time, it doesn't look too difficult.'

Anna grinned at him. 'I'll make the first batch of pastry then, and you can make a start on peeling the apples.'

When it was Jamie's turn to make the pastry, he found that it wasn't as easy as either Caroline or Anna made it look. But practice seemed to be the key ingredient, and after a few false starts Anna judged his pastry good enough to line some of the foil pie dishes they'd bought.

'The counselling's going well...' He was still curious about the things that Anna didn't talk about, and it seemed to Jamie that if he were candid with her, it might encourage a similar response.

'Yes?' She grinned at him. 'That's good.'

'My counsellor said she was relieved to find that *I* wasn't going to be billing *her*.'

Anna snorted with laughter, dropping the apple she was peeling into the basin of water in front of her. It landed with a plop, scattering water all over the table. 'I'd be wanting to get that one sorted out as well.'

'Yeah. We've made the demarcation lines a bit clearer. These sessions are part of a learning process for *me*, not the other way round.'

'It's a bit of an occupational hazard, I suppose. When you're so used to counselling the kids in your care.'

Jamie chuckled. 'Thanks for letting me off the hook. Although I suspect it's a bit more to do with the fact that I reckoned that it was all about what Gill and Jon did, and that I didn't bear any of the blame for what happened.'

'I'm sure your counsellor didn't say *blame*, did she?' Anna was mopping up the water on the table.

'No, you're quite right, she didn't. She said *responsibility*. More flour?'

'Yes, just sprinkle a bit more on the board before you roll it out. It'll stop it sticking… So what areas of responsibility have you owned up to? If you don't mind my asking.'

'No, of course not.' Jamie thought back through the twisted strands of everything that had happened, and the beginning of it all seemed very clear now. 'Gill and I met on a train. She was sitting opposite me, staring at me, and finally she asked if I was Jonny Campbell. Jon and I looked a bit more alike in those days.'

'Oh…' Anna's face twisted into pained expression.

'Yeah, I know. It's ironic, but… Actually, that just about sums it all up. We started talking, and laughed about it a bit, and I dismissed the idea that she'd actually rather I was Jon. But, looking back, I think she always wondered if he might be a bit more exciting than I am.'

'That's not very fair. You're exciting.'

The way she flew to his defence was nice to hear. 'Not quite in the way Jon is. Gill liked to go out a lot, the fancier the place the better. She didn't have a lot of time for the work I do with the charity, she rather felt that got in the way. She made no bones about the fact that I could be a bit boring about it sometimes.'

'She sounds a bit boring herself.' Anna winced at her own reaction. 'Sorry. I didn't mean to be rude. I don't even know her.'

'I appreciate the vote of confidence. Gill and I were just different. I had what I really wanted, and when there were conflicting claims on my time, I chose the charity over her. She was right to leave me.'

'Not in that way, Jamie.'

'No. Not in that way.' He shrugged. None of that seemed to matter so much now. 'So what about you?'

'Me?' Anna was suddenly uncomfortable, and it struck Jamie that she was just pretending not to know what he meant.

'I've appreciated the way you've encouraged me to talk. Can't I return the favour?'

Anna shook her head quickly. It seemed she wasn't even going to consider the idea. 'It is what it is. I've nothing to talk about and...so I don't.'

'I'm always here. If you change your mind.'

'Yeah. Thanks.' Something about the finality of her tone told Jamie that she wasn't going to change her mind. 'Oh, look out! You've got a hole...'

Jamie looked down at the pastry in front of him, and saw he'd rolled it a little too thin. Anna nudged him out of the way, folding the pastry over deftly so that he could try again and dusting the board with flour. The moment was gone.

Fair enough. If she didn't want to talk then he shouldn't press the point. He turned his attention to rolling out the pastry, and together they filled the rest of the foil pie dishes.

'Perhaps we should mark those three.' Anna pointed to the pies made with Jamie's pastry. He chuckled.

'With a skull and crossbones? Eat at your peril?'

'No! Your first home-made, home-grown apple and blackberry pies. You need to know when you're eating them.' She pulled a face, deftly cutting three capital J's from the scraps of pastry on the counter, and sticking them down on the top of the pies with a splash of water.

'Do we get to bake them all now?' The idea of filling the house with the scent of baking seemed suddenly thrilling. As if he was making a new start, in a new home.

'No, I think it's better to freeze them unbaked. We could keep one back to have tonight, though.'

'Sounds good. I'll do the washing up and then lay a fire in the sitting room...'

CHAPTER ELEVEN

PICKING APPLES AND making pies. Right now Anna couldn't think what might make a day better. But in truth it wasn't any of that which had made her day perfect. It was Jamie.

They sat on either side of the large grate, eating apple pie and cream. It tasted so much better made with apples that had still been on the tree this morning. Jamie laid his empty plate to one side.

'I'm not sure that even I can manage a third helping.'

'No. Neither can I.' Her stomach was full, and she was warm and relaxed after a day's work. They'd achieved something that might not be as important as the challenges they both met every day at work but it was more clear-cut. A task that had been started and finished, without any of the loose ends that medical treatment had a habit of presenting.

And now... He was so handsome in the firelight.

Anna bit her lip. She had no business thinking such things, it was way beyond the terms of their agreement. And it was that agreement that allowed her to be here, the one that stipulated that spending time together was just that, and not the precursor to something that neither of them could consider.

'Maybe we should think about making cider next year.'

We. Next year.

That was a promise that couldn't be kept if they strayed past the boundaries they'd set.

'Yes, that sounds…interesting. Do you know how to make cider?'

Jamie shook his head. 'Not a clue. There's a first time for everything.'

She got to her feet, reaching for the empty plate that lay next to him on the table. Maybe walking out into the kitchen and washing up would shake the spell that seemed to have settled around them.

'Leave that…' Jamie reached out, catching her hand. In the firelight it was impossible to tell what colour his eyes were, but she could still see everything that mattered in them.

'I had a really nice day today. Thank you.' Anna could hear her voice tremble. One move from him, and she'd forget everything she'd been telling herself.

'So did I. Thank *you*.' He was leaning forward, raising her hand slowly to his lips. Every moment seemed laced with powerful magic.

He made just one, gentle movement. She could have taken her hand from his and resisted him easily. It was her own desire that pulled her down, and that welcomed the feeling of his arms around her. But sitting on his lap, curled in front of the fire was just too delicious.

'This is nice.' Jamie's chest rose and fell, as if he'd

been starved for air for a long time and finally he could take a breath.

'Yes.' She curled her fingers around his. 'Not what we agreed, though.'

'We both said that we didn't want a relationship. I don't recall us mentioning any rules for our friendship.'

'Oh! So you've found a loophole, have you?' She dug her fingers playfully into his ribs.

'Not so much a loophole. Something that wasn't originally covered.'

'That's exactly what a loophole is,' Anna protested, although she still didn't move. 'Although…you're right. We never did define what kind of friendship we'd have.'

He chuckled quietly. 'Maybe we should thrash out the terms of that agreement in more detail. Clearly we need a more rigorous negotiating stance.'

And Anna had the perfect opening gambit. Moving in his arms, she turned to face him, leaving only inches between his lips and hers. 'No talking about the future, Jamie.'

'Agreed. You want it in writing?'

'No. This'll do.' She brushed her lips against his and heard him catch his breath.

'Anything else?'

'We're friends first. We don't need to be joined at the hip, and we can respect each other's lives.'

'That sounds more than fair.' He caught her hand, pressing her fingers to his lips. Then he kissed her palm, working his way across to the base of her thumb. Anna felt herself start to tremble.

'Anything else that happens is…'

'Entirely a matter between ourselves?' His eyes

darkened suddenly. Maybe it was a trick of the light, but the way his body felt against hers was no trick.

'Yes.'

He was still and silent for a moment, staring into her eyes. Everything that she wanted was right there. She kissed him and his tender response couldn't completely hide his hunger.

'Stop me, if I go too far...'

'You're not going far enough, Jamie.'

His hands moved. One rested at the back of her head and the other began to explore. It was a slow, agonising expedition into just how much pleasure a moment could contain, and Jamie was watching her silently. When he cupped her breast, his thumb moving across the fabric of her shirt, she caught her breath.

'Oh!' The agony of frustration was only bearable because she knew now that she wasn't going to allow him to stop.

'You're so beautiful.' He kissed her cheek and she felt it burn. Slowly, deliberately he undid the buttons of her shirt. His fingers traced the edge of her bra, straying across her breast, and she gasped. He was drinking in her pleasure, his eyes fixed on her face.

She wanted his pleasure, too. And she wanted to tease it from him slowly. She wriggled out of his embrace, backing away from him and slipping out of her shirt as she did so. Anna felt the warmth of the fire against her skin as she undressed, the heat of his gaze as he watched her.

'Come here.' She crooked her finger and he was on his feet in an instant. Anna took her time about unbuttoning his shirt, sliding her hands across his shoulders, feeling his heart thundering in his chest.

'Anna…!' He groaned out loud as she ran her tongue across his nipple, so she did it again. He was so strong and yet so entirely in her power. And then when his gaze swept hungrily across her body, she was entirely in his power.

Finally they were naked. This was so much more than just lust, it was loving friends who wanted to see everything. Feel everything, before the inevitable climax robbed them of this trembling anticipation.

When they embraced, she felt the tautness of his body against hers. Then he fell to his knees, one hand still pinioning her tightly against him, the other sliding between her legs. She felt his mouth against her breast, and she cried out, hanging onto his shoulders.

'Too much?' His eyes shone teasingly in the firelight as he looked up at her.

'Not enough, Jamie. It's not enough…' She gasped as she felt his arms around her sweeping her off her feet and lowering her to the floor.

The hearth rug was warm against her back. In the heat of the moment all she wanted was to feel him inside her, but Jamie had other ideas. His hands and his mouth were everywhere, and she cried out as he pulled her legs apart. He was pushing her close to her limit, and she felt a bead of sweat run across her brow, then further, past her limits, to a place where she responded only to his touch.

Then he slowed. She felt his weight on her, and she wrapped her legs around him, desperate for the sweet friction of his body against hers.

'More…please…' She'd never begged a man before, but that didn't seem to matter right now.

'More?' There was something steely in his gaze. It

told her that he could break her, and that was exactly what she wanted him to do. Break her and then hold her tight, before he did it all over again.

'Jamie! Please…' Her fist beat weakly against his shoulder, and he moved. Running his fingers from her neck to her navel, then right back where she wanted them. He was searching for the exact place that gave her the most pleasure, looking for clues in her face. When he found it, his lips curved in triumph.

A little faster. A little more pressure. She guided him as best she could, but he didn't need much help. He seemed to know when it was just perfect, and lifted his weight a little to allow her body to arch under his. When she felt his lips touch her nipple she came. So hard, so quickly. Maybe she screamed, maybe not. When she stilled and wrapped her arms around him, she felt a long sigh rack his body.

'You are amazing.' He rolled over onto his back, pulling her on top of him.

'Me? You were the one who seemed to be doing all the work.' She snuggled against him. 'Although don't think you're going to get away without doing a little more. Do you have any condoms?'

'I'll find them.' He kissed her cheek, tenderly. 'Don't you want to rest a bit?'

No. Not now. It was warm in front of the fire, and she was comfortable here. But Jamie had awakened a rolling desire that hadn't been slaked and was fast gaining momentum again.

'I want to feel you inside me. You want that?' She moved against him and he gasped. He flexed his hips a little and his erection hardened against her leg.

'What do you think?'

When he picked her up, carrying her out into the hallway, the chilled air made her shiver. His bedroom door was opposite that of the guest bedroom, and she'd only ever seen the outside of it. Jamie pushed it open, but she didn't much care to look around her, all she needed right now was him.

He laid her down on the bed and she felt the warmth of his body against hers as he leaned over to kiss her.

'Stay there. I won't be a moment...' She saw his shadow move and there was the sound of him opening and closing drawers. It was cold in here and Anna pulled the duvet over her. Jamie seemed to have found what he was looking for, and his shadow moved to the end of the bed. Then a large brick fireplace suddenly glowed into life as a gas fire ignited.

Flickering light filled the room, and his shadow was more substantial now as he moved towards her. Anna sat up, and he bent to kiss her again.

'You want warm and comfortable?' He tugged at the duvet, his mouth curving into a smile.

Warm and comfortable was nice. She wanted more than nice. 'What do you want?'

He leaned forward. 'I want to be able to see you, and for you to see me. I want to be what keeps you warm.'

Hot desire started to course though her veins. They could make use of every inch of the large bed, unencumbered by bedding. And she'd be able to see it all.

'That's what I want, too.' Her fingers tightened on the duvet, holding it firmly around her, and she leaned forward to kiss him. 'Take it...'

She heard his quiet laugh and then he wrested the duvet from her grip. His hands were still cold and he was making full use of them to make her squirm and gasp under his touch. Suddenly she was on her back, Jamie's knees planted on either side of her hips. His hands closed gently around her wrists and she felt hot desire flooding through her body.

'I want you to take *me*, Jamie...'

His grip tightened, and he pinioned her arms above her head. Raking her body with his gaze, and then covering it with his. She wrapped her legs around him, and he kissed her mouth, hard and searching.

They were the same. They both took pleasure in moments of exquisite tenderness and the long, slow build-up of desire. Whispered words, waiting and watching to see the reaction to every new caress. But when passion got the better of them, she was bold. Unafraid to challenge him, and unafraid to *be* challenged.

Anna was his match. Equal and opposite forces, they fitted each other's desires perfectly.

Her hair glinted in the firelight, spread across the pillow. When he pushed gently inside her, she seemed to bloom under him, and Jamie was carried away by the sweet ebb and flow of her lovemaking. Suddenly strong, because she had no hesitation in showing him how much he pleased her.

Sweat trickled down his spine. Every muscle quivered at her touch, and when she pushed him over onto his back, he knew one thing for sure.

'I'm in real trouble now...'

'Yes, you are.' She bent over to kiss him. 'And you can't talk your way out of it...'

He knew. When Anna climbed astride him, taking him inside her again, it seemed that everything else was just a whisper in his imagination. Only she was real. She twisted her hips and he couldn't help crying out.

She bound him in sweet, silken bonds of pleasure. All he could see was Anna. She was all he could feel. Her pace quickened a little and he reached up to caress her body, knowing that she was close to breaking. He wanted to watch, but when he felt her muscles tighten around him he couldn't hold on any longer. He roared out her name, as his own release crashed over him.

It was a long time before he was able to speak. Jamie just held her, feeling her heart beat against his in a crazy rhythm. What they'd just done together had been frightening in its intensity, but he couldn't let her go.

'That was the very best kind of trouble.' He kissed her forehead.

'Mmm…' she agreed sleepily, snuggling against him.

All he wanted to do now was to hold her in his arms, feeling the soft rhythm of her breathing against his chest. He wanted to drift off to sleep and find her there when he woke up. And if this really *was* asking for trouble, a loophole in their agreement that neither of them should have opened, he didn't care. He'd worry about that later.

Jamie dreamed that he was caught in a web. Sticky and oleaginous strands held him fast, and every time he broke free there seemed to be more in every direction. He could hear Anna's breathing, feel it almost, and he knew that he had to protect her but he didn't know how. In the distance, an alarm was trilling. Something was wrong, and he had to get out.

'Jamie… Jamie!'

He came to suddenly, still locked in the folds of the dream. His alarm actually *was* sounding, on the bedside table, and Jamie reached over to silence it. Something got in his way, and he realised that Anna really was there, too.

'Uh… Sorry.'

'That's okay. You were dreaming?'

'Yes.' The alarm was still boring into his brain, but he'd have to lean across Anna to shut it off. Jamie realised that he was naked, and that she was too. That hadn't seemed like a problem last night…

This morning it was an obstacle for both of them. Wrapped firmly in the duvet, she slid across the bed, hitting the snooze button on the alarm. That was the first problem of the morning, and quite possibly the simplest.

'You have to go, don't you?'

That wouldn't have been so difficult if Anna hadn't echoed Gill's words. She'd seemed to like the fact that he was often on call at first, she'd said he must be important if everyone needed to call him so often. But after a while she'd frowned when his phone had rung in the middle of the night or at a dinner party, and Jamie had even considered not answering a few times. But he *had* to answer. Each one of these calls could be a child in trouble, and he'd promised to be there for them, day or night.

'I'm sorry…' That was what he'd always said to Gill as well. This was turning into a re-run of old memories and old mistakes, and it was just what Jamie had been trying to avoid, for both their sakes.

'That's okay. We're not joined at the hip, you know. Remember?'

He did, and suddenly everything seemed okay. Better, at least. Anna had only been to basketball practice once, but she'd obviously enjoyed it, and become more involved than Gill ever had.

'I remember. But it's bad timing.'

Anna raised her eyebrows. 'Not really. I'd come with you, but…twice in a row…' She shrugged. 'You don't want everyone gossiping about you.'

'If it keeps them out of trouble, they can gossip all they like. If you want to come, then come. If you want to stay here and have a lazy morning, then I'll be sparing a few jealous thoughts for you.'

She flashed him a sudden smile. 'I've brought my sweatshirt, and it seems a shame not to use it. I'd love to come, thanks.'

That was the first thing settled, and the overwhelming dread that Jamie had felt when he'd woken was beginning to subside. Anna seemed less awkward and embarrassed too, but in order to get to the court, they had to get up. And under the covers that Anna was holding so firmly around her, they were still both naked.

He reached forward, touching her hand. After last night his reticence seemed laughable, but he thought he saw a flare of panic in Anna's eyes, too.

'Last night. I won't ever regret it, Anna.'

Her cheeks flushed a little. 'Neither will I. It was nice, wasn't it?'

'Nice doesn't really do it for me. Try amazing. I'm not forgetting what we said, and I don't presume to lay claim to you, or any of your time. But if you wanted to spend some more of it with me, I'd honoured.'

She leaned towards him, kissing his cheek. The duvet had slipped a little, and some of the madness of last night reasserted itself. Only it wasn't madness. In the cold light of day Anna was just as beautiful, and just as desirable.

'Thank you. I was a little worried and… Sorry…'

He laid his finger across her lips. 'Don't be. I don't want you to be sorry for anything, because I'm not.'

The duvet slipped a little more as she gave him a hug. Jamie could feel the softness of her skin against his, and he regretted having missed the feeling of waking up next to her in an embrace.

'I'm sorry for one thing. That we don't have time now…' She nodded towards the clock, ticking relentlessly on the table beside the bed.

Maybe he shouldn't. It was better to leave while they both still wanted more than to overstay his welcome. But that was ridiculous, wanting more couldn't be changed by whatever happened next.

'My alarm's set to go off twice. If I get up on the first ring, then I get breakfast. The second ring means I get coffee in the car…'

'The car's really the only place for coffee.'

He kissed her, pulling the duvet out from between their bodies. 'Yeah. My thoughts exactly.'

Sex was a great way to begin the day. Sex with Jamie…? What could go wrong on a day that had started in his embrace?

She'd feared that it would be so different. When she'd woken from a deep sleep, just ten minutes before the alarm started to sound, it had felt as if she'd messed everything up. Allowed her feelings for Jamie to get the better of her, and lost everything.

But he'd meant what he'd said last night. That they

could be loving friends, and that he wouldn't ask her for anything more than that. It seemed too good to be true, but maybe she should just take her good fortune and make the most of it. If making the most of it meant another night in his arms, then the risk seemed paltry in the face of the rewards.

Their long, playful lovemaking last night, had taught him how to take her from nought to a hundred in sixty seconds flat. And Jamie clearly loved the challenge. He fed off her arousal, the way she fed off his, and it all just worked between them. Effortless beauty.

There was even time to snuggle against him afterwards. Quiet moments, when the world began to expand from the complete and blissful circle of his embrace.

'I like your room.' His bedroom was in the same style as the rest of the house. Bare walls that contrasted with the high polish on the wooden bedframe. A large, brick-built fireplace that had provided them with warmth and light in the darkness.

He grinned. 'Only just noticed?'

'I've had other things on my mind.'

'Yeah, me too. You're welcome back anytime to get a better look.' He followed her gaze to the metal post that ran from floor to ceiling in the middle of the deep bay window. 'That's not part of the overall plan. It's just temporary.'

'I was wondering. It doesn't seem either old enough or new enough to be here.'

Jamie chuckled. 'It's a jack post. There was originally a window seat in that bay, with a wooden beam that supported the ceiling in the centre. It was rotten and I had to take it out. I was planning on getting a carpenter in to redo the whole thing properly, but that's going to have to wait.'

'No time?'

'No money. Or, to be more accurate, it was a choice between doing that and laying a floor in the community room at the youth centre. I think the floor's been a little more useful, and in the meantime the post is stopping the ceiling from falling in.'

'Sounds like a good decision.' There was a lot to respect about a man who could put his charity first when he needed to.

'I thought so.' He turned the corners of his mouth down.

'Someone else disagreed?'

The alarm went off suddenly, and they both jumped. Jamie reached across, banging his hand rather harder than he needed to on the button at the top.

'Yeah, Gill did. But there's no need to talk about the past. Unless, of course, you want to talk about yours?'

'Mine's simple.' Anna climbed over him, getting out of the bed. 'I was married and it didn't work out. I don't want to repeat past mistakes.'

That was all she wanted to say. If she told Jamie the truth, maybe he'd swear it didn't matter to him that she couldn't have children. Maybe she'd believe him. And it would all too painful when he realised that he really did want to be a father, the way Daniel had.

Jamie flung himself back on the pillows in an expression of frustration. 'Nothing's that simple,' he called out after her as she made for the shower room and turned on the water.

'Can't hear you. And anyway we have to get going, or we'll be late.'

CHAPTER TWELVE

FOR ONCE, TIME was on Jamie's side, pushing him towards the weekend, when he'd see Anna again. Three incredibly busy days working in A and E had flown by. Thursday and Friday were spent at the clinic, and in between seeing Jon and sorting out various issues to do with the charity, Jamie was fully occupied. Anna was working on Saturday morning, then they drove down to Hastings together.

The call came just as they'd arrived in the car park of the local pub for a late lunch. Jamie looked at the caller display and frowned, then accepted the call.

'Hi, Philip. What's up?'

He listened carefully to whoever was at the other end of the line. Clearly something *was* up because his brow darkened.

'Okay, let me make a couple of calls. I'll let you know.' He ended the call, puffing out a breath as he turned to Anna.

'I'm sorry. I have to go.'

'What's happened?'

'It's Spark. She's gone missing. Her parents called Jen, apparently, and she says she doesn't know where she is.'

'You think she does?'

He quirked his lips down. 'Maybe. Let me try her.'

He flipped through the contacts list on his phone, leaning back against the car and putting the phone to his ear. He shook his head, ending the call and redialling.

'You can't get hold of her?'

'She's not answering.' Jamie frowned. 'Now I *know* something's up. Her best friend's missing and she's not answering her phone?'

He had a point. Jamie waited, ended the call and dialled a third time, staring up at the sky in a silent signal that he could do this for as long as it took until Jen answered her phone. Then he gave a brisk nod...

'Hey, Jen. It's Jamie. Where are you? Yeah, I can hear you're on the bus. Where's the bus?'

He listened to Jen's reply, rolling his eyes. 'Pull the other one, Jen. Spark's missing, today of all days, and you're going to the cinema?'

It was an approach. Maybe not the most tactful one, but Anna imagined that tact had already been tried. And Jamie's relationship with all the kids was honest. He told them what he thought, and they repaid the compliment.

'No, Jen. I'll take you wherever you want to go in the car, no questions asked. If Spark's not where you think she is, then we'll keep looking. Please don't do this on your own.'

He listened again, his face grave.

'No, it's not because I don't trust you. It's because this is too much responsibility for one person. In your place, I'd need someone with me...' Jen seemed to have capitulated because Jamie nodded. 'Okay. I'll meet you at the bus stop in Hedge Lane. Wait for me there, I'll be fifteen minutes.'

He ended the call and turned to Anna, a look of apology on his face. 'Um… I'll drop you off at my place. It's on the way…'

'You will not. I can help, can't I?'

Jamie smiled suddenly. 'Yeah. Thanks, you can help.'

'So what's going on?' She waited until he'd manoeuvred the car back out of the car park and was on the road.

'Spark's younger brother died of leukaemia four years ago. She started coming to the club when he was really ill, and she met Jen there and they became friends. Spark used to talk a lot about how her brother felt, and how her parents felt, but nothing about herself. She was all about looking after everyone else.'

'Oh, poor Spark. You got her to talk?'

'Eventually. It was a while before she'd even admit to feeling anything when her brother died. Jen really supported her, though she's got problems of her own, and she understood what Spark was going through. Even if Spark didn't tell Jen where she was going, I guessed she might have a good idea.'

'Why now?' Jamie had said *today of all days.*

'It's the fourth anniversary of her brother's death today. Maybe Spark's finally found some space in her head for her own grief.'

'Her parents must be beside themselves.'

'Yeah, they are. They called our weekend helpline, and Phil told them that we'd do all we could. I'd better get back to him…'

'Let me do that. You keep driving.' Anna picked

up his phone from the dashboard. 'What do you want me to say?'

'Tell him that we're on our way to meet Jen to see if she knows anything. He's calling round to see if anyone else has seen her, and he'll liaise with the police and her parents.'

The car slowed suddenly as the lights up ahead of them turned red. Jamie cursed under his breath, tapping his finger impatiently on the steering wheel. More than anything, his reaction made her fear the worst.

It took them thirteen minutes. A bus that was travelling ahead of them stopped, and Anna saw Jen get off and slump down on a seat in the bus shelter. She was taking her phone out of her pocket as Jamie drew up alongside her. Anna opened the car door, getting out of the front seat and beckoning to Jen to take her place.

'Where to, Jen?' Jamie's voice was suddenly calm.

'The railway lines, up by the station.'

Railway lines? Anna climbed into the back seat of the car, trying not to betray her concern.

'Seat belt.' Jamie waited while Jen fumbled with the seat belt, then started to drive. 'Why there?'

'Spark's brother was in hospital in London at the end. Her parents used to go down there to be with him and Spark stayed with her aunt.'

Jamie nodded. 'Yes, I remember. I went round there to see her a few times.'

'She used to go and watch the trains. I went there a couple of times with her. We never told anyone, she was just watching.'

'For her parents to come back?'

Jen shrugged. 'No, not really. We wouldn't have

seen them even if they had been on the train. She said
that she was at one end of the line and they were at
the other, I guess it made her feel more connected to
them. We just used to sit on the embankment for an
hour and then go home.'

It was an intensely private and personal admission
for Jen to make, and it showed the depth of trust that
Jamie had built up with the kids that he tried to help.
Two young girls, doing something that made no sense
but somehow made them feel better. If only that something was in a slightly less isolated and safer place.

'Okay. So we'll start at the road bridge closest to
Jen's aunt's house?'

'Yeah. I reckon so.'

Jamie drew up in the centre of a wide bridge, and
before either of them could stop her Jen tumbled out of
the car, running across the pavement to the high railings. Jamie turned in his seat.

'You'll keep an eye on her?'

His gaze met hers and Anna nodded. One second
of contact, but she knew that he trusted her to look
after Jen while he searched for Spark. Warmth flooded
through her, and she got out of the car, hurrying over
to Jen.

The three of them scanned the embankment on either side of the lines. Jen was crying now, and Jamie's
face was impassive as he concentrated on looking for
some trace of Spark.

'There!' Jen screamed, pointing to spot on the embankment to one side of the bridge. The small, black-
clad figure was sitting almost under the bridge, with
her legs drawn up to her chest, as if she was trying to

make herself as small as possible. And she was heart-stoppingly close to the tracks.

Jamie didn't even look back. He started to run and Jen went to follow him, but Anna grabbed her, pulling her back.

'Let me go...' Jen swore at her.

'Wait. Wait!' Anna held her tight, waiting for her to stop struggling. 'Listen to me, Jen. You need to calm down if you're going to help Spark.'

Jen gulped down her tears. She saw the sense in it, and the only thing she wanted now was to help her friend. Anna just had to convince her that maybe she wasn't the best person to do that, and that she should leave it to Jamie.

'Do you know how she got down there?' A high fence bordered the embankment, and Anna knew that Jamie was relying on her to try and find a way through for him.

'There's a hole. Just there, by those trees.' Jen indicated a spot close to the end of the bridge.

'Okay. He's nearly there...' Anna waited for Jamie to turn and look back at her, and he did so right on cue. She pointed towards the spot that Jen had indicated, and he vaulted across the low railings that separated the pavement from the rough ground beyond, sliding down the steep incline towards the fence.

'No...' Jen was gesturing furiously. 'Further along...'

Jamie saw her, and turned. Then he gave a thumbs-up signal and disappeared behind the clump of trees and bushes that Jen had pointed out.

'I've got to go... Let me *go!*' Jen started to pull away from her again.

'Jamie's nearly there now. He'll bring her back.'

'But you don't *understand*. She's not trying to kill herself.' Tears were streaming down Jen's face again.

'He knows. She's feeling so much pain right now, and she's just trying to find a way of expressing it. Jamie understands that.'

Jen wiped her face, calming suddenly. 'She cuts herself, too.'

Anna wondered if Jamie knew that. He must realise it was a possibility, and he'd be taking everything into consideration right now. She put her arm around Jen's shoulders and they watched as Jamie appeared, slithering down the steep slope of the embankment and then starting to walk towards Spark.

He stopped thirty feet away from her, and must have called to her because Spark turned. His movements were slow and controlled, all his body language reassuring. He took a couple more steps then sat down on the grass.

He edged closer, stopping when Spark flailed one arm in his direction in a gesture that told him to back off. They seemed to be talking, though, and slowly Jamie started to move closer again. He leaned forward, wrapping his fingers around her arm, and Anna heard Jen exhale sharply. They'd both been holding their breath.

Then Spark turned, almost flinging herself into Jamie's arms. He hugged her tight for a moment then got her to her feet, moving her away from the tracks. Carefully he helped her back up the embankment, the two figures disappearing behind the trees as they made for the fence.

'Oh! He did it...' Jen shook off Anna's arm and

started to jog towards the end of the bridge. Anna let her go. Spark was out of danger now, and the two girls needed each other.

Jamie had wrapped his jacket around Spark's shoulders and was helping her over the low fence, his arm around her as they walked to the pavement. Jen caught up with them, throwing her arms around Spark, and the two girls hugged each other. Anna felt a tear form at the corner of her eye and wiped it away. He was so gentle with the two girls, protecting them both but giving them a little space as well to walk together towards the car.

'Why don't you go and sit in the back of the car for a moment? Then we'll take you back.' Jamie opened the car door and the girls climbed in. Then he turned to Anna.

'She's okay.' He answered the question before she'd had a chance to ask. 'She's cut her arm, but it's not too deep. Maybe you could take a look at it when we get back to the youth centre?'

'Of course. You're not taking her home?'

'She says she doesn't want to go home and I didn't push it with her. I'll give Phil a call now and get him to ring her parents and tell them we've found her. They don't live far from the youth centre and they know us so it might be better if they came there to collect her.'

He took his phone from his pocket and made the call. Then he looked up at Anna, his eyes shining.

'Thank you.'

'It was a privilege to be here. Thanks for trusting me.'

Jamie smiled, a trace of fatigue showing suddenly

in his face. 'I honestly never even thought about it. I knew I could rely on you.'

'I'll show you how much I like that you said that.' Anna leaned towards him. 'Later…'

Phil's car drew up outside Jamie's house. Jamie shook his hand, thanking him for all he'd done today, and got out of the car, stretching his legs. As he walked down the drive, he could see that the lights were on in the kitchen. That one, simple thing filled him with warmth. He felt as if he was coming home.

The smell of cooking reached him as he opened the front door. And then Anna walked out of the sitting room to greet him with a kiss. He held her tight, his limbs trembling.

'How did everything go?' Anna looked up at him, her eyes full of concern.

'Good. I think things are going to be fine.' He'd walked out of the youth centre feeling satisfied at a good outcome to the afternoon. It was what he'd found here that had brought him close to tears.

'You're sure?'

'Yeah. Absolutely.'

'Well, I've made a shepherd's pie and I just need to put it in the oven for half an hour. Then we can eat. Would you like something to drink?'

He followed her into the sitting room. This was turning into a fantasy. Arriving home to find the lights on and a fire in the grate. The smell of cooking and a kiss. Anna wasn't wearing an apron but then aprons were highly overrated. She looked wonderful, her long hair cascading down her back in a blonde shimmering waterfall. All that was missing was the knowledge that there was a sleeping child upstairs who looked just like its mother.

He cleared his throat, trying to shake the picture of a perfect domestic scene. 'I have some beer in the fridge. Would you like some?'

'Yes, I'll join you.' She shot him a smile. 'Sit down, I'll fetch it.'

The temptation was just too much. Jamie lowered himself into a seat in front of the fire and Anna bustled out into the kitchen, returning with two open bottles and two glasses. Instead of just giving him his, she started to pour his beer for him, tilting the glass carefully so that the head didn't fizz up over the top.

'Too much?' The look of mischief in her eyes said it all.

'Yeah. Far too much. I can pour my own beer.'

'I know.' She set the empty bottle down. 'I just thought…'

Jamie chuckled. 'I know what you thought. But you shouldn't wait on me like this. I'm perfectly capable of coming home and making my own dinner, I do it all the time.'

'I can make a bit of a fuss of you, can't I? On a *once in a blue moon* basis?'

'On that basis it's very nice. As long as I get to do the same for you once in a while.'

'Of course.' She smiled brightly handing him the beer, and Jamie put it down onto the table.

'That's yours. I can pour my own.' He caught her hand, pulling her down onto his knee and kissing her. 'That's the only welcome home I really want.'

'What!' She sat up straight in a motion of mock

outrage. 'Are you telling me you don't want my shepherd's pie?'

'I crave your shepherd's pie. It's just that I'd crawl across a hundred of them in order to kiss you.'

'That's all right, then.' She picked up her glass, taking a sip of beer, and leaned back into his arms. 'So tell me what happened after I left this afternoon.'

'Spark's mum asked me to say thank you for the stitches.'

'It was my pleasure. The least I could do for her.'

It wasn't the stitches. It was the care that Anna had shown Spark. No asking her why on earth she'd cut herself or making her feel small. She'd allowed Jen to help her clean the wound, and when she'd finished she'd kissed Spark on the cheek and told her that she was glad she was okay. Anna knew that the hard part was going to be in the conversation that followed, and she'd trusted Jamie and the other staff at the youth centre to do that right.

'Did you see any other scars?'

'A couple, but it didn't look as if the cuts had been too deep. I don't think she's done it a great deal before now.'

'No, that's what she told me.' He was glad to have Anna's confirmation of that, though.

'And how did things go with her parents? Did they mind that you didn't take her straight home?'

'No, they were fine with that. They know us and I think that they were much more comfortable with having someone there to help mediate. Everyone got to say their piece, and Spark understands how traumatic it was for them when she went missing.'

Anna sighed. 'She must be hurting so much. To do something like that.'

'The worst thing is that she's always been so determined not to show it. When she saw how upset her parents were, I think she realised that they can cope with her grief and she doesn't need to protect them from it. What they can't cope with is her disappearing without a word.'

'Well, I'm glad you're there. For Spark and her parents. Will you be working with them again?'

'Yes, I suggested that they might like to come to us for family therapy, and her mum and dad were really keen on the idea. I think there are a few things they need to talk about as well.'

'I so wish I could help her.' Anna turned the corners of her mouth down. 'But there are some things that no one can ever put right.'

'Yes and no. We can't bring her brother back, and we can't make all that grief go away. But we don't exist to do that. Our aim is to help show our kids that there's still a way forward.'

Anna fell silent, staring into the fire, her fingers clutching tightly at his shirt. Jamie hugged her, wondering what she was thinking. He was becoming more and more sure that there was something that *she* couldn't put right. Something to do with her marriage, which had hurt her so badly that she'd chosen a way forward that didn't allow for it to ever happen again.

Maybe she'd tell him. He hoped so, because it stood between them, a silent barrier that he couldn't tackle because he didn't know what it was. For the moment, though, he had to be content with just holding her.

'So what about this shepherd's pie, then?'

Anna shook herself out of her reverie. Kissing him, she gave him a bright smile. 'I'll just go and put it in the oven…'

CHAPTER THIRTEEN

'Would you show me your software?'

'Is that a proposition? Or are you really interested in computers?'

Jamie's soft chuckle sounded from the other end of the phone. 'It would be a proposition if this wasn't a Wednesday. I'm sticking to computers today.'

It was an odd arrangement, but it worked. For the last two and a half weeks Jamie and Anna had been professional whenever they saw each other at the clinic. Never asking about what they were doing that night, never mentioning the Hastings Hustlers, apple pie, or anything else that belonged to the weekend. Never taking the other's presence for granted, because they had their own lives.

The weekends were theirs alone, and they'd become what Anna liked to call *loving friends*. They didn't go on dates. They just did things together. And their nights were full of tenderness and passion.

'Okay. When are you free?' Anna pulled her business diary across the desk.

'Jon's being discharged tomorrow, and I'm going to take him down to Caroline's, he's staying there for a while and travelling back up to London for counselling and to see Dr Lewis. But I'm free after about four o'clock.'

'I have patients until five. Say half five? What exactly do you want to do with my software?'

His quiet laugh wasn't exactly appropriate for a Wednesday. Anna ignored it, because it was so nice. 'We're holding a workshop at the youth centre next week on body image. A few of the kids have asked for one, and it's an issue that affects most of them in one way or another. I was wondering whether you could take me through a typical consultation process and show me the software you use to indicate the difference that surgery will make, so I can answer any questions about that.'

'Fine. No problem, I'll see you then.' Anna adopted a brisk, businesslike tone and Jamie followed suit, confirming the time and giving a brief goodbye.

He appeared in the doorway of her office at five thirty sharp the following day, holding two coffees. Anna had brushed her hair and refreshed her make-up, but she'd do that for any meeting. Probably. He pushed one coffee across the desk and she thanked him.

'Shall we get started, then? I'll just give you a quick demonstration and you can ask questions as they occur to you.'

Jamie sat down in the chair she'd placed next to hers at her computer. She opened the software, aware suddenly of his scent. Enjoying that was okay as long as she didn't mention it.

'First I need a picture. Hold still a moment and don't smile…' She pointed the camera at the top of the screen at him, and he stared solemnly at it.

'Then I can smooth out any imperfections.' Anna peered at the screen, frowning. She couldn't see anything that she'd want to change about Jamie's face.

'Like the little scar, there?' He pointed to a tiny mark on his forehead.

'Oh, yes. I didn't even see that.' She punched keys, and the scar obligingly disappeared.

'Hmm. I'm not sure that I can tell the difference.' Jamie stared at the screen and Anna smiled.

'I think that's an important point. Everyone has their own idea of what they don't like about themselves, and they assume that everyone else notices those same things. That's not always the case. Plastic surgery can be an objective choice when function is impaired, but in cases where someone simply wants to remove a disfigurement, it's subjective.'

Jamie nodded. 'Yeah. So, in terms of surgery, I've a reasonable idea of what's possible. But what guidelines do you find most useful in advising people?'

'Obviously if it's a matter of restoring the function of a particular part of the body, then it's exactly the same medical considerations you'd use. But cosmetic remodelling is entirely about how the patient feels. Jon's an obvious example.'

'The scars on his face are hardly noticeable now.'

'Yes, exactly. The tissue viability nurse has worked with him to make the skin more comfortable, and he has a very different attitude to them now than when he first came here. Maybe he'll be back to have some work done on them, and maybe not. As long as it's his decision, either choice is okay.'

'I suppose being twins makes a difference.' Jamie

leaned back in his seat. 'I've been thinking a bit about how we identify with each other even now.'

Anna nodded. 'Yeah. How you see yourselves as either the same or different is important in a lot of ways.' Jon and Jamie's relationship was changing. They were working things out and there was no longer the push and pull between them that had made their reunion so difficult.

'So, show me a bit more about how the software works.' Jamie leaned forward, studying the screen.

'I'll show you something that I do when I take workshops. I'll take your face as an example.'

'Sure you want to do that?' Jamie grinned at her. He was entirely unaware of his own beauty.

'Well, I'll give it a go. I don't do this with patients, it's just a fun exercise. First of all I can take one half of your face and mirror it.' Jamie watched as she manipulated the image, raising his eyebrows when Anna frowned.

'What? I can't see any difference.'

'Neither can I. Let me try the other side…' She quickly made a third image, putting it next to the first two on the screen and scanning them. 'Well, it's official, Jamie.'

'What's official? What have you done?' A trace of panic showed in his beautiful eyes.

'You have a perfectly symmetrical face!'

'Is that good?' Jamie had clearly never given his looks much thought.

'It's surprisingly uncommon. Let's try something else. During the Renaissance, painters worked out something called "The Golden Ratio", which mapped out the proportions of a perfect face. Obviously our definition of beauty has changed over time, and there are variations according to different ethnic groups.' This was getting interesting.

'Okay. Do your worst.'

There wasn't a worst to do. Anna was usually able to predict how the results of these simple photo manipulations would turn out, but with Jamie she couldn't. She wondered if maybe subconsciously she'd known...

'Well, that's just outrageous! Did you *know* that you have a perfectly proportioned face?'

He grinned. 'You make it sound like an accusation. And, no, I had no idea.'

'It's really unusual. Mine's way off, I'll show you...'

She reached for the mouse but he pulled it away from her, his expression suddenly serious. 'Your face is perfect. I don't need anything to tell me that you're the most beautiful woman I've ever seen.'

Anna could see in his eyes that he meant it. The temperature in the room seemed to rise suddenly, and playing with pictures of their faces became irrelevant.

'I...guess that's my point. It's impossible to define beauty.' Jamie's was way beyond definition.

'You make your point very well.' Jamie's gaze was still fixed on her face. Anna knew that she wasn't classically beautiful, but he made her feel that way.

'I've got some notes from talks I've done in the past.' The lump in her throat was entirely inappropriate for a work environment. 'Would you like to borrow them?'

'I would, thank you. Or can I persuade you to come and take part in the workshop yourself? It's next Saturday afternoon.'

This was blending their weekends with their jobs.

But although she'd tried to keep the two separate, Anna couldn't think of a single reason why she shouldn't.

'I'd really like that. Saturday afternoon, you say?'

He nodded. 'We'll have a few different people giving short presentations, and then we split everyone up into groups to talk.'

'That sounds good. Um… I'll send you my notes, then. They cover some of the more serious issues as well…'

'That's okay. I don't need to see them.' He smiled as Anna's eyebrows shot up. 'I trust you. Just come along and be perfect, the way you always are.'

'I'll drive down on Friday evening?'

Jamie nodded. 'I'd love that.'

The conversation was turning into one of the long, slow seductions that belonged to the weekend. Sitting too close. Staring into each other's eyes as they spoke. A little blurring of the boundaries was acceptable, but this was going a bit too far, and a hint of panic made her hand quiver as she grabbed the mouse. This was her office, and it was supposed to be for work.

'Okay. I'll see you then.' She shut down her computer, aware that his gaze hadn't left her face.

Suddenly he stood. 'Yeah. Thanks for the…demonstration. I appreciate it. I'll look forward to seeing you tomorrow.'

'Yes. Me too.'

He left with a smile, and Anna resisted the temptation to open up her computer again and stare at Jamie's picture. That would be courting trouble, because she could only contemplate their loving friendship if it stayed within the entirely arbitrary rules that they'd set.

'Stupid rules!' She murmured the words to herself,

knowing that the rules weren't stupid at all. She could never have all of Jamie, and this arrangement allowed her to have at least part of him. When something good happened, it was wise not to meddle with it.

Jamie sat at the back of the community room at the youth centre. Community room was a bit of a grand title as it doubled up as a basketball practice court, a chess hall and a large enough area to do any number of things. But at the moment it had just one purpose. Anna was standing at the centre of an arc of chairs, several rows deep, and holding everyone's attention.

She was giving much the same message as the two other speakers, but without the clichés or the solemnity. He'd noticed that Spark and Jen, who were sitting to one side of him, had been fidgeting a bit through the first part of the afternoon, but now they were captivated, turning to each other and nodding from time to time when Anna made an important point.

Jamie was spellbound, too. He knew that Anna had chosen her bright red top to stand out and be seen. That the jokes she made were to reinforce serious points. But he still couldn't take his eyes off her.

She smilingly announced the fun part of her talk, switching on the overhead projector and displaying the picture of herself from her computer, and comparing it with the 'ideal' proportions of a woman's face. She gave herself an electronic rhinoplasty to straighten the slight kink in her nose, which Jamie happened to love very much. She also shaved her jaw, taking out some of the determined air that Jamie also loved. Finally she'd made her eyes bluer, obscuring the pale magic of her gaze.

'What do you all think?' She folded her arms, looking up at her work.

'I prefer the *real* one.' Jen spoke up, waggling her finger at the screen, and Spark nodded. A murmur of agreement went around the hall.

'Well, that's a relief.' Anna grinned. 'And the lesson that I've learned from showing this simple example to a lot of people is that it's the things that are different about us that make us who we are. It's very unusual to find someone who has a perfectly proportioned face, and I'm loving all of the different faces here...'

'And here's a little puzzle for you.' She shot Jamie a momentary glance, and he felt the back of his neck begin to tingle. 'By chance, I happen to know that there is one person here who *does* have a perfectly proportioned face. See if you can guess who it is.'

Everyone looked round and Anna laughed. Jamie saw Spark nudging Jen furiously, and their heads both turned toward him. He chuckled, spreading his hand across his chest in a *who, me?* gesture, and Jen rolled her eyes disbelievingly.

He was going to take some stick for that as soon as Spark and Jen got to share their suspicions with the others. Jamie didn't care. Anna had opened up a conversation, and everyone was thinking about what she'd said and the more serious points she'd made.

There was some lively discussion, and Anna answered the difficult questions that were fired at her honestly and with a large helping of common sense. The speakers were all thanked, and then it was time for drinks before everyone split up into their discussion groups. A group crowded around Anna almost immediately, and he could see her animated and smiling in the centre of it. Jamie knew that a lot of thought had gone into her presentation, and a lot of experience into her answers, but she made it all seem so natural and personal.

He saw Joe's father making his way towards him, while Joe and his mother hung back a bit. 'Hi, Steven. I'm glad you could make it.'

'We wouldn't have missed it, I thought that all the speakers made some very valuable points. Is there any chance that we might have a few words with Miss Caulder?'

'Anna? Yes, of course, I'll go and fetch her. Would you like to go into the sitting room and see her there? It's a bit noisy in here.'

Steven nodded. His son Joe had was eleven years old and the transition from junior to secondary school hadn't been easy for him. He had a dark red birthmark on the side of his neck and jaw, and some of the older kids at his new school had started to bully him. Steven and his wife were at a loss for some direction about what to do about it, and had contacted Jamie about the possibility of counselling.

'You go ahead, then. We'll be with you in a minute.'

Jamie caught Anna's eye, beckoning to her. She smiled, extricating herself from the group of people that surrounded her.

'What did you think?'

She shouldn't even need to ask. 'I thought you were great. There's someone I'd like you to see, if you don't mind.'

'Of course not, that's what I'm here for. Do I need my laptop?'

'You could bring it along, just in case.'

Anna fetched her laptop, and he led her to the small sitting room that adjoined the hall, quickly telling her about Joe. When they entered, he introduced her to Steven and Josie and she smilingly shook their hands, saving her special smile for Joe.

'Hi, Joe. It's nice to meet you.' She plumped herself down in a chair. 'I hear that you've got some questions for me.'

Steven started to explain, and Anna nodded, watching for Joe's reaction to everything. Haltingly, Joe started to join in, telling her about the bullying. Anna's face darkened.

'And what's the school doing?' She asked the obvious question.

Steven sighed. 'We went to see the headmistress and she said she'd do what she could. She suggested that having the birthmark removed might be a way forward.'

'Oh. Well, I don't think that's a particularly helpful attitude.' Anna's outrage made Steven smile. 'Joe's quite fine as he is, it's the bullies that need to change.'

Slowly but surely she was coaxing Joe out of his shell. He began to talk to her, and then quite of his own accord he got up from his seat, walking over to Anna. 'Do you want to look?' He gestured towards his neck.

'Thank you, Joe. Yes, I'd like to see your birthmark.' Anna waited as Joe took off his sweater and unbuttoned the neck of his shirt. Carefully she examined the skin around his neck and jaw.

'So what do *you* want, Joe?'

The boy frowned. 'Can you show me what I'd look like without it?' He gestured towards Anna's laptop. She glanced at Steven and Josie and Steven nodded.

'Yes, I can do that. Come and sit here beside me and I'll take your picture…'

She was doing it all without suggesting any one solution, letting Joe dictate what he wanted. Jamie saw Josie slip her hand into Steven's as they watched. This was clearly what they'd been waiting for someone to do with Joe.

Anna showed Joe the software first, and then turned the screen away from him while she altered his photograph. 'Do you have an email address I can send these pictures to, Steven?'

'Yeah.' Steven gestured towards his wife, who quickly pulled pen and paper out of her handbag. 'We really appreciate this, thank you.'

'It's my pleasure.' Anna turned to Joe, tipping the screen towards him so that he could see it. 'I'm going to send these pictures to your dad and so you can have another look at them. If you want to email me back, I'd really like to hear what you think.'

Joe stared at the photographs. Steven and Josie were both holding their breath.

'That's who I am.' Joe pointed at the picture of himself that Anna hadn't altered.

Anna nodded. 'Yes, it is.'

The whole family started to talk. Anna sat back, listening and answering questions. This was what she was really good at—opening avenues of communication.

'Here's my card.' Anna handed Joe one of her cards from the clinic, and he looked at the elegant script. Anna was treating him like a grown-up, and he was responding. The boy who always seemed to be clinging to one or the other of his parents had already gained a little confidence.

'You can get your mum or dad to call me anytime, if there's something you want to talk about.' She glanced at Steven. 'There'll be no cost involved if you want to bring Joe along to see me and discuss his options.'

'I'm sure there should be.' Steven narrowed his eyes. 'But thank you, Miss Caulder.'

'Anna, please. The important thing is that Joe makes his own decision about what he wants to do. When he's done that, I can make a few calls to make sure he gets whatever he needs'

Jamie nodded. 'We can help with that, if necessary.'

'And in the meantime…' Anna moved on smoothly '…I'd like to write a letter to you, outlining some of the things we've talked about today. It's my view that Joe doesn't have an issue with his birthmark, it's the bullying. His headmistress needs to understand that and perhaps a surgeon's letter will reinforce the point.'

'Thank you, Anna. I think that'll really help, don't you, Steve?' Josie turned to her husband and he nodded in agreement.

'And Joe's having counselling here?' Anna's gaze turned to Jamie.

'Yes, that's right. We'll be seeing you again next week, won't we, Joe?' Jamie reckoned that the counsellor might be speaking to a different boy than the one she'd first met last week. Joe's brief talk with Anna seemed to have set him firmly on the right track, and it was just a matter of following up now.

The chatter from the main hall was subsiding a little, and it was about time for the organisers to divide everyone into discussion groups. Anna reached for her laptop and closed it.

'Is there anything else you'd like to ask? Joe?'

Joe shook his head, and Steven answered. 'We've already kept you long enough. We really appreciate being able to talk to you.'

'It's been my pleasure. I enjoyed meeting you.'

Jamie guided her back to the community room, pointing out the group leaders so that Anna could visit each group and talk to them. She turned her smile up towards him. 'I'm not enjoying this at all, you know.'

Jamie laughed. 'No, I can see you aren't. They don't love having you here either.'

She gave a mock sigh. 'I suppose it's a boring old evening again afterwards.'

'Yeah. Dry as dust.' Even thinking about it sent shivers of pleasure down Jamie's spine.

'Oh, well. Better get on.' Anna's finger found his hand, her light touch giving him a first taste of the evening ahead. There was an undeniable joy in her step as she walked away from him, making for the first group and sitting down with them.

He didn't need to tell her that she'd done wonders here today—she'd seen it on Joe's face and in the faces of the other kids. She didn't need to tell him that tonight would be anything but dull. It was all unspoken between him and Anna, and that was nice, but Jamie was beginning to want more.

CHAPTER FOURTEEN

EIGHT O'CLOCK ON a Friday evening. Another week had flown by, and the weekend was here again. Jamie heard Anna's car draw up in the drive, and he greeted her at the door. He'd been cooking, and when she stepped into the hallway she wiggled her nose at him.

'I know what you've been up to.'

'Yes. Would you like me to pour you a drink?'

She chuckled, taking off her coat and hanging it on the stand. 'I can pour my own beer, thank you very much.'

'That's not what I had in mind...'

Jamie had never felt as happy as he did now. In the month he and Anna had been together she'd spent every weekend here, with him. They'd come a long way. They'd explored trust, and found that came easily and naturally. Honesty had come naturally too, even if Anna was steadfastly honest about not wanting to talk about her marriage. They'd spent a great deal of time exploring wonderful, tumultuous, tender lovemaking and had shared a hundred everyday things, which felt special when he did them with Anna.

She'd changed him. In ways that he'd never thought

possible. And although she was perfect already, there was just one thing that he wanted to change about her.

He led her into the sitting room, gesturing for her to sit down by the fire. He could feel her gaze following him as he walked over to the polished sideboard, from which he'd cleared the usual clutter of books, and switched on the lamp. The light reflected off a row of bottles, a silver ice bucket that he'd found in a junk shop and which had polished up nicely, and two slender glasses.

'Cocktails. I have…um…well, tell me what you want, and I might have it.'

'Mmm.' Anna's gaze ran along the bottles. 'Surprise me.'

That was turning into one of his bounden duties in life. 'Suppose we start with something…as near to virgin as it gets. We can work our way onto something a bit stronger later.'

'Sounds good to me.'

Jamie measured out the liquids, pouring them carefully so that the rainbow effect of the different densities of liquid wasn't disturbed. A dash of spirits, and then a cherry on top. He carried the drinks over to the sofa, and they sat down together.

'This is all very nice.' She took a sip from her glass. 'And that's lovely. So what's the occasion?'

Jamie grinned. 'Oh, it's Friday evening. You've been working hard all week, and you've just driven all the way down from London.'

'That's it?'

'Well, I know it's not my birthday. It's not yours, is it?' He knew so little of the minutiae of Anna's life, but still he felt he knew everything about her.

'No.' She slipped off her shoes, tucking her legs up underneath her. 'Although if it meant getting one of your foot massages, I could always change it.'

'It's Friday. That's sufficient excuse for a foot massage.'

'Ah, wonderful.' She leaned forward, kissing him. 'You are a dream.'

Jamie wanted to be *more* than just a dream. He wanted to be part of Anna's reality. But he'd ask about that later.

'We'll eat first, though? I'm not planning on stopping with just your feet...'

'Mmm. Good idea. Do you want a hand?'

'No, everything's sorted. Just relax in here for ten minutes and then we'll eat.'

It was really nice of him. He'd made a tasty chicken casserole with roast potatoes, and they ate in the dining room rather than the kitchen. There was a snowy white tablecloth, heavy silver cutlery and candles on the table, and after crème brûlée for dessert he served coffee.

'There's something I wanted to ask you.' His eyes were sparkling in the flickering candlelight and he looked so handsome. Anna was sure that her answer was going to be *yes*.

'What is it?'

'We've been seeing each other for a month now. We've shared so much and... I want you to trust me.'

A flutter of uneasiness beat suddenly in her chest, and it occurred to Anna that this wasn't going to be the automatic *yes* that she'd thought. 'Trust you? With what?'

'I want you to trust me enough to tell me what hurt you so badly. You always say that your marriage is in the past, but I know there's something you can't break free from.'

The flutter became a determined beat of panic. Jamie had asked before, but there was something about his manner that told Anna he wasn't going to back off this time.

'I don't want to talk about it, Jamie.'

She *couldn't* talk about it. If she told him why Daniel had left her then he'd know that she couldn't have children. Maybe he'd say that he didn't care, and she'd believe him. Anna suddenly realised that it would hurt a great deal more if Jamie did as Daniel had done, accepted her as she was and then changed his mind. And he *would* change his mind, Jamie so obviously wanted kids of his own.

He was shaking his head slowly. 'I need to know, Anna. What we have now…'

She stared at him. What they had now was suddenly changing. She dreaded it, but it seemed unstoppable.

'I need to know that you trust me, the way I trust you.' His voice was as gentle as a lover's sigh. 'I made one huge mistake when I blundered blindly into a relationship with Gill, and… I want ours to be different.'

'But…' Anna shivered. He'd used the 'R' word, and they'd promised not to do that. It seemed Jamie had already found a promise to go back on. 'We said this *wasn't* a relationship, didn't we?'

'Yeah, I know. But things change, Anna. I think about you all the time, and I want to share everything with you. You've changed me on a level that I just didn't realise anyone had access to. And I love being with you.'

He reached forward, catching her hand and pressing her fingers to his lips. Despite herself, Anna smiled.

'I love being with you, too.'

He took one ragged breath, his gaze tender. 'All I've been thinking about lately is a future with you, Anna. I know that's not what we agreed, and if you're not ready for that it's okay. But if you are... I want you to know that I'm ready for it too.'

Anna squeezed her eyes shut and shook her head. She'd hung onto the notion that she and Jamie would never get to the point of having this conversation. That he was as damaged as she was, and that they could continue on together with no thought of commitment or the future. But it seemed that somewhere along the way Jamie had done some healing.

'Okay. That's fair enough. Whenever you're ready.'

She was never going to be ready. Jamie might have moved forward, but Anna couldn't.

'Look, Jamie, I know that you've been through a lot, and I'm really glad that you feel that you can put that behind you now. And I know you believe that it's possible to mend things in the future...' Anna shook her head.

He gave her an uncomprehending look. 'I *have* to believe it. I believed it when I went to medical school, and managed to stay the course despite my dyslexia. And the kids I work with are making better futures for themselves, too.'

'There are some things you can't mend, Jamie. They're just facts of life and it's not possible to make them any different. You just have to accept them.'

'So…you won't even accept that we might have a chance? I don't understand, Anna.'

Jamie wasn't going to give up. She was going to have to tell him. She was going to have to see the look on his face before she could fully believe that he was capable of breaking her heart.

'Jamie, the reason my marriage broke up was because I can't have children. My husband knew that right from the start, and he said that he was fine with it. A year after we got married he suddenly decided he wasn't fine with it after all and he left me.'

He stared at her. Somewhere deep down she'd still believed in a fairy-tale world where it wouldn't matter and she could love Jamie the way she wanted to. But then she saw it. Denial.

'Are you sure?'

A tear rolled down her face. This was the beginning of an end that couldn't be averted now.

'Yes, I'm sure. I'm a surgeon, Jamie, do you really think that I haven't explored all the options?'

He was staring at her, shaking his head. Jamie never gave up, and she loved him for it. The trouble was that he didn't know when he was beaten either.

'I have a congenital abnormality that affects both my Fallopian tubes and my uterus. I can't have children.'

'I don't care.'

He was still holding on. Still believing in a future that just couldn't happen.

'Have you ever thought you might have children?'

He shrugged. 'Well, yes, of course, but—'

'But nothing! I've seen you with your niece and nephews, you love them. You're going to make a great dad, but you can't do it with me.' Anna stood up. She had to go. There wasn't enough air in the room and she was going to suffocate if she stayed.

'Wait. Anna, will you stop second-guessing me? Can you give me a moment to process this, and then we can talk about it?'

Talking wasn't going to change anything. 'No, because you're going to tell me that it doesn't matter—'

'Right in one. It doesn't.' His face darkened with anger.

'And then I'll believe you. And I'll believe we have a future. Don't you dare make me do that, Jamie, because I know for sure that it's going to break me when you come to your senses and decide you want a family of your own.'

'Sit down!'

'Do *not* tell me what to do, Jamie. We never promised each other anything, and I'm leaving now. I won't be back.'

Anger propelled Anna out into the hallway. She picked up her coat and the overnight bag that she'd left there when she'd come in tonight, and ran out to her car. She couldn't stay. She couldn't face his disappointment or his pity or whatever else it was he had to throw at her. She just had to get away.

Jamie stared blankly at the table in front of him. She wouldn't. Anna couldn't.

The silence that had seemed to damn him in Anna's eyes had been shock. Sudden understanding of all the little things he'd wondered about. But she'd seen it as rejection. She'd think about that for a moment and realise she was wrong and turn around so that he could tell her the one obvious truth. He could give up any-thing else in his life as long as Anna stayed…

Then he heard the front door bang. When he walked to the window, he saw the headlights of her car flip on and then slowly arc across the driveway.

He could have borne whatever Anna cared to throw at him. He could have borne her silence. But he couldn't bear it that she'd just left before he'd even had a chance to take in everything she'd said properly.

Gill had done that too. He knew now that there had been a lot wrong with their relationship, and it was unlikely that anything either of them could have said would have mended it. But she'd never allowed him the opportunity of any understanding or closure. Had just walked away. And now Anna, the person he be-lieved in more than anyone else he'd ever known, had done the same thing. They could have made it work, but she wouldn't even try.

Perhaps she'd feel differently about it in the morn-ing. It was a great thought, but Jamie knew that it was never going to happen. He could call and she wouldn't answer. He might even sit down and laboriously write an email, setting out everything he wanted to say to her, but he'd never know if she'd even read it because she wouldn't reply. Once Anna had made up her mind about something she stuck to it.

Anger coursed through his veins. So much for can-dlelight and a nice dinner. He pinched the wicks of the candles to extinguish them, cursing when he burned his fingers. Then in a sudden blind rage, directed at him-self, Anna, and the rest of the world, he swept his arm across the table. Plates and candlesticks went flying, hitting the floor with a crash, which somehow didn't satisfy him as much as it should have. Walking out of the house, he stood on the veranda, shivering and watching the rain fall.

When Anna popped her head around the door of the waiting room, Callum and his aunt were sitting alone. She'd expected that—she hadn't seen or heard from Jamie in the last three weeks. That was partly due to the fact that she'd been judiciously avoiding him.

This would be the last time she'd go through this kind of heartbreak. She'd been with Jamie for four short weeks, but in that time she'd known he was the love of her life. 'The One.' If it was impossible for her to stay with him, then there would never be anyone else. She'd never be hurt again.

Callum looked up and saw her, giving her a smile. Anna switched on the smile she'd been hiding behind ever since she'd walked out on Jamie.

'Hi, Callum. How are you doing?'

'Great. Thanks.'

He didn't look great. That was generally the case with patients who came for a second laser treatment for tattoo removal, they knew what to expect this time. She beckoned for him to follow her and his aunt gathered up her coat and came too.

'So. Let's take a look at your hand, then.'

Callum brightened a bit. 'It's looking really good, don't you think?'

Anna examined his hand carefully. All of the inflammation had gone down now, and the tattoos were now a faded collection of disjointed lines with no discernible meaning.

'Yes, I'm really pleased with the results, these

should only need one more treatment and then we can get started on the other hand. Generally tattoos need a great deal more work before they fade, but these small amateur tattoos are sometimes easier to remove than professional ones, because of the depth of penetration and type of ink.'

Callum grinned. 'I'll remember that for the future.'

Anna glanced at Callum's aunt, who had frowned suddenly in response to her nephew's joke. She felt a tingle at the back of her neck. A remembered reaction to the expected interjection from Jamie. But he wasn't here.

'You have to think very carefully before getting any tattoo, Callum. I'd say that if removal even crosses your mind, that's a pretty solid reason not to get one done in the first place.'

Callum nodded. 'I've learned my lesson. I won't be getting any more. Jamie said I should focus on how my hands are going to look when this is finished, and how I'm going to keep them that way.'

Anna resisted the temptation to ask Callum exactly where and when he'd last seen Jamie, and how he was. 'Yes, that's a good suggestion.'

'He said to say hello.'

'Did he?' Anna obviously hadn't managed to conceal her surprise and consternation because Callum shrugged.

'Well, he didn't actually *say* it. I expect he forgot. I'll tell him hello back, shall I?'

Anna thought quickly. Maybe the Hastings Hustlers had noticed something and this was a heavy-handed attempt to open the lines of communication between her and Jamie again. On the other hand, Callum might just be trying to be polite, it was difficult to tell.

'How is he?'

'Okay. Pretty much the same as always.'

'Right. Well, I'm glad to hear it. Don't bother to tell him hello, I should probably give him a call. I'll say hello myself.'

'Okay.' Callum turned his attention back to his hand. He clearly had more important things on his mind and he was looking nervous again.

Jamie was right, fixing his attention on the results of the procedure would help Callum through the discomfort. Even now, after everything they'd been through, Jamie was still there in her head. The worst part of it was that even though it hurt, she welcomed it because it was the last thing she had left of him.

'Right. Would you like to say goodbye to these?' She smiled at Callum, indicating the remnants of the tattoos. 'It may well be the last you'll see of them.'

Callum laughed. 'Good riddance more like.'

'I think so too. Let's get started…'

'What do you think?' Jon handed Jamie the playlist, which had been typed in double spacing to make it easier to read. Jamie studied it carefully.

'That'll be great. You're accompanying "Everywhere" on the mandolin?'

'Yes, that was a great suggestion of yours. Just right for the unplugged version.'

Jamie and Jon were sitting in armchairs on either side of the fireplace, where a blazing fire was chasing away the chill of an October evening. Good food, long tramps in the countryside and intensive counselling had done their work, and Jon was looking a great deal better now.

'You're sure this isn't too soon? You don't *have* to get straight back to work, you know.'

Jon shrugged. 'I know. I really want to do it, though. Getting back to my roots a bit, playing small venues with a few new arrangements of the songs. It's only going to be four dates, and I'm really looking forward to it.'

'Well, I'll be keeping an eye on you.'

'That's another thing I'm looking forward to. Having my big brother keep an eye on me.'

They'd come a long way together. They'd talked about everything, all of the things that had gradually built up resentment and pushed them apart. Then finally they'd talked about Gill. Jamie had acknowledged that his relationship with his ex-fiancée had been quietly deteriorating for some time, and Jon had acknowledged that his behaviour had been inexcusable. Then they'd forgiven each other.

'Caroline says she's coming along, to the final gig. She's bringing Jessica.'

Jamie chuckled. 'Doesn't that make you feel old? That your niece is grown up enough to come to one of your concerts?'

'I quite like it. Feels like a new lease of life.' Jon stretched his arms out, holding his hands towards the fire.

'I hope it's not going to be too cold.'

'Nah. Big tent in the park. What's not to like? If anyone gets frostbite I'll hand them over to you.'

'Because it's always useful to have a doctor around?' Jamie smiled.

'Yep. You can never have too many doctors.' Jon frowned suddenly. 'I wanna say something.'

That usually meant it was something that he didn't want to hear. But Jamie felt numb these days. The pain of missing Anna had made everything else seem trivial. 'Yeah, go ahead.'

'It's none of my business…'

'Whatever. Say it anyway.'

'You're bloody miserable, mate. Caroline's noticed as well.'

Jamie stared at his brother. Since he hadn't spoken about his affair with Anna, he'd told himself that no one need know about the break-up. Silence had been his way of keeping it all together, because it hurt too much to put into words. Clearly he hadn't made as good a job of covering his feelings as he'd thought.

'I'm okay.'

'Yeah, pull the other one. One minute you and Anna are joined at the hip, and you're looking like the cat that's got the cream. The next minute she's gone and… Look, I'm the last person who should be mentioning your love life to you.'

Jamie shrugged. 'Didn't we say that we were going to put that in the past? Now that we both understand a little more about why it happened, we can let it go.'

'That's what *you* said. And I'll always be grateful for it, because it's given us a future. That's not my point, Jamie. My point is that when I hit rock bottom it was because I'd lost my faith in anything ever changing. You were the one who showed me I was wrong.'

'It's complicated, Jon.'

'It always is. Until it's not.'

Jamie didn't answer. He didn't want to think about

it, because Anna had been the best thing that had ever happened to him. And losing her had been the worst.

He stared into the fire, watching the flames dance. Anna had taken his heart when she'd walked away. He'd been angry, and she probably didn't even know that he'd do anything to be with her.

An idea occurred to him. It was crazy, a chance in a million... But it had been a long time since the Campbell-Clarke brothers had taken their one chance in a million, made a song out of it, and it had shaped both their futures.

'There is something...'

Jon looked up at him. 'Yeah? Name it, big brother.'

CHAPTER FIFTEEN

EVERYONE AT THE clinic was talking about Jonny Campbell's new song. It had been released free on the internet, and in the first few hours had been downloaded over a million times. When Anna had listened to it, it had made her cry. 'Whatever' was a love song. One that promised a true and faithful heart. Whatever the cost and whatever happened.

The ticket had arrived by courier, and Anna had been called down to the clinic's reception desk to sign for it personally. There was a note inside from Jon, asking her to come to the first of four concerts, which would be taking place in one of the central London parks, the following week.

She couldn't go, of course. She'd made discreet enquiries, and it seemed that no one else at the clinic had received a ticket so she'd been singled out. If Jamie was behind it, it would only lead to more heartbreak.

But she couldn't shake the words of the song. It had the same haunting quality as 'Everywhere'. What if Jamie had written it?

The Saturday of the concert was a bright, clear day, and Anna couldn't help herself. She had to go. Whatever the cost, and whatever happened.

There had been a frenzied demand for tickets, and security was tight at the entrance to the area where the tent was pitched. She'd heard that it held a thousand people, and it was enormous, with a stage at one end ringed by security. Her ticket got her into the front section, just yards from the stage.

Excitement hung in the air, and Anna stood alone to one side, watching the hubbub around her. The promise of new, 'unplugged' versions of Jonny Campbell's greatest hits had attracted both young and old, and there was a friendly, almost holiday atmosphere. Anna felt sick from the cacophony of feelings that were tugging her in so many different directions. She was about to leave when a roar went up and the crowd surged forward as Jon stepped out onto the stage.

He looked good. There was a spring in his step and he'd lost the haggard, disconnected look that he'd had when he'd first checked into the clinic. He'd ditched his signature leather trousers in favour of jeans and a casual shirt, but he hadn't been able to resist a leather jacket, lined with studs across the back. The scars on his face were still there, but they seemed less vivid against the healthy colour of his face. It was good to see the change in him.

He started to speak, thanking everyone for coming, and receiving a cheer in response. There were a few jokes and some banter with the crowd, and then Anna froze.

'My brother Jamie is half an hour older than me, and a great deal better looking. He wrote "Everywhere" when we were eighteen, and since then we've been through a lot together. So it's my great pleasure to welcome him here this afternoon...'

She wanted to run, but that would only draw attention to herself. And this was what she was here for, wasn't it? She'd been drawn like a moth to the flame, needing to find out if this new song was what she didn't dare hope it might be. She pulled the woollen hat she'd brought with her from her pocket, putting it on and stepping behind a group of people so she couldn't be spotted from the stage.

There was a cheer when Jamie came onto the stage, and he acknowledged it diffidently, sitting down on one of the two high stools at the front of the stage and picking up a guitar. Jon joined him, reaching for a mandolin, and the two of them started to play.

The new arrangement of 'Everywhere' was more beautiful than the original. Anna couldn't tear her gaze from Jamie. He was so close, but she knew he couldn't see her, and she felt tears of frustration and uncertainty run down her face.

'You like this version?'

A roar of approval answered Jon's question and he laughed, caught up by the sheer delight of being on stage.

'Okay, it'll be released in a couple of weeks. Jamie wrote "Everywhere" sixteen years ago, and it's taken a very special lady to make him pick up his pen again. Anna, if you're here, this one's for you…'

Everyone was looking around. Anna felt her cheeks burn. 'Whatever' really was her song? Jamie seemed determined not to look at the crowd, and walked over to the piano, sitting down to play the first few chords. Jon began to sing, and was walking up and down at the front of the stage, seeming to be scanning the audience.

Suddenly she knew. The song said everything. Jamie

wanted her, and he'd always love her. He could give up anything else in his life, but he couldn't lose her. Anna waved, desperately trying to catch his attention, to show him that she was here, but he seemed oblivious of everything but the piano keys. But Jon saw her, and signalled to one of the security men around the stage. The man cleared a path through for her, and she ran forward.

'Jamie! *Jamie!*' He had to look up and see her.

Jon stopped singing, leaving the backing players to continue with the melody. Then Jamie looked up and saw her. His reaction was immediate, and he ran to the edge of the stage.

'Looks as if my brother's got something more important on his mind than playing the piano. I'm gonna need some help. Do we have the words…?' Jon looked round at the screen that was suspended over his head and the precious words, which were all for her, flashed up. He started to sing again, and the crowd joined in. Jamie jumped down from the stage, and Anna flung herself into his arms.

'You didn't look for me?' She had to press her lips close to his ear so that he could hear her.

'I was too afraid you wouldn't be there. I had to ask Jon to do it for me.' He kissed her and suddenly everything was all right.

'Do you really mean it, Jamie? That you'll love me whatever happens?'

'Of course I mean it. I've just said it in front of a thousand people, and I was going to keep saying it until you heard me. Loving you isn't just what I do, it's who I am.'

'It's who I am, too. I love you, Jamie.'

Somewhere, far away, the crowd was cheering. But Jamie was kissing her, and nothing else mattered.

EPILOGUE

Three years later

'JON'S ASKED ME if I'm going to write another song.'

'And are you?'

'Nah. The only songs I'll be writing any time soon are lullabies.'

Anna and Jamie were curled up together on their bed. It was early still, but they couldn't take their eyes off the two cradles by the side of the bed, where their one-week-old twins were sleeping.

'We're so lucky, Jamie. Everything worked out.'

'You thought it wouldn't?'

'I knew it would. But I'm so happy it worked out like this.'

When they'd got married, Jamie and Anna had promised to love each other and trust in the future. And the future had repaid their trust and given them more than they ever could have hoped for. Tests had shown that although she couldn't conceive or carry a baby, Anna could produce viable eggs. Caroline had been the one to suggest that she could act as a surrogate for them and their twins, a girl and a boy, had been safely delivered last week.

'I don't think I'll ever be able to thank Caroline enough.' Anna snuggled against Jamie's chest.

'I think you've mentioned that to her. Once or twice. And even if you hadn't I think that your offer to look after her kids for two weeks, while she and Harry have a holiday together next summer, was nothing short of heroic.'

'You don't mind, do you?'

'Mind? I'll be camping out in the garden with the boys. You and Jess can make your own arrangements.'

'I thought I might take her for a pamper day. Get our hair and nails done maybe.'

Jamie chuckled. 'She'll like that. You think we could persuade Caroline and Harry to make it three weeks?'

'We could try. You never know.'

Never knowing had become one of Anna's greatest joys. They hadn't known that the updated version of 'Everywhere' would outsell the original, and help finance the expansion of Jamie's charity, allowing him to devote all his time to it. Or that the London Central Clinic would offer her a two-days-a-week contract so that she could spend more time at home, enjoying being a mum. Or that Jon would finally find some peace, and was managing to combine a successful solo career with a stable home life.

'Jen called me yesterday. She's got the day off work and she and Spark are coming over. She said she hoped I hadn't bought any more sleepsuits.'

Jamie winced. 'Tell me they haven't decided on skulls and crossbones this time…'

'I wouldn't like to make any promises. Since she's been on that textiles course at college, Spark can make just about anything.'

'Yeah. The Hastings Hustlers sleepsuits she made are great. I can't wait to show them off to the team.' Jamie folded her in his arms, hugging her tight. 'I can't wait for any of it, Anna. As long as it's with you.'

Anna laughed, kissing him. 'That's just as well, because you're stuck with me now. I'm not going anywhere.'

'That's all I'll ever want, Anna. You're stuck with me, too. Always.'

Whatever happened. They'd completed the process of being vetted as adoptive parents, so there might well be more children to share their love with. The charity was growing, and Jamie had set innovative programmes into motion that had caught the attention of other youth agencies. The future was an endless stream of possibilities and Jamie's restless energy was tempered by an obvious contentment, which matched Anna's own.

'What's that tune?' Jamie was humming something that didn't sound familiar.

'I'm not sure.' He hummed another few bars of the melody, and then sang a few words. *'"You never know…"'*

'I thought you weren't going to write another song.' She grinned at him.

'I couldn't help it. It just popped into my head.' He kissed her forehead and then started humming again.

Anna reached for her phone, switching on the audio recorder. 'Here, sing it again before you forget it.'

He hummed the tune again, with a few more words this time, and then switched the recorder off, putting the phone down on the bed. 'I do know one thing.'

'Me too.'

They both knew that they loved each other, and their beautiful babies. And that was the only thing that either of them needed.

* * * * *

COMING SOON!

We really hope you enjoyed reading this book.
If you're looking for more romance, be sure to
head to the shops when new books are
available on

Thursday 26th June

To see which titles are coming soon, please visit

millsandboon.co.uk/nextmonth

MILLS & BOON

Coming next month

TEMPTED BY THE BROODING VET

Shelley Rivers Good grief, could the man make it any clearer that he regretted asking to kiss her? What other reason explained his disagreeable attitude since her arrival? Was he scared she might take it into her head to embrace him in front of the other staff members? Or perhaps try and seduce him in a consultation room when no one was looking?

She'd never attempted such behaviour in her life, and she didn't plan to start with him.

'With me?' she asked, just to be certain.

'I'm not sure how to act around you,' he admitted. 'But, seeing as we're going to be working together, maybe we should just forget that last night I asked to…'

'Kiss me?' she taunted, unable to stop herself from reminding him. A perverse imp filled her with mischief. 'And you held me snugly against your half naked body.'

Alex cleared his throat. 'Yes.'

'Fine,' she said brightly. 'Because until you mentioned it I hadn't considered it a big deal or wasted much thought over it.'

Pleased she'd managed to keep her voice casual and indifferent throughout the lie, she resumed cleaning the area. No reason for Alex to know she'd relived that moment over and over for most of the night. Mentally rerunning each stimulating second until she'd wanted to scream with frustration and track him down to demand he give her the proposed kiss.

He frowned at her reply. 'Really?'

She bit hard on her inner lip to prevent a smile. The man certainly didn't like hearing that she found his romantic moves unmemorable.

'If you want to forget what happened—or rather didn't—then just be yourself when we're in the same room. Otherwise people might start to notice and that would create talk.'

'Are you sure I should?' he asked, not sounding convinced.

Unable to stop herself, she laughed. Alex's self-consciousness was rather refreshing and endearing. Every time the man forgot his stiff reserve passion smouldered from him. It intrigued her how his personality had two such different sides.

'I swear my hesitation had nothing to do with you or your request,' she said. 'It was all me—I promise. So I'll help you on Saturday at the stud farm?'

'Thanks. I'd appreciate it.'

Continue reading
TEMPTED BY THE BROODING VET
Shelley Rivers

Available next month
www.millsandboon.co.uk

LET'S TALK
Romance

For exclusive extracts, competitions
and special offers, find us online:

f facebook.com/millsandboon

🐦 @MillsandBoon

📷 @MillsandBoonUK

Get in touch on 01413 063232

For all the latest titles coming soon, visit

millsandboon.co.uk/nextmonth